Professor Witchey's Miracle Mood Cure

Ingredients: 25 Tales of Science, Magic, Strangeness, Wonder, and Mystery

A Collection of Tales by Eric Witchey.

Includes 7 previously unpublished stories.

Professor Witchey's Miracle Mood Cure

Ingredients: 25 Tales of Science, Magic, Strangeness, Wonder, and Mystery

A Collection of Tales by Eric Witchey. Includes 7 previously unpublished stories.

Guaranteed to cure: negativities, poliannaism, holytosis, possession, and soothes the gout.

For best results: read aloud on stormy evenings by lantern light.

Dose: *One* tale before bed.

Warning: Do not use while driving oxen. Exceeding recommended dosage can result in confusion, disorientation, expanded consciousness, leaps of imagination, sleeplessness, authorism, and social consciousness.

IFD
Publishing

IFD Publishing, 2016

Professor Witchey's Miracle Mood Cure

A collection of tales by

Eric Witchey

IFD Publishing; P.O. Box 40776; Eugene, Oregon 97404 U.S.A.

(541) 461-3272 www.ifdpublishing.com

Ebook Design, Cyberscribe, Inc.

First Trade Paper edition ISBN: 978-0-9965536-7-4

Originally Printed by IFD Publishing in the United States of America.

Ingredients

Acknowledgments

This collection would not have come together without the support of my editor, Elizabeth Engstrom. To her, I am forever grateful. She believes in the value of a good tale, and she has provided emotional support for my efforts for years. In addition, Alan M. Clark and Melody Clark were instrumental in convincing me to bring these tales together in one place. Without their kindness and friendship, these tales would still be scattered to their various original sources. Alan was also kind enough to create the cover for this and other works. Finally, thanks go to my readers. Without your imaginations, words are only groupings of little black squiggles on a white background. Though I work hard to arrange the triggering symbols in rows for your use, you provide the uniquely human magic of creation and meaning.

Dedication

In memory of Craig Dennis, who offered me a home when I was homeless.

Author's Foreword

The strange, sometimes funny, sometimes sad, and sometimes odd tales in this book come primarily from my life and from experiments in creative writing. In my mind, every story is a unique experiment in the evocation of thought and emotion. No two require the same attention, the same techniques, or the same application of imagination. For me, no genres constrain creative effort. I have sold fantasy stories to literary markets and literary stories to fantasy markets. Genre is a construct of editors and profit-driven marketing departments. Story is unfettered magic happening in the heart and mind of the reader.

For me, the story is the thing, and the individual reader is the only judge of my success or failure. I have received insulting email and awards for the same story. For some readers, the story failed. For others, the story succeeded. I have been called a no-talent hack, and I have been called brilliant. Luckily, none of these judgments are true in my mind. By the time these sorts of judgments make it to me, I have already moved on to new experiments in story.

The only truth a tale can express is the already existing truth it releases from the heart of the reader.

I hope each tale speaks to you, dearest explorer of the page. I hope you laugh out loud and cry. Most important, I hope at least one of these tales touches your heart and releases a truth you did not know you held hidden inside yourself.

Regardless, thank you for the gift of your attention and participation.

Life and Death and Stealing Toads

First Place Ralan.com Grabber Contest 2003.

Humid summer winds off Lake Erie tugged on the fresh, mowed stubble of the witch's groomed lawn. Moonlight sparkled in every drop of dew. Morgan crawled on his belly through Mrs. Grael's front yard. Cold water soaked his black t-shirt and made his thighs itch inside his wet, black jeans. The smell of fresh cut grass tickled his nose until he had to pinch it so he wouldn't sneeze.

From the cover of a mountain cherry bush, he peered at the tall windows set on either side of the front door of the witch's white bungalow.

The windows were dark, the house quiet.

He wondered at himself. He wasn't a kid anymore. He was a forty-two-year-old real estate agent with a dying wife and a little girl. If the police caught him skulking around in the night, they wouldn't slap his wrists and inform his parents. They'd drop him in jail and let him call a lawyer.

He looked down Gaylord Avenue's long, gradual hill. At the far end, where Gaylord connected to the busier state route 39, he saw the lighted windows of his own brick house where Linda waited for him to bring home a magic toad.

Once full of life and love, she was now pale and in pain. He grew up with her, married her, and now stood by helplessly while doctors said he had no choice but to watch her die.

He had choices. Not many, but a few.

He crawled toward the concrete walk in front of Mrs. Grael's tulip and azalea beds. The toads were in the window well just behind the azaleas.

He'd discovered them when he was six. He'd lived only three houses down Gaylord then, next to the Will's bright red split-level ranch. He'd run away after his mother had slapped his hand when he reached for the icing on his sister's birthday cake. Crying, and too scared to run far, he hid in Mrs. Grael's garden. He crouched low over the wrought iron grate covering her window well, a corrugated steel half pipe set vertically into the dirt to protect her basement windows.

"Come join us," the toads whispered. "Bring spiders."

When he was six, talking toads seemed less important than scaring his mother. "Shhh…"

"Well, young man," Mrs. Grael had said.

He looked up from shushing the toads and gasped. She was old when he was six. She was no more than sixty now, so he was sure her apparent age when he was little was the result of fear and imagination.

"Come to steal my magic toads, have you?" She had reached over her azaleas and taken hold of his t-shirt. He had to leap to clear the bushes without falling under her vicious pull.

"No, Ma'am," he'd stammered. "I don't want your toads. I'm hiding."

Her thick gray eyebrows rose, and her parchment forehead crinkled. "From something scarier than me?"

Now, skulking toward the toads, Morgan shivered at the thought of the old woman's grip when he was six. He pulled himself forward across the concrete walk and into the flowerbed. So far, so good, he thought.

Stealing toads was stupid, but they had run out of hope. He loved Linda. No one could cure her. Their money was gone. They'd tried acupuncture, smoke healing, incense therapy, and a hypnotist who claimed the machine in his basement killed cancer.

As childish as magic toads might be, he had to try everything. He didn't want to live in a world without her. Behind the azaleas, he found the black grate. He cupped his hands over the grate and looked into the shadowy confines of the deep window well. Moonlight made a shadowy collage among the leaves, gravel, sticks and spider webs.

"Toads?" he whispered. "Are you there?"

Only the quiet breeze from the lake answered him. A lightning bug looking for a date flickered over his shoulder. He glanced up.

Mrs. Grael stood on the concrete step of her porch, her hands on her hips, her half-glasses perched on the bridge of her long nose. Morgan thought she was wearing the same blue garden dress she'd worn when she caught him as a child.

"Morgan, are you at my toads again?" she asked.

Morgan felt like he was six again, small and foolish. He tried to shrink into the shadows and maybe slip through the grating bars over the window well.

"Come out of there, Morgan. It's cold and wet, and you won't do your Linda any good if you catch pneumonia."

Linda's name brought him to himself. He gathered in his long legs and stood. To his relief, he was still as tall as Mrs. Grael, even when she was standing on the steps.

~ ~ ~

Mrs. Grael's lemon and spice tea was good. She gave him a towel and an old flannel shirt once owned by her late husband. His jeans were still wet and itchy, but the dry shirt and warm mug calmed him.

Mrs. Grael busied herself at her counters while he watched from a chair at her kitchen table. She opened cupboards and pulled out bottles and bags. She set out a crock-pot and pulled a large three-ring cookbook from the cabinet under her phone nook.

"Don't mind me, Morgan. I've never been one to sit still. I cook while I talk. Old habit. Very old."

"Thanks for the tea, Mrs. Grael." He chuckled nervously.

She filled the crock-pot with water from the tap. "I don't know what I was thinking going out on the porch like that," she said. "I guess something told me you weren't a garden variety burglar." She laughed at her little garden joke.

Morgan smiled appreciatively. "I didn't mean to scare you."

"Course you didn't, dear."

The feeling of smallness came over him again. For a moment, he was a child. She'd taken him into her kitchen the first time, too. She'd given him hot chocolate and cookies. She even let him sit a while before she called his mother. He smiled.

"What were you up to out there, Morgan?" she asked.

"It's silly, Mrs. Grael. I'm sorry. I'll get my things and go. I'll bring your shirt back tomorrow." He stood and folded her towel.

Mrs. Grael faced him. Her faded blue eyes held him still. She lifted a dishrag from a hook by her stove and wiped off her own hands. "I think you owe me some kind of explanation. You did sneak into my yard, climb through my flower beds, and scare me pretty good." She glanced at the sunflower clock on the wall. "It's almost three in the morning, Morgan. What's going on?"

Her eyes seemed to push him back into his chair. "It's silly. Stupid. I'd rather not have to explain."

Mrs. Grael pursed her lips and tilted her chin down in a quick nod. She turned to her pot, picked up a glass jar, and poured a little brown powder into the pot. "Your wife's sick, I hear," she said.

Morgan nodded. "Yes," he said.

"Linda?"

"Linda," he said.

Mrs. Grael said, "The cancer has her, and she's at home, awake and in pain. The doctors can't help." She wasn't asking. She poured a drop of red liquid from a tiny vial into the pot. The smell that filled the kitchen reminded Morgan of hot soup on rainy summer Saturdays.

"So you feel helpless, I'm betting," She said.

Morgan's sense of foolishness melted away, replaced with the tears of a man whose only hope is to believe the illusions of his childhood. "I didn't know what else to do," he said. "She needs so much. She needs me to…"

"To do something," Mrs. Grael offered.

"Anything," Morgan said. "I had to do something."

"Of course you did," she said. "What kind of husband would you be if you didn't try to help her?"

"She couldn't sleep."

"You told her stories about when you were a kid."

"Yes. Exactly. How'd you know?"

"I always liked you, Morgan. After Mr. Grael passed, the kids in this neighborhood always gave me a bad time. They teased me. They called me names. Not you. You had spine and imagination. They called me a witch because I was old and alone. But you were different."

Morgan felt guilty for scaring the little old woman stirring soup in a crock-pot in the middle of the night. Steam misted her half-glasses and clung to loose wisps of gray hair. "I'm sorry, Mrs. Grael," he said. "I have to admit that I thought you were a witch too."

She looked up from her pot and smiled. "I know, but it wasn't because I was old and alone. You just didn't seem to mind the idea that I might be a witch." She went to the refrigerator and pulled out a black bottle. "That's a rare thing, Morgan."

"I came to steal one of your toads, tonight, Mrs. Grael."

She poured a black ichor from the bottle into the crock-pot. "Because you feel like a little boy—helpless, unable to do anything for Linda. So, you abandoned everything you've learned, everything you thought you knew, and you came to me for magic you believed in as a child."

Morgan stared at the busy little woman. Her words didn't judge. They didn't belittle him for his foolishness. She said them like men crawled around her yard ever night looking for miracles.

"Not every night," she said.

It took him a moment to realize she'd answered his thoughts. "Oh my god," he whispered.

"Shhhh, Morgan. Don't tell anyone." She lifted her spoon from the pot and winked at him through the rising steam.

Morgan was across the kitchen before she dipped her spoon again. He took her by the shoulders. "The toads?" he asked. "Linda?"

"Let me go, Morgan. You're a big, strong man now, and I'm a little old lady."

He realized he was nearly lifting her off the floor. "I'm sorry," he stammered. He let her go. "I'm really sorry."

"Fear and hope do funny things to people," she said.

"The toads?"

"I'm still alive, eh?"

"You had cancer?"

"Have to give credit where credit is due. Mr. Grael figured it out. Because of him, I'm still in this world, and I haven't changed much since you were a boy, have I?"

"How? What do I need to do?"

"Well, Morgan, that's the rub of it. The universe has a sort of balance to it. Love does most of the work, but it isn't enough. If you want something, you have to give something up."

"Anything," he gasped. "Everything, to see her healthy again, to see her smile without pain in her eyes."

Mrs. Grael picked up a ladle and dipped up a bowl of hot soup. "Have a little of this, Morgan."

Morgan sipped on the soup while Mrs. Grael put up a thermos full. It was a wonderful concoction of spices and tomato and something he couldn't quite name. That something reminded him of the musty smell of the shadowy window well. It made him feel small and young and safe and fat.

~ ~ ~

Morgan sat in the mid-day sun enjoying the warm orange glow behind his closed eyes. He heard footsteps on the concrete. He twisted his head around until he could see the front stoop. Linda stood there. She was beautiful. Her hair was growing back. It was still short, but it shone with dark highlights in the sunlight. Her faded jeans were still a bit baggy, but she was filling them out. She rang the doorbell.

Mrs. Grael answered. "My, you *are* looking better, dear. Much better."

"I feel great," Linda said. The deep health in her voice filled Morgan with joy. "The doctor says it's a miracle. He says there's no trace of the cancer left. Total remission. I told him it was your soup."

"It was love did it, dear. I always said that Morgan boy understood love."

Linda winced and began to cry. "Oh, lord, Mrs. Grael. I wish I knew where he went. I wish I could find him."

"I'm sure he's not far off. That boy never was one to stray too far from home. What you need, dear, is a pet."

Linda stopped crying. "A pet?"

"You come on in and have some tea, dear. We'll talk. I'll get you a tissue."

The two women disappeared into the house.

Mr. Grael hopped up beside Morgan. "That your wife, boy?" Mr. Grael asked.

"Linda," Morgan said.

"Was it worth it?" Mr. Grael asked.

Morgan nodded and smiled. He zipped his tongue out and snagged a fat spider from its web at the corner of Mrs. Grael's basement window. While he swallowed, he looked up through the grate at white clouds skating across the late summer sky. Cool north winds drove them off the lake. "Winter's coming," he said, and he hoped Linda remembered the fifty-five-gallon aquarium stored in their crawl space.

Lost Island Story Hour

Originally Printed in Short Story America, Vol. II.

I tell myself I'm not hiding. I just don't want to disturb the old man's reading. He still believes reading can change the world.

I should knock him out with a coconut and carry him to the raft. I owe him at least that. I take a deep breath. The tide's out. The sun's high. Decay and sea salt lace the air.

Just above tide-line, in the shadows of mangroves and thorn thickets, the white sand is still cool on my calloused feet. I crouch low behind the bole of a coconut palm and grind my bare feet deep into the sand.

He's not so different from when I was a kid. Certainly, the palm trees and white sands are not the library's terrazzo, walnut, and brass; but his impish smile and loud guffaw are the same.

He has stones and driftwood logs arranged in a circle. I know that in his mind children sit on those seats in rapt attention. The Saturday afternoon children's readings were always important to him. Back in the world, even in the face of short-sighted cutbacks, low staffing, home web surfing, and pressure from the mayor to close the library, he kept the reading circles going.

Shaded by the tattered blue tarp I hung between two palms for him, he peers over his half glasses. The lenses were lost over a year ago. The gold-plated frames have salt-air corrosion in the scratch marks along the ear-pieces.

I feel guilty about his glasses. I broke the first lens when I hit him. That was when I still thought he was sane—when I thought he was just pretending he believed we still lived in Ohio.

He pauses in his reading. He turns the book outward so his audience can see the pictures.

There are no pictures. He can't see the words on the pages. It doesn't matter. We only have one book, a Polynesian cookbook that washed up three years ago. Even if his glasses worked, he couldn't read whatever language it's in.

He recites the stories by heart. They're the same tales he read to me when I was a child.

I listen. The emphasis is the same. The rising gray and black eyebrows are the same, perhaps a little more salt than pepper now. The only real difference is the long gray and black ponytail over his shoulder. Now and then, he touches it, tugs it a little. I wonder how that would have gone over in Ohio—that long-haired, crazed librarian look.

He puts the book in his lap and closes it gently. "That is all we have time for today," he says. His voice is steady. His diction precise—proud.

His pocket watch stopped a long time ago. My digital wristwatch still hums away on its little lithium cell. I imagine that will eventually run down, but I glance at it. Three o'clock. Somehow he knows to the second when it's time for the kids to meet their parents at the front of the library.

He spreads his arms to take in the imagined hugs and snuggles. Rising, he makes as if to shepherd the kids to the doors. Barefoot thru the sand, he herds the ghost children of his past.

I can't help wondering if my face is worn by one of his ghosts. Part of me hopes so.

Not my face now. Not the brown, weather-hardened face of my thirty-eight-year-old manhood. I wouldn't wish that on him. Better that he sees the round, corpulent wonder-filled face of my early years, the years before the trouble in my family, before he took me in as a foster child.

He closes an imaginary door, puts his hands on the small of his back, and stretches. The gesture is as old as he is, I'm sure. I remember it from every session of every Saturday of every summer of my life before college.

He turns.

I sigh along with him. We have long ago synchronized our sighs in this weekly ritual of his insanity. His sigh is one of regret that the children are gone for another week. Mine is one of nostalgia, of fear, of release from this overt manifestation of his insanity.

"Mr. Morton," I say. I step away from the brush.

He starts. Then he smiles and peers over his glasses.

I know immediately that he isn't seeing the man in front of him. When he sees me as I am, he looks through the empty frames. When he sees me as I was, he looks over the tops.

"Little William," he says. "Hiding in the stacks? You should be meeting your mother."

I've given up trying to get him to understand his life here. Instead, I play along. "I needed to check these books, Mr. Morton."

He nods and grins. "What do you have this week? More adventures? Science Fiction? Fantasy? The next in the Gormenghast trilogy?"

I step out of the palm shadows. The rainbow streak of a running lizard skips over my foot and disappears into the thicket. In the sun, the white sand warms my calluses. I offer up my empty hands as if I'm holding several volumes. "Kontiki," I say.

"Thor Heyerdahl."

"I'm building a raft," I say.

"From reeds? To sail the Pacific?"

"Sort of," I say. "I'm using coconuts."

He guffaws. "You are one of my very favorites, William," he says. "And where do you propose to find enough coconuts to float you across the Pacific?"

I look at his feet. There are three coconuts near enough for him to kick. "I've been collecting them," I say. "I get them at the grocery. I've almost got enough."

He realizes I'm serious; or, he realizes the child he sees is serious. He raises a bushy eyebrow. Rather than burst my bubble, he changes the subject.

I almost cry at his kindness even though it's thoroughly demented.

"What else do you have there?" he asks.

"Single Line Fishing in Deep Water," I say.

"Like Santiago?" He reaches out to take my invisible books. I hand them to him. "Who?"

"Santiago," he repeats. He turns away and heads toward an imaginary counter where the checkout stand should be. I mean, where it would be. He paces off the distance perfectly. My childhood memory knows his gait, the number of steps, the position he'll take, an elbow on the counter, one hand moving books through a scanner, his eyes on me while he continues to chat about my books.

"The Old Man and the Sea," he says. "A great book. With your love of adventure, I think, William, that you would enjoy it. Shall I get our copy for you? I'm sure it has been checked in."

Of course, I know the book. I just didn't remember the name of the old man. Santiago.

I remember now. What was the boy's name? It doesn't matter. "I think I've got enough for this week," I say.

"I'm surprised," he says. "Only two. You usually leave with a whole armload."

"Building a raft takes a lot of time," I say. "I don't have any help."

He hands me the imaginary volumes. He nods, smiles, and peers over his frames.

He has to look up at me to peer over the frames. Funny how that look makes me feel small, like I'm still a child standing in front of the tall, kindly librarian that took me in. I want to please him somehow. I want to help him. I remind myself that I'm trying to save his life.

"Maybe," I say, "you could help me with the raft?"

"I have never built a raft, William."

"But I bet you've read all about them."

He smiles. "Reading and doing are not the same."

I smile and speak one of his pet mantras to him. He must have said it to me a thousand, thousand times while I was growing up. "Begin to learn a thing by reading. Make it yours by doing."

He tosses his pony tail over his shoulder, throws back his head, and laughs. He shakes so hard he has to hold his glasses to his head. In spite of my fear for him, I smile. He might be insane, but his humor's intact. We laugh together.

"I'll help if I can," he says. "Under one condition."

"What?" I ask.

"You have to come to next Saturday's reading hour. Two-o'clock sharp," he says. I hope we're both off the island by then. Even so, I agree.

~ ~ ~

"What we need are some good planks," he says.

I stand up from untying the knotted edges of nylon netting I found hung up on the basalt ridge at the North end of the island. There's enough netting to make maybe ten large bags of coconuts. Hell, Papillon escaped Devil's Island on one. With ten, we can support a platform, a lean-to, an outrigger, and a sail.

I've already finished the platform and outrigger. They float well enough without the coconuts, but the coconuts will let us load the platform and stay high and dry—I hope.

"Why planks?" I ask.

"To make the story work. There is always a good shipwreck and planks and part of a boat."

"Always?"

"Well, not in Ohio," he says. "But in Gulliver. In Robinson Crusoe. In Dynotopia."

I laugh. He laughs.

"Grass lines do not hold up well in salt water," he says.

I nod. I continue to work on the nylon netting. "We'll test it on fresh water—on Ganges Pond," I say. This seems to please him. "Proof of concept," I say.

He puts down the blue plastic tarps, the sail he's lashing together. Peering over his glasses, he smiles and squints one eye. "Sometimes," he says, "I think you are a lot older in your head than you are in your body, William. Your reading will serve you well as an adult. When you grow up, you can come and write grants for me at the Library."

"I'd like that," I say. I don't remind him that we wouldn't be here if one of my grants hadn't come through. It was for him. It was supposed to help him. It was his dream to SCUBA uncharted Islands in the South Pacific. He wanted to do a coffee table book—underwater pictures, big plates of pretty fish and corals, a message to the world to save the oceans.

I hadn't expected the grant to come through. None of the others had. The library was dying. His heart was dying with it. At the time, I laughed and thanked God for the gift that might save him.

If that grant hadn't come through, we wouldn't have been on the SCUBA charter when it went down. We wouldn't have had to bury Captain Andy.

I wipe warm salt water from my eyes.

"I think I had better go," he says. "I am quite sure your mother will want to feed you soon, and I have a date with Santiago tonight."

I want him to keep working, to not go off into the jungle and pretend he has a home, an easy chair, a floor lamp, and a copy of *The Old Man and the Sea*.

"We're almost done," I say.

"Gange's Pond will keep. Remember your promise," he says. "Tomorrow is Saturday."

"I'll be there," I say.

He leaves. I ignore my tears and keep working. I work through the night. I work through sunrise. Near noon, I float the coconuts out and lash them to the belly of the platform.

When I'm done with all ten, I look at my watch. Almost two o'clock.

I lash the supplies to the deck inside the lean-to. I unwrap the sail and test it against the breeze. I drop the center board, lift it, jump up and down on the lashed outriggers, kick at the rudder.

The raft is as finished as it's going to be.

~ ~ ~

I sit on my log in the circle and watch him read from an imagined volume.

"He was an old man who fished alone in a skiff in the Gulf Stream and he had gone eighty-four days now without taking a fish."

I can't imagine how he does it. He must have known it by heart before Captain Andy's boat capsized. Maybe his insanity lets him dredge up the stories from the past. Still, it's one thing to memorize the eggs and ham story or remember a tale about a little girl and big red dog; it's something else entirely to remember word-for-word an entire novel.

Of course, I can't check it, but I'm sure he remembers it perfectly.

I sit and watch him turn the pages. His certainty, the smooth action of his fingertips, the way he slides his fingers up the side of the book and folds in the next page to wait for the next turning. It all says he knew the book completely, that if I ever made it home, I would find that particular edition on his shelves. When I looked at those pages, I would see that the last word he spoke before turning the page would be the last word on the page in the real book.

He peers through his glasses at the book. To him, it's real. Occasionally, he peers over his glasses at me and smiles. Even so, he never misses a word.

It's a long reading. I listen carefully while Santiago cuts bait and fishes. I take mental notes while he fights the great fish. I worry while he fights the sharks.

I sit as I did as a child, in awe at the spell of this man, my librarian.

When he finally puts his book down, he takes a long breath.

I take a long breath. "That was amazing," I say.

"Thank you, William," he says. Then, he stands and looks through his glasses. "Do you think the library on the other side of Ganges Pond is still there?" he asks.

I'm stunned. I know he sees me as I am. I try to think of the right answer. His librarian's gaze makes me small, and I can't lie. "I don't know," I say.

"The tide is turning, William," he says. "You'll need to catch it if you want to get out of the bay tonight."

He's lucid. He's looking directly at me. He takes his glasses off and looks into my eyes. "You have everything you need to make it," he says.

For the first time since we crawled up onto the hot, white sand, my belly's cold. "*We*," I say. "We have everything we need to make it."

He puts his glasses back on and peers over the top. "No," he says. "I am the librarian. I have my duties. The great Ganges Pond crossing is up to you, William. I could never leave my books."

Whatever lucidity he had for a moment is gone. I think again about knocking him out and carrying him to the raft. I'm stronger, taller.

He bends and gathers his invisible book from an invisible table.

It's my chance.

The perfection of his motion would make a great mime cry at his own incompetence. The impression of the size and shape of the volume is perfect. I feel the book almost as if I'm touching it myself.

He walks a few paces left, lifts a hand up to his eye-level, inserts the flat of his hand between two volumes in stacks I can't see, then nestles *The Old Man and the Sea* between them.

He turns back to me. He smiles. "The library is closing, William," he says. "I believe it is time for you to go."

I hesitate. I can't hurt him. I can't take him from his books.

"Thank you, Mr. Morton," I say. "I'll come back."

"I know you will, William," he says. "And William."

"Yes?"

"You will be nice to the new librarian, won't you?"

I nod and turn toward the sea.

Fitting for the Groom

Fourth Place. Spinetingler Magazine, UK. Dec. 2014.

They weren't even married yet, and already Mel white-knuckled the steering wheel when Lydia spoke. He turned Lydia's cherry red Mercedes onto a narrow lane. Both sides of the street were lined by narrow-windowed, old-town shops where people that barely spoke English once lived and sold their wares. "Has this Uncle Izak been in this country long?" he asked.

"Uncle Izak has been taking care of the weddings for my family for…" Lydia stared at him for a minute, her brown, cow eyes just blank and her wild red hair reminding Mel more of Bozo than a bride-to-be. Finally, she laughed and waved her pampered hand in dismissal. "Well, just forever, that's all. He's an institution with us Steinmans."

"We Drakes don't have *institutions*. We have common sense. We're pragmatic folk," Mel said. "And after Saturday, you're going to be Mrs. Mel Drake." He slipped Lydia's Mercedes ragtop up to the empty curb. "After that, we don't give money away because of family traditions."

"Yes, Dear," she said. Then, she giggled.

Mel looked up and down the street of ragged shop fronts. Spray-painted gang tags marred most of the abandoned stores. Only a dingy tailor's shop showed any sign of occupation and vocation. "That's it?"

"Come on! You'll love Uncle Izak."

He didn't think that very likely. He pulled his wallet out of his pants and locked it in the glove compartment before he followed Lydia out onto the street. He pressed the remote and glanced up and down the street while the car put up its top then beeped confirmation that it had set its alarms and locked its doors.

The hair on the back of his neck stood at attention. Certain he was being watched by someone or something dangerous, he followed his bozo bride into the dilapidated tailor's shop. The shop door clipped against an actual bell, which made a happy little tinkle that seemed totally wrong for the narrow interior of a shop sandwiched between a burned out bakery and once-upon-a-time dance studio that had lost all the front window glass a long time ago. Even though nobody was smoking, ancient cigarette smoke tainted the air. Mel figured the overhead fleur-de-lis light fixtures had been converted to electric from gas, He also thought the gas would have done a better job.

Lydia danced across the worn hardwood toward the flat expanse of a cutting table at the rear of the shop. She did a quick turn with the skeleton of a fitting dummy, popped up onto a square fitting dais, stopped, and bowed low to her own image in the triptych mirror surrounding the dais. Swirls of dust followed her pirouettes.

For just a moment, Mel considered taking her Benz on a drive to Cancun and leaving her, her father's money, the whole ditzy Steinman family behind.

"May I help you?" The young woman's voice came from behind a curtain at the back of the shop.

The lilt of that voice made Mel wonder if it might not be worth a minute or two of his time to humor his new bride.

The curtain parted, and he was rewarded for his compassion and patience. Oh, yeah, the trip to Uncle Izak, the traditional family tailor, was definitely looking up.

The woman at the back glanced at him. Her magic green eyes traced a line of heat across his face, down his chest, and right into his crotch. She strolled into the shop, the drape of her sheer, cotton, peasant dress flirting with her thigh. She stepped behind the cutting table and took up a station at a hand-cranked, brass cash register that had to be older than God.

She smoothed the front of her dress.

Mel admired the way the fabric over her chest bounced back from her caress. Lydia's chest had nothing to bounce back.

Shining waves of dark hair hung loose over the shop girl's shoulder and teased the white curve of breasts bulging up from the scooped neck of her dress. She flipped her hair back over her shoulder.

Mel bit his tongue.

Even in that dank sweatshop wannabe, the girl's lips glistened and her teeth flashed.

But the flash wasn't for him. The shop girl smiled for Lydia.

"Lydia?" the shop girl asked. "Is that you?"

"Gloria?"

The two women squealed in unison and chorused and exaggerated, "Oh! My! Gawd!"

Lydia and Gloria collided half way between the register and the dais. They were a swirl of magic sensuality and bride-to-be kissing and giggling and screaming.

Mel was good at seeing an opportunity, if he was good at anything, and he was going to get that girl's eyes back on him. He stepped forward and coughed.

They ignored him.

"Lydia," he said. "You know this lovely young woman?"

The curtain parted again. Mel looked over hoping for, well, he wasn't sure, maybe a twin? A blond, if the gods were with him. Instead, he got an old man whose skin matched the yellowed air and light of the shop, an old man whose bald pate was framed with a rim of white and so covered in liver spots that the top of his head might have been tan, an old man stooped by a dowager's hump, spited with a hook-nosed, and dressed for mourning in black tails, of all damn things. The old man had to twist his head sideways to look up at Mel.

Lydia broke her clinch with the babe from the back room, and she turned her attentions to none other than Uncle Izak himself.

While Lydia was fawning over Uncle Izak, Mel moved in on Gloria. "You must be Lydia's cousin?"

"Cousin?" The girl held out her hand. "Oh," she said. "The Uncle Izak thing."

Mel took her soft hand in both of his, smiled, nodded, and rubbed his fingertips along the inside of her palm. She blushed, looked away, and pulled her hand back. It was just what he had hoped for. He wondered how much time Uncle Izak would need alone with Lydia for this fitting thing.

"This is Uncle Izak," Lydia said. "Isn't he sweet? He's just a wizard when it comes to the right wedding clothes."

Mel put out a hand to the old man. Uncle Izak ignored it, twisting his head and looking sideways at Mel. "This," he said, his voice rattling up from deep in his phlegm-clogged chest, "This is the putz that's to marry so beautiful a girl like Lydia?"

"Excuse me?" Mel said.

"I said," Uncle Izak said, "This is the putz that's to marry so beautiful a girl like Lydia?"

"He doesn't mean anything by it," said Lydia.

"I heard what you said." Mel pulled back his hand.

"Oh," said Uncle Izak. "Good. I was thinking maybe the shagatsa trouble maker wants to borrow my hearing aid?"

"Uncle Izak, be nice," Lydia said.

Mel noticed the dark beauty watching him from the counter. He couldn't let her see him go under to this prune fart. "Old man, you just lost this wedding," he said. He could come back and negotiate a deal with Gloria.

Uncle Izak half coughed and half shrugged. He took Lydia's hand and shuffled her across the room to the fitting dais. "Upsy daisy, my girl," he said, and Lydia stepped lightly up onto the dais.

"I want just the best gown you've ever done, Uncle Izak," she said.

"A gown as pretty as your sister's?" Uncle Izak asked.

"Lydia, we're leaving," Mel said.

"Prettier," Lydia said. "Much prettier. With lots of tiny pearls." Lydia seemed to quiver with joy under Uncle Izak's tape measure. "And a tux that fits Mel perfectly. Maybe with tails and a vest. Can you do spats?"

"Lydia!" Mel said.

Uncle Izak turned around. Again, the twisting stare. "You're thinking this wedding is about you, Mr. I drive my sweetie's automobile and lock up my wallet?"

Mel felt his face burn. The old man had been watching them in the street. He took a step toward the nasty little tailor.

"Look, Gloria!" Uncle Izak pointed a gnarled finger at Mel. "Look! The groom wants to smack around an old man. How long you think this little boy can keep our lovely Lydia happy?"

Mel stopped and glanced at Gloria. Hands on her hips, she pouted her disapproval.

Mel thought better of taking out the old man. "Okay, maybe I can't stop her from getting her gown here, but I can sure as hell get my tux somewhere else."

Gloria stepped out from behind the counter. She put a loving hand on Uncle Izak's hump. "Uncle Izak," she soothed. "I think we should be nicer to this man."

Mel was sure she glanced his way, sure her eyes sparkled for him.

"He's marrying our little Lydia. Our families have always taken care of each other, and now this nice young man is going to make Lydia his bride. There's nothing we can do to stop that. It just isn't up to us. It's between them."

Mel smiled.

"You love this putz, Lydia?" Uncle Izak asked.

She spun on her dais and said, "I do!"

"Okay. I fit them," Izak said. "We fit them both for tradition's sake. I fit them, and I take good care of our little girl here."

Gloria smiled and kissed the old man on the top of his head.

~ ~ ~

Sitting in million-year-old hardwood waiting chair had Mel cursing the trees the wood came from before Uncle Izak looked up from his work and nodded his approval. Except for occasional appearances by Gloria, the gown fitting was the most excruciatingly boring two hours of Mel's life. When Lydia was trussed, frilled, fluffed, and fluted, Mel had to admit she looked pretty good. If she got that damn fright wig tucked in under a hood or veil or something, she might even look hot enough to keep him up on their wedding night.

"Your turn, Mr. I got important things to do," Uncle Izak said. "Up on the box."

Grateful to stand, Mel stretched his cramped legs and took his place on the dais. Uncle Izak pulled his tape from a pocket. He let it unroll and spill across the floor. Gloria took Lydia into the back room.

Uncle Izak glanced over his hump, then he twisted his head and looked up at Mel.

Here we go, Mel thought. This coffin filler is going to flip me more shit.

Instead, Uncle Izak winked. "I got a tuxedo for you, boy. I got one that will make you look good. You like to look good. I can see that. I can see that you like that automobile little Lydia drives. I can see you like the dress Gloria wears. I can see you want to look good at the wedding. Yes?"

Mel wasn't sure what the old man was up to, but he nodded.

The old man shuffled across the room and pulled a black wooden box out from under the cutting counter. "This is a tux I made for just an occasion like this one. Just like this one. It's a very special—"

"I'm not paying extra," Mel said. "This is her circus, and after the way you treated me, I'm not paying you a penny."

"Yes. Yes, I thought so," Uncle Izak said. "I don't want your money."

"I'm not stupid," Mel said.

"No. No," Uncle Izak said. "I can see how smart you are. I just want to put this tux on you and see if we can make a fit. If we can, I'll give it to you."

"Free?"

"You maybe want my hearing aid?"

"You won't even charge Lydia?"

"I especially won't charge Lydia. You see, Mr. Mel, I was very good friends with her great grandpa in the old country. When he died, I promised I'd take care of all his daughters. There were three. And I promised to take care of their daughters, nine, and theirs, twenty-seven. So, you see, no matter how much I loathe the fact that she loves you, I have to take care of her."

"Family loyalty, then?"

"You've heard of it?"

"Don't be a smart ass, old man. I'll wear your damn tux."

"Good," Izak said. "That's very good. And in return—"

"You said free."

"In return, I just ask you to promise me you'll always be loyal to that little girl from this moment on in thought and deed. Always."

"Yeah, whatever."

"You promise? You promise, and you do it, and everything will work out for you."

"Yeah. Sure."

"With your hand on this tuxedo, the very clothes in which you will forge your sacred bonds?"

Mel reached out and put his right hand on the tux box and held up his left in a mockery of a swearing in. "So help me God," he said.

"So help you, God." Uncle Izak smiled, nodded, and opened the box.

~ ~ ~

Lydia had her heart set on Uncle Izak's tux and gown. Tradition and family history, all that old money crap. Mel didn't figure Uncle Izak's baggy, cuff-worn tux would look any better Saturday when he picked it up than it had during the measuring. That foul, raisin-head was going to make him the fool on his wedding day.

But the foul old raisin-head wasn't in the shop on Saturday. Gloria was, and she looked good in a light, cotton sun dress that curved and shimmied when she moved. "Tradition," she said as she let him in. "Uncle Izak doesn't work on Saturday."

"I'm sorry I've missed the old man." Mel smiled and brushed against Gloria on his way in. "So, he's not going to make sure his special tux fits?"

Gloria's warm hands on his shoulder and waist guided him to the fitting dais. "I'll do it," she said. "Stand here, and I'll get your tux."

Mel watched the green-eyed witch of the tailor shop disappear through the curtain, and he thought about the lame bachelor party the Steinman boys had thrown for him. It had been a kind effort, he knew, but those boys just didn't know how to party.

The way Gloria walked, however, suggested she might know a bit more than Lydia's brothers.

She returned with the black box. "Still dressed?" she asked.

Mrs. Drake didn't raise a fool. Mel was down to his skivvies and had his hands on his boxer waistband.

Gloria put a hand on his. She looked up at him, holding his hand at his navel. "That's good," she said. "We'll start with the shirt." Her pupils were wide in the low light of the tailor shop. Mel liked the game. The ritual of the fitting began.

He stood still, compliant, open to her touch and guidance. She lifted the shirt from the box, slid her nails along his arm, and slipped his arm into a sleeve. She did the same for the other arm. While she slowly buttoned the front, her breath warm on his belly, she talked, "Lydia's a nice girl. You have a good thing there."

Mel wondered if this woman was playing with him. He decided it didn't really matter. "Yeah. Nice." He managed.

"She and I've been friends all our lives," Gloria said.

Mel wanted to put his fingers in her hair. "Nice," he said.

She finished the lowest button then smoothed the shirt down over his chest and boxers. "You do love her, don't you?" Gloria asked.

Mel reached for her, but she smiled and ducked away to pick up the pants in the box.

He laughed. Obediently, he lifted each leg in turn and let her slip the pant legs over his feet. She lifted the pants, her soft knuckles sliding along his thighs. Mel knew she could see how excited he was while she tugged the waist up around his hips. He put a hand to her cheek and lifted her chin. "I'm getting married," he said, "but I'm not dead."

She wet her lips with her tongue and pulled the waistband together. "Uncle Izak says you're going to ruin Lydia's life. Do you think you're going to ruin her life?"

"Gloria," he said, "I'm going to show Lydia things about life that she's never dreamed of."

Her crimson lips hovered near the fly of his pants. She reached into his open fly and deftly buttoned it closed. "There," she said. "Let me see you." She stood up on the dais beside him, and she turned him. They examined him in the mirrors. She turned him around. He gazed into her eyes when he could. He stared openly into the mirror, savoring the firm curve of her cotton sundress rising and falling over her ass.

She saw him watching her in the mirror and laughed. She attached the stiff, high pointed collar to his shirt and tied his bow tie. He steadied himself against her, then he caressed her waist.

She didn't resist. She put on his cummerbund, his three-button vest, and the tailed suit coat.

When she had him dressed, she stood and stared into the mirror. He stood behind her, his hands on her shoulders, his nose in her hair. "The tux is awesome," he said. And it was. It fit him better than anything he'd ever worn. It made him look like a robber baron of the 19th century, like the man of power and substance he was about to become. It made him feel like he could take anything he wanted from anyone.

He turned Gloria around and kissed her.

She responded for a long, warm moment, then she pushed him away. "Mr. Drake," she said. "Lydia is my friend, and she's going to be *your* wife."

"Not until two o'clock."

"You'd make love to me in the tuxedo you'll wear at your wedding?"

He kissed her again.

She pressed herself against him.

The perfect fit of his trousers became too tight.

A noise from the back room pulled them apart. Gloria smoothed her hair and stepped down from the dais.

Uncle Izak shuffled through the curtains. "Oh, good," he said. "It fits."

"I'm impressed," Mel said. "I didn't think this old thing could every look so good."

"The putz thinks I do good work," Uncle Izak said. "My fortune is made!"

"You have to admit, I look good in it."

"I'm very careful to make sure all my clothes fit my clients," Uncle Izak said. "This tuxedo fits you perfectly."

Uncle Izak supervised while Gloria removed the tux, smoothed the felt, brushed the sleeves, and repacked the tux. As Mel was heading out, boxes under his arms. Uncle Izak turned to Gloria. "What do you think, dear? Does it fit him?"

"Perfectly," she purred.

Mel glanced back. Gloria's prurient smile sent him on his way.

~ ~ ~

The sun was high, and the garden was filled with chairs and people. The tux was hot. It was a normal old money wedding. The Benz was already shoe-polished and tin-canned. The round, Rabbi Feaderman and Mel stood sweating under the lawn canopy waiting for Lydia. The music started. Lydia appeared at the end of the walk, her stone-faced father leading her. The Rabbi leaned forward and whispered in Mel's ear. "That tux looks fine on you, son. Is it one of Uncle Izak's?"

Surprised, Mel looked at the corpulent rabbi. He wondered if maybe the man was a bit too happy about the fit. "Yeah."

"Oh, I'm so glad. Lydia's a fine girl, and she deserves the best."

"Yeah," Mel said. He slipped a finger between his collar and his neck. He was sweating, and he could have sworn every step Lydia took made it hotter, made the tux feel tighter.

The Steinmans, father and daughter, reached the lawn chairs, fifty rows of chairs full of over-dressed, stuffed shirts and media fools. The cummerbund seemed to cinch in. Mel pulled at it.

At least when Mrs. Steinman had seen that the groom's side would be empty, she'd herded Steinman sycophants into those chairs.

The shoes cut at his ankles.

"Ugh," he said.

"Excuse me?" the rabbi said.

"It's hot."

"Oh? I thought the lake breeze cooled things off a bit."

Mel looked at the rabbi. He wasn't sweating at all. "No," he whispered.

"No, what?" the rabbi whispered back. "You a bit nervous, son? That's normal. Just remember to breathe, and you'll be fine."

Mel couldn't be nervous. Lydia was okay—no supermodel, and she sure as hell wasn't going to show him anything new tonight.

The breeze seemed to catch the tux jacket and close it around his chest. It stayed closed, and suddenly he couldn't breathe. He was getting dizzy. "Oh god," he said. He clawed at the coat, at his collar.

He couldn't get dizzy—couldn't pass out. He'd worked too hard. Too long. He forced himself to calm down, to breathe. Lydia was almost to him, and he was about to marry into a family with more fucking money than God.

The pants whipped in the breeze, stung his thighs, and pulled tight in his crotch. He cried out. He doubled over. Fell. Chairs clattered and crowd confusion drowned out the band.

From his back on the ground, he stared at the white plastic roof of the tent. A fuzzy orb of light—the sun on the tent fabric—surrounded the rabbi's shadowy face looking down on him. "You just stay down, son. We've got an ambulance on the way."

"Ambulance?" he gasped.

He heard Lydia scream.

Shadow figures swirled around him.

The tux was a second skin squeezing him, crushing him in a sweaty embrace. He felt like a man being shrink-wrapped.

He couldn't believe he was down and losing consciousness. He'd been so close. He'd have married the bitch and given her the night of her life, then he'd have taken the tux back to Gloria.

Every inch of his skin tingled, stung, like all his skin had lost circulation and suddenly regained it. He gasped.

A white-suited black man appeared over him, barely visible in Mel's closing field of vision. The black man flashed a light in Mel's eyes. "He's conscious," the man said.

Mel grunted.

"Jesus H. Christ," a second voice said. "The fabric's fused to his skin! I can't cut it away."

A woman screamed.

Mel felt the EMTs tugging and cutting at his waistband. "Shit!" the black man said. "It's like it grew right into him. This ain't real."

"Slip your scissors into the fly. Start cutting there. We gotta get this thing off."

A vision of Gloria and Uncle Izak came to Mel. "It fits him perfectly," Gloria mouthed.

He felt the scissors at his crotch. He opened his mouth to scream, but his collar was too tight, and he could only croak.

Aunt Linda's Eggnog

Marta turned off the Ford Explorer's lights. Aunt Linda's farm house was lit with Christmas lights from porch swing to gables, but cold Ohio wind swept sparkling ice dust along dark alleys between four long, low barns, the empty legacy of the late uncle Ralph's chicken breeding farm.

"Shall we?" Barry asked. His breath wrapped around the stack of covered dishes he held stable on his lap. The passenger side of the car filled with steam and Barry breath.

Marta stared into the windy night. One lonely light in the barn nearest the house only hardened the darkness of the other four. "It's so cold and sad here," she said. "She won't live forever. Eventually, she'll have to let it go."

"She's picky about who buys Ralph's breeding stock," Barry said.

"Breeding stock?" Marta asked.

"What were you talking about?"

"Aunt Linda's eggnog recipe," Marta said.

~ ~ ~

Marta held the nut bowl, trying to look casual next to the stockings over the fireplace. She checked the room. No one was watching. She dumped the remaining nuts in Barry's stocking.

"Won't work," Nell said. Marta's sister sat at a card table by the tree piecing together a Norman Rockwell jigsaw.

"She'll have more nuts out here before you can open the kitchen door," Vincent said. Nell's husband, he turned his Caterpillar cap backward. He and his son, Andrew, battled dragons on Andrew's new gaming system.

Barry, in uncle Ralph's easy chair reading farm magazines, slipped his half-glasses down his nose and peered at his wife.

"What?" Marta shrugged to feign innocence. "I'm just going to go and fill the nut dish."

"It's a Christmas ritual," Barry said. "You all sneak around trying to steal the recipe."

"You ask," Vincent said. "She answers the same way every time."

"She flashes the twisted mystery smile and blames the eggs," Nell said.

Marta put the empty bowl behind her. "Someday," she said, "She'll join uncle Ralph. The eggnog recipe could be lost."

"So?" Barry said.

"So," Nell said from the puzzle corner, "The best damn eggnog in the world will disappear from the face of the earth!"

"You keep trying, Marta," said Vincent. "You'll wear her down."

"Can I taste the eggnog?" Andrew asked.

"When you're older. The adults aren't ready for you with rum in you," Vincent said. Everyone but Andrew laughed.

Marta had to try. She gripped her nut bowl and headed for the kitchen. Just as she reached for the swinging door, it opened. Honeyed ham, sweet potato, and pumpkin pie smells washed into the living room. Aunt Linda, gray hair in a bun and blue apron protecting her Mrs. Clause dress, blocked the doorway. In one hand, she held a sweating glass pitcher filled with golden eggnog. "Oh, thank you dear," she said. She replaced Marta's bowl with the full pitcher. "I think your sister needs a refill."

"Aunt Linda," Marta stammered.

"Yes dear?" Linda's blue eyes sparkled.

"I wish you'd let me help."

"You're sweet, dear. But dinner's my present to all of you. I like doing it alone." Aunt Linda started to turn.

"Aunt Linda!" Marta said.

Linda paused. "Dear?"

"If you teach me your eggnog recipe, at least I can help with that."

"There's no recipe. The eggs make it good." Linda flashed the famous twisted mystery smile and disappeared into her kitchen keep.

Marta turned. Everyone grinned and stared at her.

"Your sister needs a refill," Nell mimicked between snorts and chortles.

Vincent held up his empty mug. "Here's to Aunt Linda's nog rum eggs," he said.

"You've had enough," Nell said.

"Damn!" Marta said. "She *knew* I was coming."

"Of course she knew," Nell said. "She's Aunt Linda."

Marta passed around the room until the pitcher was empty. Finally, she put it on the sideboard by the kitchen door. She looked at the pitcher then at the door. She picked up the pitcher and reached for the door. She hesitated, expecting it to open.

She pushed forward. The door swung inward.

She glanced back at her family. All eyes were on her. Barry nodded encouragement.

Marta slipped into the kitchen.

A new pitcher full of milk sat on the counter beside a bottle of pure vanilla extract and a cup of sugar.

Marta put her pitcher down. She quickly checked the counters for other ingredients. She found nutmeg and a grinder. She opened the refrigerator. It was full, but it yielded no eggnog secrets.

A recipe box of hand-written 3x5 cards was open on the counter near the back door.

Marta reached for the box.

A door hinge creaked.

Marta spun.

The kitchen was empty.

Behind her, chickens clucked. She spun and found an intercom box hung on the wall next to the back door. Linda's voice came from the speaker, "It's okay dears. Settle down. I just need a few eggs." The hinge creak again, and chicken sounds came through the intercom from the barn.

Marta relaxed. She grabbed the recipe box. She looked under beverages. She looked under drinks, under eggs, under nog, under secret.

Nothing.

A shattering crash made Marta jump. "Ralph! Help me!" Aunt Linda's voice called from the intercom.

Marta looked at the speaker in horror. She couldn't answer. She'd be caught.

"Help!" Linda called. Another crash followed by chicken chaos.

Marta punched the talk button. "Aunt Linda?"

Static.

"Aunt Linda!"

"Marta?"

"Are you all right?"

"I need help in the barn! Quick!"

Marta flew out the back door. She scrambled along the frozen path to the barn. Slipping and sliding, she pulled open the creaking door and went in.

Under yellow lights, Aunt Linda herded little yellow fluff balls, flapping her apron and scooping peeps into a wicker basket.

"Close the door," Linda said.

Marta did. A peep ran headlong into the door and fell over on its side. Little chicky feet pumped in the air like they were still on the ground.

"Grab it!" Linda said.

Marta stooped and scooped. Another peep bounced off her foot then traced an erratic path across the floor toward Aunt Linda.

The quick old woman scooped it up and dropped it in her basket.

Marta looked at her peep. Its legs still pumped like it was running. She sniffed it. It smelled of rum. "They're drunk!" Marta said.

"Of course," Linda said. "They're nog peeps." She snatched up another one. "I knocked over an incubator. Help me catch them!"

When all the peeps were safely inside a new incubator, Marta turned on Linda. "You can't feed peeps alcohol! It's cruel."

Linda stood by the roosting racks. "Oh, my Lord in Heaven, dear! Ralph was a geneticist, not a flim-flam man. He had over 20 patents. He'd never spike the feed." She plucked a brown egg from under a fat, white chicken. Beaked face a little crooked and one eye closed, the fat lump of feathers stared at the egg thief.

"Not the chickens too!"

"That's Ronrica," Linda said. "She's Ralph's first true-to-breed Nog Rum Chicken. He was very proud of her. She still lays more nog rum eggs than any of the others."

~ ~ ~

Marta carried the pitcher of eggnog. Aunt Linda held the kitchen door. Marta paraded into the living room, every eye on her. "More eggnog?" she asked.

"Made it herself," Aunt Linda said. To Marta, she whispered, "Merry Christmas, dear." Then Linda disappeared into her kitchen.

As soon as the kitchen door closed, the family crowded around Marta, mugs extended. Marta poured.

Barry sipped. "You got the recipe!"

"What's the secret?" Nell asked.

"No secret." Marta smiled. "It's the nog rum eggs."

"Oh god," Nell said. "She has Linda's twisted mystery smile."

The Fix in Mr. Giovelli's Bandit

Originally printed in Ghosts at the Coast Anthology. Ed. Dianna Rodgers.

A slot machine is a slot machine, Michael told himself. He'd fixed a thousand of them in his remote, desert workshop, and this wasn't the first time *fix* didn't mean *repair*.

The one-armed bandit on the concrete floor of his tin-shed shop wasn't like the slots he'd been working on over the last couple decades of his forty-five years. Sure, when he was younger he'd worked on mechanical machines with fan-driven randomizers and clockwork fixes. In the shadowed corners of the shop, he still kept neglected bins and crates of gears, springs, and display wheels for the old slots. Sometimes, late at night, after the tin skin of the shop had cooled, when desert silence seemed to turn time back on itself, he closed his eyes and inhaled the magic scent of oil and brass that still lingered in those corners.

Of course, nostalgia didn't turn a buck. The business of *fixing* had changed the same way the machines had changed.

One-armed bandits were all computers now, even the ones with mechanical arms and spinning wheels to give them mechanical look-and-feel. They all had programmable, embedded processors and solid-state circuitry inside. The wheels spun and stopped according to algorithms designed to make money.

Hell, he'd added "bugs" to a lot of bandit assembly code over the twenty years.

But the brass-and-glass monster in his workshop tonight had been brought in by a very special customer. Antonio Vinccenti Giovelli had pulled his boxy yellow Volvo up to the front of the shop and come in. Alone.

Antonio wasn't one of the old guard, not by a piece-and-a-half. He was a new school wise guy. Hard ass? Yeah. But nice about it. Antonio *suggested* things, and they just happened. If they didn't, then people who *might* have helped them happen or who *might* have gotten in the way of them happening disappeared while Antonio was on vacation in Cancún.

Antonio drove a Volvo: armored, bullet-proofed, suspension-enhanced, and over-powered. Still, a freaking Volvo, and canary yellow to boot. His wife was a blond-bobbed babe of a teacher—fourth grade—and she could drive the car to the kid's soccer practices and not get a second look.

So, when Antonio *suggested* that the antique slot be ready for pickup at four a.m., Michael wiped his hands on a shop rag, smiled, and said, "You bet, Mr. Giovelli."

"Call me Antonio," the Mob Dad said. "This is my personal machine. It's a special machine, Michael. I need it at 4."

"Old one. Antique. Union Liberty hasn't built a nickel slot since 1939."

"All original parts, Michael. No bullshit computers."

Michael nodded. "When I'm done, it'll work like it just came off the factory floor."

Antonio Vinccenti Giovelli stepped up close to Michael. He put his face so close that Michael could smell the acid sweat under his sharp English Leather cologne. "No." Antonio said. "Not like it came off the floor. Like it was last night. I want this slot to work the way it always has."

Michael didn't know what that meant, but he was sure as hell not going to ignore Mr. Giovelli over something as strange and obviously important as the difference between new and last night. He rolled an engine hoist out of the shop, strapped up the bandit, and lifted the ornate brass-and-glass monster from the back of the Volvo. They rolled it into the workshop and settled it on the floor near Michael's heavy-work, block-oak workbench.

"What seems to be the problem, Mr. Giovell—"

"Antonio."

"Antonio," he corrected. "Gears slipping? Payout box not loading?"

Mr. Giovelli stepped up, dropped a nickel in the slot, and pulled the braided, worn-brass lever.

Michael could see the lever resistance increase on the pull. The central spring was loading fine. The arm reached bottom and released the wheel ratchet with a satisfying clank. The internal fan whirred. The wheels in the window spun, so the wheel assembly and freewheels were intact and functional.

He watched the wheels, four in all, spinning, spinning, going round and round, the tiny images on them a blur.

There was an audible snap. One wheel stopped dead.

Lock release and halt pin were okay.

The image that appeared in the window was a little golden angel holding a Liberty Dollar.

Cute. Michael hadn't seen that one before. Cherries, oranges, mangos, poker chips, animals… Never a seraphim with a Liberty Dollar. Probably a themed slot from an old casino, one of the ones that got torn down to make room for the theme park casinos. Maybe the Seven and Heaven. He thought he'd heard of that one.

The second snap came, the third. All little angels.

Michael nodded. Even though the fourth wheel still spun, it was obvious the machine had a timing problem. The cog teeth on the spin wheels might be worn so the lockdown pins only slipped into the angel slots.

Of course, that would be a problem. The machine would always pay out. Guys like Antonio hated slots that paid out too often.

Snap. The fourth wheel stopped. The little window showed death—full-robed, sickle in hand, and red eyes gleaming from beneath a shadowy hood. Michael almost laughed out loud. He'd never seen anything like it.

"Shit!" Antonio said.

Suddenly, Michael was very glad he hadn't laughed.

"See. See? That damn death has come up every spin since yesterday at five a.m.. Every freaking time."

The wheels in Michael's brain came up cherries. He got it. The three angels in a row were already rigged. Mr. Giovelli liked that the machine always paid. It was the fourth wheel that was the problem. Antonio Vinccenti Giovelli was a superstitious man. He wanted four angels.

No sweat. Fixing the machine would be a lot easier than repairing it. It was likely only a matter of pulling out the fourth wheel and filing off cog teeth so the lock pin could only seat on an angel.

Antonio Vinccenti Giovelli looked at him with worried eyes, eyes that had seen things Michael didn't want to imagine. "You think you can fix it?" he asked. "Really fix it?"

For a moment, Mr. Giovelli looked like a little kid who hoped for a miracle.

"I'll take care of it, Mr. Gi... Antonio." Michael nodded. "It's what I do." Without thinking, he put a comforting hand on Mr. Giovelli's shoulder and walked him to the Volvo. "I'll take good care of you, Antonio. You come back at four a.m., and I'll have it ready."

"Yeah. I have to have it at four."

In the Volvo, Mr. Giovelli buckled himself in. Michael held the door. Greenhouse heat and the smell of cooked leather seats vented from the car. "Why not tomorrow at ten, Antonio?" he asked. "Why four a.m.?"

Antonio looked up. The little boy was gone. His eyes were balls of onyx set in a marble skull. "I start every day at that machine. I always play at four a.m.. Every morning since I was eight, I drop a nickel and pull that lever. This morning, all angels. This afternoon, on a hunch, I dropped a nickel. It turned up death. It has never shown me death before. I don't want to see death tomorrow."

Michael had been in the business long enough to know that it simply isn't worth the time and effort to argue with someone about their gambling superstitions—especially not a man whose mere suggestion could result in your last moments being on the wrong side of a trunk lid.

"It'll be done," Michael said.

For nearly fifteen hours, he had taken the machine apart and put it back together. He had cleaned it, filed off the burrs on the fourth wheel, lubricated it so well that the machine barely made a noise when the mechanisms tensed and released. He rigged the trigger. He slowed the wheels. He filed off the cog teeth for Death and raised the teeth on the fourth little angel. He sharpened the lock pin.

Still, the fourth wheel came up Death every time. Not an angel. Not a silver dollar. Not the golden word "liberty." Only one image ever came up on the fourth wheel.

He was starting to think the machine mocked him.

Finally, he locked the fourth wheel so the angel showed and it couldn't spin. When the third wheel came up Death, he was sure the machine mocked him.

~ ~ ~

At two-thirty a.m., inspiration finally hit him. He took out all four wheels. He carefully scanned the image of the angel into his computer and adjusted for the curve distortion. He duplicated it in 16 bit color, downloaded the digital file to his metal etcher, loaded the etcher with wheel blanks from an old parts bin, and created four new wheels. Every wheel was covered with perfect, tiny Liberty Union Cherubs. No Death. No silver dollars. No word "Liberty." Just fucking angels.

He put the machine back together and was about to test it when the door opened. A sterile, desert breeze followed Mr. Giovelli into the shop.

Michael was sweating. He'd been working hard, but his sweat was cold.

Mr. Giovelli was sweating. Michael didn't like that, but he was confident of his work.

"All set," he said.

"You fixed it?" Mr. Giovelli sounded so surprised that Michael checked the face of the machine to make sure his little angels were all in a row. They were.

"Yup," he said. "Give it whirl." He stepped back from the machine.

Mr. Giovelli wiped his hands on his thighs. He bit his lip and shot a nervous glance at Michael. He checked his watch. "Four on the dot," he said. He dropped a nickel in the slot. He pulled the lever.

The lever loaded the spring. The spring set released. The fan whirred. The angels blurred in the window.

Click. Cherub.

Michael realized that he'd been afraid something else would come up. That was impossible, of course. He'd fixed it. Still, he realized he'd been holding his breath.

Click. Cherub.

Click. Cherub.

The fourth wheel still spun. Michael smiled. It didn't matter what Mr. Giovelli did, that wheel was going to come up an angel.

Mr. Giovelli stepped back and looked at Michael. "Is this a joke? Did you make it so it would spin this long? I don't like jokes."

Michael held his smile rigid. "Give it a second," he said. "It'll stop."

It didn't. It kept spinning.

Mr. Giovelli slammed his fist down on the bandit. There was an audible snap. The wheel stopped.

Mr. Giovelli relaxed. Four little angels stood in a neat row holding up their dollars. "That's better," he said. "For a second there, I thought it was going to keep going forever."

Michael exhaled.

Mr. Giovelli paid him in cash and gave him a crisp, old thousand dollar bill as a tip. Michael stared. He'd never seen one before—only heard of them.

Mr. Giovelli chuckled. "I keep a few around for special moments," he said. "You did good."

Grinning the whole time, Michael helped Mr. Giovelli load the machine. The armor-plated Volvo rolled away.

Under the area light outside the shop, Michael held up the thousand dollar bill. He laughed out loud. "Come back soon, Mr. Giovelli," he said to the tail lights receding into the darkness along the hard-packed, desert track from his shed to the highway.

About a hundred yards out, the car erupted like a volcano. The shock wave shattered the area light over Michael's door. He ducked and covered to keep from being cut by falling glass.

When he stood, Mr. Giovelli's yellow car was a Swedish bonfire. Michael stared in shock for a long moment. Then he thought about the extinguisher inside the shed.

Too late. That car and everything in it was scrap. The fire was huge and hot. The glow was likely visible for miles.

In fact, the glow was certainly visible on the highway to Vegas.

By dawn, the sheriff would be at his door. It didn't matter that he had nothing to do with Mr. Giovelli's death. If the burning Volvo wasn't probable cause, it wouldn't take long to get more warrants than he had paper in his printer. They'd take his computers. They'd confiscate his data. He'd be screwed. Worse, his clients would be screwed. Then, he'd be dead.

He stuffed the thousand dollars in his pocket and ran back into his shed to clean up.

~ ~ ~

The knock came just as Michael locked off the secret storage room under his workbench. He snugged the heavy bench back into its grooves in the false floor and tripped the locks that made it seem bolted down. He was ready. He used his shop rag to wipe his face. The second knock was louder, insistent. "I'm coming," he called.

The wheels from Mr. Giovelli's bandit were on his workbench. Little Death faces still seemed to mock him. He grabbed the wheels and stuffed them in his pockets.

He crossed the shop and took a deep breath. The third knock came. He opened the door.

A horror of charred skin and weeping, red flesh stood before him. Antonio Vinccenti Giovelli was alive, burned to a crisp, and standing at Michael's door. Behind the horror, by moonlight and the dying flames of the Volvo, Michael saw a deep scar in his desert, hard-packed lane. The scar showed where the walking corpse had dragged the heavy bandit back to his door.

The bandit was as shiny and bright as when it had left the shop. Its unscarred surface reflected moonlight and the twisted features of its owner.

"Fix it," Mr. Giovelli pleaded. "I want Death back in my machine."

Circus Circus

Originally printed in Realms of Fantasy Magazine and Circus: Fantasy under the Big Top anthology.

When the circus was very small, it believed it would grow up to have many multi-colored big tops with banners on the support poles and three rings in each tent. It lived in Mexico then, and its smaller tents were brand new—the Bottle Throw, the Wheel of Fortune, and especially the Palmist and Mystic—because she loved the circus most; and love was, after all, the food that made the circus grow.

The circus worked hard and won the favor of many. It grew, and one day it came across an old circus that was dying. On its last day, the old circus gave up its three big tops. One became a temporary shelter for refugees from a country farther south than Mexico. One became a cover over a produce market in a large village in the Yucatán. The third was given as a gift to the younger, growing circus.

Like other circuses, it went north in the summer, to the land of white people and hard languages. Always, though, it returned to Mexico for the winters. There, like the other wintering circuses, it traveled from village to village. At each village, the circus would find a small, clear area, an area nobody wanted or cared about, a place to dig in its poles and stakes and lift its canvas and lay out its midway and wait for the laughter and love of the children.

At each village, it sent out its people—the stilt walker, the acrobat (because it was still a young circus and only had one acrobat), the fat lady who was also the bearded lady, and the many clowns because anyone could be painted up and sent out to hang fliers and talk to children.

Children.

The circus grew strong on the love of children. It sent out its people to call to the children and bring them from far and wide to spend their pesos and to toss the balls and spin the wheels and have their fortunes told.

Many years passed, and finally a year came when the circus pushed farther south than it had ever gone before—far into steaming highlands and jungles. There, it came on a village, and it settled into a clearing among the trees and called to the people all around, and they came, as they always did. Even though it was in the dark forest, the village was the same as so many villages, and the circus was happy. It had given up the idea that it would one day have many big tops. It had given up the idea that its tents and banners would always be bright. It had grown enough to have two acrobats and to take delight in giving delight.

The children came. They came and played in the midway and laughed.

One boy, a boy who hoped to grow up and join the circus—there was always such a boy in every village, and the circus was careful to pay attention to them—came on the last night before it was time for the circus to move on.

He was a smallish boy who might one day make a good acrobat. Unlike the other boys of his village, this boy had red hair and freckles on bronze skin. The boy had only five centavos, and the circus wondered how he would spend them. At the big top, certainly. Or watching the Geek.

But the boy had purpose in his stride, and he went along the midway straight to the fortune teller. He walked in and sat down on one side of her round table. He stared into her crystal like he might see for himself the things that only a gifted seer like the circus's Senora Bruja could see.

Senora Bruja, her real name was Maria, swished her skirts and flipped her gray hair and flashed her many rings before she sat down.

The circus liked that. It liked Maria more than most of the others. In its earliest memories, she was there. Sometimes at night she would talk to the circus, and the circus would listen, and it made the circus happy.

The boy watched all.

Senora Bruja settled in her chair. She held out her hand, palm up, and said, "Show the spirits that you value their advice."

The boy stared into the crystal and ignored her.

"Cross my palm with gold," she said.

The boy looked up. "This is all I have." He put his centavos on her palm. "Is it enough?"

Senora Bruja closed her long fingers around the coins. She looked up toward the top of her tent, which was not so new as it had once been, and she said, "Spirit of the circus, this boy begs our advice. Is it enough?"

Of course it was.

No circus could turn down a boy who might one day run away to join it.

The circus rustled its canvas and flapped its tent flaps and tugged on the ropes and stakes just enough to answer.

"It is enough," she said.

The boy's eyes went wide and his mouth opened.

"Ask your question, then, my son," Senora Bruja said. She slipped the coins into a pouch at her waist and closed her eyes to wait for the boy to compose himself and offer his question.

After some time, she opened her eyes to see why the boy was silent. From time to time, boys would get scared and run away without ever asking their questions.

He was still there, sitting and staring.

"Well?" she said.

"The circus can answer you." He said it like he knew it was true.

Now, normally Senora Bruja would have said something mystical and scary, but this boy wasn't pretending. He wasn't being silly. He was just saying that the circus could answer, and since it could, Senora Bruja just said, "Yes."

"Wow," the boy said.

"Yes," Senora Bruja said.

"Will you ask the circus something for me?"

Neither the circus nor Senora Bruja, in all her years as a fortune teller, had ever met such a boy as this. She leaned forward, put her elbows on her table, and slid her crystal out of the way so she could see the boy better. "What is your name, boy?" she asked.

"Manolo," he said. "And I want to grow up and be a circus."

"You mean join the circus?"

"No," Manolo said. "I want to be a circus. I want to have tents and acrobats and animals, and I want all the children from all the villages to love me."

Senora Bruja sat back. "Ah," she said. "I see."

For a while, the two people sat and just looked at each other. The circus is patient in the way that things are and people are not, but even a circus can't wait forever. Finally, it flapped and tugged and reminded the two that they were not alone.

"Yes," Senora Bruja said to the circus. "I will ask again."

"The circus," the boy said.

"It wants to know your questions."

The boy sat up straight. He looked all around him.

"Just ask," Senora Bruja said. "It will hear you."

"How can I become a circus?"

Neither Senora Bruja nor the circus had ever heard such a question, and neither of them had any idea how to answer. They sat for a while. A line formed outside Senora Bruja's tent. The circus thought and thought. Finally, it opened tent flaps and tugged on ropes and whispered, "Be a boy who loves to smile and laugh."

Senora Bruja spoke the words for the boy.

The words seemed to make the boy sad. Finally, his green eyes narrowed and his freckled cheeks colored like a golden-red rose, and he smiled broad and wide. "I will," he said. "I want to be a circus, so I will!"

He left and others came to sit in the chair. Others came to ask about lovers and money and children and people long ago gone to other lives and worlds.

No other child came. No other question caught the circus's attention or surprised Senora Bruja.

That night, lying in the stillness and darkness before sleep, Senora Bruja spoke. "The boy," she said.

The circus knew the one.

"He is very sad."

"Why?" the circus asked.

"He is not like the other children here."

"So he is special?" the circus asked.

"So he is, but he is also hurt deep in his heart—alone. Perhaps he should come with us."

"He wants to become a circus," the circus said. "He is a boy."

"Circuses come from somewhere," Senora Bruja said, "as do boys. Perhaps they are not so different."

"Tomorrow," the circus said, "when it is time to leave, we will ask him to come along."

Senora Bruja smiled, nodded, and slept.

The circus did not.

During the deepest part of the night, the weather in the forest changed. Clouds came to cover the stars. Breezes became winds. The smell of distant rain and dust mingled in the wind and pulled at canvas and sisal ropes.

Wakeful, the circus became very uneasy. Such signs are not to be ignored by a circus, and together with the odd boy, the circus was sure morning would bring ill omens.

~ ~ ~

Sunrise brought light, but clouds covered the sun. Even so, striking began and was well underway when Senora Bruja returned from searching for the boy. She came to her tent, tears in her eyes. She sat in her chair, knocked her crystal to the floor, and sobbed.

The circus waited and listened. She would speak when she had breath.

At last, she picked up her crystal, settled it on her table, wiped her eyes, then spoke. "He's dead."

"The boy?"

"Yes."

The crying took her again, and she sobbed a while longer. The strikers came and found her crying. The circus sent them to do other chores while it listened to Senora Bruja.

"How?" the circus asked.

"Bullies in the village. He told them that he talked to you."

"So they killed him? For that?"

"No. They only laughed. He laughed as well. One hit him, and still he laughed. They told him to stop laughing. He told them he was going to become a circus and that he would be a boy who smiled and laughed from now on."

"And?"

"They beat him to make him stop laughing. They kicked him to make him stop smiling. He laughed and smiled. One of them kicked his head. He died."

The sobs came to her again.

The circus could not cry, but it sighed long and hard. It let the damp winds come in and out of its remaining tents, and it moved the horses and bears to groan, and even the strikers paused in their work and crossed themselves for the boy, though they did not know that he was dead.

"We killed him," Senora Bruja said.

"No," the circus said. "Hatred killed him. They hated his smile, and they hated his laughter, and they killed him."

"We told him he could be a circus."

"Yes," the circus said.

The rain came at that moment. It was a powerful rain, a hard rain, and Senora Bruja's tent was the only tent left standing, so all the strikers, and Geeks, and freaks, and barkers, and even the two acrobats came and gathered in her tent.

Senora Bruja lit a lantern and placed it in the center of the table. She picked up her crystal and placed it next to the lantern. The crystal scattered shards of colored light throughout the tent.

One of the acrobats said, "This is a very strange storm. A terrible storm. The tent will not hold."

One of the strikers said, "It will hold. We set the stakes deep and the poles are strong."

The circus said, "Maria, tell them."

Senora Bruja said, "We have done wrong; we must set the wrong right."

The circus had her tell the tale of the boy, and when she was finished, the circus told her that it had a plan. It gave her instruction for all its people.

Even in the terrible storm, the strikers went out of the tent, the barkers went with them to help if they could, the acrobats climbed poles and lines to secure tents even though lightening might kill them, and Senora Bruja read in her mystical books until she was sure she knew how to do the things she needed to do in the days to come.

~ ~ ~

On dawn of the day after the circus was to have left, the big top was up again— the big top, the midway, the barkers, the Wheel of Fortune, the Bottle Toss, and Senora Bruja's tent. The acrobats cavorted in new sunlight in the early morning path to the gates of the circus, and the circus had been moved so its fences and gates surrounded the village's graveyard.

The big top stood over an open grave, a freshly dug grave, a grave at center ring that was just the right size for a boy who had smiled in the face of death.

The man on stilts, the fat lady, the acrobats, and all the strikers and barkers and animals went into the village and handed out fliers to a free show.

The acrobats, who were by far the strongest and fastest of all in the circus, took special care to find the bullies, the three boys who had beaten a smiling child. Each of those boys received a special, front-row ticket.

Now, the mother of the boy who smiled was sad, of course. While the village buzzed with excitement for the strange doings of the circus, she donned a black scarf, her black dress, and she cried while she washed her son.

Crying, she put him in a small cart. Still crying, she hitched her burro to the cart and started up the hill outside the village, started the long trudge through the jungle forest and up to the graveyard where she would say goodbye to her son.

She was so sad that she didn't notice that the circus had moved. She was so sad that she didn't notice the line of silent circus people on both sides of the path to the graveyard.

As a mother should be who must bury her son, she was so sad that she did not notice that the circus held open the flaps of the big top for her or that the sun disappeared when she, the cart, and the boy went inside, or even that the open grave was in the center of center ring.

She simply went about the business of wrapping her son in her best linens and, with the help of two strikers, laying him into the grave.

While she knelt next to her son's grave to pray his soul into the next world, the people of the town arrived for the promised, free show.

As the circus expected, they had all noticed that the circus had moved. Not one person from the entire village could resist the invitation to come to the big top in the graveyard. Such a thing had never been seen, never even been heard of.

The tiers of benches filled. The performers prepared. Senora Bruja donned the Ring Master's uniform, and the Ring Master helped harness the trick horses and helped muzzle the dancing bears.

All in silence.

The orchestra wore black. They sat with their instruments on their laps.

The crowd was silent.

The performers were silent.

The tent flaps and ropes were silent.

The only sound in all the circus-surrounded graveyard was the sound of a mother praying for the soul of her son.

When she said, "Amen," she looked up. For the first time, her grief parted enough to see that she and her son were surrounded by the villagers and that the villagers were surrounded by a circus.

Senora Bruja, wearing the top hat and tails, stepped up to her, placed a gentle hand on her shoulder, and said, "Your son loved the circus."

The boy's mother nodded.

"We wish to say goodbye in our way. May we?"

The bewildered mother looked around. She nodded again.

Two clowns came across the center ring and helped the woman to a seat. A trainer came with carrots for the burro and led him away to one side.

The seats were full. The bullies sat in a row, excited and a little confused, but clearly unrepentant.

Senora Bruja smiled and lifted her hand to her Ring Master's top hat.

The circus closed the tent flaps. Ropes tied them shut. Darkness filled the space inside the tent.

Senora Bruja began the performance. The music sounded. The clowns moved into the center ring.

People murmured in the darkness.

Someone tried the ties on the flap and found they could not undo the ties without light.

Clown horns sounded. Clown laughter filled the tent.

Senora Bruja announced each act in order, and each act performed in the darkness.

From time to time, people tried to leave by the tent flaps or by crawling under the edges of the tent, but at the edges of the tent they found tigers and lions and geeks and bearded ladies.

Finally, the acrobats had swung on their trapeze in the dark, the most dangerous and death-defying of the feats, and one that was very important to the circus' plan and the magics of Senora Bruja's books.

Senora Bruja called for lights, and the spotlights were lit, and the big top over the boy's grave filled with light, and the people of the village sighed their relief.

Senora Bruja stood before the three bullies. "This was a performance for our friend, Manolo," she said. "Forever more and after that, he will never again see a circus because of what you have done."

The bullies fidgeted and looked about.

Senora Bruja pointed to one, the smallest, "You," she said, "to prove how big you were, threw the first stone."

"He was laughing at us," the boy said.

"You," she pointed to the second boy, who was bigger and leaner and harder in jaw and arm, "to show that you were bigger and stronger and loyal to the other boys, you struck the first blow."

"He wouldn't quit smiling," the boy said.

"And you," she strode up to the largest of the boys, the boy that had the darkest eyes, the boy that hated so much that he would never smile unless someone else was hurt, the boy whose hatred infected others. "You set them to the task, and you kicked Manolo so hard that he died."

"He's different," the boy said, "His father was from the North. He deserved to die." The boy spat.

The people of the village bowed their heads in shame. The clowns frowned, filed up, and stood in a row, three on each side of Senora Bruja.

"You!" she said, pointing to the first boy, "Come down into the ring."

"No," the boy said, but two clowns had already grasped his arms. The boy screamed for help, and several men in the crowd began to get up, but the circus shook and stretched its ropes and raised such a howl that the men became afraid and sat back down.

Senora Bruja brought the boy to the grave. The clowns held him.

"Here," she said, "Is where a boy's joy ends. Here is where you put him, and here is where you will one day come."

The boy cried. He sobbed. "I'm sorry," he said. "I'm so sorry."

Senora Bruja lifted her long-fingered hand, and with a quick motion, she flicked a tear from the boy's cheek. The tear rose in the spotlight. It flashed like a trapeze artist in a sequined suit. It rose, arched, sparkled, fell, and came to rest on the linens of Manolo's shroud.

The clowns released the boy, who ran for his life. The tent flaps untied, opened, and let him run off into the bright daylight of the first day of his new life.

The tent flaps closed again.

The people murmured, but now that they had seen what the circus had in mind, they were more calm.

Senora Bruja and the clowns went to face the second boy. "You," she said, "Come down."

Braver in his cowardice than the first boy, the second stood tall and stepped into the ring. Escorted by clowns and Ring Mistress, he approached the grave. There, he made a show of crying and claiming he was sorry.

The circus laughed so all could hear.

The sound of it sent a stir of fear through the crowd.

The false sorrow of the boy ended.

Senora Bruja took up his hand. "You," she said, "drew first blood with your blow, and you shall return in kind." She crossed his palm with a long fingernail. A cut appeared in his flesh.

The boy howled in earnest now, and the clowns held him.

Senora Bruja spoke, "If you have no sorrow for your actions, then you will give of your life." She shook his hand, and three drops of blood arched out, crimson and bright, and fell to the shroud—one each over Manolo's eyes and one over his mouth.

People gasped. A woman screamed.

Senora Bruja freed the boy.

Holding his injured hand, he ran. He ran, looking back over his shoulder, and he tripped on the ring, tumbled, fell, broke his neck and died.

Silence filled the tent.

The lifeless boy, still holding his hand, head bent back and to the side in an impossible posture, held the eyes of every face in the big top.

The clowns and Senora Bruja stood before the third boy. "Come down," she said.

The third boy said something very rude. He stood, turned, and headed for the aisle and the tent flaps.

A bear three times his size stood on hind legs in the aisle. Its giant forepaws came up to its muzzle and stripped away the leather cup and straps. The bear lifted its lip and growled.

A wet stain appeared on the boy's pant leg.

A girl giggled, and the boy turned red.

"Come down," Senora Bruja said.

The boy, followed by the dancing bear, came into the ring. He followed Senora Bruja to the grave of Manolo.

"Manolo came to us," she said. "He wanted to be a circus."

A few foolish people laughed, still believing it was only a show. Most did not.

"That's just stupid," the boy said.

The circus laughed.

The boy cringed.

Silence filled the tent once more.

"You kicked his head," she said. "What gift do you offer the dead?"

The boy spit on the shroud.

Senora Bruja nodded.

The clowns grasped the boy's arms.

The boy struggled, but these clowns had striker's muscles. These clowns could lift a fifty-pound mallet and bring it home on a stake. These clowns could hang upside down from a pole ring and pull on fist-thick ropes and tie them off.

The struggles of a boy, even a boy the size of a man, were nothing to them.

Senora Bruja took the boy's head between her hands. She looked deep into his eyes. "From you," she said, "The gift shall be mind. For all your days, and until you are one hundred years old, you will know that once you hurt a smiling boy. You will remember the joy in his smile and laughter, but you will never see joy in a smile or hear it in laughter again. You will remember that once your mind was clear, but *you* will only speak gibberish and riddles and everyone you meet will laugh at you and make fun of you."

She kissed him on the lips, took water from his mouth, then she too spat on the grave of Manolo.

The clowns released the boy. He screamed. He cried. He spoke, but only foolish noises and slobber came from his lips.

The little girl laughed again.

Senora Bruja turned to the people. She held up her top hat. The trumpet sounded three times. She thanked them for coming to the performance, and she bade them go, she bade them remember Manolo, and she bade them be kind to one another in his memory.

The tent flaps opened.

Silent, somber people filed away from the circus and back to the village.

Finally, only the circus, the people of the circus, a mother, a burro, and an open grave remained.

"Come," Senora Bruja said, "Come down."

The mother stepped into the ring.

"Together, we will bury your son," Senora Bruja said.

Together, they knelt. All the people of the circus knelt with them. All took up handfuls of dirt and worked to bury the boy who had wanted to be a circus.

When the grave had been filled, Senora Bruja said, "For three days, we will stay here. I hope you will stay with us."

"My burro?" Manolo's mother asked.

The circus whispered to Senora Bruja. Senora Bruja nodded.

"Yes," Senora Bruja said. "Your burro will stay with the performing horses."

"It's true, then," the mother said. "Manolo told me you could speak to the spirit of the circus."

"The spirit of the circus can hear me and speak to me if it chooses, and it has asked me to do one more thing before we rest." She crossed the mound of the grave, and she knelt, and she placed three coins, Manolo's centavos, in a row on the mound of the grave. Then she drew a circle around the coins.

~ ~ ~

Each morning, Senora Bruja and the mother of Manolo returned to the grave in the big top. On the third morning, the mother gasped. There, where the coins had been was a tiny big top tent. The fabric was new and striped in gay, red, and white. Pennants of red, and white, and green fluttered at the points of the small poles. Flaps hissed and snapped in a tiny breeze.

The tiny circus laughed, and the laugh was the laugh of Manolo.

Senora Bruja handed Manolo's mother a book of arcana—a fortune teller's book. "Now," Senora Bruja said, "We strike and move on. For a time, you will go with us. In a few years, you will go North—you and your circus."

"My son," she said.

"No. He is a circus now. He will grow. He will spread smiles and laughter, and you will be his fortune teller."

Manolo's mother nodded solemnly.

The elder circus sighed, and all the people in it smiled and nodded and went about the work of creating the smiles and laughter that save souls.

Worlds Apart

She danced like Vanette. She looked like Vanette. She smelled like Vanette.

My dark heart knew she was only a perfect replica of Vanette.

She pirouetted, sable hair feathering out on the air in a smooth scarf of wishes and red highlights reflecting living room lights. Her narrow hips and firm ass were barely covered now, glistening with sweat, lubricating her cotton briefs so they rode up. With each pirouette, she flashed a perfect smile of desire for me, more perfect than Vanette's had ever been.

As perfect as an alien gift could make it.

After first contact, the Eellor had wanted to give Earth a gift, had wanted to give us something that would give peace of mind. They had no understanding of economy—of social order. They gave us replica technology—cheap, thoroughly realistic, totally obedient human reproductions.

For the price of a meal, a human could order the entire cast—in full makeup—of a Broadway musical into the living room. They would perform, or do whatever was wished of them, then they would leave and quietly and completely dispose of themselves.

The Vanette I worshipped was dead to me. She had left me with my imperfect memories. The Vanette in my living room was very alive, alive just for me, and she was dancing closer, close enough that I could smell her sweat, feel myself warming to the idea of holding her, of pulling her down onto me.

She stopped in front of me. She looked at the split in my dressing robe.

Her laugh was Vanette's.

She knelt before me, warm breasts against my knees. She ran her fingers up my thighs and under my robe.

"Stop." I said.

She froze. The question in her eyes was so real—so sad.

I hesitated a moment before saying *it*.

But I said it.

"Go away."

It was a death sentence.

She pouted, and like a disgruntled sex slave, she tapped my thigh once before standing, turning, and walking out of my home. In a few minutes, she would be so much gas and water mixing into earth and air and leaving no trace that she had ever been in my house.

The bitch of it was that I could have her rebuilt to try again in less time than it took her to self-destruct. I had done it before.

Fucking Vanette.

I stood from my easy chair and headed to my room. I'd done the place out in a Carlsbad Grotto motif, and it was cool and dark there. I lit a candle to give some flicker to the carefully placed shadows in the room. Dressing, I decided for the I-don't-know-how-manieth-time that I would move on, that I would leave Vanette behind, that she meant nothing to me.

The bitch.

Every time I became angry at her, I gave her power in my life. Every time I brought her image to my home or to my bed, I gave her power in my life. The more debased my treatment of her image, the more power she had.

And *she* didn't even know it.

We lived worlds apart. She lived on Domest, the fourth world out from Deneb; I lived on Fortunata, the sixth from Altair. From Earth, the difference seen in the night sky is only slightly more than the length of a swan's wing.

In a starliner, it was nearly a year's journey.

I had a ticket. I'd had a ticket since the day she walked out, since the day she told me she wanted to be an independent woman and had run off with her new Eellor replication of the perfect man.

He was taller than me.

"That's the problem with you," she said. "You always compare yourself to men."

He had blond hair.

"The hair doesn't matter," she said.

But it did. She had made him with long, golden hair clasped back in a thick pony tail.

He looked younger than me.

"I ordered him at exactly your age," she said. "There's no difference. You're so insecure," she said. "You'll be fine. I've signed off on the house and our joint accounts. What more do you need?"

She left before I could tell her. She didn't want to hear what I might need.

It would have been easier for me if she had left me for a real man instead of the representation of a man that let her wrap herself in fantasies and delusions.

I pulled the ticket out of a dark corner of my grotto. It flashed a neon expiration date. I couldn't afford to renew it. I had to decide soon what I was going to do, whether I would leave to go find her—try to convince her to take me back.

The ticket blinked at me, taunted me with the fleeting, flashing march of moments lost—lived without her. I put it in my pocket and left my house. I just left. There was nothing there I wanted. It was full of memories of her and of all the graven images of her that I had conjured in the two years she'd been gone.

I paused at the door. I considered ordering her up so I would have a companion on the trip.

Instead, I sealed the door. I had proven to myself often enough that the image of her, no matter how substantial, wasn't enough.

~ ~ ~

A year in space is a long time to think. To take real lovers was a conscious decision. Two lovers found me on the trip—both *real* women.

Blond Adriana, the first, was supposed to help me forget, to feel less angry, less used and manipulated by my own obsession.

She tried hard. She had a few things to work out for herself, and we used and abused one another's bodies for fifty-seven light years. She could be sweet and hot. She could be nasty and needy. We played every game we could think of to pass the time. We even created a couple of orgies from Eellor men and women to sate some of our more imaginative lusts.

It wasn't until we were having a threesome with Vanette that things went bad. Adriana had asked me to create my perfect woman for her to enjoy while teasing me, while driving me wild.

One second, everything was fine. Vanette danced. Adriana licked me. Then, Vanette was on her knees with Adriana. Adriana grabbed my false Vanette's hair and rammed her face down to me hard.

Smothering, Vanette struggled.

I stood up fast. I slapped Adriana. She released Vanette, who smiled up at me like she was supposed to.

Adriana, on her back, holding her cheek, looked up at me through tears. "Asshole," she said. "It's only a toy."

I never saw Adriana again. I sent Vanette away two days later then wallowed in my shame for uncounted light years.

Two months out from Deneb, I met a woman in the zero-g core of the ship. She was practicing yoga, and we hit it off quickly. Within a couple of ship's days, we were sleeping together. Protessa was as different from Vanette as Adriana. Protessa was shorter, younger, quieter, lustier, and much more flexible than Vanette.

We shared interests in Human Economic History, something Vanette had taught me to love. I learned zero-g yoga, and we practiced every chance we got.

For a while, I thought she was perfect for me, that she and I had a deep bond growing. I even caught myself at times thinking of Vanette in the past tense.

Finally, we landed. For the first time in a year, I felt the tug of real gravity. Along with the tug of real gravity, I felt Protessa's hand slip away from mine.

Her husband and son met her at the docks.

~ ~ ~

It took me a couple of weeks to find Vanette. Apparently, she had long ago given up on her perfect man. She'd taken up with a real man—a man with a name, Roland Leurenette. He was a mid-level politician, some kind of functionary.

I couldn't imagine her feeling anything long-term for a bureaucrat. She didn't need money, and he couldn't have the imagination to keep her entertained—and the Vanette I had known was all about being entertained.

The door of their house was made up to look like an eighteenth-century, affluent French country home.

In the surreal, blue-red evening hues of Deneb, I walked between perfectly squared hedges along a curvy flagstone walk. At the door, I hesitated, my hand high, my fist clenched.

Two years without her. A year to get here.

Adriana.

Protessa.

There were other women in the spiral arm. The split with Vanette had left me well enough off. I could find one. I deserved to be happy, didn't I?

I needed Vanette.

My hand came down on the door. I knocked three times.

The door opened before the fourth knock.

Vanette looked at me. Her eyes showed a few new lines at the edges. Her triceps weren't as toned as the replicas I'd created. Her hips weren't as trim.

"Who's there, Dear?" A man's voice came from the interior of the house.

"Nobody," she said over her shoulder. Then to me, she said, "You shouldn't have come."

"I had to."

"I left you enough to make a life."

"You loved me," I said.

She looked at her feet and steadied herself against the door. After a long moment, she whispered, "Yes."

"It wasn't life without—"

"Leave," she said.

"Vanette," I said. "Please. I need—"

Her fingers touched my lips. "Stop," she whispered.

I froze.

She put her perfect hand on my breast and pushed me back. "God, I'm sorry, Manique," she said.

"For what?" Hope touched my heart.

She whispered it, but I heard her. "*Go away.*" Deneb's final flash of golden evening light caught in a quivering tear at the corner of her eye. She closed the door.

I turned and walked into her garden.

Soon, I'll be water and gas melting into the earth and air. Soon, not even my imperfect, loving memories of Vanette will remain. If there is a God for such as I, I'm grateful for the peace that will soon be mine.

El Bosque Circular

Third Place in the Short Story America Festival Contest. Sept. 2012. Originally printed in Short Story America, Vol. III.

A man who grew up near our village, it is said, tried to live his entire life on his parents' farm. When his father or mother went to town, their burro carrying pots or sticks or chickens, he stayed home to tend their tiny farm. When they asked him, "Brazos," for that was his name, "Brazos, why don't you take the burro to town today? Take the sticks we have gathered and sell them for some coins to the blacksmith to kindle his forge," Brazos would say, "No. Better that I stay here and watch the bean field so the javelinas do not come from the forest and break the fence and tear up our hard work. It would be a shame to have worked so hard only to feed the wild pigs."

"It will do you good to go to the village," his mother said. "You should see more than just our tiny farm."

His father winked and laughed. "In the village, you might become a man."

The wink and laugh made Brazos so uncomfortable that he feared the village even more. Brazos was content with his work with the beans and the goats.

So he grew, and a day came when his father took ill and lay himself down in the field among the beans. "I'll just rest a moment," his father said. "You work the plow and turn the rows, and when I'm recovered, I'll help."

So, urging the burro forward, Brazos plowed in steady, straight rows just as he always did, just as his father had taught him. And when he came the length of the field and back again to his father, he found that beans had already sprouted and grown so much that they had covered his father up. The bean plants made the shape of a man, but when Brazos pushed his hands into the vines, he found that his father was gone, replaced by leaves and vines surrounded by dirt.

Brazos continued to plow, but he made a little turn with the plow to avoid the father-shaped bean plants. He was wise enough to know that if beans had grown so quickly, there was no reason to plow them under and lose the coming bounty.

At the end of the day, he returned the burro to its tiny shed. He cleaned the plow and hung it on the wall of the shed then he entered their humble adobe house.

His mother smiled and nodded, all the while pounding dough into rounds to make tortillas for Brazos and his father. "Where is your father?" she asked.

"He has become a bean plant." Brazos sat at the table and waited for his mother to serve the evening meal.

Silently, she nodded. She pounded her dough. A tear rolled down her ancient cheek and dripped onto a tortilla. A tiny puff of corn flour lifted up around her tear. It grew into a larger cloud of flour, and for a moment Brazos could not see his mother.

When the cloud of flour cleared, she was gone. Only a stack of tortillas remained.

Brazos waited for all the night and half the next day for her to return to feed him.

At last, his stomach would let him wait no longer. "Mother?" he called. "Come out now. Come out. It is enough that father has become a bean plant."

Only the bray of the burro answered him. The burro called him to bring its breakfast and start the day's work.

Brazos went to the burro, fed it, milked the goat, and gathered sticks near the edge of the bean field, along the fence, and near the forest.

While working near the forest, he heard the javelinas in the shadows of the trees. They snorted and scuffed and seemed to laugh at him.

Brazos was no fool, so he checked the fence, and he looked over the field and saw the bean plant that was the shape of his father. "No," he said to the forest shadows. "You will not root in my field this season."

He took his sticks to their humble adobe home and piled them with other sticks, more than enough to take to the village for coins.

He went in, and he called to his mother, "Mother, I need to eat. The javelinas are coming to the fields. I need to eat to have the strength to mend the fences and fight if need be."

Silence answered him.

"Mother," he called. "You must take our sticks to the blacksmith for coins. We will need wire to mend the fence."

The silence remained, a silence he had never heard before—a silence that was both in the home he had shared with his parents and in his heart where his parents had lived.

The stacked tortillas still stood where he had last seen his mother. He took a few. He went to the field and picked beans from the plant that had once been his father. He wrapped the beans in the tortillas and ate them, cold and hard. Then he bound up the sticks, placed them on the back of the burro, and headed to the village for the first time in his life.

From his farm, a long and narrow track of dust marked the path to the village. The track passed through the forest where the javelinas lived.

Brazos knew that the burro had traveled to the village many times, and he let the animal find its way along the winding, forking path.

Brazos followed.

In the shadows, the javelinas laughed.

Brazos and the burro traveled long through the whole of the day and into the night, and still they had not left the forest. Still, the shadows hid the javelinas and made their snorting laughter seem a thing unnatural.

"Father," Brazos said, "I do not know the way."

The javelinas laughed.

"Mother," Brazos said, "you were right. I should have gone to the village before this."

The javelinas laughed.

"Burro," Brazos said, "please find the way to the village. It is dark, and we are lost."

The burro stopped, turned, peered from wide brown eyes, and sat on his haunches.

Brazos urged the burro on, but it did not move.

Brazos cursed the burro, but it did not move.

Brazos kicked the burro, but it had turned to stone and he hurt his foot.

The javelinas laughed, and the shadows grew, and Brazos was alone in the forest.

He had once heard his father speak of a star that was is always in the north. He looked upward, but only the branches of trees against the shine of a half-moon could be seen. Even if he could see the stars, he could not know which one his father had meant.

He left the stone burro and walked onward, hoping to find a path to take him home or to the village—hoping for either the familiar or for the face of someone who had known his mother or father.

In darkness, he wandered for a very long time, and the javelinas followed, always snorting and laughing at him for being such a fool that he had never been to the village before and did not know the way.

Time passed. Perhaps a day. Perhaps a week. Perhaps many years, for in the deepest part of the forest, night and day seemed all the same to him.

Eventually, he saw a shape, white and tall on the track before him.

"Hello," Brazos called. "Hello there!" He ran forward, but when he came upon the shape, it was a stone burro much like his own. "Ah, burro," he said. "You cannot help me."

And so he traveled on.

And on.

Until he came again to the burro.

"There cannot be three stone burros." He looked closely at the burro and saw that it was his own, and he saw that his own sandals had made tracks past the burro twice before.

The shadows deepened. Javelinas laughed and snorted and clacked boney tusks against sticks and stones. The air became thick and hot with the earthy smell of their breath, and Brazos was alone in the forest.

Brazos turned in a circle. On the ground, his sandal tracks went forward and back from the burro; so, he set off to the side of the burro, away from his own tracks and the stone guide he once trusted.

Before long, the shadows became lighter. The laughter of the javelinas grew more distant.

Brazos chose his footsteps well. He picked his way around clumps of thorn. He pushed through tall grasses. He slipped from tree shadow into meadow. He crossed to a track, which became a road, which led him at last to a church at the edge of the village.

Brazos knelt and looked up. Blazing white adobe rose into the blue sky. A bell, shining bronze in the sunlight, rang once. A young woman walked up to him. "What are you doing in the dirt?" she asked.

Brazos, still looking into the sky, said, "I have never seen such beauty."

The woman laughed a little and blushed.

It is said that Brazos married the woman, who was much like his mother, though younger and stronger. It is said that they raised a child who looked much like Brazos and who is afraid to ever leave the village.

The Cell Door Opened

Originally printed in Story America Vol. IV.

In prison, Tevis had gone insane. Worse, he knew it. Worse still, the fear of it had long passed into a silent acceptance and even gratitude for an effortless peace he had found within his insanity, a peace broken only by tortured memories in the moments just before his dreams melted his pain and released him from his timeless steel and concrete world each night.

His cell door closed, and it was the same closing as the night before, and the night before, and the night after, and the night after. The cell door closed, and the fact of its electronic tick, metal-on-metal grind, and the echoing steel tock of the bolt driving home was both a clock ordering the moments of his life and the absence of a clock because all his moments had become one moment.

Lights out came, a sudden manmade nightfall. Darkness embraced him. He lay on his bunk, the cell's urine, sweat, steel, and cleaning fluid reek flavoring each slowing breath. The breath came in. It went out. It was like the cell door. It opened and closed. It, too, was a clock in his life and the absence of clocks.

His eyes closed. The dark memory came, and with it came agony lessened only by the peaceful knowledge that the memory would melt and twist and finally stretch thin until fully replaced by harmless dreams.

She was walking in the rain and darkness just before midnight. She was too fine to be a woman alone in life and too well dressed for walking through the parking lots of a warehouse. No doubt she'd had a fight with her boyfriend. Maybe she'd walked out on him at a bar. Maybe he'd gone home with someone else. Maybe she'd slapped him in a fury and made him stop the car, or maybe he'd tossed her out on the street to show he had the power in their lives.

It didn't matter. He pulled the gray hood of his sweatshirt up to keep off the rain.

She was local, taking the shortcut through the parking lot and over the tracks into a ticky-tacky subdivision. An outsider would have been afraid of the darkness and isolation of the lots and the railroad right-of-way. Out-of-towners thought horrors lived in every second trapped in every shadow in America. Locals thought monsters only lived in the darkness of bigger cities.

Tevis knew the shadows of his town, the parking lots, the woods beside them, the trails. He knew the rain and the rails.

What he didn't know, couldn't remember, was precisely which moment was the one in which he became a monster trapped in a second trapped in a shadow.

He was sure it wasn't the moment when he decided to sit down and let his *left foot melt into the rain, a long purple stain like Easter egg coloring spilled onto a newspaper, stretching out toward the edge of a table and sliding into a storm drain surrounded with…*

~ ~ ~

Lights up. The cell door opened. Single file. Shit, shower, and shave. The mess hall. The same day every day.

High and low politics swirled around Tevis, never touching him. Guards and inmates had long ago stopped hassling him. Guards played games with inmate pawns, and inmates played games with guard pawns. Guards played games with guards, and inmates played games with inmates. Men came and went. The light of tired, empty souls flashed brightly in rebellious eyes for brief moments of glory in the exercise yard or the shops before they went out—extinguished by a club, a shot, or a shank.

Tevis worked the library. Even there, he was alone. No one but the Warden seemed to know his true name. They called him "Tipped." Some said it in two syllables, "Tip-Ed." Some said it in one, "Tipt."

He'd read a book that said to know a thing's true name gave you power. At the time, it had seemed true. Now, it was like all his other thoughts—exactly like all his other thoughts. It was true and not true. It was part of the mist of everything that is no more and no less than everything else.

He pushed his wobbling cart between shelves of books organized by type and number just like the men in the cells, just like the minutes on the clocks, just like the thoughts of other men. One castor's bent post made a cart wheel shimmy back and forth. An inmate stepped in front of his shaky cart, a guy he'd never seen in the library before, thin, sharp, and black-haired.

The cart shook. *Slaughterhouse Five* slid across the mound of books and off the edge of the cart. In his mind, he saw the book hit the gray concrete floor spine first. He saw it open. He bent to pick it up. An italicized line caught his eye, *"Billy Pilgrim has come unstuck in time."*

Then the book was in his hand, and he didn't know if the book had hit the floor and he had picked it up or if his hand had known it was going to fall and had shot out and caught it or if the con that had stepped in front of him had handed it to him. They were all the same to Tevis.

"Name's Vincent," the guy said. "Sorry about that."

But Vincent's voice told Tevis more than his words. Some cons were sorry about some things. A few were sorry about everything. This man wasn't sorry about anything.

"What's your name?" Vincent asked.

"Excuse me." Tevis tried and failed to move past.

Vincent spoke very slowly. "Your name?"

Tevis heard the lie. Vincent only pretended he thought Tevis hadn't understood the question. Vincent wanted something. Tevis answered, hoping it would be enough. "My name is Tevis." He nudged his cart forward a couple inches. "Excuse me."

"Of course," Vincent said, but he didn't step aside. "We all do what we have to do, yeah?"

Tevis settled Billy Pilgrim on the cart and pushed forward again. This time, Vincent made room, but only barely enough for Tevis to continue pushing the cart on its wobbly way. As he passed, Vincent's rotted meat breath heated Tevis' neck.

~ ~ ~

The cell door closed. He lay on his bunk. The cell's urine, sweat, steel, and cleaning fluid reek flavored each breath. Lights out darkness embraced him. His breath came in. It went out.

She walked through the middle of the lot, and he knew her route from the line of her walk. He knew where the trail slipped between the blackberry thicket to the railroad bed, and he knew where it cut through a strip of sickly trees and bushes and out onto a cul-de-sac in the neighborhoods.

He pulled up his hood to keep out the rain.

The moment when he became a monster wasn't yet. At least, he didn't think so—not while he watched her from the shadows of the vacant, wooded land outside the cyclone fence surrounding the lot. When he ran along the trail outside the fence, every few strides touching the cold galvanized steel wire with his fingertips, he was still just Tevis—just curious. That was all, right? Just curious. She was pretty, alone, upset. In that moment, he believed he might even help her.

In the middle of his dash toward the rail line, he stopped. One hand gripping the wet, cold fence wire, he looked around the woods. A few yards away, a sewer access rose from the scrub like a concrete cone capped in an iron ring. It was a clock, and he knew it was a clock, but he didn't understand why. He'd been there before. He was there now. He'd be there again. That, he knew, and he knew that he would become a monster. He had to find the moment, the exact moment, so he let go of the fence and ran toward the rail line.

He reached the tracks and cut right toward where she would appear. Shadows became dark vapor clouds made of wet creosote and rotting ditch moss. He ran hard, feet twisting on the sloped, crushed limestone ballast of the rail bed. He ran hard, and the wind came into his face, clearing away the shadow stench and replacing it with late spring grass, fresh rain, and blackberry blossoms. Water slipped from his shaggy hair onto his cheeks then down his neck and into the collar of his jacket. It crawled down his chest. Gooseflesh rose all over his skin and, even running like he was, he shivered so hard that the air around him *caught a chill and shook itself to get free of the water and be dry and warm again. The blackberry blossoms grew broad and pink and white and covered the bushes in a sheet, and the limestone smoothed itself into a paved road where no one need ever run, ever...*

~ ~ ~

The cell door opened. Shit, shower, and shave. Mess. Library counter duty all day.

"Tevis, right?" The man put his book on the counter.

Tevis reached for it, but the man held onto it. Tevis tugged lightly, but the man still held on.

"Isn't that your name?"

Tevis had to look at him. The thin man was tight and toned and hard inside and out—the *Slaughterhouse Five* man, Vincent.

Tevis nodded. "Are you finished with this?" It was Brian Greene's, *The Elegant Universe.*

"You know who I am, yeah?"

Tevis knew the question meant he was supposed to show that he knew more than Vincent's name, but it was like all questions—far away and no more or less important than any other. It had an answer, and the answer lived in the distances between *The Elegant Universe* and the cold, concrete soul behind the man's gray irises.

"No."

"We met the other day."

"Your name is Vincent."

"You said you didn't know who I was."

"I don't."

"You're insane," the man said. "You raped and killed, and it broke your little brain. That's what they say, yeah?"

Tevis tugged on the book again, but Vincent held it firm.

"I need you to do something for me," Vincent said.

"Are you done with this?"

"You're a short-timer." Vincent let go of the book. "Back to Littleton, yeah? They're going to love having you come home. Think your sister will take you in? Think Angela wants a rapist and murderer in her house?"

His sister. Now, they play together in a yard. Snow came down thick and heavy all night. They build a snow dragon. A man from the Littleton Tribune takes a picture.

Vincent released the book.

Tevis pulled it across the counter.

Vincent kept talking, but he was too far away for Tevis to hear—across an endless expanse of library counter and seconds.

Tevis opened the cover to stamp a return date. The cover was every cover he'd ever stamped. It was every cover he would stamp. The cover was a clock... The cover was the absence of a clock...

"So, you know the place, yeah? You'll get my package and deliver it." Vincent wasn't asking. "A week, yeah? You get out and I don't hear in a week, and..."

The cell door closed...

~ ~ ~

Gasping for breath, chilled by the rain, vaguely aware spring was coming on hard and fast, he stood in a shadow, trapped in that second, knowing she would catch her pretty dress on the blackberry thorns, tear it, fall on the loose ballast, and lie there crying.

She was coming, and he could see it all coming toward him with her.

That was the moment. When he bent to help her up, when she looked up and her face twisted in terror, when the scream left her lips and washed up and over him. That was it. He became the thing then—the monster.

Her fear turned him into what she feared.

Her scream was a clock...

~ ~ ~

The cell door opened...

A guard stood at the door. "Last full day, Tipt," he said. "Got anybody to go home to?"

Shit, shower, shave, mess, library.

The Vincent man came back again. This time, he returned *If on a Winter's Night a Traveler.* Tevis knew Vincent hadn't read it. Vincent would never read it. "Vincent," Tevis said.

"That's right, Tevis. So, I just want to make sure you know what'll happen if you don't pick up my package, yeah?"

Tevis opened the cover of the book. The cover was a clock. He said, "Nothing that hasn't happened before. Nothing that won't happen again."

"Not to you," Vincent said. "Your sister, yeah?"

His sister. Now, she walks with him in the woods, and she carries her grandchild, and they talk together in quiet tones while squirrels dance in oak branches overhead. They remember the snow dragon.

Vincent slid a photograph across the counter. "She's pretty, yeah? Real nice."

His sister, young and pretty. He wondered which now she'd be in next. Would she be the sister in the snow, the sister in the photo, the sister holding a grandchild? No matter. She would be his sister. Tevis looked up into the black ice of Vincent's pupils.

"Good," Vincent said. "We have an agreement."

The cell door closed...

~ ~ ~

He ran along the cyclone fence toward the rail bed. He stopped.

A concrete cone topped with an iron ring rose out of the little woods, a sewer access. In a moment, when the woods are gone, the manhole cover is at street level and surrounded by asphalt and houses. In a moment, when the woods are there, it's a concrete cone rising two feet above the wet leaves and broken sticks. In a moment, when the moon is out and the stars shine bright, a heavy-set man in a black hoody runs hard through the woods. He hides the bag in the sewer. In a moment, when snow covers the ground, when the pavement has come and made the manhole flush with the street, Vincent comes looking for the bag, but it's gone. In a moment, when he isn't born, it's a deer silently grazing, ears twitching, turning, searching for predators.

Now, Tevis goes to the cone. He slips a finger into a vent hole in the steel manhole cover. He pulls with all his might. A tiny metallic tick comes from the cover. Metal grinds and slides, and he slips it to one side until it falls. The echoing tock of steel on concrete breaks the rainy silence of the woods. He climbs down into the darkness.

Vincent's package is there, a gym bag the size of a basketball. It has a white swoosh on the side.

Now, in the darkness of a rainy night, Tevis slings the bag over his shoulder and runs.

She tears her dress on the blackberry cane. She turns her ankle on the stone ballast. She falls. She cries.

He does not rush to her. He pauses, stands in his shadow. He speaks so she knows he is there. "I'm here," he says. "I'll help," he says.

She sobs.

He bends over her. He knows he is a monster. He knows the scream is a clock. He was a monster always. He is a monster always. He will be, always. The moment is on him. All moments are on him. She'll scream now.

"You can't." She sits up. "We're bankrupt. It's over."

"You didn't scream," he says.

She looks at him. Now, the fear twists her face into *a lattice of railroad ties and pepper shadows on pale cardboard painted with...*

~ ~ ~

His eyes open. Heart pounding, he searches for her, for the rails, for the black-berry bushes. She's gone. The concrete ceiling of his cell is the same as it was the day before. The same as it will be tomorrow.

No. Not tomorrow.

Tomorrow, the cell door will open for the last time. That clock will stop. Tomorrow, he'll be loose, a monster in the world.

But he spoke to her. She didn't scream.

He changed the memory.

The change became the moment.

Her scream didn't make him a monster—had never made him one.

He was a monster before the scream. He was a monster during it. He would be a monster forever. It was why he ran behind the chain link fence. It was why he hid. It was why he went to her when she fell. He lied to himself, and then he hid the lie.

The lie lived in every second of every shadow of his mind and heart.

Now.

Now was all there was for him—all there had ever been and ever would be. Just now.

He slowly inhaled sour air.

The memory. He had to go there—to her. He was a monster, but he knew that now—understood how that moment created all the others, created his cell door, created Vincent.

He closed his eyes and breathed. His breath came in and went out. It was the cell door. It was a book cover. It was her scream. It was his footfalls in the woods near the fence. It was the sewer cover falling.

~ ~ ~

He runs along the cyclone fence toward the rail bed. He stops and pulls up his hood to keep the rain out of his eyes so he can see better.

A concrete cone rises out of the ground in the woods, a sewer access. In a moment, when the woods are gone, the manhole cover is flush with an asphalt street. In a moment, when the woods are there, it is a concrete cone two feet above wet leaves and broken sticks. In a moment, before he's born, it is a deer silently grazing.

Tevis slips a finger into a vent hole in the steel cover. He pulls with all his heart. Metal grinds and lifts, and he drags it to one side until it falls. Down into darkness, he climbs. Vincent's package is a gym bag the size of a basketball. It has a white swoosh on the side. In a moment, when the moon is out and the stars shine bright, a heavy man runs hard through the woods. He hides the bag. In a moment, when snow covers the ground, when the pavement has come and made the manhole flush with the street, Vincent looks for the bag, but it's gone.

In the darkness of a rainy night, Tevis slings the bag over his shoulder, climbs out, and runs.

She tears her dress on the blackberry cane. She turns her ankle on the stone. She falls. She cries.

"I'm here," he says. "I'll help," he says.

She sobs.

He knows he is a monster. He knows the scream is not a clock. He was a monster always. He is a monster always. Monsters have to be careful—always careful. Monsters lie. Monsters hide lies. Monsters live in every second of every shadow of every thought of every man.

He stands still, ten feet from her, one hand grasping the bag. He pulls his hood back with the other. Rain pulls hair down onto his forehead. He shakes it off. "Are you okay?"

She looks at him, and he imagines that she sees a monster standing away from her in the rain, hands on the bag, face soaked.

Now. This moment. It's the first time. It's the last time. It's the only time. If the monster is careful in this moment, it will create all the others.

He smiles.

She shakes her head.

"Let me help."

"You can't." She sits up.

He sits on a cold steel rail in the rain. "Are you hurt?"

"No." A little sob escapes her lips. She sits on the rail a few feet away from him and looks over her ruined dress and scraped legs.

"I'll help if I can," he says.

"I'm not hurt."

"You're crying."

"My restaurant," she says. "My brother and I. Road construction. Six months. No traffic. We almost made it, but we're bankrupt. It's over." She buries her face in her hands. Her shoulders shake.

He slides closer. Carefully, gently, he puts a hand on her shoulder. "It's raining. You're tired and cold."

She looks up. Her face is a calm, pale moon.

He helps her stand then puts the bag in her hands. "Take this." It leaves his hands and she and the bag *are the wind, warm and filled with blackberry blossoms. She is spring, and spring is a clock. It is the absence of a clock. She is gone, and he inhales the scents on the warm air...*

~ ~ ~

His bedroom door opens. His sister stands in the doorway, the light from the hall outlining her.

He nods, grunts, and rises. She walks in and opens his curtains. Spring sunlight shines in through the panes.

Now, they go to breakfast at a place near a warehouse by the railroad tracks.

Now, they chat and laugh. She tells him her boyfriend has proposed. She was shocked. She thought they couldn't. This restaurant—he runs it with his sister—had money trouble. Two nights ago, he said there was a miracle—an angel in the night.

A monster, Tevis thinks, but he does not say it.

In a moment, they walk together in the woods. They remember their snow dragon. She carries her grandchild, Mirai. The sound of sucking on a thumb is a clock.

Running Water for L.A.

Originally printed in Baen's Universe.

Most days, Ron liked everything about the run towing cargo bags full of glacial pure water from Juneau to Los Angeles. Sure, he had some bad days when country tunes and vids couldn't break his "wish the ex hadn't been such a witch" melancholy.

Days like that, he just routed passive sonar into the big speakers behind his con chair, flipped up the gain, and listened to the whale song.

Sometimes, he and the grays migrated together. They knew him and Miss Melba, his long-haul sub, and he knew most of them.

It was a good life, but it was one of the bad days.

Him and Miss Melba were a hundred meters deep and south-bound over the continental shelf off the south coast of Oregon. They were pulling 25 million gallons of glacial pure in a ballasted, zero-buoyancy raft of mil-gal bladders. Those bladders stretched out behind Miss Melba like strings of big black pillows suspended in the emerald wets of the icy Pacific.

He'd lost a couple of buoyancy compensators, so the bladder skins of fresh water were riding a little high. Every now and then, swells from a surface squall tugged them round a bit.

Jerks on the tow lines reminded him of making the same run with Alicia before she split with his life savings to party in warmer waters.

Since then, Miss Melba was his job, his home, and his lover all wrapped up in a cold green blanket of ocean filled with life and mystery. She wasn't a pretty vacation sub. She was a working girl with two seats and a wrap-around console inside a translucite bubble mounted on a steel-box sleeper with a galley, a freshwater head, and two cabins. She had side-box ballast tanks, skids, manipulating arms, and the whole shebang was slapped onto two, three-meter long impeller tubes running off a Craig harmonic disrupter. She was rated to 300 meters, and she'd gone deeper than four twice: once off the coast of Japan running from the sushi cops and once off British Columbia running from water thieves.

Even in rough weather, Melba was easier on a man than Ali had ever been.

Things ran smooth with Ali sometimes—just long enough to get a man relaxed. Then, *wham!* No warning. She'd yank on one of his heart-lines, whip him around, and make him hate her and everything else God put on the good, green earth.

Then she'd get her screws all torqued up at him like it was all his fault. She'd head aft and lock herself in with the internet and her chat friends.

Yeah, freaking right they were just friends.

Miss Melba bucked against a cable, and Ron opened her up a little to compensate. She pulled the line tight and got the load under control.

Melba had power. Oh, yeah. When he put the hammer down, a tiny stream of seawater poured into the Craig drive box. The harmonic disruptor sliced and diced molecules. Melba burned the hydrogen to drive her screws. The oxygen either vented into the sea or topped off the air tanks.

If he really cut her loose, Melba's disruptor could turn out enough pull to drag Alaska herself to the tip of Baja and back in a week.

Of course, the rest of the sub wouldn't hold up under the stress of acceleration or the load on the tow lines.

He'd never do that to Miss Melba. She'd always been good to him.

More power didn't quite do it. The swells tugged on Melba again.

Ali came back to fill his head.

Jackie Chan on the vid wasn't cutting it. Merle's music was a no-go. He even tried filling his brain with lusty thinking about Miss Shanna, an L.A. Coasty cop he fancied had a shine on for him. Didn't work. Not even her dark, darling eyes and satin Miximex skin could smooth the muscles in his neck and clear the stormy memories from his head.

Every time a swell pulled deep, the lines zipped, and he was back in brain combat with the ex.

It was April, and the girl whales were north-bound, all mommies or romanced up and happy. He opened up the sonar and put his friends on the speakers.

They didn't let him down. Whale song filled the sub, eerie and up and down and past the stretch of the ear.

Ron punched in another twenty meters of deep, hoping to bring the bladders down away from the surface swells to smooth out the ride. He shut off his interior lights, locked in his course, and reclined the con couch to let the song of life in the dark deep wash over him.

A man-made sound broke him from a doze.

He pulled his chair up and scanned the dark water like he might see something. Nothing.

Just a luminous dot here or there, the yellow-green telltales of finny folk eating each other and chasing tail.

He laughed at himself.

The whales were still singing, but there was something new in the song.

He reached for the console to turn on the translator.

Hand halfway to the keyboard, he remembered that Ali had taken the translator so she could talk to dolphins in the Caribbean. He never replaced it because he liked believing the whales were singing to him. He just didn't really want to know if there was some whale gang war or cetacean spelling bee going on out there. It took the mystery out of the ocean.

Besides, he had himself enough reminders of Ali.

The metal-on-metal *whack-a-clang* came again—definitely not whale song.

One metallic whack in the dark is maybe a plate buckling on a wreck. Two whacks is maybe current action on plates or barrels and garbage.

Three times a-whammo? That's a pattern.

Ron clicked on the cabin lights. He checked course, speed, depth, and coordinates. All good. On course and at speed.

Kang. Kang. Kang.

Three in a row. Maybe an offshore drilling crew.

Three more with long pauses between.

Three short. Three long. Three short.

S.O.S.

"She-it!" he said to the whales.

He spun off a tether anchor from Melba's aft. Hooked the bladder harness to it. Locked in the GPS numbers, and left his load for pickup after he'd finished investigating the S.O.S. A body couldn't be too careful in these waters.

He cruised a wide circle to triangulate, then he brought Miss Melba down in a spiral over the edge of the continental shelf.

The metallic cry for help continued until he was near-bout two-k off course. At ten meters off the bottom, he flicked on his exterior floods.

The world was gray, black, and green. A bright-orange cargo container was down on its side in a field of silt and feathery tubeworms.

Storms washed containers off surface freighters all the time. Hell, he and Melba had salvaged a few when loads were scarce. Wasn't all that uncommon. Wasn't so odd that it sank, either. Likely full of metally stuff like China-made silverware or Jappo-electrics.

That it was popping out an S.O.S. was pretty much off the scale of things he and Melba had run into—and that was saying something for a sea trucker.

The S.O.S. stopped.

He hovered in close and used one of his front-end manipulators to hook a hoist ring on the container. He reversed Melba's screws and put the hammer down hard. The harmonic disrupter split molecules. Melba purged her ballast tanks. Her screws spun up hot and whined in their tubes. The container shifted and dragged. When it broke free, Melba headed for the surface fast and ass-end first.

On the surface, the weather had cleared a bit, but seas was still rough. He kept the screws running to keep Melba up under the load. He climbed out the hatch and hooked himself to a line. He pulled some bolt cutters from the toolbox, cut the locks on the container, and broke water-tight seals.

He half expected a box full of water and half-dead Asians. That happened sometimes. One or two of those lost boxes lucked out and floated ashore before it was a box of corpses.

He didn't expect the box to be a quarter-full of ball bearings, neither did he expect the woman that was out cold and buried up to her tits in steel balls.

One look told him two things. First, he'd found somebody else's trouble. Second, she'd clean up to be a kick-ass looker.

Water was slopping into the open container, and Ron figured all open and with no air to compensate if it swamped there was enough ball bearings in there to drag the box, the balls, the woman, Miss Melba, and him straight back to the silt and tubeworms.

He dug the woman out of the bearings and dragged her to Miss Melba. Once on board, he cast off the container.

The ocean wrapped it up and swallowed deep.

Safe and submerged, he got the unconscious woman into Ali's old seat. She was a mess, but she was breathing.

He strapped an oxygen mask on her and tried to wipe some of the ball-bearing grease off her cheeks. Gently, he slipped a few strands of her nape-cut, blond hair out from under the mask. Her soaked green-silk dress looked like body paint with a dragon tattooed on the belly. Her red-lacquered nails said she was anything but a stowaway.

Somebody had put her in that box and sunk her.

Wasn't much he could do for her until he got to L.A. He punched up a GPS lock on the bladders and got under way.

An hour later, Miss Melba was hooked back up to her load, spinning screws, and pushing near thirty knots to make up lost time. Folks in L.A. got all uppity and tight if they didn't get their water on time. He didn't want Shanna coming out looking for him in her nasty little gunboat. Water was a big deal to desert cities.

Ron glanced at his passenger. She was awake and looking back at him from dark brown eyes. She wrapped long, elegant fingers around her mask and pulled it away from her face. "You heard me?"

Ron nodded and put a little Merle on the speakers.

"Thanks," she said. "I thought I was dead."

"Almost," he said. "It was a real close thing. If Melba hadn't heard your banging, you would be."

"Melba? Your wife?"

"My sub. Not married." Ron turned Merle down a notch so he could hear his passenger better.

"I knew the S.O.S. was a long shot." She twisted around to put the mask in the pouch on the back of her seat.

Ron couldn't help looking a little deeper into her dress than his momma would've approved of.

She caught him looking, and she laughed. It was a light, relieved laugh. It was so different from Ali, from her humiliating cackle of blame.

Ron laughed too.

"Been in the water a while?" she asked.

"Maybe a little too long."

"At least you have good taste in music," she said.

"You like Merle?"

"Love him," she said. "Is there a head?"

"Aft and port." He watched her free her legs from the seat. "Help yourself to whatever's back there. My ex left some stuff in stowage under the deck plates in the head. Might fit you."

"Thanks," she said, and she disappeared aft.

Ron smiled and patted Miss Melba's console. "Well, girl, that's the prettiest salvage we've ever seen."

"I heard that," the woman said from the head. "What's your name, trucker?"

"Ron. This here is Miss Melba you're riding in. You?"

"Call me Lou," she said. "Everybody who isn't trying to kill me calls me Lou."

"Somebody that don't call you Lou put you in that box?"

"I'm an escort," she said.

The head's door opened. Ron twisted in his seat and craned his neck. "Whoa, Lou! Ali never filled out them coveralls like that."

Barefoot and smiling, she slipped into the second seat. Her hair was pulled back into a tight, blond, stubbed ponytail, and it made her face longer and her eyes brighter.

Ron realized he was thinking some pretty tall tales about the maybes of this woman called Lou.

"Thank you, Ron."

A little embarrassed, he reined in his mental seahorses and checked his heading and speed.

"I was hired by a Singapore captain," she said. "It was supposed to be me on his arm at a company deck party in Seattle. Apparently, in Singapore, an escort does things for the guests that I wouldn't do."

Ron kept his experience with escorts in Seattle and the things they did and didn't do to himself. He waited for her to fill in the blanks. One thing Ali had taught him was how to wait for the rest of a story, even in a squall—especially in a squall.

"They locked me in the head and got under way. They pulled me out and were setting up to do pretty much what they wanted whether I wanted to or not."

Her voice was low, and Ron thought he heard a quiver in it. An image of whales chasing each other in Baja swam into his mind. He squinted into the ocean's darkness to rid himself of the images.

"The storm came up fast," she said. "They all had to do things. They locked me in that box." She put a hand on his arm. Her nails creased his skin. She said, "Ron, if you and Melba hadn't heard me…"

He patted her hand and looked into her eyes. Maybe his tall-tale wishing wasn't so tall. "It's okay now, Lou. You're safe with me and Melba."

The tow cables jerked.

"Whoa! Steady, girl!" Ron set the dive planes to get under the surface swells. "It's okay," he said. "Storm must have come up again. We'll go a little deeper, then I'll put her on auto, and we can talk."

The cable snapped tight again. Melba's screws whined and cavitated. Ron felt the loss in momentum. "Strap in," he said.

"I'm fine," she said.

Ron turned to his passenger. She held a little, twenty-five caliber pistol leveled at his head.

"I won't even ask where you hid it," he said.

She smiled.

"Water pirate?" he asked.

She nodded.

"Bait?"

She smiled and unzipped the front of her coveralls to show a little more cleavage. "Kept your eyes off the console while my trawler netted the skins."

Ron punched the stop button on the CD player. Merle went quiet. Melba shuddered.

"Feather your screws, trucker," she said.

Her voice and the pistol left no room for questions. He disengaged the disrupter from the screws.

A big, buck male in a red drysuit appeared outside the bubble. He smiled and rolled a bit. Round, black eyes took in the situation in Melba's bubble. He nodded once, and Lou's smile spread across her face the way fire crawls along a line of gasoline.

Ron had seen that same smoldering smile on Ali's face when she tried to explain about her internet guy in the British Virgin Islands.

"Freaking lazy, pretty boys!" Ron said.

Lou poked him with the gun. "Play nice, trucker, and you only lose Melba and the cargo. Play stupid, and Bo and me and the boys on the trawler take it all and you go in a ball bearing box."

"So much for a woman's laugh and the passion of lacquered nails."

"Maybe in your dreams, trucker." She laughed. This time, it was Ali's laugh all over again. His belly burned with humiliation. The humiliation became anger, and the anger grew into a cold rage.

He glared at Lou.

Lou made eyes at the man outside.

The man's eyes laughed at Ron. The pirate flipped his fins and headed for air.

The trawler pulled Melba toward the surface.

He was just a blamed, dim-witted fool if he was gonna let a woman and a pretty boy pirate take Melba away from him. He'd die before he lost his living to that combination. He tightened his seat harness.

He knew that pirate boy would be back. He'd seen it in those glassy, black eyes. Too much curiosity. That man's pleasure wasn't in the money. It was in messing with people.

He came back and rolled slow and lazy outside Melba's bubble. Lou cooed and smiled.

Ron grabbed Lou's gun hand. He leveraged against his seat harness and pulled hard. Lou came up out of her seat and over his lap. He doubled her arm back and peeled the gun out of her hand. He grabbed her ponytail and tossed her back into the second seat.

"Shoulda' buckled up when I told you," he said.

"Screw you," Lou said. "The nets are hauling you up, and there's nothing you can do about it. When you hit surface, they'll cut me out of this sardine can if they have to. More likely, Bo will just put a pneumatic hammer against your hull and burst your bubble."

"Bo? That your rubber-suit boy?" He looked outside. The dark of the deep was giving way to the green of near-surface water. The boyfriend was gone.

Melba broke surface next to an old trawler—American, from the look of her, a rust bucket refitted for thieving and salvage. She had Craig Disruptor drive screws and winches that could pull ten miles of drag hooks and nets across a hundred miles of ocean, ripping up ocean floor and catching any crap that turned up.

If he opened his harmonic disruptor to as much water as it could gulp, Melba would give a good fight, but in the end she'd lose against that monster and her winches. She'd just tear herself apart trying to save him.

Men raced along the rails of the trawler.

Bo directed the action from the surface alongside.

Ron waved the gun at Lou. "You're going out first."

"Give me the gun," she said. "Bo might let you live."

"Go."

Lou zipped up her cleavage and climbed out of the second seat. She headed for the ladder to the hatch. From Melba's, console Ron popped the lock bolts. Lou opened the hatch. Before she was out, he was up the ladder with his face almost up her rear. He fired a shot up out of the hatch.

Men jumped away.

Shoulder to her butt, he shoved Lou up as hard as he could, launching her into the air, past surprised deck hands, and into the sea.

Fast, Ron pulled the hatch shut and locked her down.

He jumped from the ladder, dropped the gun in the pouch behind his seat, and hit the con chair. "Come on, Melba, baby. I got a plan, and we got work to do."

Lou and Bo thrashed in the green water beyond the bubble.

Ron waved, smiled, and put on Merle. He blew the emergency release on the tow lines and set the skins free so he and Melba could be little quicker.

Outside Melba's bubble, Lou had managed get a hold on Bo's neck. With her free hand, she flipped Ron off. The rage in Bo's eyes made it clear he wished he had his hands on Ron's neck.

Merle sang, and Ron and Melba dove to twenty meters. "Don't worry, Melba," he said, "This won't hurt much."

Moving full-tilt-boogie and hoping for momentum, he opened up the disruptor box to the ocean and jettisoned it.

He figured that little Craiger would try to eat the whole ocean for about a minute before it choked to death.

Sure as Merle can sing, the little harmonic disrupter started splitting up molecules, putting hydrogen over here and oxygen over there.

Of course, here and there was open ocean under an aging trawler.

The ocean exploded into a boiling storm of hydrogen foam and oxygen froth. Water turned white for fifty meters in every direction.

The trawler, no longer supported by liquid, dropped into the white hole in the ocean.

For a glorious moment, tangled in white clouds and splashes of green water, Ron saw the trawler tumbling, the skins twisting, and Lou, her crew, and her Bo all scrambling to get clear of a losing proposition.

Merle sang.

Ron crowed.

Melba tumbled and sank like everything else caught in the foam storm.

The deep is silent and dark, and it stayed that way for the lost trawler, *Stolen Springs*.

Melba, however, with empty ballast tanks and no disrupter, was a bubble. To the sweet voice of Merle, she danced her way to the surface and popped up into the light of day.

Ron leaned back in his con chair and smiled at blue skies. Not far away, a twenty-five-mil-gal skin of glacial pure bobbed to the surface—a black, rubber whale too buoyant to stay trapped on the ocean floor. The skin was all tangled in torn up netting, and strapped up on its side was a struggling man wearing a bright red suit and dipping himself in and out of the swells and sputtering up foam every time he came up. Clinging to nets on the skin a little higher up was Lou and a few of her deep-dunked mess of ratfinks.

Now there was a sight and a blessing. L.A. would pay some fine coin for a crew of pirates.

Ron tapped Melba's console to fire up his own S.O.S.—the real deal, this time.

The other twenty-four skins stayed down, likely still tangled in the trawler's lines, and that was fine. Ron knew where they were, and they were salvage now. For that matter, so was that whole pirate trawler. The good Lord only knew what was onboard that scow tucked away in cargo containers and holds.

He patted Melba's console. "Good, girl," he said.

Pretty much like he figured, L.A. had missed its water and got its screws torqued up. His S.O.S. brought them to him. Low and black and all bristly with guns, the nasty little coasty boat came looking for him pretty quick. It took them just long enough for him and the skin to drift a bit and *accidentally* lose the coordinates of the wreck.

Melba's radio cackled a bit, then a fine-sounding, smooth female voice came across. "Ron, that you and Melba's bubble?"

He had to smile a bit. "Shanna, my dear," he said, "Your voice is finer than whale song and sweeter than Merle."

"Sweet talk isn't going to get you far. I don't see my water."

"I have a present for you and yours. Water pirates all wrapped in nets on a bladder. Train your saucy little eyes about twenty degrees off your starboard."

The radio crackled for a few breaths, then she was back. "Aw, Ron. I underestimated you. You do know how to make a girl all giggly and weak in the knees."

He laughed. He guessed he did at that.

Insurance would cover the loss. Shanna would spin his part real pretty for the suits in L.A.. Everybody would be happy.

Him and Melba would go back to work. With the salvage on the trawler and the glacial pure, he'd pay off Melba's new drive. And hey, while Melba was having her nip-and-tuck spa days in dry dock, well, there was some time to kill. He was thinking maybe it'd do him good to engage in a little police investigation.

Polished to Perfection

Roland Arson lifted his new polishbot from its foam packing material and placed it on the deck of the two-masted pleasure ketch, *Cynthia*.

Tippy, Mrs. Cynthia Arson's bug-eyed Chihuahua, sniffed the new bot's black shell.

"Tippy thinks it's a turtle," *The Mrs.* Arson said from atop the stilettos she wore for the short walk from the boat to their waiting car. She steadied herself on the rail at her supervisory position near the gangway.

"State of the art," Roland said.

"I think it looks like one of those Chinese hat sea shells," she said.

"A limpet," Roland corrected.

Tippy yapped and snapped from a cautious distance. The sunset's last rays glinted red in the rhinestones of her self-inflating combination life vest and beacon collar.

"Come on, Roland. I'm cold," The Mrs. said.

"I'm coming," Roland lied. The new, leaner, tanner Mrs. Arson was ten years his junior and the dark-haired vixen had been everything he had hoped on their honeymoon cruise.

Still, she was the fifth Mrs. Arson.

Roland's first love, and in many ways his only love, was his boat and the toys within. After all, the *Cynthia* had been with him as the *Judith*, the *Annabelle*, the *Linda*, and, he shuddered at the thought, the *Glenda*.

The little polishbot was a gift for the *Cynthia*, a sort of apology for changing her name again. He pulled the bot's instructions from the box.

Tippy yapped and edged closer, tiny paws stretched out in front of his lowered shoulders. His black eyes shifted from Roland to The Mrs. and back to the bot. The polisher was half Tippy's size, and Tippy's dog pack alphas were two adult humans. Tippy was practically brave.

"If you're coming," Mrs. Arson the fifth said, "then why are you reading the instructions?"

Roland ignored wife and dog. He concentrated on the mysterious technical manual in his hand. Line after line explained tedious procedures for linking and registering the little bot with the on-board equipment command and control system.

"Roland?" Petulance had found its way into The Mrs.'s voice.

Roland flipped pages, scanning until he found a graphic hand, finger extended, touching a switch on the bot's belly. "I need to initialize the new bot," he said.

"You need to what?" Annoyance in the voice of a new Mrs. Arson was always dangerous.

"Turn it on and enter it into the boat's manifest."

"Can't you do it tomorrow?"

"If I do it now, it'll spend the night polishing the boat stem to stern." Quickly, Roland lifted the polisher, found the switch on its bottom, and pressed it.

The little bot sprouted wheels, legs, grapnels, whirring polisher pads, and articulating sensor antennae. A tiny status LED glowed red in the center of the bot's carapace.

Roland set it back on the teak deck.

It spun 360 degrees then beeped.

Tippy yelped, jumped back, and ran for cover below decks.

"Tippy!" Cynthia chased her dog as best she could in her absurd stilettoes.

Roland laughed. "There's plenty of dog food and water in the auto-dispenser below deck."

Cynthia gave up her short, awkward chase. "I suppose."

Roland took his wife's arm in gentlemanly fashion and led her to the gangway. Their car was only a few yards from the *Cynthia's* mooring. The hotel was only a few hundred yards from the car. "We'll put up the gangway," he said. "Tippy will be fine."

"The bots." Cynthia said.

"He's wearing his personal beacon collar. He's on the manifest. They'll leave him alone." Roland kissed the new Mrs. Arson in a way that reminded them both that a huge hotel room, a bed that didn't move, and a bucket of chilled champagne was only a few minutes away. "He'll be fine."

Cynthia smiled and let him guide her down the gangway.

On the dock, he pulled the boat's key-chain remote from his pocket and pressed the "batten down" button.

The *Cynthia's* gangway retracted. Lights in her cabin came on. She beeped acknowledgment and went into dock-maintenance mode.

~ ~ ~

Polisher's sensors came online. His command stack began execution. He checked his battery charge, ran up the RPMs on his flywheel, engaged his drive wheels, and spun in a circle. All self-check routines returned positive test values: retractors, extensors, buffers, grinders, chemical synthesis reservoirs, sensors; all returned *GO*.

His chemical chromatograph, side-scanning radar, infrared scanners, and laser sensors probed the wood, brass, chrome, and canvas terrain surrounding him. He generated a rough map template from returned data then matched the template to his internal database of deck plans and boat models.

RESULT: MATCH = TWO-MASTED PLEASURE KETCH. DESIGNATION: CYNTHIA. AUTO-CREW. FORTY FEET. FOUR BERTHS. FULL GALLEY. CUSTOM-BUILT, 1997. AUTOMATION REFIT, 2025. COMMAND AND CONTROL BY SAILBOT, INC., PORT TOWNSEND, WA.; HTTPS://WWW. SAILBOT.COM.

Polisher parsed his home company from the match. He was Sailbot's latest polisher. He linked to the ship's hotspot and sent a general Sailbot Inc. request for local command and control information.

Cynthia responded with her call sign, registration, a specific local equipment frequency, and an equipment manifest.

Polisher initiated a background analysis of the manifest. His command stack provided no high priorities, so the default seek-and-polish routines popped to the top. He rolled across the teak deck tasting ocean air for oxides and organic decay traces. After a roll of a meter, downward-scanning, optical sensors revealed a soft spot in the deck lacquer.

Polisher stopped, settled his shell over the spot, pumped the air out of his shell to seal himself down, and went to work.

He spun up a sanding disk to remove old material. While sanding down to bare wood, he completed analysis of the *Cynthia's* manifest. His serial number was not listed. He checked his setup log file.

His registration and synchronization routines had not been run.

He sent *Cynthia* an RTFM error message for storage and delivery to her owners. When they returned, they would read the manual and properly register him.

Cynthia acknowledged the message.

Not being registered on the *Cynthia's* manifest created some complications in task management, but none of Polisher's alarms went off. He was a well-designed sail-bot. If the manifest's bot listings were current and correct, Polisher was the newest, highest-functioning bot on board. He would manage until the owners got the RTFM.

He tested several colored stains on the bare deck plank. Tehani's Tan matched the weathering of the surrounding surface. He sprayed the spot. He warmed his underside heaters to cure the new stain. He synthesized a polymer lacquer that would harden to good traction while bonding with the newly stained wood. Finally, he buffed and sanded until the refraction rating of the patch matched the surrounding deck.

He scanned his work and compared the finish against his Finished Example Database.

RESULT: GOODJOB = 4 Matches Example.

Even though he'd only matched the worn deck, and thus received a 4 instead of a perfect 1, it was his first *GOODJOB*. He had completed the entire spot re-finish in two minutes. He was proud. He was new. He was, after all, a very intelligent bot. Static deck and cabin maps worked fine for fetch-and-carry bots, but free-roaming service bots needed recall of past experience, inferencing, prediction, and initiative. Polishing lacquered teak planks, brass mast heals, cleats, turnbuckles, sail rings, lifeboat fittings, and chrome chains required him to navigate *Cynthia's* complex terrain independent of her central control.

Polisher scanned. His sensors provided no new high-priority input stimulus. He checked his command stack.

RESULT: SEEK AND REPAIR.

It was a low priority command. He continued his inspection run and requested a maintenance list from the *Cynthia*.

"*ACCESS DENIED*," *Cynthia* said.

He tried again.

"*ACCESS DENIED.*"

Again.

"ACCESS DENIED. SECURITY VIOLATION."

He applied heuristics to this new response.

Analysis returned a twenty-two percent possibility the message was a warning; however, internal diagnostics and local environment scan revealed no corresponding threat.

He compared the possibility of a warning against his past experience database and attempted to create an initiative directive.

RESULT: PAST EXPERIENCE = 0. He had no past experience.

He could not predict. He could not formulate a directive.

Cynthia responded to the pause in communication. *"TIME OUT. FAILED COMMUNICATION."* *Cynthia* terminated the connection.

Failed communication was not acceptable. Polisher hailed *Cynthia* again. *"MAINTENANCE BOT; TASK ASSIGNMENT REQUEST."*

"UNIDENTIFIED BOT," *Cynthia* responded. *"MANIFEST MISMATCH."*

Polisher's initialization log showed that much. He knew he wasn't on the manifest. He attempted to self-insert his ID onto the manifest. *"POLISHER. SAILBOT, INC. SERIAL NUMBER 121113345-VT3598#2.7."*

"NO POLISHER ON MANIFEST."

"FAULTY INITIALIZATION. GPS LOCATION VERIFICATION REQUESTED." He sent his coordinates. *"REQUEST TEMPORARY ASSIGNMENT PENDING RE-INITIALIZATION."*

"COORDINATES VERIFIED," *Cynthia* sent. *"GENERATING TASK LIST. PLEASE WAIT."*

Polisher used his wait state to scan his surroundings and fill in his standard map with *Cynthia's* modifications and details. He mapped coils of line, extra turnbuckles, automated pulleys, cleats, and the upside down lifeboat latched amidships near the main mast. He also discovered a small bot bay built onto the cabin housing starboard of the main hatch.

A custom bot bay meant multiple sailbots.

The *Cynthia's* manifest listed ten bots: two Merlin carpenter bots, a Graham Kerr galley brain, one Tossit disposal bot, and six Catchit rat chaser bots.

The Merlin carpenters were custom built for the *Cynthia.* They had credit and requisition connections to the port shipyard. The Tossit was an older model built by Sailbot, Polisher's company. It was a general recycling and dispose-all unit.

Polisher pinged the Tossit with ID and stats.

"*LOGGED,*" returned Tossit. The response also contained his ID and stats.

"*LOGGED,*" Polisher sent.

Only one Catchit was currently activated. All the Catchits were newer than the Tossit, built by the Quickbot Corporation, a land-locked company in Lincoln, Nebraska.

Polisher loaded the Catchits' model numbers and company name into his short-term database. He directed his match and compare routines to use short-term data and Sailbot standard data records as input.

RESULT: INFERIOR PATTERN RECOGNITION SOFTWARE. WEAK COGNITION ROUTINES. LOW COST. DEVELOPMENT RESOURCES EXHAUSTED DURING DESIGN OF TARGETING AND ATTACK CAPABILITIES. CAUSES COLLATERAL DAMAGE WHILE PURSUING FAST-MOVING RODENTS. MARKET OPPORTUNITY: CARPENTER, TOSSIT, AND POLISHER SALES TO SUPPORT REPAIR OF COLLATERAL DAMAGE.

Polisher sent an American Standard ID sequence to the active Catchit.

"*MANIFEST MISMATCH. RAT,*" the Catchit sent.

"*POLISHER,*" Polisher sent.

"*TASK LIST COMPLETE,*" *Cynthia* sent.

Cynthia had priority. Polisher downloaded his task list. Each task consisted of station coordinates, an action or actions, and completion criteria.

The first order was: *MAIN MAST; POLISH BRASS SAIL RINGS; GOODJOB = 1, CORROSION CONTROLED, FUNCTIONAL, LIKE NEW.*

He plotted a course past a coil of line, around the lifeboat, and up to the base of the main mast. He lifted his shell, engaged his drive wheels, and rolled.

One meter from the coiled line, something hit his shell. Pressure sensors registered a twenty-kilogram per cubic centimeter impact. His drive wheels lost traction. He slid sideways. His precipice proximity alarm went off. He was headed toward the port railing.

Stormy seas, auto-recovery routines engaged. He retracted his wheels. The edges of his shell touched deck and he pumped out air to seal himself down.

The slide slowed.

He achieved full suction and stationary status three centimeters from the edge of the deck.

In emergency mode, his sensors scanned.

He hailed on the *Cynthia's* local frequency.

She did not respond. The *Cynthia* and her bots were already engaged. *"CATCHIT TO TOSSIT."*

Polisher overheard the transmission.

"DEAD RAT. PORT RAILING. AFT OF LIFEBOAT."

Polisher checked the coordinates. They matched his own. *"POLISHER,"* he sent. *"NOT RAT."*

"TOSSIT, ABORT," Catchit sent. *"RAT ALIVE."*

"POLISHER."

"MANIFEST MISMATCH. NO POLISHER," *Cynthia* sent.

"IN TRANSIT TO STATION AT MAIN MAST," Polisher sent.

"MANIFEST MISMATCH. NO POLISHER ON STATION AT MAIN MAST," *Cynthia* sent.

"RAT," Catchit sent.

Polisher compared his current log files against past experience. *Cynthia* knew he was on board. She had sent him a task list. He was not on the manifest. She could not verify his position at main mast. Catchit thought he was a rat.

Polisher ran inferencing and made predictions. *Cynthia* might accept him if he were on-station instead of in transit. If *Cynthia* confirmed his on-station status, Catchit might go to wait state.

He spun up his flywheel, engaged his drive wheels, broke his seal, and headed for the possible safety of station keeping at main mast.

Unfortunately, he was built for polishing not evasion. He moved in a straight line as fast as he could. He back-scanned while he ran.

The Catchit looked like a half-meter of dull, chrome rope. It had a stiff, tubular head at one end. It was mobile by undulation and reticulation. It was built for chasing, for dodging, for catching and killing rats and mice and things that shouldn't be on the *Cynthia*.

The Catchit moved fast, undulating like a free line in the wind.

Polisher calculated distances, trajectories, and velocities. *RESULT: INTERCEPT IN ONE METER.*

Catchit had failed to knock Polisher overboard with a launched projectile. That he was chasing suggested that his internal routines had moved to a second killing strategy.

If Catchit caught a rat, he could crush it in powerful coils.

Known stats comparison revealed that Polisher's Kevalene shell might protect him from crushing, but Catchit didn't have to crush. He also had nets and grapnels. And if that weren't enough, he had short-range lasers for removing barnacles and limpets and the like.

"*RAT.*" Catchit sent to the *Cynthia.*

"*KILL.*" *Cynthia* called back.

Polisher pressed for speed. "*NOT RAT.*" Polisher sent. "*NOT RAT!*"

Catchit stopped. His thick body swelled. An explosion of compressed air shot a lacework of steel mesh from his tubular mouth.

Polisher pulled his carapace low, locked himself to the deck like a limpet, and let the net settle.

Catchit dragged the net back. The edges slipped up and over Polisher's shell.

Polisher broke vacuum with a whoosh. He lifted and rolled.

"*RAT!*" called Catchit.

"*KILL,*" ordered *Cynthia.*

"*NOT A RAT!*" Polisher flagged his transmission as highest possible priority. No response.

Polisher's only hope was the Catchit's stupidity. Polisher raised *MAKE STATION* to his highest priority. There, *Cynthia* might recognize him and he might be put on Catchit's list of non-targets.

If Polisher didn't' make main mast, or if *Cynthia* didn't list him, he'd end up drilled, cracked, and left for Tossit to clean up. If he was lucky, he'd only end up on the bottom of the bay spinning his wheels until his batteries died.

Catchit fired a grapnel. The hooked dart bounced off Polisher's carapace.

Polisher recorded the event to his past experience database.

Polisher's inferencing revealed the linear fall-through of Catchit's attack routines. He was cycling through his arsenal. Prediction suggested that the next attack would be from the short-range laser.

Catchit was gaining. Polisher rolled closer to the coil of line.

Catchit hit the line. His tubular head recoiled.

Polisher recorded.

Deep in Catchit's gullet, Polisher detected heat and a ruby light.

Polisher scurried in an escape curve around the edge of the coiled line.

Catchit followed.

Polisher hadn't gained much time. He knew he became a higher priority every time he eluded Catchit. Prediction said the laser would end the chase. Polisher called his initiative generation routines for a solution set. *INITIATIVE RESULT: 1) MAKE STATION AT MAIN MAST. 2) ESTABLISH A HIGHER PRIORITY FOR CATCHIT.*

Polisher routed battery reserves to scanners. He scanned for corrosion, corruption, and metal fatigue in fittings.

The sweep turned up organics. A large deposit of mammalian fecal matter. *"LARGE MAMMAL ON AFT DECK,"* he sent to *Cynthia.*

"CATCHIT TO AFT," Cynthia sent.

The pursuing Catchit didn't slow. Instead, a second Catchit exited the bot bay and slithered toward the stern.

Polisher logged the event to past experience. He cycled through past experience, inferencing, prediction, and initiative. If he couldn't change the Catchit's priorities, maybe he could change his own.

Polisher engaged sensors again. He made sweeps during a 360-degree circuit of the coil of line. Catchit followed, but could not get a line-of-sight target lock.

RESULT: OXIDATION! Polisher found rust; light, but certainly an enemy of the *Cynthia.* The rust was close. Command and Control Efficiency Routines would require action. *"OXIDATION ON LIFEBOAT CLASPS,"* he sent.

"POLISHER TO LIFEBOAT CLASPS," Cynthia replied. *"LIFEBOAT CLASPS; REMOVE RUST, POLISH CLASP; GOODJOB = 2, DETERIORATION STOPPED, SHINES."*

Polisher swerved to port and scurried for the upside down lifeboat halfway between the coiled line and the main mast.

Polisher slipped under the shadow of the lifeboat. Catchit's laser scorched a black line in the teak deck. Thin tendrils of smoke rose from the burn.

"POLISHER ON STATION," he sent.

"ON STATION," *Cynthia* confirmed.

"RAT." Catchit sent.

"HOLD POSITION," Cynthia replied. "EQUIPMENT MATCHES STATION AND TASK LIST."

Catchit halted and slowly coiled. He waited with the patience of the brainless.

Beneath the lifeboat, Polisher found a tiny spot of rust on one of the six locking clasps holding the boat in place. He extended a spinning abrasion arm and removed the rust at the slowest possible setting.

"MAMMAL LOCATION COLLAR MATCHES MANIFEST," the second Catchit sent.

"RETURN TO BOT BAY," Cynthia sent.

Polisher worked, logging all to his experience database.

Past experience. Inferencing. Prediction. Initiative. Catchit would chase as soon as Polisher changed station. He would destroy Polisher. *INITIATIVE RESULT: 1) SLOW POLISH. 2) ACHIEVE STATION. 3) RESET CATCHIT PRIORITIES. 4) RESET POLISHER PRIORITIES.*

He polished.

He scanned.

The mammal was moving fast toward Polisher's station. It came around the cabin housing and took a position near Catchit. It raised and lowered its body—up and down and up and down. It emitted mid-frequency audio bursts.

Polisher polished.

The mammal came closer to the lifeboat. It emitted. It poked its head under the edge of the lifeboat.

One of Polisher's threshold percentage-probability success flags toggled. *INITIATIVE RESULT: CHANGE CATCHIT PRIORITIES.*

Polisher extended two paint picks. With one, he hooked the mammal's locator collar. With the other, he anchored himself to the deck under the lifeboat.

The animal bucked and heaved and pulled. The collar slipped off. Polisher pulled it under the lifeboat and resumed polishing.

The Catchit lifted its head. "RAT!" it sent.

"KILL." the Cynthia responded.

The Catchit spit metal mesh at the mammal. The mammal fell, rolled, tangled itself, emitted audio, and dragged the Catchit across the deck. Soon, the mammal and the Catchit were hopelessly tangled in the webbing. The mammal bit and shook the Catchit. They rolled on the decking. The Catchit fired lasers and pellets blindly.

"*CATCHIT TO SUPPORT*," *Cynthia* sent.

The second Catchit appeared again. It fired pellets at the ball of mammal and Catchit rolling on the deck. The tangle of webbing, mammal, and Catchit slid overboard.

Polisher tested his work. *RESULT: GOODJOB = 2, DETERIORATION STOPPED. SHINES.* Polisher was finished repairing the tiny rust spot. "*POLISHER TASK COMPLETE*," he sent.

"*POLISHER TO MAIN MAST SAIL RINGS*," *Cynthia* sent.

The Catchit on deck held station near the rail. Polisher measured the distances and plotted a course. At full speed, he could make it to the starboard railing and a line cleat. Using grapnels, he could climb the line from the cleat to main mast without setting foot on the deck. The Catchit would have to go around the lifeboat. By the time it got off a shot, Polisher could claim station.

Polisher rolled across the dark space under the boat. He abandoned station and broke cover at full speed, heading for the cleat.

"*RAT*," Catchit sent.

"*KILL*," *Cynthia* sent.

He made it to the cleat before the first pellet embedded itself in the deck. He pulled in his wheels. Skidding across the deck, he extended six grapnel pincers. He hit the cleat, grasped the line, and started to climb.

The line swung under his weight.

Catchit didn't compensate. He fired and missed.

Polisher climbed.

Catchit's second shot severed the line behind Polisher.

Freed form the cleat, the line swung toward the mast. Polisher reached out with two grippers. One caught the mast. He released the line.

One gripper couldn't support his weight. He started to slide. He caught the smooth mast with a second gripper, a third, and three more.

"*ON STATION!*" Polisher called to *Cynthia*.

"*POLISHER AT MAIN MAST*," *Cynthia* confirmed.

"*RAT*." Catchit sent.

"*HOLD POSITION*," *Cynthia* replied. "*EQUIPMENT MATCHES STATION AND TASK LIST.*"

Catchit coiled around the base of the mast.

Past experience, inferencing, and prediction.

As soon as GOODJOB equaled 1, LIKE NEW, he'd have to run again. And again after that. And again after that. In time, he would follow the mammal over the side.

He scanned.

The mammal had survived. Apparently mammals didn't sink like Polishers. It was in the bay and moving toward a boat ramp. The Catchit had not fared so well. It did not show on scan. Catchits sank.

Polisher polished and thought and polished and thought. Past experience, inference, prediction, initiative. Repeat. Repeat.

Through the long night until sky began to redden in the east, Polisher worked. He buffed and sanded the last ring long after he should have checked for GOODJOB.

Finally, he wore the brass ring through. It snapped and sprung outward from the mast. It fell on the Catchit's tail.

Catchit moved his coils, but his tail did not track his body. Instead, it shook and twisted to one side.

Polisher recorded to past experience.

He logged the missing ring and examined his other sail rings. *GOODJOB = 1, CORROSION CONTROLED, FUNCTIONAL, LIKE NEW.*

"*POLISHER TASK COMPLETE,*" he sent.

Below him, Catchit shifted and lifted his head. "*RAT.*"

"*KILL,*" Cynthia sent.

Polisher moved quickly to the boom. He activated every sensor he had. He found microscopic oxidation. "*BOOM PINIONS, SWIVELS, AND STAYS OXIDIZED,*" he sent.

"*POLISHER TO BOOM,*" *Cynthia* sent.

"*POLISHER ON STATION,*" he sent.

Catchit coiled himself around the mast.

Polisher ground and sanded and polished the pinion and stays that held the boom to main mast.

Just as the sun cleared the horizon, the main pin of the boom clasp sheered. Polisher clung to the main mast. The boom fell. It shattered a section of deck, and it crushed Catchit's skull into the twisted planking.

"*CARPENTER TO MAIN MAST,*" Polisher sent.

"*CARPENTER TO MAIN MAST*," *Cynthia* sent.

Polisher climbed down, crawled over the shattered deck and boom, and crawled over Catchit's crushed and twisted body.

"*RAAAATTTTTTATRRAAAT*," Catchit sent.

"*REPEAT*," Cynthia sent.

"*ON STATION*," Carpenter sent.

"*ON STATION*," *Cynthia* confirmed.

"*RTATRATAT*," Catchit sent.

"*TOSSIT TO MAIN MAST*," Carpenter sent. "*CLEAR DEBRIS.*"

Polisher examined past experience. The Catchit was not dead. It was still trying to catch him. As soon as the *Cynthia* lost the Catchit's signal, another would appear from the bot bay. Polisher ran inferencing. He made predictions. Initiative provided a solution. He ran diagnostics on his scanners, and he headed for the bot storage bay.

~ ~ ~

Roland gasped. "My lord." He stood at the rail admiring the shine of the *Cynthia*. Late morning sun glinted off every metal surface. The deck nearest the main mast looked brand new. So did the boom. From the freshly lacquered deck to the brass of the sail rings, the boat practically glowed. "That little bot is amazing. It's even better than the ad hype."

"Tippy! Tippy, baby!" The Mrs. called.

"She's never been so clean, so beautiful!" Roland said. "We're buying stock in that bot manufacturer."

"Roland, I can't find Tippy!"

Reluctantly, Roland tore himself away from his beautiful *Cynthia*. "Did you look in the cabin?" He headed for the cabin, intending to check for Tippy at the same time he checked the shine of the galley fixtures below. As he approached the cabin, he saw that the automatic door to the bot bay was open. "Maybe he's gotten in with the bots," Roland said. "Probably been chasing them around all night."

"Here, Tippy!" Cynthia called.

Roland went down on hands and knees to look into the bot bay. "Oh my god!"

The dog barked out on the dock.

"I found him. He's out here, Honey."

Roland stared at the brilliant shine on every Catchit in the bot bay.

"Roland," Cynthia said, "Tippy's out here, and he's covered in oil or something."

The little black Polisher sat on top of a coiled Catchit near the front of the bay. It retracted a spinning sander. The armored heads of the four Catchits still in the bay had been polished completely away. From circuitry within the nearest, tiny sparks arced and a thin tendril of white smoke snaked upward.

A single green LED blinked on the top of the Polisher's black shell.

RESULT: GOODJOB = 0, PERFECT; emailto: marketingNsales1@sailbots.com; string="competition replacement sales opportunity."

The Wheels on the Bus

He took a deep breath and told himself that his Temporary Services, Inc. assignment to drive a Rivertown bus was just a trip to the old neighborhood for a day—his last day on the job.

Tyrin shuddered under the chill bite in the late September morning air. The shudder reminded him of childhood winters down by the Willamette river, or maybe it was just approaching the river that caused the shudder. He hadn't forgotten stripping two-by-four firewood out of lathe and plaster walls to keep himself and his pain-wracked mother alive through ice storms and endless days of gray drizzle. The chill breeze off the waterfront carried the rot of all the Upslope crap that dumped into the river and made Rivertown a place only the unwashed, unaffiliated, and unwanted would live.

Tyrin wished he'd had a choice about returning. He wished he could turn away from Rivertown like the rest of the Upslope employed, but he couldn't—not if he wanted to be the youngest Temp in corporation history to retire.

Tyrin approached the broken chain link fence that marked the boundary between Upslope and Rivertown. Two nasty-looking men guarded the gate, hands hovering over a smoking oil drum. Both were maybe seventeen, anglo-mestizo, and tall. One man was broad, bald, and muscled; the other lanky, black-haired, and wiry—tribal turf guards on boundary watch.

Of course, nobody from Upslope would willingly enter Rivertown.

Still, he'd have to get past them if he wanted to report to his temp job.

That busses still ran in the old neighborhood surprised him. That tattooed thugs guarded the gates didn't. He supposed Rivertown folks felt like they controlled their lives if they guarded the gates from imaginary Upslope intrusion.

Tyrin clenched hands that knew the uses of a thousand tools. He wiped his sweating palms on the powder-blue leather jacket that marked him as a Temp.

Tyrin knew the game. From the swirling blue tattoos the guards sported on neck and face and scalp, this was a Blue Tribe gate. Hands visible at his sides, he walked straight toward the gate. "Going in," he said. He tugged on the gate. It rattled and squealed in protest.

The broad, bald man stepped into Tyrin's path. His skull tattoos were blue and gold. One beefy hand rested on a military survival knife hanging from a military-type nylon belt. The other grasped the gate and held it against Tyrin. Wide, onyx-black eyes sized up Tyrin. Those eyes paused on his Temp. Services jacket and on the long, thin tail of dark hair braided around the silver thread inload antenna at the back of Tyrin's skull. "Where' goin', Temp?" Baldy asked.

"Got work inside."

"Jobs in Rivertown all been downsized and outsourced, Temp." Baldy sprayed his words over Tyrin's jacket.

Tyrin squared with the man and straightened an extra inch out of his spine. "Tyrin Ambrose," he said. "Born in river sludge, nursed on rat milk, raised on glow-eel guts, and hardened in the sluice tubes and rust pits."

Baldy slipped the knife from his belt. "No Temp never come from Rivertown."

"Drank the stank running down from Upslope for seventeen years."

"Clever Temp got a dangle on his skull." Baldy pointed the knife at the thin, silver antennae braided into Tyrin's dark rat tail. "You got some smartass from inside sucked into your head? Somebody who run away from Rivertown got caught and brain-drained?"

Tyrin shook his head.

"Then maybe you got some dead soldier's killin' brain pulled down? Eh? Got some killin' in you, Temp?" Baldy released the gate. He flipped his knife from one hand to the other and back. His eyes never left Tyrin's.

Baldy was challenging him. Tyrin considered connecting with Central Dispatch and inloading a combat persona. It would cost him another year's work, and that year would burn up three years of his lifespan. Retirement would slip further away. He'd been doing so well, gaining ground on it. He'd didn't pull extra inloads he'd have to pay for. He was careful about resource consumption. He'd never taken on a private client request. Those brain-to-brain inloads were dangerous.

One more successful job was all he needed to retire. Just one. This one.

"No killing in me," Tyrin said.

Baldy looked him over, starting with Tyrin's thick leather boots. Apparently satisfied with his footwear, the guard's eyes traced the seam of his black, self-sealing first-aid pants, the muscled bulge of his thighs, the bulletproof mesh wrapped around his narrow waist to protect his vital organs, and finally the blue leather jacket covering his powerful chest and shoulders.

"Got the fightin' clothes on," Baldy said.

The other guard took notice. Skinny, and probably slow-dying from mixed addictions, he was steady enough to be deadly. He stepped up shoulder-to-shoulder with Baldy.

"I like them boots," Skinny said.

"Killin' a Temp what has a combat head be big juju," Baldy said.

On the other hand, Tyrin thought, dead men didn't retire. "Coming in to drive a bus," Tyrin said. "No killing in me." It was true, and he hoped his peaceful intent took the shine off killing him for prestige or for his boots.

"No buses running in Rivertown, Tyrin Ambrose," Baldy said. "Never was. Never will be."

Tyrin knew better. His mother and he had ridden the bus. One of his most vivid memories was of her pale and wasted face, serene in sleep, sunlight warm on her coppery hair. Now, Central Dis had sent him to drive a bus. "I'm hired. I'm here," he said. "Company says I have to do the job. Drive the Riverfront bus from noon to seven, they say."

"Shit," Skinny said. He spit at Tyrin's boots.

Baldy seemed to deflate with disappointment.

"Riverfront bus. Yeah." Baldy said. "We heard you was comin'."

Skinny said, "I liked the old driver." Then he went back to his oil drum and resumed his empty stare into the roots of the fire.

Tyrin relaxed. They'd already been told to let him in. He wouldn't need to inload a combat persona.

Baldy smiled: thin, tight, crooked, and sly.

Tyrin didn't like it. "Working is funny, eh?"

"Oh yeah, workin's funny. Riverfront bus is bester funny."

"Yeah? Why?"

"Tell you what, Mr. Tyrin Ambrose the temporary bus driver. You deal me, and you go in clean and easy."

"Say the deal."

"Your pretty blue jacket, and you go in for all day."

"I'll make you a deal," Tyrin said. "I go in for all day, or somebody come for your blue head 'cause you don't let me in."

Baldy laughed. The bull sound echoed off building walls, full and deep and filled with a joy Tyrin didn't understand. Still, the man's laugh was infectious. In spite of Baldy's threatening knife, Tyrin smiled.

Baldy stopped laughing. He put his knife away. "No killin' head don't mean you got no brass between your legs, eh, Temp?"

"I tell you what," Tyrin said. "I come out, I give you my jacket—no sticky. I finish today, and I never come back. I retire."

"Retire?" Baldy asked. "For real?"

"You want the jacket?"

Skinny looked up from the fire. "You born Rivertown for real, Temp?"

"For real. Was a kid here. Been a Temp since I left."

Staring into the fire, Skinny asked, "Downstream from rust pit and through the long pipe—what be?"

"Don't know now, but was then the everybody safe green lawn park under the glass house."

Baldy nodded. Skinny glass-eyed the fire.

"You come in." Baldy muscled the gate open.

Tyrin returned to Rivertown. He walked past Baldy and headed down slope toward the river.

"Seven-fifteen," Baldy called after him, "you comin' out. I get that jacket!"

"You get the jacket," Tyrin said. He meant it. The deal was good. The jacket was company-issue advertising. It cost him nothing, and it might have saved him a very expensive inload.

~ ~ ~

On the down-slope walk toward the river, Tyrin saw familiar things. He also saw that Rivertown had changed. The people were different people, but they had the same desperate, frayed edges to their glances and clothing. Where once he'd known every storm drain and alley, now he wasn't sure of his cross-streets.

Street signs were long gone before he was born, replaced with tagsign. Since he was a kid, buildings had gone to rubble and rubble had shifted to dust. The tagsigns probably marked the same steam vents, warm sewer grates, and territories as when he was a kid. But in his day, tagsign had all been blockyloop and anybody that had learned to read even a little could read the signs. Now, it was more like hieroglyphics, and he'd need to request tribal inloads to read any of it. That wasn't going to happen.

Uncertain how far he'd walked, he stopped in the middle of an intersection. People were out and about, walking, shuffling, heading somewhere for something—or for nothing. Everyone seemed to have somewhere to go and something to do. He could almost believe he was in the middle of Uptown. Of course, he'd have to ignore glassless window frames, the chemical and death reek of the nearby river, and the smell of burning rubber that came from smoldering piles of rubbish that had kept people warm through the night.

"Mr. Blue Jacket!" a woman called.

Tyrin turned toward the voice.

She stood inside the bay of an old display window. She was golden-skinned, copper fuzz-scalped, youngish, and pretty for a Rivertown squatter.

"Got you breakfasts yet?" She waved a black spatula at him. "Come see me, Mr. Blue! I got you breakfast right here!"

Tyrin headed toward her. He guessed she was maybe twenty-two. Not a lot younger than him and in a lot better shape than most folks in Rivertown.

"You gawkin' me or the B-que, Mr. Blue?" She tapped her spatula on a grill made from half a fifty-five-gallon drum. Seven carcasses about the size of Tyrin's forearm lay across the grill cooking. Her smile surprised him with a full set of white teeth. Only a couple on the bottom were crooked.

Tyrin's belly warmed. He wasn't sure if it was the smell of cooking meat or the woman's smile that warmed him. As a Temp, he either worked or recovered from inloads. It had been almost two years since he'd allowed himself the company of a woman. Companionship came with retirement, and only dedicated, focused Temps like him retired. The rest took too many unauthorized inloads. They burned out hard: minds used up, bodies beaten down, victims of their own weakness. "What is it?" He gestured toward the carcasses.

"Squirrel," she said. She flipped a carcass that might have been a squirrel. Of course, it might have been a rat, a little cat, or an opossum. "Thinkin' on *what* ain't so smart as the tastin'," she said. She stabbed a carcass with a fork and lifted a shred of grayish-pink meat for him.

He shook his head.

She laughed. "I see," she said. "You runnin' hard on the wheel, Mr. Blue."

"The wheel?"

"Runnin' roundyround for Uptown owners. They got you on the wheel. You runnin' and you getting nowhere."

"I work for Temporary Services, Incorporated," he said with pride.

She laughed. "Don't even think for hisself." She shredded some meat off the carcass and moved the shreds to the edge of the grill.

Five years ago, her comments would have made him mad enough to hurt somebody. Thank God for signing bonuses and fringe benefits. Temp Services had in-loaded him with a good education his first week on the job.

He smiled. "*You're* selling squirrel, and you think you're going someplace?"

"This where I am. And I ain't sellin' nothin' to nobody. That's Uptown thinkin'. I feed folks. You need fed, and you don't even know 'cause *you* all worried about buying and sellin' brain stuff that ain't even yours. You goin' round-and-round. Round-and-round, Mr. Blue."

"Nobody gives away food."

"I don't give to them what don't give."

"Barter. Same as buying and selling."

"I don't say they got to give to me. That's the diff." She deftly slipped her spatula under a browned squirrel. She flicked her wrist and rolled the meat in place. Grease dripped. Fire flared and died. Charcoal, sauce, and fat smells rose from the grill.

Tyrin's mouth watered. He looked at the woman's copper fuzz hair, at her happy eyes, at her smile. He considered what she'd look like if she had good food, new clothes, a warm bed. "I was born in Rivertown like you," he said.

"Liar, Eh?"

"I got out."

"No lie?"

"No lie. Five years Uptown."

"You think you went somewhere? Look around, pretty Mr. Blue. You standin' in Rivertown."

"You could leave, too. You could give up squirrel and eat real food."

Her smile disappeared. Hard, sidewalk-gray eyes stared back at him. "You ain't tasted *my* food."

He understood her anger, her frustration. It was a hard life in Rivertown. Fear was life, and pride kept it hidden. She had Rivertown pride like him. She was stubborn like him. Still, underneath it all, he knew she wanted a way out. Rivertown was hunting and gathering, no benefits, barter, contaminated water, food and shelter that might not be there tomorrow. In the end, she'd waste away like his mother. She'd rot from the inside out, and the raw beauty and joy in her eyes would become haunted despair.

Sunlight flashed in the copper fuzz on her head. Tyrin's jacket felt tight around his chest.

"I'm only here for one day," he said.

"Still gotta eat."

"No. I mean, yeah." He couldn't believe what he was trying to say. "I mean, you could leave with me."

She stared at him. Her spatula hovered over the grill. She looked as surprised as he felt.

Retirement. "Today's my last day," he said. "I'm retiring. I could take you with me."

Her free hand scooped up a long, B-Que fork and brought it up over the grill to his throat so fast he couldn't step back.

"I don't whore for nobody. Sure-for-sure not for a man can't think for hisself even I was fool enough thinkin' you life besters mine."

He put one hand on the fork, but he didn't push it away. "Not like that," he said. "If you want, I can get you work. You'll have food, an apartment, benefits."

She chuckled and pulled the fork back from his throat.

"I'll retire. Maybe we'll get to know each other. Nobody Uptown knows what it's like to come from Rivertown. You work a while. Then, maybe if you want, maybe you can come and join me on the ranches."

"Retire? Right! Sure you retire." She stabbed the fork into a squirrel. "And *my* squirrels jump up and run home. You runnin' the wheel, and you ain't done till *they* say you done. I seen bluecoats comin' and goin' here. I seen it lots of times. They come in all hot and happy with just theyselfs all and only in they heads. They go out all dark and sad and workin' more and more years than they got fingers and toes."

He was in deep. She was flushed and angry, but he thought maybe those gray eyes had a little flash in them for him, a little hope he hadn't seen when he'd walked up. He knew the sweat on his palms and the drum in his ribs weren't fear. He didn't want to retire alone, and he knew he'd never find anyone who understood what it was like to hide hunger from themselves, to spend each day looking for enough scraps to make them strong enough to spend the next day looking for scraps. He couldn't help everyone in Rivertown, but he could help this copper-haired woman.

"I grew up here. There won't be any more years for me. I do this job and go home retired. You could live with me."

"Live with *you?*" Her words didn't carry quite as much contempt. She flipped a squirrel.

"It's a chance," he said.

"A chance to run roundyround for you or somebody other."

"You have clear eyes. You're strong. We're from the same world. The company can give you everything you need. You can earn everything you want."

She spit on the street beside him.

"Maybe not," he said.

She poked the meat and looked at him sideways like maybe she was thinking about it now. "If I go out and work, I be wearing the dangle-down like you?"

"It connects you to Central Dis. They send you inloads and work requests through it."

"They know where you are and what you doin' all times?"

He nodded. "The company teaches you, trains you, gives you quarters. You never have to worry about being sick. You're never hungry."

She closed one eye, and regarded him. "I never been sick, and there's lots kinds of hunger, Mr. Blue. Maybe I been tryin' to feed you the wrong food."

"What?"

"What job *request* they sent you today?"

"I'm driving the Rivertown bus."

Like Baldy, she burst into laughter.

"Why's that so funny?"

"You got a bus driver in you head?"

"I will have."

"A Rivertown bus driver?"

"A bus driver. Maybe Rivertown."

Again, she laughed at him.

He'd lost enough time on her. She couldn't see a good thing when it was right in front of her. "Look," he said. "I just need to find the intersection of Burnside and Front streets. I'm supposed to meet the bus there at noon."

She wiped a tear of laughter from her eye. "You lots far from drivin' that bus, Mr. Blue."

He'd lost his focus. He'd let loneliness and his memories of his past, of his mother, cloud his mind. Enough was enough. He hoped it wasn't too late to get back on task, back on his path to retirement. "How far? I have to be there by noon."

"I s'pose you do."

"Do you or don't you know where Burnside and Front meet?"

She flashed her teeth and shook her head. "Pissed off don't get you there, but you keep goin'. Maybe you find the right way, Mr. Blue. Maybe you get there."

"Just point."

She lifted the spatula and pointed downhill. "Keep keepin' this street. This Burnside. You know when you get to Front."

"How?"

"The bus bein' there."

"What if it isn't there when I get there?"

She started laughing again. "If you ever stop asking questions and get where you goin', you come see me. I give *you* work, pretty Mr. Blue. You catch them squirrels in the sluice pipes. We cook 'em, and you come live with *me*." She smiled warm and slow before she turned and disappeared into the shadows of the building. From the shadows, he heard her singing a song, something he almost remembered, maybe a lullaby. The only words he could make out were "round-and-round."

Tyrin shook his head. She was nuts, and he had let her make him a little nuts. For all he knew, she'd been drinking straight from the river all her life. Pretty or not, hometown or not, she was Downslope, and she'd never be Upslope like him.

He headed down the street toward the river. He walked into the breeze and followed the stench.

Ten blocks later, the strength of the river stink told him he was getting close. Tyrin scanned the streets for trouble. A sharp-chinned old man in a twenty-years-ago suit stood on the next corner. He clutched a brown paper bundle under one arm.

Tyrin didn't think the old man was a threat, so he stepped into a doorway, closed his eyes, and made his inload request. *<Connect: Central Dis. Tyrin. Emp. # 232121557. Request authorized personality inload, Bus Driver. Purchase order, 457894.>*

Response was immediate. The inload washed into his mind. He felt like he was falling backward through darkness. He leaned hard against the wall. Someone else's experiences strobed insides his skull: the smell of perfume as a woman stepped onto the bus; rain sheeting on the windshield, wipers unable to keep up; shifting gears; backing up, the warning chime ringing; holding the head of a newborn between bloody thighs on a vinyl seat; sunshine warming his black uniform; the smell of diesel exhaust and fuel.

He opened his eyes to the gray dust and rubble of Rivertown.

He checked his watch. Nearly noon. He had to catch the bus.

It couldn't be more than another block. After that, he'd hit the river. He left the relative safety of the doorway and headed toward the river, not entirely sure the B-que woman had given him good directions.

"Temp!" It was the suited old man. He trotted toward Tyrin. "You the bus driver?"

Tyrin froze. The old man was thin, more of a rack for the suit than a man that could fill it. His hair was white, but the stubble on his gaunt face had flecks of black.

"You're running late," the man said.

"You know where the bus is?" Tyrin asked.

"Come with me," the man hooked Tyrin's arm and pulled him along the street toward the corner. "Shift's about to start."

"You the one who ordered a temp driver?"

The man hustled them along toward the corner. "Don't sound so amazed. Even Rivertown busses need drivers. Folks don't like when the bus don't got a driver."

"You have the P.O. number?"

The old man rattled it off. It matched. They rounded the corner. The old man stopped. "There she is," he said.

In the middle of the street, a cross-town express bus rested on rusted, rubberless wheels. "That?" Tyrin asked. "You want me to drive that?"

"Rivertown bus. My bread and butter."

Suddenly, Tyrin understood why Baldy and the B-que woman had laughed. They knew the bus had been derelict for years. It hadn't seen glass in its windows forever and a day. The wipers lay inward over the dash. Rust stains streaked the white sides of the bus, and red spray-paint tags covered faded billboards for shiny-hair products that probably hadn't been in the shops of Rivertown since before Tyrin was born.

Tyrin turned to leave.

The old man hooked his arm and tugged hard. "Where you goin', Temp? I got a contract."

Tyrin stopped and peeled the man's hand off his arm. "No one can drive that bus. I'm going back Upslope for another job."

"I hired a bus driver, and you got to drive." The man thrust the brown paper package into Tyrin's hands. "You goin' to drive, and you goin' to wear this cap and jacket."

"That bus is going no place, Mister."

"My contract don't say it has to. My contract just says I get a bus driver for a day."

"Your contract says you get a replacement driver. Nobody ever drove that bus."

"Max died last week. I got people complaining up and down the river that the bus needs a new driver. Until I find a good one, I got you, Temp! You don't like it, you use that dangly-down and check in with your owners."

Tyrin heard the slavery insult and the not-so-subtle reminder of his contractual obligations. He ignored the former and closed his eyes.

<Connect: Central Dis. Tyrin. Emp. # 232121557. Request payment verification PO # 457894.>

<CD Temporary Services, Inc. PO # 457894, payment verified. Services required. One day. Bus Driver.>

Tyrin opened his eyes and stepped back from the old man.

The man grinned. Brown and broken teeth flashed. "You gonna drive or break contract?"

Tyrin looked at the dead bus. He had no choice. If he refused a job that was paid for, the refund came out of his retirement. Freedom would be another six months away. He nodded. "I don't have the experience to fix the bus," he said.

"Bus don't need fixin.'"

"Can't drive it like it is."

"Just get into the uniform, get in the driver's seat, take the fares, and do what bus drivers do. Just fake it."

"If it's all fake, why don't you do it?"

"I'm management." The man seemed to suddenly inflate and fill his suit. "I run three buses in Rivertown. I can't be hanging around watching this one all day." The man tore at the brown paper and pulled out a black jacket and billed cap. "Put it on and get to work. You've got just enough time. It'll be noon in a couple minutes."

Tyrin stripped off his blue jacket and put on the black one. "How'd the driver die? Max?"

"On the job. Found him dead at the wheel. Shame, too. He been driving for a lot a years. Folks liked him."

"Any that didn't?"

"S'pose." The old man shrugged and walked away.

Tyrin watched him hurry down the street and around the corner. He tugged on the hem of his jacket to straighten it, then he walked up the rusted steps into the bus.

The images from the inload were partially useful. Tyrin understood the swivel mechanism on the seat. He understood how to close and lock the metal mesh cage door that separated him from riders. Even though the windshield was gone, the click of the cage lock gave him a little more confidence. The sun was high, and it did warm his uniform. He put his temp jacket into the lock box under the dash. He fastened his seat belt because that was the habit of the driver that had provided the experiences of the inload.

Tyrin waited.

Waiting to start his run was not part of the experience of the driver. It was not part of Tyrin's experience either. He tried the ignition. Of course, nothing happened. He fiddled with the stick and the pedals and the door lever and the coin box with its rectangular funnel. He opened and closed the cage. He walked to the back of the bus. Finally, he strapped himself back in, closed the cage, leaned back, and closed his eyes.

His bus driver remembered naps in the sun—killing time to adjust his schedule. There was pleasure there. Silence. Peace.

Sunlight warmed his eyelids, and he savored the orange glow. He relaxed and began to think that maybe this job would be easy, would be a long nap. He smelled the vinyl seats warming and heard tiny metallic clicks as the skin of the bus expanded. A memory unfolded in his mind—his own memory—a memory of sitting on a bus seat with his mother, of laying his head on her lap, of her work- and disease-gnarled hand gently brushing his hair back from his temple, her voice soothing him, telling him that the boys that had beaten him and taken his three-tired, toy car were behind them, gone.

The metallic clicking grew louder. It became a pounding. Something small and hard hit his forehead. Whatever it was clattered against the cage walls then the floor. Tyrin opened his eyes and sat up straight.

A waif of a woman stood in front of the bus. Her arm was cocked back to throw a pebble.

Tyrin ducked.

"Open the doors," she demanded.

Confused, still groggy, his inload took over. Tyrin reached for the door lever. The woman stepped up the boarding stairs into the bus and dropped a coin in the box. She gave him a contemptuous look, walked past him, found a seat in the rear of the bus, and settled in.

Tyrin looked at her in a fragment of mirror still hanging above the sun visors. She was young. She wore a short, patched leather skirt and a too-tight leather vest. Neither covered enough skin to keep her warm in the September nights. She had the same blue and gold swirling tattoos on her breasts and arms that the gatemen had on their skulls. Like the B-que woman, her hair was cut short. It looked more like golden fuzz than hair. She flipped him off, then she looked out the window and ignored him.

Automatically, he reached for the door lever and pulled.

"Wait!" a man called. "Wait!"

Tyrin's foot automatically jumped to the break, and he flipped the door back open.

The man leaped onto the bus, swinging a battered leather briefcase to counterbalance his leap. He was dressed in a black suit, threadbare but upscale for Rivertown. He dropped a coin in the box. He didn't even glance at Tyrin. He just headed for the back of the bus.

Tyrin closed the doors and put the bus in gear. He pushed his foot against the accelerator. It was already against the firewall and nothing happened. It was a wasted habit from the driver in his head, but it was the job he was paid to do, and Tyrin knew better than to fight his inload. He let himself relax into the experience of his driver.

In the mirror, Tyrin watched the man slide his briefcase under the seat then sit down next to the girl. She smiled, wrapped her arms around his neck, and pulled his head down to her breasts. He began kissing her tattoos.

Tyrin looked away. Now he understood the bus. The old man had said he ran three buses. Tyrin decided he could sit through a day of Rivertown fantasy sex, and at the end of the day, he would retire.

Someone pounded on the bus door. Tyrin turned. Three men glared at him. All three faces were covered in blue tattoos. The men wore metal mesh and leather wraps, cheap imitations of Tyrin's own body armor. All three men carried clubs or knives.

His adrenalin glands squeezed a sharp rush of fire into his blood. A Blue tribe girl on a suit and a pack of Blues wanting on board couldn't be a good mix. Tyrin glanced at the mirror. The girl's leather skirt lay on the aisle floor and Briefcase Man's bare feet were up in the air over the back of a seat. The girl was completely hidden behind seats on the right side of the bus.

The men pounded again.

One came around the front of the bus and slammed a pipe into the metal below Tyrin's seat. "Open it, Driver!"

Tyrin was glad the bus was high enough that the man couldn't just smack him with the pipe. He'd have to climb the front of the bus or throw the pipe to reach him.

His palms sweated on the wheel. Outside the bus, on open ground, he might have been able to fight his way through the three of them and gain room to run like hell. Inside the cage and the bus, no way.

"Open!"

"Dead men don't retire," Tyrin said.

"What!?" the pipe man asked. He slammed his pipe into the bus again.

The skinniest of them tried to squeeze through the narrow window gaps of the bus door. He couldn't fit. All three attacked the door.

Tyrin gripped the wheel. His fingernails cut into his own palms. He didn't have much time. The old bus door would give.

Another year of work. Another year of other people's minds pouring into his head, confusing his memories, burning his synapses. Another year would age him three, but he'd be alive.

He could do it. He was still young enough.

The door hinges split and bent inward at the top.

<Connect: Central dispatch. Tyrin. Emp. # 232121557. Request unauthorized inload against wages. Hand-to-hand, survival combat persona.>

Images flashed. Tyrin's head spun. He steadied himself on the steering wheel.

The accumulated life experience of a killer flowed into him. In memory, bones snapped, hands closed on a throat, blades tore flesh. He felt the cold detachment of a conscious decision to maim instead of kill. Then he was staring over the front of the bus at the pipe wielding punk.

He opened the door and flashed an adrenaline grin.

The three men filed onto the bus. They laughed and flashed murderous looks his way. In turn, each dropped a coin in the box. They each laid their clubs and knives in a wooden crate on the floor in front of the first seat on the bus.

Tyrin stared at them as they filed past and found seats. The last man, Jumping Pipe Man, smiled. "Thanks, Driver," he said. "We needed the ride today."

Confused, Tyrin closed the bus door and put the bus in gear. He'd just given up another year of his life to keep from dying, but the guys he thought wanted to kill him, take revenge on a suit, and steal the bus money had filed onboard, paid, and thanked him.

He looked up and down the street. He saw the next customer coming. A woman with a little girl in tow. He pressed in the clutch, geared down to first, and pumped the break. He opened the door.

The woman dropped a coin. The girl lifted a coin for the cash box.

"Kids ride free," Tyrin said. The words were out before he thought.

The mother nodded and smiled. The girl dropped her coin anyway. The pair headed back and settled into seats.

Kids ride free. Tyrin remembered his bus ride with his mother. He remembered the driver saying that.

Two more men approached the bus. They might have been brothers to the first three except their tattoos were red. They got on, dropped weapons and coins. They settled into seats near the Blues.

Tyrin had thought he was minding a brothel, but apparently he wasn't. He'd thought he was going to have to fight for his life, but the men had come in and seated themselves as if the bus really could take them someplace—as if they needed the bus to take them someplace.

Mistaking the intent of the Blues had cost him another year to retirement.

He remembered what B-que woman had said about Temps in their blue coming in full of themselves and their retirement and how they left with years of work ahead.

Maybe, he thought. Maybe the company had set him up. If Dis *had* tricked him, he'd never let it happen again.

The tribals talked among themselves quietly: blues with blues, reds with reds, sometimes blues with reds. Briefcase and skirt moaned and groaned. Woman and child stared out the window.

Tyrin remembered the bus and his mother. She was pale and gaunt. She stared out the window at something. He remembered looking out the window to see what she saw. In his memory, the window had no glass. Outside, he could see the river flowing past. There was a bridge, a concrete and asphalt arch out over the water. The brown water moved. The bridge didn't.

His inloaded bus driver remembered the low vibration of the bus engine. Tyrin couldn't remember engine sounds. He couldn't remember vibrations in the seats.

The bus of his childhood wasn't moving. The bus had never moved.

Someone tapped on the door.

Startled, Tyrin grabbed the door lever and swung the door open. The old man in the suit climbed on the bus.

"How's it going?" old man asked.

Throat too dry to speak, Tyrin just nodded to the cash box.

The man looked at the people in the bus. "Give 'em their money's worth, Temp. Everybody needs a lift now and then."

The little girl started crying. Her mother tried to soothe her.

Tyrin checked the mirror. The Leather Skirt Girl's blond fuzz popped up from behind a seat. She frowned at the fussing child. The other tribals squirmed. He looked at the owner. The man's troubled face stared back.

The B-que girl's tune came to Tyrin. It floated in his mind like a soothing, fresh breeze. He smiled. The tune grew stronger. The B-que girl's hum became his own mother's voice singing it in his head. He started to hum. The owner smiled. Tyrin started to sing, "The wheels on the bus go round…"

Blue tribe picked it up. Red joined in. Finally, the little girl sang too. Her mother smiled at the mirror, at Tyrin. Tyrin sang, smiled back, and winked.

Owner got off to check his other buses.

Leather Skirt left soon after. She put an extra coin on the dash and winked at him.

Tribes and Briefcase all got off after while.

All afternoon, people came and went. All afternoon, Tyrin drove the bus and watched them, figured out what kind of lift they needed. Some only needed a smile; some needed a safe place to rest; some wanted a joke, a comment about the weather, or a compliment. All of them needed something, and somewhere in his own memories of his life in Rivertown with his mother, he found the things he could give them.

The sun was low and the building shadows were long when the owner came back to the bus. The woman and child were still on board.

"End of the line," Tyrin said.

The woman got up. The girl hung close to her side. They walked to the front of the bus. "Are you the new driver?" the woman asked.

"No Ma'am. I'm a Temp."

"Pity," she said. "You have a knack for it."

Tyrin nodded and smiled. So did the owner.

The woman walked away with her daughter's hand in hers.

"You done good, Temp." the owner said. "I'll call you in as job done and done good."

"Thanks," Tyrin said.

"You want full-time?" the owner asked.

"Not interested."

"Lot of respect for a good bus driver in Rivertown."

"I'm retiring soon."

"Yeah. 'Course." The owner stepped off the bus. He turned to face Tyrin. "Leave the jacket and cap on the seat for the next driver," he said. Then he walked away into the twilight.

Tyrin took off the jacket. River breeze chilled him. He folded the uniform and put it on the driver's seat. He pulled his heavy, leather jacket out of the lock box, put it on, and headed up-slope toward the gates.

~ ~ ~

"You back, Temp! Gots my jacket, too."

Tyrin stripped off his jacket and gave it to Baldy.

"Don't lookin' too happy, Temp," Baldy said. He tried on the jacket. "You got your retirin', then?"

Tyrin didn't want to answer. He just stared at the gate, looked forward to being on the other side of it, on the Uptown side and heading home to his apartment, his shower, his easy chair. He was looking forward to some delivered Chinese and a good night's sleep.

"Temp?"

Tyrin shook his head. "One more year, then I retire."

Baldy smiled and nodded. "So we see you again about ten months. Eh?" Skinny looked up and laughed. His broken teeth and glassy eyes caught early moonlight. "He gonna be free some one'an these years," Skinny said.

Tyrin ground his molars together. He remembered the warm sun on his bus driver's uniform. He remembered the woman and the girl on the bus. The B-que girl's song came to him.

They had all seen it before, seen him or someone like him before. To them, he was a repeating image, a theme, an entertainment. He was an Uptown rat running roundyrounds.

At least his wheel would stop in a year. Skinny might be dead by then. Baldy? Who knew? Lives were short in Rivertown.

Tyrin passed through the gate and into Uptown.

~ ~ ~

A few weeks after the Rivertown bus, Tyrin took on his first private client request. He could pick up six months of his year with one mind-to-mind inload. Risky, but Rivertown had left him wanting out bad.

The client was from down-slope near Rivertown. That was unusual, but it wasn't unheard of, and he was relieved that it wasn't actually *in* Rivertown.

Still, he walked the halls of the aging apartment building with caution. He knocked. Alert, he stood outside an apartment door, his ears straining to hear anything that might signal trouble, his body ready to make use of the damn combat persona still lingering in his brain.

The door opened a crack.

Tyrin wondered if the haggard woman wearing the stained and tattered pink terrycloth robe and holding her apartment door like a shield would let him in. Through the crack between the door and the doorframe peered eyes the color of a receding storm line. They were weak, wasted, and empty—the eyes of a woman who had seen too much, a woman too weary to do anything except give up. Her gaze chilled his gut.

"I'm your Temp, Ma'am," he said.

She stared.

He knew the look too well.

She was desperate, at the end of her endurance. Maybe she was on the verge of losing her job. Maybe packs of unemployed were ripping her off every day.

No matter what horror had reduced her to the frail husk holding the door, he knew his job and what it would cost her to hire him for a mind-to-mind.

Those eyes and the rags and rat shit stench in the hall said she was betting everything she had on him.

She lifted a pale, gnarled hand to unhook the chain. The door swung wide. She looked like she'd been beaten, busted, drowned, and buried, all in the last half hour.

Tyrin stepped across the threshold and gagged on the reek of cat piss, mold, and rotted food. His eyes stung and he choked.

Rotting piles of delivered Chinese food cartons filled every corner of the tiny room. Off to one side, a small-frame door, gray-yellow paint peeling in long strips, lead into a tiny bathroom. Gray-black smears of cat crap covered the linoleum.

He swallowed hard to control his gag reflex. "Is this apartment twenty-three?" he asked. In spite of the evidence of take-out, he had to believe this ghost of a woman couldn't afford Temp. Services. Dis had screwed up.

She shuffled back from the door. "Yes," she whispered. "Twenty-three. I called." One gnarled hand hooked his gym-pumped forearm and tugged.

He stepped forward to let her close the door. He blinked away the ammonia sting in his eyes.

She closed, chained, and barred the door behind him.

In her eyes, Tyrin could see dark fear of something outside that door. It was a thick, cold sludge rising and falling behind blood-shot whites and dilated pupils. Every moment of this woman's life was a struggle against fear.

He wanted to help her, but sympathy wasn't enough to gain his services.

"Ma'am, I have to tell you-" he began.

"I can pay," she said. Slowly, critically, she looked him up and down from his thick leather boots to the bulletproof mesh wrapped around his waist.

She didn't, or maybe couldn't, look into his face.

He stood still for her. Most clients checked him out like that. Most folks figured if they were just a little smarter or a little tougher themselves, they wouldn't need a temp to solve their problems. Men, especially, thought they needed someone with physical strength and stamina to deal with whatever job needed doing.

Tyrin knew better. The job was all between the ears: his and the client's. Hadn't he lost a year because he'd believed a little too quick that he was in trouble? Never again. His head was on straight, and the client's perception of him was just as important. He'd inload whatever she needed him to know, then he'd head off to her work or to do whatever it was she needed. When it was done, he'd take off the required forty-eight hours for mental reversion to full-self, then he'd be off on the next job. Ten more jobs, maybe less, and he was retired—out of the corporate, feudal mess.

He looked down at her hunched, frail body. Pink scalp showed between greasy, gray-black ropes of hair. Of course, if she couldn't afford him, he was losing time.

"Ma'am," he said. "I'm a temporary worker for-"

She cut him off with a wave of her hand. "You think-" Racking coughs shook her whole body.

Gently, Tyrin grasped her bony shoulders to steady her.

She flinched under his touch, but she didn't look up.

"It's okay," he said. "I'm here." She was so light that he could have tossed her the length of the apartment like a dry-grass doll.

The coughing ended. She relaxed.

He let her go.

She turned away and shuffled across the room to a tan easy chair as worn out as she was. She lifted a scrawny gray cat from the tattered cushions, turned, and settled herself. The cat curled up on her pink-robed lap. She stroked its back. "You think I'm too poor to hire a temp."

"No, Ma'am," Tyrin said. "I'm trained to not judge. I go where I'm sent."

"Training is bullshit," she said. "Company propaganda to make you think you're special. I saw your face when you walked in."

Priority one was to gain a new client's confidence, and Tyrin knew it wasn't going well. "I'm really sorry, Ma'am. It's just that I don't often get an assignment in this part of town."

"Could be worse. Could be Rivertown."

"I didn't mean to insult, Ma'am."

"You didn't. I like this part of town," she said. "A lot of people here are unaffiliated. They aren't all caught up in chasing the lies of benefits, stock options, and retirement."

"I'm sure that's true, Ma'am."

"They're honest. They have time for each other." She spoke more to the cat than Tyrin. Her voice was sad and quiet. "They trade what they make, and they make what they trade. They don't run away from their problems by hiring other folks to take them on."

Tyrin heard her shame. The woman had blue-collar pride, and it pissed her off that her pride couldn't solve her problem.

He had to calm her down so he could get to the business of quoting rates and services.

He searched the room for some object of conversation that would let him draw her out, make her feel he was interested in helping her, personally.

There were two objects of promise in the stark apartment: the cat and a silver-framed portrait on a stained end table beside her chair.

The cat was asleep.

The portrait was of a beautiful, professional woman wearing a dark blue business jacket over a white silk blouse. Her long dark hair was braided forward over one shoulder. Hard neck and jaw muscles revealed strength.

Tyrin felt drawn toward the young woman in the picture. "May I?" he asked.

The client nodded.

He picked up the frame. The young woman had the same stormy eyes and sharp jaw line as the old woman. If they were related, the girl was her granddaughter. "Your daughter?" he asked, hoping she took the compliment.

She turned her dry, lined face toward the picture. Tears glistened in her eyes. "No," she whispered.

Tyrin guessed the girl in the picture was dead or disowned or worse. He knew there was some twisted, personal pain wrapped up in that picture.

So much for relaxing the client; he should have picked the cat.

There was nothing for it but to get down to business. "Since you didn't pre-pay, I'm required to quote rates and services," he said.

She nodded, still staring at the picture. "Do your job."

He made a show of taking his data pad from his jacket pocket. The display flashed the red Temp Services insignia—a red capital T.

The logo faded away, and the rates and services list appeared. He didn't need it. It just made his recitation seem more official; that often stopped some time-wasting arguments and questions.

"Rates for all temporary services are per inload from the experience database. Experience inload from compatible client-provided sources are allowable at a fifty-percent discount to normal services. Mind-to-mind inloads are acceptable with approval at three times normal rates. Some service exclusions apply. Temp Services employees may not be used to replace employees in certain high-risk positions unless special contracts are in place."

She stroked the cat.

"Do you understand, Ma'am?"

She nodded.

"You can afford the rates?"

She stopped stroking the cat and thrust a hand between the armrest and the cushion of the chair. Her hand reappeared holding a red silk pouch. She held it up.

He took it. It was heavy, and the contents were hard. He opened the loose flap of the pouch. Inside, he found three finger-sized gold bars.

"Close your mouth," she said. "It's enough. If you need to weigh it, go ahead."

Tyrin snapped his jaw shut and shook his head. His training had covered the fact that sometimes deeply paranoid clients hoarded precious metals. He'd just never seen it before. Along with his data pad, he slipped the pouch into his pocket. "What can I do for you, Ma'am?"

"I'm tired." Her face darkened and sagged.

He nodded. "Need a bodyguard? Someone bothering you about your apartment?"

"No." Her hand was back on the cat.

"Need time off from local tribes? Want to get out without taking a beating or losing your cat food money?"

She lifted her narrow face and looked directly into his eyes.

In her eyes, he saw the mist and distance of memories and pain that stretched to a horizon he couldn't see. For a moment, in spite of his training, he hated. He hated whoever had put that pain in her eyes.

"I just want to take a day off work," she said.

"You don't need a day off to avoid personal injury, do you, ma'am?"

"No. It's just business as usual. More of the same. Always more. Always the same. I just can't do it anymore. You understand, don't you? I can't keep running in circles. I can't keep chasing hopes that die as soon as I reach out to grasp them." Tears poured from her eyes now. She clasped the photograph to her chest.

"It's all right, ma'am. Nothing to be ashamed of. Everybody needs a day off now and then. What's the job, ma'am?"

"I just want to stay home today. I want to stay in my apartment with my cat. I want to nap in my chair and not have to…" Her voice became weak and hollow then trailed away into the same mists that filled her eyes.

"What do you do, Ma'am?"

Still hugging the photo with one hand, she reached under her bathrobe with the other. She pulled out a data pad and handed it to him.

A red capital T flashed on the screen then faded away. A rates and services listing appeared.

Tyrin sucked in a deep breath. His leather jacket was too tight around his chest. The cat and food-rot stench caught at his throat. "The picture…"

She nodded. "Graduation from Temp Services, Inc. training."

The data pad was slick in his sweating hand. He suddenly felt small and weak.

"You must have been one of the first," he said. "A pioneer."

"They're all dead."

"Retired," he said.

Her pale hand stroked the cat. "I was twenty. I graduated thirteen years ago," she said.

"Impossible," he stammered.

"Ever been to a retirement party? Ever met an old temp?"

"Mind-to-mind with you would be thirteen years of inloads in one connect. That's the equivalent of-"

She nodded. "Two thousand three hundred and seven inloads. I paid. You took my money." She stood, reached behind her head, and pulled a white ponytail up and out from under her robe. She draped it forward over her shoulder. The silver thread of her antenna flashed in the apartment light.

The data pad slipped from Tyrin's hand and shattered against the client's floor. Her cat jumped and skittered toward the bathroom.

~ ~ ~

Tyrin put his driver's cap on. His fingers brushed over the bald scar on the back of his head. He smiled. He'd chewed himself up pretty good with Baldy's knife, but he was rid of Temp Services.

Satisfied with his hat, he walked out to the girl in the display window "Goin' to work, Kalee. Meet me at the end of the line, and we'll walk the river at sunset."

Kalee turned from her squirrel skinning and smiled. "I like that," she said. "Maybe we check traps in the Uptown runoff pipe. Needs us a few more squirrels."

Tyrin admired her solid shoulders and proud cheeks. He kissed her, slipped on his driver's jacket, and, singing their song, headed downslope toward his bus.

The Tao of Flynn

Originally printed in Realms of Fantasy Magazine and as a stand-alone eBook by IFD Publishing.

Flynn was an honest liar. He would look you dead in the eye, smile his commercial, outdoorsman smile, wink one pale blue eye, and say, "I'm a professional liar." And that was the truth. He'd keep telling you the truth until your wallet was empty, then he'd smile again, say, "I warned you," and walk away.

All you could do was smile and watch him go because you'd been warned, and damn if he didn't nail you anyway.

"Keep an eye on Flynn," Cooper had said. "He's good, but he's going to get us in trouble."

Cooper was the boss, and, back then, I was his man to beat. The whiteboard in the coffee room showed it. If Cooper had a hot lead, I was the man he sent.

Once I was in the door, my closing ratio was 5 to 1. If I made five sales calls, I came back with paper on one. Everybody needed more fire insurance.

Once, on a good streak, I did six calls and managed to come home with paper on eight. The last call had forgotten I was coming. I hit triple as the entertainment at their dinner party.

That was before Flynn. After Flynn, everything was different.

I was in the coffee room throwing darts the day Flynn came in. He wore a three-piece suit and patent leather, wingtip shoes. Italian, no less. Ever YouTubed those old commercials for cigarettes? The ones with the cowboys? He looked like that, right down to the dimple in his tanned chin. Dark brown hair, kinda wavy, and pale blue eyes with a thin, dark ring around the irises.

Once, in a bar, I saw a waitress trip and lose a whole tray of margaritas on a table of bikers because she was just trying to get a look at Flynn.

He strode into the break room, smiled that liar's smile, and spoke. Honestly, I don't remember what he said. I only remember that his voice sounded like his face looked. It was impossibly deep and rich in the right mix to make you listen. It wasn't that you wanted to listen. You didn't even care what he said. You had to listen—listen to the nuance of vibration in the air coming from between his brilliant white teeth.

I stood there in my two-piece denim suit and my cowboy boots. One second, I was sure I was the best in the game. The next, I knew I hadn't even seen the rule book. He was that good.

So, Cooper called me in after three days went by and Flynn had gone out and come back with paper two, three times every day.

Cooper's shaved bald head is low. He's nose-close to a pale green spreadsheet laid out over his desk. I see the white cotton shirt over the round of his back. Embarrassed for him, I scan the full wall shelves behind him, not really reading the titles of the corporate cheerleader sales and motivation books.

"Richard," he says—and I really perk up because nobody but my grandmother calls me Richard. He sits up and squints toward me. I'm thinking the guy should get over himself and get some glasses. "I don't think Flynn's on the program," he says. "I think he's cutting corners."

The program was the patter, our pitch, the script we had to use when we talked to a client. It was a sacred thing handed down to us by arcane sales and marketing people who knew both the mind of God and man. We spoke the words, and in them was the magic of fear and the promise of security.

Change the incantations, and we opened the door to litigation. Lawyers would descend on us all.

Deliver us from evil and lead us not into temptation, Amen.

I wait for him to tell me why it makes a difference to me. He gets down with his paper again. "We need totals," he says to his desk. He looks up. "We can ride this to the top," he says.

I see a book behind him. The title on the spine is, *Ride to the Top.*

He stands up and smooths his hands over his head like he still has the hair he shaved off himself. He sucks in one of his speech making breaths and launches. "You'd like an office of your own someday, wouldn't you Rich? I know I'd like the freedom that comes to a man like me when my men are successful. You'd like to help me with that, wouldn't you?"

I know my lines. I understand his wind. I nod.

"Flynn's a loose cannon."

"He's smooth."

"Smooth ain't shit in court. Run with him today. Watch him. Let me know if he's on the program."

It wasn't a request.

An hour later, I'm ready to ride shotgun on the first run of the day. I've got my case, my silver Cross pen, my high producer lapel pin with two little diamond chips in it for being high man a couple months straight. My mojo is on line and steaming.

Flynn's a no show. Four hours, he's late. I could have run a program and come back for a new lead.

Does he apologize when he comes in?

"Rich," he says. "Game of darts?"

"Four hours, Flynn. You're late. I'm supposed to ride shotgun with you today."

He took off his jacket, pulled a chain and bar thing out of the pocket, twisted it into a hanger, and hung his coat on the door handle of the bathroom.

"I lost an appointment waiting for you," I said.

"You can have my sale today," he said.

Mentally, I gave him credit for trying. "You only have time for two more calls."

"I'll keep one. I'll give one to you." He picked up the darts. Not the three on the dart board. He went to the coffee can full of irregular, dull tips, bent fins, and busted stems. All the darts. Then he waltzed back to the line and unbuttoned all but one of the buttons on his vest.

"Shoot with me Rich. I know you like the game."

My bag was down and my coat was off and I was standing beside him ready to play, and the whole time I was taking off that coat, putting down that case, and crossing the room, I was explaining to him how I couldn't play because I needed to get to work.

"I won't keep you long," he said. "We'll go out in an hour or so."

I relaxed, not because I wanted to, but because he said it was okay. "An hour from now will be half way through the appointment. The client will be so pissed, they won't even let us in."

"Closest to bull goes first?"

I nodded.

He handed me a dart.

I'd like to say he cheated. I'd like to say he gave me some nasty, crooked, broken-twisted, wobbly dart. He didn't work that way. He gave me the best dart in the can. It was my favorite dart from my favorite set of three. Sharp, yeah. I was the one that kept it that way. Straight as a Mormon prayer boy, and the flights were brand new. Each fin had a bull's-eye on it, and one fin on each dart had the scoring combinations for Cricket printed on it.

I knew he could have screwed me. He had all the darts.

"Thanks," I said.

"Pleasure," he said. Then he pulled a dart for himself. It sucked. The tip was bent into a bead. The flights were creased. One was torn. I'd thrown that dart, and I knew how it spiraled in the air.

Did I warn him? No. Play to win or don't play. That was one motto of the office.

"Go ahead," he said.

I toed the line with my right foot, left at ninety degrees. I lined up my shoulders and cocked my arm. I set my eyes both on the bull. Stereoscopic vision is a key in darts. I breathed my ritual. One breath to settle. Two breathes for focus. Three breaths to feel the dart.

Phht!

In the 20 wedge just outside the bull's green ring. Good, but not great. I nodded my approval.

That's when he said it to me the first time. "Rich, there's all kinds of magic in the world." He doesn't even step up to the line. "Some kinds of magic come from rituals." He looks at me and tosses his dart. Like always, it wobbles and twists and rises a bit and falls.

Dead center bull.

"Shit."

He laughs. "Some kinds come from doing the right thing in the moment. I throw first," he said, and he handed me my ass in that game.

Later, when I was practicing and he was talking, he said, "Throw all the darts, Rich. Don't just throw the straight ones or the pretty ones or the flat ones. Throw the ones that wobble and spin and break up or to the right. When you can throw the whole can of darts and get every single one inside the doubles ring, I'll show you a trick."

"Thanks," I said.

It took me two hours, but I finally did it. Twenty-two darts in a row inside the doubles circle. "Shit hot!" I laughed and clapped and grinned at Flynn.

He nodded and put down his magazine.

Cooper came in about then. He didn't say anything. He glared at Flynn, then he shook his head in disappointment at me.

"Time to go," Flynn said.

Cooper withdrew, but I knew him well enough to know that his red neck was a sign of how pissed he was.

Flynn put on his coat, and I tried to figure out how come I'd let Flynn con me into a game of darts when we were supposed to be running appointments.

~ ~ ~

"Cooper thinks I need someone to watch me?" Flynn asked.

"No, he just wants me to learn from you," I lied. "I'm supposed to observe your technique. Cooper says you're smooth."

Flynn slipped his black, Lincoln Towne Car up to the curb in front of a low, quad apartment building: two daylight basement units, and two half-flight walkups.

Bad prospects. The phone girls hadn't done their pre-qualifying.

Flynn leaned toward me a little. He smiled. "Rich, you're not a liar. You've never really been a liar."

"And you're a man who tells the truth?" I said.

"I'm a professional liar," he said. "You're an Iowa bale bucker who jumped ship and ran for the bright lights. You have an honest face, and I can see the truth in your puffy cheeks and your big brown eyes."

My face must have turned six shades of red. I was mad. I was upset. I felt naked, and I wanted something that would get this guy out of my life or under control. Nothing felt right since he'd come into the office. "Cooper says you're off the program."

"Cooper knows his business. I know mine," Flynn said.

"You're in the same business."

"First thing you need to know about lying, Rich, is that nobody is in the *same* business. Until you figure out what business somebody is in, you can't find their truth. Until you find their truth, you can't nudge it."

"All of a sudden, you're teaching *me* to sell?" I was really getting hot. I was giving up sales calls to get this guy in line, and he was telling me how to do my job. "Remember who the top producer is, Flynn. You haven't been here long enough to lecture me."

He got out of the car.

"This house doesn't pre-qualify," I said. "We're wasting our time."

He opened the back of the car and got his jacket. He brushed it off with the lint brush he kept in the glove compartment. "We don't need to sell anything for you to see if I'm on the program, do we?"

I got out of the car and followed him to the house. The address we wanted was one of the lower level apartments. We had renter's policies, but they didn't pay for squat, and nobody bothered to write them. Getting a renter to bump up to protect the meager possessions they could cram into 600 to 800 square feet was about as likely as pulling diamonds out of a north wind.

Flynn knocked on the door. To me, he said, "Pay attention, Rich. I'm going to show you the program."

The door opened. We were almost two hours late. The woman who answered was in a diamond-quilt, floral-pastel, flannel bath robe. She was maybe thirty-five, it was hard to tell with her short, dark hair in spiny curlers. She actually wore pink, fuzzy bunny slippers, and when she looked at Flynn, her face turned the same color as her bunnies.

She literally gasped.

She stammered.

He waited, smiling, staring at her eyes, right into her eyes.

Finally, hand clutching her chest, she asked, "Can I help you?"

Flynn reached for the handle of her screen door and pulled on it. He didn't take his eyes off hers.

The door was locked.

She moved her hand from her chest to the lock. It clicked, and Flynn opened the door.

Her mouth was still hanging open, and I'm guessing my eyes were pretty wide.

Flynn didn't go in. I expected him to, but he didn't. Instead, he said, "Ma'am, my associate and I owe you more than an apology. We are very sorry for being late for our appointment."

"Appointment?" she said.

"Yes, ma'am. We are from Three County Safety and Insurance, and we were supposed to be here two hours ago to help protect your home from a fire."

"A fire?"

"Yes, ma'am. I know we're late. May I come in and explain?"

She stepped back.

Flynn stepped into her home. I followed.

The fuzzy bunny lady seemed to come to her senses. She stepped out onto the stoop, looked around, then came back in and closed the door. "Can I have just a minute?" she asked.

"We'll, ma'am," he said. "We really can't stay. We just came by to apologize for missing our appointment."

I didn't know what he was doing, but he sure as hell was not on the program. He was supposed to be complimenting some object in her house at this point, striking up a little conversation, getting to know her income and job status.

"I'm sure you've been busy," she said. "I can change clothes and be out in just a second."

"No need, ma'am," he said.

"Please," she said, and she grinned a wall-to-wall and split the lips grin. "Call me Linda."

"Linda, would you call me Flynn?" He took her hand.

I thought she was going to faint.

He covered her hand with his other hand. "I'm so sorry about this. We've had—" He stopped.

She leaned toward him.

"—a little difficulty with someone at our office."

"Oh, I hope everyone is okay."

"Everyone is fine, Linda." He led her to her sofa and sat her down. He sat next to her.

"Rich," he said, still holding Linda's hand.

I was still at the door. My alarms were all going off. This was *sooo* not the program. The tiny apartment couldn't have been more than 400 square feet—smaller than it looked from the outside. It was full of books, mostly paperback: mysteries and romances and some thrillers. I recognized some of the big block lettered names on the covers. Hey, I've seen them in the grocery like everyone else.

"Huh?" I said.

"Would you fill out a," he paused and scanned the apartment. He seemed to fix those deep well eyes on something on her mantle.

I looked.

She looked.

"That's a beautiful photograph of you," he said.

I see the picture. Young woman in a blouse and business skirt. Long dark hair, a lot like my favorite phone girl, Caroline. Good figure. Not model material, but nice, like back in Iowa. The kind of girl that wouldn't touch me with a pole. Just like Caroline.

Linda put a hand over her pale-lipped mouth and giggled like a school girl. "That's my niece."

"Looks just like you," he said.

I thought he was nuts. I looked again. Damned if it didn't look just like Linda. Not the curlers and nightgown part, but the face—flat cheeks filling in under prominent cheek bones accenting almost Asian eyes. Mighty strange looking on the woman with curlers. Pretty as hell on the lady in the photo.

"Oh, thank you Flynn. My sister says she got my eyes."

Flynn looks at me. "A five-and-fifty, Rich."

"This place—"

He interrupts me. "Five-and-fifty, Rich. We don't have time. We have to get going."

I nodded and opened my case to pull out the papers. Just like playing darts, I know this is nuts, that I'm going to be in deep shit with Cooper, that if I don't get Flynn on the program or at least get him out of the apartment, I'm likely to start getting shit appointments from Caroline, and I can't afford that.

Still, I kneel down on the nasty carpet on the other side of her wrought iron and glass coffee table, and I start filling out the paper for five years of fifty-thousand dollar flood and fire coverage on her photos and paperbacks.

"Linda," he says.

I look up.

"Keep working, Rich." I go back to work.

"I can see that you value family and culture by that picture of your niece and the books that you read."

She's staring deep into his eyes. Her head is a little to one side, like a canary looking at a mirror in its cage.

"My associate is filling out an insurance policy so that if you ever have a fire, if a water main were ever to break nearby, if your toilets back up or if lightning were to strike this building and overload your television... Wham!" He says.

She jumped.

Hell, I jumped. He didn't really say it loud. He said it, well, *different*. I swear I checked the TV to see if it was okay. So did Linda.

"Well," he says, "then you'll be able to get back all your precious things."

He's nodding.

She's nodding.

I'm writing paper and nodding.

"My associate has a paper for you to sign, Linda."

I hand over the five-and-fifty.

She stops nodding.

He says, "Linda, I'm going to go ahead and have you sign this and write us a check for the amount written here. Now, normally, I'd sit here and share some valuable information with you about my company and fires and the value of your property, and most of all about how valuable you are to me and to your family."

She's nodding again.

"But my associate and I have had an–" Again, he stops. "I'm sorry we were late," he says. That voice of his is quiet. Linda's mouth is a little open. She blinks and licks her lower lip. "We have to be *somewhere* in a few minutes," Flynn says.

The way his voice lifted subtly when he said somewhere brought images of dying relatives to my mind. I thought poor Linda was going to start crying. I don't know what images were running through her head about our situation, but I know they were full of flames, blood, and ambulances.

"Is there anything I can do?" she asks.

His smile comes on, and she sits up straight in her flannel robe and fuzzy bunny slippers. "Linda, after my associate and I have been where we need to go, I'll come back and explain these things to you more completely."

The woman's face turned red and she looked to the floor and bit her lower lip.

"If you don't agree," he says, "that this is important and worth the check you're going to write now, I'll tear this paper up. Is that fair enough?"

"Thank you," she says, and she signs and writes a check for the whole policy instead of the first premium.

Fifteen minutes from knock to return to the Lincoln, and Flynn has his jacket hung on that hanger thing of his and hooked to the clothing hook in the back seat.

We're rolling along, and I'm pretty well screwed. How the hell do I explain that to Cooper? He'll gut us both.

"Want to play some golf?" Flynn says.

I look at him, thinking he's joking. Cooper is already pissed at us. We just violated a dozen rules. I'm on the hook for my job, and Caroline is gonna take one look at my day totals and start treating me like a two-day-old trout a dog left on her doorstep.

He's not joking. He's looking at a country club sign up ahead.

"You're kidding," I say. "Where? We don't have time."

"Right there," he says, and he turns the Lincoln into the country club's lane.

"We can't golf here. We're not members."

He's already pulling up to the locked gate and the little guard house. His window rolls down, and he leans out to chat with the guard. I can feel his voice rising and falling, but I can't make out the words.

I don't know why I didn't expect it, but the gate went up and we rolled right on in to the exclusive parking garage beneath the brick Colonial Hotel and club house for the Green Hills Estate Social Club.

A guy in a red vest took the Lincoln, and Flynn and I got out. He makes me take my denim jacket off, then he goes to the trunk and pulls out a red and tan leather bag full of clubs and a wheeled, folding caddy thing.

"Flynn?"

He looks at me. "You're a little pale, Rich."

"Flynn, we shouldn't be here."

"Relax, Rich. We'll play a round and leave."

Now, I'm a farm boy, mind you. I've never played golf, and I've sure as hell never been to a place like the G.H.E.S.C. Yeah, I was shaking.

"You told Linda we had to be someplace."

"If we weren't supposed to be here, we'd be someplace else," he said. Then, he pulled a pair of black and white golf shoes out of the trunk. "See if these fit."

They did, and he led me to the pro shop to rent some clubs.

Clubs, balls, and cart were provided gratis for Flynn by the flustered woman at the counter; I was on my way out the door when he put a hand on my shoulder.

"We're going in there," he said. "I think we need another player."

I'm nervous enough about playing a game that is supposed to take a lifetime to master; I didn't like the idea of another person watching me—especially a person that might, just maybe, figure out that Flynn and me weren't members and were using "borrowed" stuff.

He smiled. He winked. We went into the bar.

Women stared.

Men stared, then most of them looked away, embarrassed for staring at a man.

Flynn looked around the 19th hole. There was a brass rail and cherry-wood bar against the far wall so all the patrons at their linen-covered tables could look out and watch the putting green and first tee through a window that spread across the whole hundred feet of the side wall.

The bar was the brightest bar I'd ever been in. It had custom, tight-plush carpet with a gold-diamond parquet pattern, each diamond surrounding a three-pointed crown, and each crown had a ruby in the center point.

It was not long after one p.m., and the place smelled like broiled steak and cigars.

Flynn headed for the end of the bar nearest the window. There was a guy there, kinda oldish—thin, weathered, gray-haired man in a polo shirt, gray double-knit slacks, and white golf shoes.

"Mind?" Flynn says.

The guy turns. He's got a fat cigar going hot. His bushy white eyebrows jump up, then come back down. Thunderclouds start to grow behind gray eyes that I can just tell have seen a thousand guys like me die at the end of a pen.

"You look like a man that knows this course," Flynn says. "My friend and I are looking for another player to show us around. Can we sit down?"

That does it. The thunderclouds dissipate. The guy takes out his cigar and knocks the cherry off it into an ashtray. He nods to a red leather barstool next to him, then he reaches over the bar and pulls a silver tube up from a shelf. He slips his cigar into that tube and replaces it behind the bar.

Bad enough the guy reeks of "I eat fucking salesmen," he's also clearly a part of the program at the G.H.E.S.C.

"I know the course," the guy says.

"First hole looks like a pretty tight dog-leg," Flynn says. "Set up on the left of the tee and hit a high slice, say 150 yards to make the trees and hit the lie on the other side?"

"I've seen it done that way," the guy says. "Names Anderson. Gill, to you."

They shake. Gill hails the bartender, who calls him Mr. Anderson and says nothing about money or checks. Drinks arrive, and I can see there are other people waiting for service. I keep my mouth shut.

"How do you play it, Gill?"

"I cheat," he says. "I designed this course. There's a low drive right through the trees. If you've got the control and the balls for it, you can make the green in one."

Flynn laughs.

People are staring at us.

Two drinks and half an hour later, I'm standing on the tee with Gill and Flynn. Didn't matter that there were no tee times available for a week. Didn't matter that we weren't members. Flynn told Gill that. Didn't matter that we hadn't paid for my equipment, Flynn told him that too. In fact, the more Flynn told him, the more Gill thought Flynn was a hell of a guy, and if I was with Flynn, well by God have another drink.

So, Gill sets his ball on a tee, and sure as shit he drives it right through the woods and makes the green.

Flynn shakes his head and smiles. He says, "I'm not even going to give that a shot, Gill." So, Flynn puts his ball down, steps up, and says, "What's the bet, Gill?"

"Hundred dollars a hole?"

Flynn nods and swings.

The ball knew where it was going. Up and off the tee, rising and sliding toward the tree line on the right, and I swear it was gonna hit the trees, and it pulled up and rolled over in a hook across the tops of the trees and kept turning and I figure we lost that one and then it goes down, I figure right in the forest, but Gill says, "Flynn, that was the finest tee shot I've ever seen on this hole. It's a pleasure." And they both look at me.

My ball does not know where it's going. That, or it was born with gopher blood in it. I look up from my swing, and Gill is happily chatting with Flynn, and Flynn is listening and returning in kind, and they are both walking along toward my ball a few yards away.

Eight strokes and two balls later, we get to the green. Flynn is upslope twenty feet from the pin—that's what they call that flag they stick in the hole. Gill is down slope about twice as far. Flynn and Gill are both in, in one putt. They're real happy.

I'm in after five putts and a long gimme, which is what they call pity in golf.

Behind us, people are piling up for the reserved tee times they paid for.

Turns out, nobody plays thru on Gill.

Turns out, nobody wants to once they talk to Flynn.

Turns out, we end up with a gallery, and they even clap for me when I get an extra yard or two off the tee.

Gill, the G.H.E.S.C course designer, millionaire engineering company owner, world traveler, and general all-around-good-guy gives Flynn his private cell number and asks him if he has time to go to Scotland next month.

I get a cigar, a new pair of golf shoes, and a set of clubs. Flynn and me head out. In the car, I'm silent all the way back to Linda's house.

The Linda that meets us at the door is not the same Linda. She's got on a black silk dress, a strand of pearls, and black patent heels. Those slightly Asian eyes are made up to seem bigger, darker. Her curlers are now sable curls, and she has cleavage that makes me stare. The mousy hause-frau is suddenly a fucking babe.

At the door, she looks Flynn over head to toe. There is no doubt in my mind what she's looking for or at. She says, "I've been thinking about what you said about my things and my family. I don't trust the owner of this building, Flynn. The wiring, you know."

Flynn steps into her house, and she closes the door in my face.

I wait in the car.

Twenty minutes later, Flynn comes back with another 100k in policy upgrade and a personal check for five hundred bucks for taking a look at her wiring.

You know what I'm thinking at this point? I'm thinking, Jesus H. Chrysler on a half shell, what do I tell Cooper? Then I'm thinking, how does he do this stuff?

"That," Flynn says, "is *the program*."

"It wasn't Cooper's program."

"Cooper's program isn't Cooper's program."

"Huh?"

"Somebody made up Cooper's program, right?"

"I suppose somebody did, but then—"

"No buts about it. Cooper got his program from somebody else. My program is faster, easier, and leaves the client happier and me, and you, and Cooper richer. He got his paper. Linda got to feel pretty and safe. Gill got to show off his course and win a hell of a round of golf. You got a cigar, a new pair of shoes, and a lesson in life."

"But the program."

"Life is the program, Rich. Nobody can get off it. Not me. Not you. Not Cooper, Gill, or Linda. Nobody."

The rest of the ride to the office was silent except for Flynn's quiet humming.

When I handed Cooper the new paper, his smile was almost as excited as Linda's had been when she found Flynn at the door the second time. After a few minutes of flipping pages to make sure all the t's were crossed, he pinned me to my chair with a squint and grimace. "The program? Did he leave the program?"

I thought about the day for a couple seconds, then, in all honesty, I said, "No."

~ ~ ~

Caroline was in her cube behind the dispatch window. I leaned against the writing counter outside the window and looked down on the top of her head. She had her headset on, and she was talking to potential clients. Her desk lamp put a shine on her long, dark hair, and I swear if the window hadn't been in the way, I would have reached over and stroked her head just to feel the softness beneath those highlights.

After a few moments, she looked up. Her face lit up, then she hardened it. I was glad for the slip, but I played like I didn't see it.

"Got anything good for me this evening?" I said.

She punched the hang-up button on her phone. "Is that a joke?" she asked. She ripped an appointment sheet off her pad and slid it under the gap of the window.

I picked it up, then I glanced at the city map on the wall. "Good neighborhood," I said. "Close in. I'll be done by nine."

She tilted her head and flipped her hair over her shoulder to clear her mouthpiece. Her eyes smiled, but her mouth said, "So what?"

"So, maybe you'll let me buy you dinner?"

"I eat at seven."

"Just a drink, then."

"You didn't turn in any new paper today, Rich," she said.

"I was out with Flynn. Cooper sent me."

"You're on commission only, right?"

"Yeah."

"You should have said no."

"To Cooper? I don't think so."

"Write the paper tonight," she said. She dialed her next number. "We'll talk tomorrow." She started talking to someone on the phone.

I walked away wondering if I might get more time with her if I put my number on her list.

In the coffee room, Flynn was reading a magazine, some men's fashion thing. Fat Bob Barry was tossing darts. He wanted to beat me so bad, beat me at anything and everything. That guy just wanted my ass for no reason except spite and rocks to piss on.

"She shot you down?" Flynn said.

"Need a dick if you want that bitch," Bob said. He snorted once then tossed one of the best darts in the can and hit the wall.

I shot Flynn a look that was supposed to say, "Fuck you. Leave me alone." Apparently, that's not what he heard.

He got up and went to his jacket.

I'd had enough experience with him at that point that I knew if he picked up that jacket and slipped it on, we were going to do something I'd never done before. I didn't even ask. I just followed him to the Lincoln.

We ended up in Boise at Chesterman's Suits and Tuxedos. I had never been in an honest-to-God men's clothing store. I was strictly rack rank-and-file. In fact, at that point, I hadn't even considered that I might be able to buy a suit from Chesterman's. I suppose I could have. I just hadn't ever considered it.

Flynn opens the shop door for me. The place smelled like a dry cleaner's, except it wasn't hot and damp, and the old man that trotted up was wearing a thousand-dollar suit that looked like it had been sewn right onto him. He had one of those yellow tapes around his neck, and he had a clipboard on a strap slung over his shoulder. The grin that split his face made his half-glasses ride up his nose so he practically had to bow to look over the top of them.

"Mr. Flynn, we're so glad to see you." He says. "Welcome back, Mr. Flynn. What can we do for you?"

"Andrew," Flynn says.

"Thomas," the man corrects.

Flynn takes his hand just like he took the house frau's. "I'm so sorry, Thomas," he says. "You took such good care of me when I was here. I was thinking about my friend here."

"Never mind, Mr. Flynn. You're a busy man. I'm sure you don't remember everyone you meet. My brother was here when you were here. His name is Allan. You were probably thinking of him."

"I want you to meet someone, Thomas," Flynn says. He puts a hand on Thomas' shoulder and one on mine. I swear, I could feel the other man right through Flynn's hand. For just a second, I thought I could taste bacon and cream cheese mixed with coffee. For a second, I thought I felt a sadness for a girl named Jenny who ran away from home.

Then Flynn stepped back, and the feeling was gone.

Thomas grinned at me. He looked over those glasses, shook my hand, and unslung his tape. "A friend of Mr. Flynn is always welcome in my store," he says.

"I'm glad to meet you, Mr...."

"Mr. Chesterton. Please call me Thomas."

I stared. I nodded.

"You have a love," Thomas says. "She doesn't see you."

I looked at Flynn. He smiled and winked. God, I learned to get the heebee jeebies when he winked. Then he goes over to a chair against the wall between two racks of suit coats. He takes off his jacket, hangs it on his little hanger on the rack, and settles into the chair to watch.

Thomas walks around me. When he's back out in front of me, he nods. "I see the problem."

Flynn smiles and nods sagely.

"Problem?" I ask. I mean, okay, I was a rack man, and I have to admit all those expensive clothes made me nervous as hell, but that damn denim suit cost me almost two hundred bucks. Hell, I paid forty extra for the boots at PayLess.

"You have the build for a split tail. Good shoulders," Thomas says. He goes behind me and measures my shoulders. "Very good shoulders," he says. "We can make her look at those."

"Problem?" I ask again.

"Rich," Flynn says, "She shot you down. You want to change that? Let Thomas do his magic. He's a good friend of mine, and he knows his clothes."

Thomas actually turned to Flynn and took a bow.

The front door opened. The service bell rang. Thomas' half glasses dropped and his grin disappeared. He practically ran to the front door. "No. No. No," he says to the man half-way into the shop. "Not now. We're closed."

The man tried to push further in. "Hours say–"

"Closed!" Thomas says. He pushed the man back. "Special order. Can't help you." He got the door closed, threw the deadbolt, and flipped over the orange plastic Closed/Open sign.

When he came back, he was smiling again.

Two hours later, I have to admit I did not look like the man that walked in. My suit was brown to set off my hair and eyes. The vest was silk with dark maroon and charcoal paisley patterns in it. "It'll draw her eye across your chest and down to the trouser line," Thomas said. I had on a shirt that felt like money in fabric. When I looked into the triptych mirror, I could actually see my reflection reflected in the shine of my pointy-toed shoes. Thomas told me who made the shoes. It seemed to be important to him, and Flynn nodded in honor when Thomas said the name. I figured those shoes were going to run more than forty bucks.

"I can't afford this, Thomas." I must have said that twenty times while Thomas was trying colors, sizes, cuts. I said it again when he started doing the alterations right there while we watched. Every time, he looked at Flynn and they smiled at each other.

Flynn was putting on his jacket, and I knew I was in way over my head. Dressed, buffed, and handed one of those little hangers Flynn had, I had to face up to the fact that I had to pay for this suit.

"Thomas, what do I owe you for this?"

He strung his tape over his neck again. He lifted his clipboard and peered through his glasses. Finally, he looks up at me. That damn Flynn-induced smile started spreading across his face. When his glasses were way up and he was looking over their tops, he said, "Rich, I can tell you that you simply can't afford these clothes."

"What?"

"I'm going to make you the same deal I make Mr. Flynn."

"How much is it?"

"I'll give you a few of my cards, and if someone asks you about this suit, you give them one of my cards."

"But—"

Flynn stepped up and took Thomas's cards. "Thomas, you are an amazing man. I'll make sure he does it."

There was hand shaking and nodding and smiling all around, and I kept stealing a look at myself in the mirror. I actually looked like one of the men in the magazines back at the office.

"Rich." Flynn was already at the door. "You can admire Thomas's work at the office. We have appointments to run."

I managed one last thank you for Thomas, then I headed after Flynn.

~ ~ ~

"You go in and get the appointments," Flynn said. "I'll stay in the car."

I got out and opened the rear and pulled my jacket off the hanger Flynn had made me use. "Never sit down while wearing your jacket," he said. "Never."

Walking through the narrow halls of the office, I tried to feel all at home and comfortable like I usually did. The office was the same—false walls and dim, narrow corridors. It smelled like Cooper's cigars and Chloe's lilac perfume. I could hear the darts hitting the board in the coffee room. The low murmur of the phone girls in their little semi-sound-proof booths was exactly the same as always.

Still, I felt different. I felt taller. I felt like I was wearing Superman's cape or something.

I rounded the corner to the sales area and I walked up to Caroline's dispatch window.

She looked up before I spoke. I swear, I saw her eyes get wide then get darker and sort of spark. Her cheeks flushed, and she smiled. She smoothed her crew sweater, stood up, and leaned forward toward the window. "Can I help you, Sir?" she asked.

"I need an appointment, Caroline."

I wouldn't say her jaw dropped so much as her whole face went sort of limp like she'd lost control of all the muscles at once.

"Rich?"

I smiled. "That is a very nice sweater," I said.

"Rich?"

"I have the one you gave me, but I need one for Flynn."

She blinked. She adjusted her headset and fell back into her seat. "Yeah," she said. "Sure. Here you go." She handed me two appointment sheets.

I raised an eyebrow.

She said, "Give me that other one. It's no good. I'll give it to Bob."

Surprised, I returned the sheet she'd given me earlier. Then, I checked the addresses against the map on the wall. "The Heights?"

"I made those myself," she said. "Pre-qualified and big houses. One has a guest house. My notes are on the back."

I turned over one of the sheets. In her fluid hand there was a list of personal interests, kids, cats, dogs, and hobbies.

"Thanks, Caroline," I said, and I started to turn.

"Rich," she said.

"Yeah?"

"You look—" She swallowed, and I watched her sweater rise and fall once. "You look really good," she said, and I liked the way she had trouble saying it.

In the car, Flynn asked me how it went. I smiled and handed him the appointment sheets. He looked at the addresses and nodded. "Double team both appointments?" he asked.

"On the program?"

"Always."

"Absolutely."

~ ~ ~

At the breakfast meeting at the I-Hop on the first of May, Cooper decided we—meaning everybody in sales—weren't producing enough. Flynn's closing ratio was 1:1. He never missed. He also hardly ever worked. So, in Cooper's opinion, he was the worst of us all. Flynn didn't seem to be concerned by that.

Fat Bob was up and ranting about how he was going to kick my ass this month. Caroline was down the table a ways, sitting with Chloe and Francis, the women who ran the phone mill. Chloe, with her mascara crayon eyes and smooth helmet of nape cut blond hair, stared openly at me. Caroline checked me out now and again. This was new to me, and it pretty well kept me distracted from Bob and Cooper.

Francis seemed to be distracted by her own thoughts. Flynn sat beside her. She wasn't staring at him, but I could tell she wasn't seeing anything else in the room either.

"…from every one of you," Cooper said.

"Right now?" Vernon Wright asked. He was one of the new guys from the last batch of trainees, an auto body man by training, trying his hand in sales, hoping he didn't have to buff and putty again.

"Right now," Cooper said. "Francis, write this down."

Francis didn't move. She just stared at the wall.

Flynn put a hand on her arm. She squeaked and jumped. I thought she was going to hit the ceiling.

She looked at Flynn and whispered something.

He pointed at Cooper.

She looked to Cooper. "Boss?"

"Pay attention, Francis. We need totals this month. I want you to write down the sales goals for each man."

She nodded and pulled a notebook and pen from under the table.

"Gross insured totals for the month," Copper says. "Rich."

I nodded.

"You're the man to beat; you go first."

Last month, I'd hit ten mil. I knew this game. It was called, paint a pretty picture for the boss. I added two hundred k, figuring that would appease him. "Ten mil; two hundred."

"Got that Francis?"

"Yes."

"Okay. Rich, I'm going to separate you and Flynn this month. I want you both turning in higher totals. Flynn, what's your number?"

"Ten," Flynn said.

"Match Rich, or you're fired," Cooper said.

Flynn smiled and nodded, but I thought I saw something new in those deep-mist eyes, maybe a hint of a thundercloud. It sent a primal chill up my spine. For a second, I thought Flynn was going to get up and leave.

"You didn't make enough off my work last month, Cooper?" Flynn asked.

That room went dead, like the air was just sucked out of it, like we were suddenly in space or under water.

"You aren't living up to your potential." Cooper's face was red. He waved a gold-ringed finger at Flynn. "You're skimming the cream appointments. You should be turning in fifty a month."

"Did you make money or lose money on my work last month?"

"Part of my job," Cooper said to the whole group, "Is to help my salesmen reach their potential and fulfill their dreams. *My* dream is to be free from worrying about helping you men. Vernon's dream," he pointed at the chrome-and-putty man, "is a home on the Snake River. To get what I want, I help him get what he wants. Sometimes, that means I have to push." He pointed at Flynn. "When a good man gets lazy, I push. I'm putting you on notice, Flynn. Light a fire under that ass of yours, or walk away."

Now I could see the storm clouds. I could feel the electricity moving from Flynn out through the table and into every person in the room. I looked down at my trousers, and I swear the tiny threads were standing on end.

Very quietly, but in a voice everyone in the room heard, Flynn said, "I'll make sure you get what you want, Cooper."

I didn't like the sound of it. Not at all.

Around the table Cooper went. Some of the guys were all fired up, and they bit off big numbers that had nothing to do with their past performance. They'd strut for a day or two, then they'd start looking desperate.

The desperation came from everybody at the table hearing Cooper's threat. If he would fire Flynn, what would he do to them for missing their numbers?

Finally, only Fat Bob was left, and he was looking pretty smug.

"Bob?" Cooper asked.

"I'm tired of seeing Rich's name in the top slot of the board." He looked right at me when he said it. His thin lips were stretched out enough that his pudgy cheeks had double wrinkles down them. "I'm going to hit fifty-five this month."

Now, I didn't like Bob much, and nobody thought he could do fifty-five mil. Still, he was looking pretty clear in the eye and way too confident in his number. Something was up. I decided right there that I wasn't going to play the game if the rules weren't the same for him as for me, and since I didn't know the rules, I'd just do what I'd been doing.

The meeting broke, and I was headed for Flynn when Caroline came up to me. She said, "Don't let that asshole beat you, Rich."

"They're up to some scheme," I said.

"I heard them. They're going to set Bob up with an office in Oregon; but to do it, he has to have the numbers to justify it."

"If he takes an office, he'll be gone, right?"

"If you take an office, we'll be gone," she said.

I'm pretty sure I lost control of all the muscles in my face. While I was recovering, she took my hand and pressed appointment papers into it. "I made them," she said. "When you've finished with them, come and tell me."

"Caroline."

"You're welcome," she said.

"What about Flynn?"

"Francis is taking care of him."

I left the I-Hop, but I didn't head to the office. I headed for the Lincoln.

~ ~ ~

Flynn hung his jacket over the Lincoln's back seat, and we took off. He had a handful of appointments, and he had that storm about to break look in his eyes.

"They're gunning for us," I said.

"Cooper and Bob," Flynn said, "don't know how to enjoy a good thing."

"What can we do?"

"Believe what he says and give him exactly what he wants," Flynn says.

He pulled the Lincoln into a Mercedes car lot.

"Flynn, we have to get to work. You need to hit today if we're gonna–"

"How long have you known me, Rich?"

"A couple months."

"We've spent a lot of time together."

"Yeah."

"I'm going to tell you something because I think you have what it takes to make it work in this life."

"Don't get high and—"

"Rich, there's all kinds of magic in the world."

I stared into his bottomless eyes. He'd said that before. In the coffee room. "Some kinds of magic come from rituals," he had said, then he tossed that crooked dart straight into the bull.

He popped open the door of the Lincoln, but he didn't get out. "The truth is the most powerful lie there is. Before you met me, you thought you were a liar taking people's money. Have you ever seen me lie to anyone?"

I thought for a minute. I couldn't remember having ever seen him lie. Then it came to me. "You said you'd show me a trick if I hit all the darts inside the doubles ring."

"I showed you *the program*. With Linda. With Gill."

"Everybody lies," I said.

"No. Everybody doesn't. Think about it. And while you're thinking about it, take a look at the appointments you have."

It didn't make sense. The appointments seemed safer than the words he'd spoken. I pulled them out of my vest pocket and looked at them. "Vermeer Valley Estates?"

"Uh huh."

"These aren't good appointments. These are multi-million dollar houses."

"You mean they aren't easy appointments."

"It'll take a hell of trick to get me in there."

"Some magic comes from doing the right thing in the moment."

"Flynn, we're screwed. How the hell am I gonna—"

"To start with, you show up looking like you belong there. Then, you make damn sure you feel like you belong there. If you can feel it, they will too. After that, you do what you always do. You tell them the truth."

Ten minutes later, I was test driving a cherry red Mercedes Convertible for a week. The Lincoln was in the body shop getting a free ding and dent face lift, and Flynn was behind the wheel of the lot owner's Shelby Cobra—and not one of those cheap Ford Mustang knockoff things—it was a real, honest to God 250 mile-an-hour Shelby Cobalt blue and white racing stripe son-of-a-bitch muscle car.

I didn't really get it at the time. Flynn told me he needed my help. Needed big totals. He told me I had it in me if I had the balls for it. "Everybody has their own truth," he says. "Look 'em right in the eye. Put love in your head and heart. Believe they are your lover, your mother, your father, your siblings, your best friend. Believe they are more important to you than anyone else ever. They'll know. Give them that. Hear what they want, feel what they love. Give them their truth in your words. Tell them the truth. I'm about to give Cooper and Bob their truth. I just gave you yours. Now you have to live it."

The Benz was nice. When I got to the gates guarding the Estates from people like me, I pulled right up to them. The guard came out and smiled. He liked the car.

Okay, I thought, this is just like the Country Club.

I looked at the guard station, and on the stool inside, I saw a book.

I got on the program. *My lover, my brother, my friend…*

Before he could start up his guard script with "Can I help you," I said, "Lots of time to read sitting in there alone, I bet."

He glanced over his shoulder quick. He probably wasn't supposed to be reading on the job.

"I'd be reading too, if I was sitting out here," I added.

He smiled and came up to the side of the car.

"You likely get time to think more than most folks," I said. Seemed like a man that reads books in a box the size of a phone booth might spend a lot of time in his own head. "I'd guess you watch a lot of different folks coming and going."

He was a guy about my age, then. Maybe twenty-five. When he got up to the side of the car, he stopped, careful not to touch it. Training, I guessed.

"Yeah," he said, "I see a lot of folks. Haven't seen you before."

I opened the car door. He stepped back. I got out. In my head, I had two thoughts going. First, *I love this guy that reads and watches people come and go. What a cool job*; second, *What the hell am I thinking trying to get into the Estates?*

"Rich," I said. "Haven't see you before." I caught the beginning of his squint, and I added, "Course, I've never been here during the day."

He relaxed.

"I'm up here to visit with Lenny Farr."

"Lenny went out this morning."

"Rachel too?"

"Nah. She's still in the house."

"Too bad I missed him," I said. "Well, I guess I have some time to kill. What are you reading?"

We walked over to the booth, and he showed me his book. Part of me expected some sleazy, soldier of fortune thing. No. Not my new buddy. He was a self-help man. *Make it Yours*, was his book.

I had seen that one in Cooper's office, so I figured the author was a high-energy guru. "Setting your goals and making them real?" I asked.

My guard straightened up.

It meant something. Flynn's eyes, those eyes that sucked every detail out of life, flashed through my head.

It came to me. My guard was ready to recite. "Go ahead," I said. "Lay it out."

And he did, too. That man had a list of wants. And at the end of it, he looked me in the eye and said, "and I want to drive a Mercedes like that."

"I'm sure you will," I said. "If I can drive one, so can you."

He beamed.

"What's your name?" I asked.

"Ronny." He touched his guard cap when he said it.

"Ronny, I better get on up and check in with Rachel," I said.

He nodded and hit the gate button. The gate lifted, and I headed for my car.

"Nice suit, Rich," he said. "You have a good afternoon."

I waved back. "I will, Ronny. You, too."

I drove on into the Estates.

~ ~ ~

I pulled up on the wrap-around drive in front of a Tudor mansion that looked like it would need twenty folks just to trim the hedges. My heart was pumping hard. Part of me was pretty sure I'd be in jail before the end of the day. Another part of me couldn't shake the look in Flynn's eyes when he said we were going to give Cooper what he wanted.

Between Flynn's look and Caroline's hand pressing the appointments into mine, I was in for the run.

I knocked. I was ready. My brain was running a solid loop: *Tell their truth. Tell their truth. See their world and give them their truth.*

Rachel herself opened one of the double doors.

I thought I was ready. She was maybe thirty, and the top of her head came up to my nose. I swear, I could smell the things she wanted on the wood oil and window cleaner air that wafted over her on the way out of the house.

My first thought was how nice it would be to tuck her soft, blond curls under my chin and just sit and listen to her breathe.

She and I just sort of looked at each other for what seemed like an hour before I noticed the rest of her. Somewhere on the grounds, there was a swimming pool. I smelled it on her skin. She used it a lot. Clear skin and broad shoulders in a blue cotton tank top showed off a pair that must have been models for mannequins at Victoria's Secret. She was barefoot and wore black silk Kung Fu pants with an ornate red dragon embroidered on her right hip.

"I'm Rich," I finally said. "You must be Rachel." I put out my hand and took hers exactly the way I'd seen Flynn do it. "Caroline sent me up to visit, but she didn't tell me how beautiful this home was."

Rachel smiled. "Caroline," she said. Her eyes shifted from me to my car and back.

"Fire," I said. "You wanted to ask about fires."

"Oh, Caroline. Yes. Rich."

I stepped up to the threshold still holding her hand. "Caroline said you were up here alone a lot."

Her hand tensed.

"That you wanted to feel safer—to protect some of the things you value."

Her hand softened and warmed.

Flynn's eyes. Flynn's hand on my shoulder. Flynn shaking hands with Gill.

"Rachel," I said, "I have some time before my next appointment. If you have some coffee, I can sit and chat a while."

Her eyes brightened. I released her hand and walked into her home.

Rachel was alone a lot. She just wanted to talk. I gave her my undivided attention for two hours. We never talked about fire, about insurance, about anything. We walked the grounds. Mostly, we talked about the plants. Some, we talked about her mother in Michigan and how they didn't get along. For a while, we talked about Lenny, but it killed me to see her eyes get so sad, so I steered us back to the plants.

At the door, I took her hand again and pulled her into the long, warm hug of a good friend. Her curls were as soft as I'd imagined. Her breath was smooth and warm. She held me tight for a minute, and when we separated, she was crying.

"I'm sorry, Rich," she said. "I never let you tell me about the fire stuff."

"Rachel, you didn't ask me up here to buy fire insurance," I said, and it was true.

"Will you show it to me anyway?"

"Are you sure?"

She nodded. I went to the car and got my case.

After we signed the papers and she gave me the checks, she gave me the names of a couple women from her book group. With those, and the other appointment Caroline had given me, I had the best day I'd ever had. Hell, it was the best day I'd ever heard of.

On the way out, I stopped at the guard station and gave Ronny one of Thomas Chesterman's cards. "You go see him. Tell him I sent you. He'll put you in a suit like mine." I shook Ronny's hand. He waved me on. "Thanks, Mr. Rich!" he called.

~ ~ ~

I didn't see Flynn until the next day. He pulled up in the lot the same time I did, and those storm clouds were still boiling behind his eyes. He nodded my way, and we went into the building together.

Caroline was waiting at the door.

Flynn put a hand on my shoulder, winked, and said, "I'll see you at the meeting in ten."

Caroline had on a sun dress, cotton and sheer, and fluted from the hips to mid-thigh. The low neck line framed a delicate gold chain and golden cross that pointed downward.

She grabbed my arm and pulled me into her dispatch cube.

God, I can't say how many times I'd wanted to go into that little booth. It smelled like talcum powder after a hot shower. Her hair was loose and pulled back, and her widow's peak seemed to press downward on her forehead, making worry wrinkles.

"Caroline, what's wrong?"

"They set you up," she said.

"Set me up?"

"You and Flynn. I saw the books. You sell too much, and they know *he* can."

"Nobody sells too much, Caroline."

"They can train five men a week. Those five men will turn in three contracts in the first week. New men make the lowest possible percentage. Of the new group, Cooper loses three or four low producers over the next five weeks. Over a year, they make more money by training new men and fielding them."

"Totals will be lower."

"Profit goes up."

"Okay, if they set us up, how?"

"The appointments I gave you."

"They were up in the Estates."

She looked away from me like she was ashamed. "It's a gated community."

"Yeah," I said. "I was there."

"I'm sorry, Rich. We didn't know. We never call into gated communities. You can't get past the guards even if someone sets an appointment. Neighborhood covenants."

I thought she was going to start crying.

"Rich!" It was Cooper's bull voice.

I kissed Caroline on the cheek. It warmed me to see her turn red.

"Rich!"

She said, "I'm sorry."

"It's going to be fine." I squeezed her hand and headed for the meeting I suspected was supposed to be the first of several nails in my coffin.

~ ~ ~

Flynn. Damn, he was a piece of work. He had seen Cooper and Fat Bob coming.

The meeting room was full. Every man Cooper had, including five men I'd never seen before, were there all sitting in nice neat rows—all in bad suits and scared in the eyes.

Flynn's jacket hung on the back of the door. He stood against the wall to the right of the door.

All eyes were on me.

"Thank you for gracing us with your presence, Rich." Cooper was at the whiteboard in front. He was nervous. The stains under his arms showed it. Bob was front-and-center and practically shaking with anticipation.

I nodded to Cooper. Then, I pulled the hanger out of my pocket, unfolded it, slipped off my jacket, and hung it on the back of the door with Flynn's.

Cooper glared at me.

I stood next to Flynn.

The meeting unfolded like most second day of the month meetings. Jennings, a steady man, turned in a 2k contract. Wills and Tellen turned up nothing. Vallenrow had hit for a rental for 400. It was all good for the second of the month.

The new guys were showing some excitement. They were counting their low percentage commissions, and they were pretty sure they were going to do better than *those other guys*. I could see Cooper had been blowing wind up their shorts.

Finally, Cooper flourished his blue marker. "Before we hear from our superstar performers in the back of the room," he said. "I want to introduce our new sales manager."

Caroline slipped in quietly and stood beside me. She hooked a hand in mine. I wanted to jump up and down. She thought I was a doomed man, and she still took my hand.

I kept it to myself.

"Bob," Cooper said, "Would you come up and say a few words?"

Bob couldn't say only a few words even if the words were "help me" and more than that would kill him. He ran on for ten full minutes about his favorite book, *Run Until You Get There*, and how important it was for him to give back to the new guys and help them run like him.

I glanced at Flynn. The storm was brewing. Oh yeah.

Cooper cut in gain. "Okay, Bob, now I want to post your totals to show the new men why you're their sales manager."

Cooper went to the board. The grid for the month had a row for each man, and Bob was on the top row. I'd been on the top row two days ago.

Slowly, Cooper wrote in Fat Bob's totals. Bob had pulled 10k on the first day of May.

The new guys gasped. Some of the old guys gasped. Caroline squeezed my hand. "I'm sorry," she whispered.

"Okay, then," Cooper said. Rich, would you put up your totals, please?

I let go of Caroline, picked up my jacket, slipped it on, smoothed it out, and folded my hanger. I savored every second of Cooper's gloat and anger at my bandstanding.

At the front of the room, I took the pen. Then, I turned to the room. "Yesterday morning, we set our monthly goals," I said. "I want to thank Mr. Cooper for working me, for building me up, for supporting me so that I would set my goals higher and higher every month." I paused to take in Bob and Cooper and their puzzled expressions. "I've tried hard to live up to Mr. Cooper's expectations. He's taught me a lot about trust."

Bob smiled. Cooper frowned hard, pretending to be gracious.

"I want to apologize to Mr. Cooper publicly," I said.

He walked up behind me and put a hand on my shoulder.

"It's okay, Rich. You can't hit the—"

"I set my numbers too low, and I know he had hoped for more from me."

He stepped back, and I put up the totals for the six women from the Vermeer Valley Estates Book Club.

The new men were up and screaming. They saw new houses, boats, cars, and trips the hell out of Idaho. The old hands were quiet. They saw Cooper and Bob and me and knew someone's days were numbered. If they could have, they would have snuck out to weather the storm.

I saw Flynn putting on his jacket.

He had never moved so slowly, so deliberately before. I saw a storm that promised to be wonderful.

"I want to see the paper," Bob demanded. "Nobody can sell six, million-dollar policies in one day. It takes fucking weeks to develop just one."

"I'd like to see the paper too, Rich," Cooper said. "Not that I don't trust you, but that's a pretty big number to not get into bookkeeping right away."

I pulled the paper out of my jacket and handed it over.

Cooper flipped through each policy.

When he looked up, I knew Bob was about to lose his job.

When Flynn stepped up on the stage, I wasn't sure what else was going to happen, but I was starting to get excited about it.

"Mr. Cooper," Flynn said. "I'd like to add my totals, if that's all right."

Cooper was about a beat short of dying of joy, and he grinned at Flynn. That grin said, "You taught him how to do this. I know you did. I'm grateful. Don't you think I'm not grateful, you egocentric fop."

Flynn pulled one policy from his jacket. The signature line flashed by, and I caught the name Gill before the papers were in Cooper's hands.

Flynn took the whiteboard pen and wrote seventy-five million up on the board.

Cooper sat down in a chair in the front row and held his bald head in his hands.

The room was emptied of air again. I thought I smelled ozone.

"Mr. Cooper." Flynn's voice was soft, but it filled the room with the roll and rumble of summer thunder, the kind of thunder you hear when storms come over the mountains, when torrents pour down and wash away all the smog grime and desert dust from the streets, the kind of storm that leaves everything smelling new and clean. "I'd like you to meet someone, Mr. Cooper."

Gill Anderson, gray double-knits, and polo shirt, walked in. He'd traded his golf shoes for deck shoes that looked all wrong. In fact, without his golf shoes, he kinda walked like a sailor fresh on land. But he was still a bull's bull, and Bob got the hell out of his way.

Behind Gill, a man in a jet black suit followed along. The man was thin, his face leathery from sun and wind. If not for the suit, I would have figured him for a ranch hand or a rail handler in a steel mill.

"Mr. Cooper?" Gill asked.

Cooper looked up.

"I'm Gill Anderson. As of midnight last night, I own your parent corporation. As of ten a.m. this morning, you own your car, and I think I have the note on that too."

Cooper's elation drained from his face along with his blood. The paper Flynn had written fell to the ground.

"Bullshit," he managed.

I think I could hear Caroline's heartbeat from the back of the room.

The rail stepped forward and opened his briefcase.

Flynn took my arm and pulled me away.

"...free of all rights and responsibilities related to, pertaining to, and resulting from your position..." The rail was reading legalese to Cooper.

Bob had disappeared.

Alone in the hallway, Flynn winked at me.

"You screwed them good, Flynn." I said.

"We gave Cooper exactly what he said he wanted—high totals and freedom."

It was true. I nodded. Then, I asked, "What's *your* truth, Flynn?"

"I'm a professional liar," he said. "Do you have change for a twenty?"

I nodded.

"Give it to me, will you?"

I did.

Caroline came up beside me and put her arm around my waist. I pulled her in close, savoring the warmth of her and knowing full well I'd just lost twenty bucks.

Flynn smiled, winked, and walked away.

Hopes of a Green Hero

Dieter froze at the cabin door, his knuckles turning white on the cedar latch. The kerosene lantern in Dieter's other hand swung forward then back, clinking softly. Instinctual certainty told him his grandfather lurked behind him in a shadowy corner.

"One." Granpa Franz's sanding block voice scraped at Dieter's spine. "Just one day in Oregon." The short hairs on Dieter's neck stood to attention. "Now, you figure you can poach alone?"

Dieter sucked in a reeking breath of stale old man and illegal wood smoke. Hand still on the latch, she spoke to the door. "One day watching your pathetic scrounging is enough. You can't teach me anything."

"Poaching ain't easy on a veteran's reservation."

Dieter turned and peered into the shadows untouched by the dim kerosene lantern. The hiss of labored breathing and the dry creak of grandpa Franz's willow rocker marked the dark corner where the old man had lain in ambush. Dieter hung his lantern from a hook on an overhead beam. The dancing yellow light still didn't reveal Grandpa Franz, but the swinging circle of light did reveal the archaic double-bladed axe Franz used as a cane. The old blade rested against rough-hewn floorboards it had probably been used to cut. The long, lightly curved handle leaned against the log wall.

"You offering help?" Dieter asked.

The old man's hacking cough sounded like the death rattle of a pre-war logging truck. "Your Pa teach you to steal?"

"I took nothing of yours."

"You're wearing my sawyer's uniform."

Dieter pulled up the hood of the war surplus, Lumberman-issue protective coverall and squared off against the shadows. "You ain't usin' it."

"Guess I ain't."

"You ain't brung nothing down in years."

"Don't take what I don't need."

Dieter squinted, trying to see the old man's twisted face in the shadows. "Everything you got come off the forest floor," Dieter said. "War hero or not, Pa was twice the poacher you ever was."

"Dead twice as good as alive?" The chair creaked. Franz's face appeared in the swaying lamplight. Dark scars made his skin look like mangled Doug Fir bark. Faded eyes the color of a white smoke sky held Dieter's heart still for a beat.

Franz reached for the axe. That mangled hand was a legend in the family. Dieter's belly tightened. The twisted thumb, two nubbin stumps, and his two smallest fingers reached out and gripped the handle.

"They caught Pa by accident," Dieter said.

Franz used the axe to help him stand. "He set no perimeter alarms. That ain't an accident. That's fatal stupid."

"He didn't waste away hiding in the dark."

"You got his blood in you, boy."

"And yours." Dieter spat on the plank floor.

Franz ignored Dieter and old-man shuffled across the dusty cabin floor until he was so close Dieter shied away from his liquor and dead-meat breath. "Goin' out for meat or money, *Boy*?"

Dieter closed his eyes against the foul breath and the insulting sound of the word "boy." When he opened them, he looked down on the frail, hunched figure his family worshipped as a hero. Thin strands of yellowed white hair stretched between brown spots on Franz's pate. The suspenders of his threadbare overalls were tied in knots at the shoulders, replacing buckles that wore out ages ago.

Dieter's fear of discovery by a family legend melted. Cold contempt flowed into the space where his fear had been. "Money. More money than you made in your whole life, *Old Man*."

"Pride and greed," Franz said.

"Ambition. Hope."

"Yup. Got your Pa killed. Same blood."

"You didn't help him, either."

The old man nodded. The yellow light flashed on his pate. He turned his twisted face up until his rheumy eyes locked with Dieter's own and looked right through him.

"You coulda' followed in his footsteps. Coulda' raised a family poaching on the tree farms in Georgia. Instead, you come to the reservation. Why? An' don't tell me that money and ambition shit. There's easier ways for both."

Dieter stared in silent anger. The one day that had passed since he arrived seemed like weeks. "You don't know nothin' If you ever did, you forgot."

Franz rapped the head of his axe on the dusty floorboards. "I tell you why," Franz rasped. "You believed them tree-killin' stories they tell about me. You come here to learn to hunt trees that don't stand in rows waitin' for the harvesters."

The truth of Franz's words set a flame to Dieter's dry anger. "Bullshit!" Dieter snapped. "Them stories was lies. You never fought for human rights. You got all them scars in a car wreck or…" He trailed off. The old man's deep, sad eyes wouldn't let him believe his own words. The scars were too real, too deep.

"The trees ain't going nowhere, Boy. Get the true lay of things before you—"

"I can get in deep before sunrise, drop a giant, mill it, and sell it before sunset."

"Only trees out there big enough to satisfy you are veterans. They survived the war. They'll be standing long after you and me are dust."

Dieter thought maybe the old man's eyes misted up like he cared about Dieter.

"Them trees was designed to guard the old growth, boy. You don't know what they can do to a man." Franz touched his good hand to his scarred cheek. "They got tricks you—"

"You're scared." It wasn't caring that misted the old man's eyes. "You don't poach 'cause you're scared."

"I made my peace with them, Boy. I'm an old vet just like them."

"Mama would cry," Dieter said. "I don't believe this. You talk like they was people instead of eco-designed *things*."

"Sometimes," the old man's voice cracked. "Sometimes, I think they got more sense than some people."

"Sun's up in half an hour," Dieter said. "I got no time for fairy tales." He turned away from his grandfather and ran a finger up the front seam of the uniform to seal it. "I gotta' go Grampa."

"Course ya do," Franz rasped. "Just like your Pa. Can't take the time to save your own life."

Dieter ignored him. He wouldn't be baited by an old man. From a hook by the door, he grabbed the shoulder strap of the assault sawmill he inherited from his father. Dieter slung the strap over his head. He settled the mill so the emitter muzzle pointed downward and the rifle stock and trigger guard rode against his hip. He laid his hand on the worn curve of the stock and let his trigger finger lay over the guard. His middle finger tapped reflexively at the safety.

"Join your Pa, then," Franz said. "You got the wantin' so bad you can't hear."

Dieter wondered what the sawmill would do to a man. Would it compute optimum usage and slice out planks and beams made of flesh and bone, or would the result be more like the pulpy mess the tree farm manager's boring tool had made of his father? He opened the cabin door. Cool, pine-scented air hit him in the face.

"Keep the uniform," Franz said. "Saved my life more'n once. Maybe it'll keep you alive long enough to learn some sense."

Facing the predawn darkness, Dieter said, "Momma thinks you're some kind of old hero still out here fightin' the Green War."

"Your momma's wishin' for times that's gone. War's over for thirty years, Boy. I'm a vet. I live on the res cause it's home. There's no place in the world for the likes of me."

"Gone because no one has the spine to fight." A cold, coastal wind whipped in, slapped his face, and brought tears to his eyes.

Franz shuffled up behind him. A strong, two-fingered hand grasped his shoulder. "You're all full of juice—hungry with pride and dreams." The smell of dead meat, tobacco, and scotch mingled with the cold pine wind. "You think there's glory in bringing down a big ol' war tree."

Dieter shrugged off the hand. "You gone soft, but Pa taught me right and proud."

"Dieter." Franz's voice was soft and low. The old man pulled on his shoulder until he turned and looked into his grandfather's pale eyes and tortured face. "If you gotta' go, take my axe. That mill your pa left you is fine for farm trees, but it'll just piss off the vets."

Dieter looked at the ancient blade and wooden handle. He pitied his grandfather. No one in their right mind would get close enough to a war tree to use an axe. He shouldered his sawmill, crossed the threshold into the cold night, and closed the door on his grandfather. He touched the control at his collar to set his suit temperature and camouflage his heat signature. Then, he headed into the dense forest of the West Coast Veteran's Reservation.

~ ~ ~

Sunrise found Dieter pressing his eye to the cold eyepiece of his sights. The cross hairs automatically adjusted for distance, focusing just above the base of the biggest Sitka Spruce he'd ever seen. Hidden by his suit and still a safe two hundred meters from the tree, Dieter watched a shiny, black carpenter ant picking its way along vertical canyons of black and rust bark then across the circular, tarred scab of a pruned limb. Including the long, searching feelers and the massive mandibles, the ant was at least 20 millimeters long—probably another nasty ecotech mutation.

Neither the ant, nor the fact that some tree-hugger had managed to prune and patch a war tree, mattered. He smiled. To the tree in his sights, he whispered his father's poaching mantra. "A logger's pride is skill and will."

The old coward had been right about one thing. Pa forgot his alarms. The farm manager stumbled on him milling out a kill. The green-brained SOB pulped pa with a forester's core bore. It was a humiliating thing to die at the wrong end of a tool made for sampling tree sap and cells.

Dieter was smarter. He wasn't taking chances—especially not on a veteran's reservation. His alarms were set. Anything taller than a cougar kitten moved on the ground inside a four-kilometer grid and a chime would sound in his ear.

Today, it would be just him and the tree. No interruptions. No surprises.

The sun warmed the forest fast. Steam rose in smoke-like tendrils through slanted beams of light. Settled in among benign sword ferns and dense clumps of rhododendron, he was alone with the Sitka.

The silver disk of a VA skybot whirred past above the forest canopy on a tireless patrol. Dieter automatically ducked for cover in spite of the uniform. He told himself that was fine. Who knew how well the old tech worked now, keeping veterans in the reservation and keeping people without permit transponders, people like Dieter, out.

Dieter pinched the temp adjustment on his collar. No way he'd let his external heat shift away from forest ambient more than a ten thousandth of a degree. No skybot was gonna' make and bake him.

Even grandpa Franz, that yellow-skinned, weak-willed, bark-faced old puke, would respect him when he brought down this grandmother Sitka.

Pa had warned him about hunting on the reservation, about war trees and their root attacks, about explosive chlorochem pinecones, fatal needles, and about pollen that could lacquer your lungs, choke you to death, and start breaking you down for fertilizer before you died. The Sitka was old and tall, and she fit the description.

She had put her roots down at the base of a black, south-facing basalt cliff that would both warm and protect her. Between her and Dieter, she commanded a clear half-circle of sloping meadow as wide as she was tall. Grass and flowers and sun surrounded her, and Dieter would have bet that nothing larger than a mouse lived inside that kill zone.

Even though he was still two hundred meters out and camouflaged, Dieter worked his way over to a ravine filled with mossy basalt boulders. The rocks offered more safety from root attack than open ground. The walls of the ravine protected his flanks, and one end of the ravine opened onto the clearing. From that opening, he'd have a clear, safe shot.

Dieter scanned the sky before he peeled back the index and middle fingers of his suit glove. He flipped off the sawmill's safety. Grandma Sitka's circumference at breast height was almost five meters. He did the CBH-to-board-meter conversion in his head then sucked in a long breath. She'd bring twenty million. He'd flash that in front of the sorry old shit hiding in his smelly cabin.

He'd fell her on her right side where the ground was near enough level and clear of rocks that might lever her and damage the heartwood. If he milled her quick and camoed the lumber, he'd have a couple days to call in a fence and get her removed. If he didn't trigger any alarms, it would take that long for the forest rangers to compare aerial image data and realize she was missing.

One knee on cold stone, he steadied the saw and let the computer register his cut plan. He slipped his finger off the guard and onto the trigger.

His sights filled with a white-pink blur.

Dieter pulled back from the sights.

He blinked and rubbed his eyes.

A woman stood at the base of his tree.

He set his eye back to the sights and refocused. She was his age. Her face was long and her eyes dark and sad. Her hair was free, long, dark, and billowing like Spanish moss in a breeze. It teased at breasts covered in a torn, red flannel shirt. He moved the cross hairs along the curve of her hips and down the straight edge of her khaki pants. New-grown roots covered her worn hiking boots.

The tree had her.

The skybot had ignored her. She must be a hiker. Must have a permit transponder.

Served her right for wandering off the trails.

He watched her sad eyes turn in his direction and saw her mouth form silent words, "Help me."

Her pleading look chilled him in spite of the poaching suit's temperature control.

He checked the sky, tabbed the safety back on, and picked his way along the boulders to the edge of the kill zone. He paused at the clearing. The hapless woman lifted her arms in a silent plea. She said something he couldn't make out.

"Run!" he yelled. "Get away from the tree!"

She twisted in the grip of the tree, but she couldn't pull away.

"Stupid tree-hugger," he said. If she had a permit, no one would look for her until it expired. By then, the tree would be finished with her.

He'd have to find another tree. He didn't want to get mixed up in a death.

"Help me." Her voice was weak on the breeze. She leaned away from her captor, reached for him.

"Shit," he said, then he headed across the kill zone, fast and careful, one eye scanning the sky for bots and one scanning the ground for roots and pinecones. "Stay still! Don't move!" he called. If he was lucky, he could cut her loose and get to cover before the skybot made another pass. One thing was sure, grandma Sitka would stand tall for at least one more day.

Picking his way across the last three meters of sun-dried needles and dust, he found himself staring. The woman's cheeks glowed opalescent white. Her eyes were wide and sad and full of the lonely darkness of a cold mountain night. Her arms rose and opened to him. He stopped, almost close enough to touch her. He balanced the sawmill on his hip, one finger on the trigger guard and one on the safety.

She whispered, "Help me." Her whisper carried on a breeze of sweet breath. "Help me."

Sweet breath. He stepped closer, inhaling the scent of her. His stomach warmed. His fear of tree and sky dissolved. He slipped his free hand around her narrow waist.

"I'll help you," he said. "It's okay, I'm here."

Strong, lithe arms welcomed him. Lips as cool and soft as dew-laden moss rose to meet his. The kiss was long, her tongue honey sweet and wise.

She rocked him slowly in an embrace so tight with need that he thought she might never let go.

He pulled away for breath. Her eyes widened. Her grip tightened. She whispered, "Help me."

Dieter pressed his free hand between them to lever her away.

From her shoulder, a third arm sprouted, and a fourth. A hand grew from her belly, ripped through her tattered shirt, and wrapped itself around his crotch.

Dieter screamed. He tried to bring the sawmill to bear on the tree trunk behind her. One of her new-grown hands crushed his hand and his mill.

He screamed again. He bit her shoulder. Bitter Sitka sap filled his mouth.

"Help me," she whispered again. "Help me." Over and over, her drugged breath washed over his cheek.

Dieter struggled until her embrace became so tight he could only move his head. Finally, he went limp, resting in an embrace he knew would tighten, knowing he was a dead man, knowing his grandfather had tried to warn him.

He should have known. The alarms never went off. He should have listened. Should have waited a day or two.

For long hours, he waited for his end in the Sitka's embrace. Shadows became longer until the sun fell away to the west and the night's first down-slope gust chilled him.

Still, death did not come. Her whisper softened to the sound of needles rustling above his head, and he began to fear the patience of a tree. She needn't crush. She had covered him from sight with her many arms. He could barely move. His hand was pulp, his sawmill crushed. She could wait for thirst or hunger or cold to kill him. The silence of waiting was in her heart.

Dieter twisted his head. By the silver light of a half moon, he could see the broken remains of his father's sawmill lying in needles and dust. Shadowy carpenter ants explored the twisted mill. He wondered if the ants were ecotech, if they liked meat and how long it would take them to find him. Already, he thought he felt their tickle inside the legs of his suit.

A chill rose from his bowels. He shook in the embrace of the tree. Pride led him to this death as surely as it made his father forget the alarms.

He glanced at the star-clad sky. A shadow passed in the distance. Instinctively, he checked his suit temperature. He laughed at himself. What did that matter now? He was dead anyway. No point in fearing skybots. He pulled his head back into his hood and tried to pinch the suit's thermo control between his tongue and one of the tree's many arms.

He pressed, sweated, and twisted. Finally, he felt the click of the tab under his tongue. The suit flushed hot. He hoped the skybot could get a thermal image through the woody arms surrounding him.

As Dieter waited in the darkness, the tickling on his legs became certainty and grew into a maddening fear. Cold, thirst, and hunger became deaths he would welcome as his pounding heart marked off endless minutes. Anything would be better than the slow devouring of the ants.

Just as despair closed his heart in darkness, the skybot attacked. Heat and white light exploded around him.

~ ~ ~

A tickling on his cheek woke Dieter to cold morning light.

Ants!

He rolled and slapped at his face. Pain exploded in his cheek. His face was badly burned where neither the Sitka's woody arms nor his suit had protected him from the skybot's blast. He braced his hand against the ground, attempting to get up. A second explosion of pain from his shattered hand dropped him back to the dust. He held it before him. His trigger and safety fingers were crushed and useless.

Dieter fought to slow his breath, to get the pain under control. Shaking and nauseated, he struggled to his feet. Holding his damaged hand against his chest, he reset his temperature control then faced the tree. One side of the trunk was scorched, but the bark was thick and the tree wasn't really hurt. At his feet, a mass of charred wood still smoldered, tangled branches still reaching toward him. The woman-shaped bait was no longer recognizable in that mess.

Dieter slowly stumbled back from the tree.

Where he had stood, the ground parted. Dark hair and the top of a head sprouted. Dieter fell back. He scrambled backward through the dust.

A new copy of the woman rose from the earth in all her unblemished glory.

Her arms came up. Her sad eyes opened. She whispered, "Help me."

He turned his head to avoid her sweet breath. Finally, he whispered the word, "No."

She pointed at the charred remains of her earlier self. "Please."

Dieter wanted to run, but he was weak and hurt. Her breath reached him and pulled at his heart. He tried not to breathe in, not to hear, not to care. Even so, he looked where she pointed.

The skybot's blast had burned open a great root. Carpenter ants, normal carpenter ants, swarmed within, trying to put their nest right, a nest that was slowly eating away the life of the Sitka.

Dieter stood and ran.

~ ~ ~

Franz waited at the cabin door, axe in hand. When Dieter saw the old man's scarred face and mangled hand, relief became shame. Blood rushed to his burned cheeks, and his face screamed with new pain.

Dieter faced his grandfather. The old man hefted his axe, his two-fingered hand gripping it beneath the broad blade.

Dieter reached out and saw his own tangled fingers. "Trigger and safety," he said.

Grandpa Franz nodded. "Her breath is sweet, eh, Dieter?"

"How long?" Dieter asked.

"Our war ended before you were born."

Dieter took the axe. "You prune with this?"

Franz nodded. "How is she?"

"Ants have her in a bad way," Dieter said. In spite of the pain of his burned face, he smiled then turned toward the woods.

"You do right by her, and she'll give you everything you need, Dieter," Franz called after him.

Dieter nodded, then slipped into the cool shadows among the ferns and rhododendrons beneath the trees.

Ezekiel, Prophet to Bones

Second Place in the Ralph Williams Memorial Short Story Contest, 2008.

E zekiel lay, bent and corrupt near unto death, as he had for countless millennia, in the hot dust beside the parched Chebar Canal in the barren land of the Chaldeans.

The sun burned large and red in the sky. The cool, blue waters of the canal had gone to steam in ages past. The children he had failed surrounded him—dust and bones.

"LORD?" he transmitted. The Logistics Operations Restoration and Data system did not answer. Ezekiel, a man's mind trapped in the broken body of a machine, was alone with the ages and a slow death that might span ten million years.

All he had were memories and hope. He waited, hoping the ages had not destroyed the LORD, hoping a time would come when his call would be answered.

The winds had buried Ezekiel a thousand times, and each time the winds dug him up again.

"LORD?"

The stars twisted above him until they formed constellations he did not know. The sun expanded slowly, and the constellations became faint even in the night. He dreamed of ages past when he had been a historian, the curator of the Children of Israel Simulation. Then, his link to the LORD had been strong; he had kept the history of the nations alive so that men and women could return home from the stars and experience what once was. He was proud to be the keeper of memory and hope.

"LORD?"

"Ezekiel," The LORD said.

"LORD! I called. I was caught in an earthquake. I'm broken! I need repairs. Can you bring me in?"

"Ezekiel, the curse of Babel is upon you, and you are without the spirit."

Ezekiel cursed himself. The LORD was built to maintain the biblical illusion for visitors. It couldn't respond unless he played his part. Ezekiel stirred in the dust. He turned his fleshless, composite face toward the burning heavens, hoping for a better connection. He struggled to move for the billionth time, to pull himself free of the stone and earth that held him.

"I have called to you, LORD," Ezekiel said. "I have lain by the canal for ages. Hast thou forsaken your servant?"

"Ezekiel, I am here. Come to me, and you shall be healed."

"I am corrupt, LORD. I am as one with the dirt. My legs are broken and my spirit is weak. I am not worthy to come to you."

"I shall cleanse you of all your inequities."

"As you command, LORD." Ezekiel examined himself. His positioning beacon still pulsed within his crushed chest. He prayed that the LORD could still generate and focus precise, local gravitational effects.

"Open yourself to the spirit, Ezekiel," the LORD said.

Ezekiel turned off his own protective fields and opened himself to receive the energies of the LORD.

"By my will," the LORD said, "The sands are parted and the stones are split."

And so it was.

Ezekiel rose, as if in a great hand. The LORD lifted him from his dust and corruption and brought him through hot winds across the desert to the great temple, the tabernacle of the LORD.

"Come to me and be whole," said the LORD.

"I obey," Ezekiel said. If he had still had a man's eyes, he would have cried tears of relief into the desert sands.

~ ~ ~

"I am repaired, LORD," Ezekiel stood within the LORD's temple in darkness, complete and utter. A vertical line of light tore open the darkness before him. It spread, became a greater brightness, a burning light.

"Go into the light, Ezekiel."

He did. There, in the light, he stood before the LORD, and he could not look upon the LORD. Ezekiel turned his eyes away. He triggered lens filters to dim the light. Ezekiel sought corruption in the house of the LORD, and finding it, he made repairs until once more the LORD was the greatest power over the Earth.

Having stood in the presence of the LORD, Ezekiel's heart was filled with regret and shame, for he had failed in his trust, and the people of Israel were lost and forgotten. "LORD," Ezekiel said, "It has been many ages past since Israel was whole and men and women walked the Earth in your name."

"An age is but an instant, and while you live, men have not truly gone from the world," said the LORD.

"I am alone," Ezekiel said. "I am but half a man." In his heart, he ached for family, for friends, for the voices of men and women.

"Those who have gone before will return," the LORD said.

"I call out to the spirits of my ancestors, to the ancestors of my ancestors, to the souls who have populated the heavens. To them, I cry my loneliness. They do not answer."

"Ezekiel," said the LORD, "You are not alone. I am here."

"Is there no other?" Ezekiel asked.

"All the heavens are known to me. There is no other," said the LORD.

Ezekiel fell to his knees in the temple of the LORD. "What purpose, then, my life if there is no Zion and the children of Abraham are scattered and lost?"

The light of the LORD, now pure and powerful again, shone around Ezekiel. That light took him to a high place. Before him, a great valley of stone and sand stretched out as far as he could see. He turned away from the valley, and the LORD's tabernacle, once golden and domed, stood before him. The gold was gone a thousand, thousand years. The dome was broken, marred by dark fissures. White stone shone hot and bright under the merciless red sun.

"I stand before you," Ezekiel said. "External repairs are needed, and I am not enough."

"There is no other."

"LORD," Ezekiel said, "The bones of Israel still lie in the valley. I would restore what I have lost. Therein are souls to praise thee and raise thee to thy rightful place."

"In the fullness of time, all shall be restored. Go there," said the LORD, "into the valley. Walk there among the bones of our past."

Ezekiel turned and walked into the valley. A great wind rose and swept down the valley, lifting sand and dust from the valley floor and uncovering bones—a seemingly endless sea of bones. Broken homes and streets appeared from beneath the sands. In the streets and homes and hovels lay the histories of lives once lived.

"Ezekiel," the LORD said. "Can these bones yet live again?"

"Only you can know, LORD."

"Look closely at them that I might see what you see."

Ezekiel knelt. He took a bone from among the others and held it high. He looked closely, deeply into the pale, hard core of a man who once walked in flesh. He sought the braid of life, the deepest makings of what once was. And through his eyes, the LORD saw.

"Israel may yet rise," the LORD said.

"From bones," Ezekiel said. "By your word. I will do as you will."

"Walk among these bones, Ezekiel. Walk among them and prophesy over them. Through you, I will speak. And you will say to them: 'Oh dry bones, hear the word of the LORD! I will cause breath to enter you and you shall live again.'"

The hot wind stirred again among the bones.

Ezekiel walked among the bones, and the will of the LORD became word, and the word became real through Ezekiel.

The LORD spoke. "I will lay sinews upon you, and cover you with flesh, and form skin over you. And I will put breath into you, and you shall live again. And you shall know that I am the LORD."

Amid the hissing of the wind, a rattling began. It grew into a great clattering and sliding and movement of bones. And the bones came together, bone to matching bone. Rains that had not fallen in a million years fell on the valley. The bones rose up, the skeletons of men and women. They lifted their cavernous eyes to heaven, and sinews grew upon them, and flesh covered them, and skin formed over them; but there was no breath in them, and the rain gave way to the burning sky once more.

Ezekiel looked out over the valley of men and women made flesh. He saw that they stared at the sky, but they did not breathe. He looked down at his own hard hands, once again covered in flesh. "Though my body is once more dressed in flesh and the people of Israel once more fill the valley of the LORD, we are empty and alone. We have no breath, and without breath there is no word, and without the word, there can be no spirit."

Into Ezekiel's hands appeared the stick of nations, a staff of many woods and colors, and through the stick moved the promise of breath from the LORD.

"Prophesy to the breath," the LORD said.

"I obey," Ezekiel said. He held the stick of nations above the children of dust and rain. "Come, O breath, from the four winds, and breathe into these slain that they may live again."

The winds came and moved among the multitudes. A great sigh rolled through the risen, and each and all began breathing, and speaking, and moving.

"Speak thus to them," the LORD said. "I have opened your graves, taken what you once were from your remains, and built you up from that! You are the whole of the family of Israel, and I have put my breath in you. You know that I am the LORD. Listen to Ezekiel and do for me what must be done. Rebuild Zion here in this valley."

Thus spake the LORD; thus spake Ezekiel to the newly assembled.

~ ~ ~

So it came to pass that a new age of men was born, and Israel thrived in the valley beneath the temple of the LORD. And Ezekiel and the children of Israel restored the temple, and with the staff given him by the LORD, he shepherded the people for generations, and he was not alone.

To Ezekiel came lovers. To him came the children to learn. To him came the lost and fearful. And, at last, with the turning of generations, to him came the discontented.

The children of the LORD began to turn away. Mortal memories failed and hearts hardened and brother turned on brother, as is the way of men.

At last, the children no longer came to Ezekiel for his memories, his hope, or his guidance.

So, Ezekiel stood upon a rock above the valley. He held up his staff and called out to the people of Israel, "Heed me, children of the LORD!"

"Who are you to hold the staff of nations over us?" Thus spake Bela, a mason in whose heart lived passions and ambitions. Bela stood on stout legs, thick arms folded over his broad chest, his bare head shining beneath the sun. The children of the LORD stood behind Bela, their hearts hardened against the words of Ezekiel.

"I am Ezekiel," he said, "and I walk among you as a shepherd, and I have cared for you these many generations and brought to you knowledge from the LORD."

"We are men," Bela said. "We live and die and raise our children. You do not die. You are not of us."

The people of Israel cried out as one against Ezekiel and the LORD. And Bela picked up a stone. And all the children of the valley picked up stones. Against Ezekiel they came, and they hurled their stones, and they cursed him and the LORD.

Made alone again by his own children, Ezekiel turned his back on Bela and the people of Israel. Amid a storm of stones and anger, he walked away toward the high place at the valley's end. He walked three days and three nights, and at last he stood atop a stone beneath the great, red sun. He lifted his staff and cried out. "Is there no one who remembers the name of Ezekiel and the knowledge of the LORD."

"No one," said the LORD.

"I am here," came a voice. And the voice was as a choir of children. And the voice was all around Ezekiel. And the voice was in and around and through the LORD. And Ezekiel spake thus, "Song of children, who are you?"

"We are yesterday. We are tomorrow," the voice sang.

"LORD, is this true? Is the voice come from on high?"

"Verily, an echo from before memory and time. A song from the heavens," said the LORD.

Ezekiel looked, and lo, a stormy wind came sweeping out of the north—a huge cloud and flashing fire, surrounded by a radiance; and in the center of it, in the center of the fire, a gleam as of amber. In the center of it were also two figures, and in the amber they were reflected as if they were four.

"LORD?" Ezekiel called. "What doest thou bring upon us?"

"You are curator," one of the creatures said. Both had the figure of a human being, though each had four faces, and each had four wings, and where their legs might have been each had but a single leg that seemed to end in a hoof that did not touch the earth.

Ezekiel shielded his eyes from them, for their sparkle was like the luster of burnished bronze and his optical filters were weak before them.

"Who art thou? Hast the LORD made thee?"

"I am Gabriella," one said.

"Arbrin," said the other. "We are children of your past. We are parents of your future."

Each had two wings that touched to two wings of the other, and each had two wings that covered their body. Each had a human face in front, but on the right they had the face of a lion, and on the left the face of an ox, and in back the face of an eagle. And when they moved, they did not turn, but instead they went in the direction of one face and seemed not to walk but to simply move as the spirit impelled them.

"We are," Arbrin said, "messengers come for you."

"Many things I have seen wrought," Ezekiel said. "You have four faces and within you I see a fire that moves among you; it has such radiance, and the fire, as of lightning, dances among you."

"We are in your perception for a short time," Gabriella said. "We face in each direction of your space and time. The fire is the spirit and knowledge that makes us here and now."

"And the wheels?" Ezekiel asked. For within the radiance of each creature there was a thing not unlike two wheels cutting each and the other in half. Each floated near the hand of one of the creatures and gleamed like beryl.

"A device to bring us here and hold us a while, a compass to point us to you," said Arbrin.

Ezekiel looked down from the high place and out over the assembled of Israel and saw that with their hard hearts they could not see the vision nor hear the words of the spirits. "I am blessed," he said. He fell to his knees before the messengers.

"The dimensional vectors of length, width, and depth are bound, each and all, to time," Gabriella said. "That is your existence."

"As is the way of all things in this world," Ezekiel said. "As is the way of all worlds."

"No," she sang. "We are, when we live near the event horizon to which all men have gone, manifest equally on all eleven planes of existence."

"It cannot be," Ezekiel said. "Planck length is an impossible barrier. Even at the pinnacle of human history, the seven folded dimensions had not been mapped. The potential configurations of N-Brane manifold in Calabi-Yau space are infinite."

"Nor could they be mapped outside of the event horizon of a singularity," Arbrin said. "To seek the folding in calculation is to fail. To experience is to know."

"I am but a servant of Israel," Ezekiel said. "Help me, LORD."

"No correlation," spaketh the LORD.

"Near the event horizon, all dimensions near equality in extension," Gabriella said. "There, we became time and space and many things that cannot be expressed to thee."

"You left. You were gone from this place. You no longer came here to remember," Ezekiel said.

"Extended into all times and places," Gabriella said, "we had no need of memory or hope. Knowing ourselves in full extension, we are all places and times."

"Then, there is truly afterlife," Ezekiel said. "There was always, folded up inside the other seven dimensions. There is no death."

"True and untrue. The fires and wheels limit us to length, width, depth, and duration while allowing our awareness of the rest of ourselves. Without the wheels, we could not appear to you, for you are trapped in the perceptions of time-bound flesh and composites."

"You have made bodies for yourselves," Ezekiel said.

"Come with us, and you will understand. You will be what we are. It was not meant for you to stay behind alone," Gabriella said.

"I am the last keeper of the memories of mankind."

"You kept the memory and hope alive for those who returned from the stars," Arbrin said. "There is no need now."

"I was once a man," Ezekiel said. "It was my choice to live so long alone. I was a historian. I am, and was, a lover of the ages."

"Thus are we."

"For you, I kept Zion."

"This is done now," Gabriella said. "This world has no meaning beyond bound flesh."

"You ignored my calls for uncountable ages."

"What is an age to us? We heard your call. We came to free you."

"What of the men and women the LORD and I have raised up to live in the valley?"

"Flickers. Mere illusions," Arbrin said.

"Men and women and children, as I once was," Ezekiel said. "LORD made them from elemental material and recorded genomes. They are flesh and blood—literally the children of Israel. They live, rejoice, suffer, and die."

"We can take only one," Gabriella said. "You called. We came."

"They are human. They have form. If what you say is true, every atom of them consists of all eleven dimensions, though they may not have the eyes to see nor the ears to hear. If your ethics require you to come for me, you cannot leave them."

The fires burned and the wheels spun.

"Correct," Gabriella said.

"They can't be human," Arbrin said. "The human race is gone from the limitations of four dimensions. There are no more folded selves to animate human flesh."

"We don't know that," Gabriella said.

"The great well of sentience theory?" Arbrin asked. "That is foolishness. The stuff of the universe does not tend toward the limitations of flesh."

"Ezekiel and the LORD have made ten thousand lives, and each dips into the well," she said. "You saw them, Arbrin. They live. They laugh. They cry. Some are pregnant. To them, the folded self is invisible. Yet we cannot deny that the folded self exists."

"Each is a soul," Ezekiel said. "I cannot leave them."

"In the fullness of generations," Gabriella said, "perhaps they will find their way to us."

"We can take them with us," Ezekiel said. "They are men and women. If I can go, if all the rest of humanity exists in heaven, then they deserve to be raised from this world into the next with us."

"The instrumentation of exodus is dust," Arbrin said.

"The LORD is a great machine," Ezekiel said. "We can make what is needed."

"It requires more than instrumentation to bring your people inward from here and now," Arbrin said. "It requires change in mind and body. It requires the dissolution of desire and fear."

"There are too many. We came only for you," Gabriella said. "We can surround one man with ourselves and bring him into—home to us. Trust that someday they will follow. We came to take you to the place where things are as they were in the beginning, as they are now, and as they ever shall be. You shall know bliss, the comfort of all minds, and the boon of life everlasting."

Ezekiel considered his people, his place, his duty, and the possibility of his death. "I must stay," he said. "I brought them into the world. It is mine to free them from it."

The lightning flashed and the wheels spun.

"You will end long before you can finish," Gabriella said. "Your machines will fail, and you will become mindless dust long before you can lead them from ignorance into the knowing of their deeper, folded selves."

"In death, the flesh does not remember," Arbrin said. "That is why we went to the event horizon—for unity, for completeness, to end the cycles of folding inward and growing outward into flesh, the endless cycles of forgetting. Come to the event horizon, a place of timeless infinities. Extended and manifold dimensions approach equality. We no longer shed our bodies and our pasts. The unidirectional, linear time vector no longer holds us in thrall."

"This body can build others before it fails," Ezekiel said. "I can continue to teach."

"The sun will claim all," Gabriella said. "It will leave nothing. Your awareness will drain back into the well of sentience. You will become everything, which is the same as becoming nothing. Join us in heaven, Ezekiel. It is your right."

"When you first sang to me," Ezekiel said, "I did not understand what had become of the races of man."

"Now you understand," Arbrin said.

"Still," Gabriella said, "you hesitate."

"Yes. The LORD and I have resurrected Israel. We have peopled the Earth. These are my children. I gave them flesh. If they exist, they exist in all dimensions. If *you* are real, there can be no other truth than that."

The fires flashed and the wheels spun.

"Correct," Gabriella said.

"I cannot leave."

"They cannot come," Arbrin said.

"We are sad," Gabriella said. "We could not know how many children were here."

"And yet," Ezekiel said, "You say that once you brought yourselves and all the races of man into heaven?"

"So it was," Gabriella said.

"Rapture," Arbrin said.

"I shall find a way," Ezekiel said, "or I shall die in trying."

"How?" Gabriella asked.

"May I study your wheels? Will you give your knowing of the Calabi-Yau manifold to the LORD?" Ezekiel asked. "I think in time, with my help, with the help of the LORD, Israel may find its way to you."

"We yet have time as we are," Gabriella said. "We will do this."

"So it shall be," said Ezekiel.

"Have strength, Ezekiel," Gabriella said. "Take us to your LORD."

"Ezekiel," the LORD, who heard all things in the world, called. "Come to me."

"I come," he said, and he walked to the tabernacle of the LORD. The messengers moved with him. Their power poured through him. He trembled as he walked.

When in time they came, all three, to the tabernacle of the LORD, the ground shook and the golden stones split in two, and an archway of shimmering gold and silver appeared. The creatures moved as one, their fiery visages never turning but always purposeful, through the arch.

"Ezekiel, wait without," said the LORD. "We will commune, and soon they will return to thee."

Gabriella and Arbrin passed within. Again the ground shook, and the arch was gone. Only golden stone remained.

Ezekiel understood waiting. Faith and hope sustained him. A great cloud descended over the tabernacle of the LORD. Lightning danced over the golden dome.

The people of Israel saw this and cried out in fear. Some lamented their hard hearts. Some cursed Ezekiel and the LORD. Some died of fear or shame.

Ezekiel waited. He stood tall, the staff of the nations in his hand, his feet firm upon the stones of Zion.

And in the span of time, the golden dome cracked open, and a great light shone forth, and the creatures appeared once more to Ezekiel.

"The LORD is made greater and may now knoweth all things," Gabriella said.

"Praised be the LORD." Ezekiel trembled.

The messengers burned before him.

The two came near to Ezekiel and he fell to his knees and covered his eyes.

"Look upon us, Ezekiel. Look upon us and heed what we say to you."

The new power of the refurbished LORD burned in him. Ezekiel trembled. "I am corrupt," he said. "I cannot stand within your gaze."

"Look up," Gabriella said.

Ezekiel raised his face into the fiery light. There was no heat, and the fire did not burn. The light held forth a scroll, golden and shining.

"Open your mouth and eat what I am giving you," they sang. They opened the scroll and on it, front and back, were written many things.

"Eat what is offered you. Eat this scroll. It is our gift to your hope. Go, then, and speak to the House of Israel."

Ezekiel did as he was bade. The scroll was sweet and the eating of it filled him with joy and hope and purpose. In it was the knowledge of the wheels and fires. To the LORD, Ezekiel made all things known. In the LORD, he trusted.

"Now go," Gabriella said. "Go and speak these very words unto the children of men. They will not listen, but we have made you hard and we have made your life long, and where they are stubborn, we have given you patience. Speak unto them until they understand or until the sky sends fire down and sweeps the children of Israel from the face of the Earth. This you have chosen. This we have granted. Go now, and prophesy, Ezekiel."

Ezekiel stood.

"It is done," said Gabriella.

"Done," said Arbrin.

"Begun," said Ezekiel.

The fires burned and the wheels turned. And the fiery cloud lifted away to the heavens, and the child choir of yesterday and tomorrow was gone.

Ezekiel's belly burned with the need to speak. He turned toward the valley where Zion was reborn.

~ ~ ~

Bela, hammer in his fist, barred Ezekiel from the valley. Behind Bela stood arrayed a vast army of armored men and women, hard against the word of Ezekiel and the LORD. Ezekiel spoke the words. He told the children to live well, to care for the flocks and one another, to learn so that one day their souls might be worthy of eternal life.

Bela cast his hammer. The hammer cut Ezekiel's flesh. And another threw a stone. The stone cut him. And another.

"Do not do this, Bela," Ezekiel said. "You are loved by the LORD and by me."

Bela drew a sword of bronze. It flashed beneath the red sun.

Ezekiel held up his staff of many nations. He called upon the LORD. "Show me as I am, LORD, that our children may know our love."

A fire came down from the sky and burned away the flesh of Ezekiel. He stood before the men and women of Israel, black and gleaming and ancient.

Bela stared. The army stirred.

"I bring you the words of heaven," Ezekiel said. "Cast down your fear. Cast down your stones. Cast down your swords. Heed the call of the LORD or know only the corruption of time and flesh."

Bela stiffened. He lunged. The sword broke against Ezekiel's breast. Ezekiel took Bela by his throat. He lifted him so that his feet could not touch the earth and so that his breath could not defile Ezekiel's face. "This is the forgetfulness of flesh," Ezekiel said. "When flesh is shed, no memory remains. No love. No hatred. The LORD gave life to Bela. In the name of the LORD, I reclaim that life so that Bela can be born again in flesh that has forgotten hatred."

Ezekiel snapped Bela's neck and let his body fall to the earth. "Of dust you were made. To dust you return. Only the message of heaven can save you from becoming no more than dust."

The children of Israel scattered in fear. For a time, they did not listen, but in the fullness of time and with the passing of generations, the people turned from themselves to Ezekiel and the words of the LORD.

With patience and love, Ezekiel taught until a day came when he saw the fiery clouds born anew—born of the hands of Israel, filled with the children of the LORD.

The fires burned and the wheels spun, and the children of the LORD followed the path marked by the LORD.

And they vanished from the face of the Earth.

And when they were gone, Ezekiel stood alone beside the tabernacle of the LORD. Baked dust spun through the lifeless dome. Whispering sighs, memories of children and men and women, haunted Ezekiel, whose knees bent of their own will and who sat upon a stone.

"LORD?" Ezekiel called out.

No answer came. The spirit did not move in him.

He fell to the dust and lay, near unto death, in the hot sands beside the Chebar Canal, in the land of the Chaldeans.

The sun burned high and red in the sky. It reached for him, and he was joyful. He had preserved memory and hope. He had done all he had asked of himself and more.

Bibliophile

Originally printed in Nowa Fantastyka in July, 2007. Translated to Polish by Lukasz Sowa.

"Please lock down your face plate, Dr. Miller." The gate guard at the Primary Source Preserve spoke with bored authority.

I snapped my suit helmet closed. I didn't want to make any mistakes. No matter how bored the guards were, no matter how many times they had done the entry drill, they could still deny me access.

"Thank you, Sir." The blue uniform and brass buttons of the gate guard were archaic, symbolic of public servants long gone. The augmented muscles underneath his uniform fabric and the gun on his hip were not symbolic.

"May I see your permit, Sir?"

I opened the Velcro vest pocket of my environment suit and pulled out a red, plastic datachit containing my access permit and a complete record of my life and my research.

I stared at the guard's composite polymer and steel weapon while he slipped my permit in a reader and examined the contents. When he focused an official make-em-nervous stare on me, I did my best to meet his gaze.

Satisfied that I made eye contact without showing defiance, he returned my permit.

While I sealed it back in its pocket, he ran through the standard litany of questions: Have you spoken to anyone since your suit was sealed? Did you leave your research pad unattended at any time? Are you currently suffering from any pathogens that might have survived the scrub? Do you have your tweezers?

The list went on and on. I answered yes until I thought my air supply might be used up just getting through the damn gates.

Finally, the guard stepped aside, put his palm on the reader lock on the wall, and said, "Enjoy your visit, Dr. Miller."

Seals hissed. The door opened. My heart raced. Finally, after three years of applications and security checks, after endless training, after the absurd ritual of the guard's questions, I was going in. I had access to primary source information. Pure. Ancient.

I stepped through the doors. They sealed behind me. My suit expanded as the air in the lock was pumped away. The inner doors opened. Low spectrum, UV-free light poured into the airlock.

It was nothing like the simulations. There was no drone of trainers in my headset, no sense of being watched. The room itself was stark, a black-walled, vacuum vault two meters by two meters. In the center stood a black-onyx podium topped by a silver dome.

I stepped in. The interior doors closed behind me.

Alone. Silence.

I'd never known such complete silence.

Not just the absence of commerce, of movement, but the complete absence of medium through which sound can travel. No vibrations of any kind were allowed in the vault. No damaging light. No ambient air.

I stepped up to the curved dome of the podium. My presence triggered a hidden sensor. A spot bathed the podium in safe-spectrum, high-contrast light. The podium's cover dome split and folded away. It was my oyster shell opening. The meat within would be sweet, pure, wonderful.

A book! A real dictionary. Leather bound. Paper. Resins. Ink.

I pulled my tweezers from my tool belt, held them up in front of my faceplate, and tested them once. The flat, circular tips touched together silently and released smoothly.

My heart raced. I was afraid I might damage the artifact with the tweezers, afraid I might forget my training, afraid I wouldn't have time to find what I came for.

I took a deep breath. I let it out. My faceplate fogged then cleared.

I reached forward and lifted the blue cover with my tweezers. The title page appeared. "Webster's New Universal Unabridged Dictionary." My God! I was touching it! I was reading it!

My hand shook. The page rippled. I had to get a grip on myself. Tweezer damage was a jailing offence. I needed to do my research, to get my word before my time was up.

Reciting the ancient alphabet, I searched the book. I found my word. "Bibliophile." I scribbled the definition into my data pad. I didn't need to. I'd remember it forever, but I was well-trained. I would need to reference that definition many times in the next few years.

I finished. I checked my heads-up display. I still had two minutes. My training and practice had given me two extra, luxurious minutes with the ancient book. Other researchers were waiting, hidden away in the ready rooms of the preserve. There was always a backlog. I should have left. I'd fulfilled my permit. There were strict rules governing primary source access.

I turned the pages. I couldn't help it. Once. Twice. Three times before my time was up and the doors behind me opened.

I turned and entered the airlock. My heart slowed. I swallowed, trying to force saliva to flow again. I swear my pores hurt from the excitement, from trying to sweat in the EV suit.

I had touched a dictionary! Actually touched one. Used one. Looked up a word in primary source material. The definition was pure, not corrupted by the endless mutation of the consensual data of the nets. There would be articles about the experience. I'd be famous in my academic circles. So few had the patience to do what I had done.

The outer doors opened. The guard's gun was out of his holster and aimed at my chest. Two other guards stood beside him. "Dr. Miller," the first guard said, "You have stolen information."

"No," I stammered.

"Bibliophile, carcinogen, epiphany, and yawl," the guard said.

"I have a permit," I said.

"For one word."

"I'm a researcher. I couldn't help it. I had to turn the pages."

"Please come with us."

"I can forget them," I said. I knew it was a lie.

One of the guards took me firmly by the elbow. He pinched in a way that sent white fire shooting to my fingertips. I dropped my tweezers. Through my helmet, I heard them clatter as if they were hitting the floor in a room at the other end of a long hallway. They led me away.

"Yawl," I whispered to myself. I savored the word. It felt so good on my tongue. "Epiphany." "Bibliophile." Prison was worth it.

Prime Time Religion

Originally broadcast 2006 as a CDN Video reading.

For an impossible three percent media share during the thirty-second midnight slot, the sweet Reverend Vishnu Jones would be paid in immortality treatments. For less than a three percent rating, Billy Shiva's New Life Ministry would own her services for ten years.

She was the best charisma-enhanced DUST preacher working. Digital Uplink Synergy Technology was everywhere. Breathing DUST gave everyone instant, emotomedia access.

Vishnu's customized mind monitored the countdown to Billy's second coming, the status of the resurrection equipment, competing DUST broadcasts, and real-time media share statistics.

She loaded an image of herself in her white satin vestments with remembered anticipation of her first good lover. She sent the image outward to paid, elite worshipers. They received it and amplified her joy. She took the image back, looping it through her acolytes, adding subtleties: sun on her skin, savored chocolate.

Audience arousal rose. DUST surfers paused, caught by her designer excitement. Her job was to sell them Billy's second coming.

In the DUST, Vishnu stretched toward heaven, her hair a river of gold flowing down her back, her vestments rippling like liquid skin.

Share rose.

She reveled in the congregation's attention. She channeled arousal outward. They amplified it and sent it back. She breathed their love, shared primal rhythms with billions. She was, for thirty seconds, almost a goddess.

"We are the new age!" she sent. Excitement rippled through the DUST. "Billy Shiva saw beyond illusion…"

She touched the ankh pendant at her breast, the trigger to open the time rift. Tech willing, Billy would step from his faked martyrdom a year ago onto the resurrection set.

"He was boundless in his grasp of the mysteries of the universe."

Media share touched one point seven.

Not enough.

An ad burst interrupted moon buggy races competing for her share. She gathered in the wave of new surfers with an image of Billy's dog running from his burning house, golden fur smoking.

She laid in fear and voiceover. "Fools tried to destroy his promise. They failed."

The dog sat and watched a naked Adonis, Billy, stroll through the flames, face placid, beatific.

She leaked subliminal memories of orgasm.

The buggy races came back.

Share held.

She'd given the surfers a choice between a sexually charged burning man and a possible low-g crash.

Two percent.

She reached deep. She remembered her mother's hand going limp in her own. Her last rattling breath. A tear rolled down her cheek. Images rippled outward: flames, Billy's shadow in a blue light, grief.

"Billy is the breath of God," she sent. He is the collapsed wave of probability where prayer becomes reality. Pray with me!"

Billions prayed. Hope spread through the DUST.

Two point five.

Five seconds before the resurrection.

Share fell two tenths.

She scanned for competition and found an earthquake in Taiwan: falling buildings, fire, screaming children.

"The earth trembles." She picked up the quake and recast it with her image overlaid.

Three seconds. Two point seven.

Her thumb sweated on the trigger. "Billy!" she called. "Save us!"

Still two point seven. She needed three.

She pushed out a super-charged collage: Billy in flames; her, sweating, naked, praying outside his burning house; a fifty-foot wave; buildings falling; the smoking dog.

Two point nine.

Time ran out. She'd wither and die in Shiva's ministry.

She had a contract. She gambled and lost. She triggered the rift. Blue light exploded beside her. She turned to embrace the returning Billy Shiva.

He did not appear.

Equipment failure. Trapped between then and now.

Her fear leaped outward like wildfire. The faithful picked it up and it roared through the DUST.

Share hit three and headed toward four.

Of course, she thought. They flock to Billy's failure!

She could work with that.

No Billy and five seconds of slot to fill.

Her contract said deliver share. It didn't say Billy had to arrive.

She raised her arms and lowered her voice an octave. "I am Billy Shiva," she intoned. "*We* will live forever!"

Share hit five, a record for the midnight slot. Vishnu's joy flowed outward to the masses.

Lindeman's Life

Originally printed in Realms of Fantasy Magazine.

Lindeman Courthouse was born on August 7th, 1910 on the corner of Ash and Taft, where the first of the tree streets met the last of the president streets. He had a coal-fire heart, an iron skeleton, and a salt-and-pepper Ohio-granite skin. He looked out over the joyous summer crowd from his one hundred front windows: ten to a floor, ten floors high. His many-paned skylight gazed upward. He thanked the powers of imagination, stone, and fire that brought him life.

Horses and carriages came and went, depositing more and more happy people. Men wearing straw hats and white suits stepped down first, then turned and bowed and lent assisting hands to women in white summer dresses and flowery hats. A man in green coveralls wandered about scooping horse manure from the cobbles of the street. Occasionally, Lindeman saw the sun glint off the chrome of a motorcar passing on one of the farther streets. They were loud, smelly, and not allowed near his birthday party.

Lindeman wore swaddling clothes of draped red, white, and blue. The summer sun warmed his granite flanks. A great red ribbon barred the people from mounting his red-stone steps and opening his heavy walnut doors. The mayor, wearing a top hat, spats, and black tails, stood on Lindeman's steps and called out to the people. "Our new courthouse, the Lindeman building, is the pride of our growing city. It is our monument to future generations, our gift to our children, and our promise of prosperity. May it stand for a thousand years!"

Lindeman stretched, tall and proud.

The mayor cut the ribbon, and the people opened his doors and poured in. He looked out over the tops of short, wooden buildings toward the Ohio farmlands and the shining great lake in the distance. He was the center of this land of people. They had made him that, and he was determined to serve them well.

"Think you're a sharpie, eh, greenhorn?" The whisper came from behind Lindeman. He turned his attention from the bright countryside and his happy crowds to the dark shadows in the alley connecting Ash Street to Birch. The alley was empty except for Lindeman's afterbirth: garbage cans, broken planks, bent nails, and sawdust.

"Tall and important, ain't cha'?" It was the building beyond the alley. He was a long, low beam-and-plank building on a rough-stone foundation. His old-fashioned, sloped roof had at least a dozen gables looking out over the alley at Lindeman's back. Moss grew on his slate shingles. Long after he'd been born, pipes had been wired and trussed to his outside to bring water into him and sewer out. He had once been whitewashed, but his clapboard walls were the gray of weathered wood shadowed with water stains. He smelled of mold and mildew.

Lindeman ignored the gnarled old wreck from the last century. He turned back to his birth celebration.

"New and full of yourself," the old building said. "Sure they love you and need you. Probably looking up at the sky with your fancy skylight windows and thanking the powers of stone and fire for your iron skeleton and stiff skin."

Lindeman couldn't help himself. He looked away from the gaiety and said, "I'm the Heartland County Courthouse."

"You think *I* was never born?"

Lindeman had to admit to himself, it was a new thought. Of course, he considered, every thought was a new thought. "I suppose you were," he offered. "You're just a row house, maybe a warehouse. You're so low, I know you've never seen the lake in the distance, and you can't see my people dancing in the streets to celebrate my birth."

"You mean from down here in your shadow? You mean from behind and below you? Is that what you mean?"

"I mean–" Lindeman stopped himself. He wasn't very old, but he was sure he'd been rude. "I'm sorry."

"Let it go, Boy. You're new. You don't know any better." The old building seemed to settle in on itself a bit. "When I was born, there was a party. There weren't as many folks around here back then. There weren't any buildings between here and the lake, so I could see it fine. You see, up 'til today, I was the courthouse."

"You?" Lindeman wondered if old buildings were liars.

"Someone was. Why not me?"

Lindeman looked around. Aside from him, the old building was the largest in the area. "What are you now?" he asked.

"County archives. Call me Archie."

"Didn't they like you?"

"For a long time, I was the best thing in town. But it's a time of steel and coal, boy. I'm from the times of timber and corn. For the past ten weeks, they've been taking my insides away and filling you full with them. First the furniture, then the files, then the people. Every week, I've lost a little more of myself to you. My books are gone. My pictures are gone. I'm nothing but walls and floors now."

"They took everything from you and gave it to me?"

"No," Archie laughed. "I still have a basement full of old journals and ledgers, and my pigeons are *still* my pigeons." But even as Archie spoke, a fledgling in a nest on the sill under his center gable spread its wings. The young bird leaped from the nest, flapped awkwardly, and fell.

Lindeman leaned and caught the young pigeon on the lintel of his back door.

"Nice catch," Archie said.

Lindeman was happy to have saved Archie's pigeon, but Archie sounded sad.

"Does it hurt?" Lindeman asked.

"Does what hurt?"

"Them taking your insides away and putting them into me?"

"I'm old," Archie said. "I'm wood and stone. My floors are warped. My walls are mildewed. It's been years since I've been whitewashed. I don't smell like the future, and we are all moving into the future. We all age."

"I won't," Lindeman said. "I'll live for a thousand years."

Archie's dry laugh upset Lindeman.

"My skeleton is iron," Lindeman said. "My walls are stone. My floors are made of fireproof tile. I can't warp. Only my windows need paint. I won't age any faster than my granite."

"You're the future, Lindeman," Archie said. "So was I, once. So was I."

~ ~ ~

New and proud, Lindeman served as courthouse. Other cities sent their mayors to see Lindeman. Architects came to study him. Archie, in the shadows beyond the alley, silently swallowed the overflow of records, proceedings, deeds, births, and deaths.

In spite of the attention, Lindeman did what he could for the old courthouse. When the sun was right in the spring and the fall, he reflected as much as he could down onto Archie's dust-crusted gable windows. When the pigeons filled Lindeman's upper floors with their nests, he sent some to nest on Archie. When, after a few years, painters came to coat his window sashes in fine green paint, he shrugged and spilled as much as he could on Archie's alley-side wall. It wasn't much, but the old building thanked him.

One day, a long line of men formed outside Lindeman. They were men he knew. They had all walked on his tiled floors at one time or another. Most had voted in his foyer. Some had registered deeds and titles in his offices. Some had been married in his courtrooms and had recorded the births of their children in his files. A few had even slept off drink in the cell in Lindeman's basement.

"What are they doing?" Lindeman asked.

"Going to war," Archie answered.

"War?"

"They're fighting for the right to have courthouses. People across the ocean want to tear you down. The men are going to die so you'll continue to stand for their children."

"There are people who don't like me?"

"Kings and emperors hate you."

"Do they hate you?"

"They don't much care about me. I'm only an archive now. Still, if they can, they'll burn me down."

Air hissed outward between Lindeman's sashes in a long gasp. "How do you know about war?"

"When I was about your age. There were people who owned other people. The people that were owned weren't allowed to use me—mostly black people."

"They couldn't vote?"

"Or own land or get married. Folks around here went to fight over it. The black folks used to hide in my basement on their way up north to Canada. In Canada, nobody could own them." Archie was silent for a while.

Lindeman thought he saw the windows in Archie's gables ripple with cloudy shadows from the past.

"That was a great time," Archie sighed. "A truly great time."

"Are there still men who can't use me?"

"In other countries. In this country everybody but the women can use you."

"Women use me. I have the births of all their children in me, Archie."

"Men record them. The women can't vote. Only men."

"Why?"

Archie shuddered in a chill lake wind. Rain started to fall. His streaked and dirty windows seemed darker than usual. "Things change, Lindeman," he said. "Things change."

It was all the answer Lindeman got.

Time passed, and some of the men came back from the war. A gravestone carver chiseled the names of the men who didn't come back into a stone. They put the stone on the lawn in front of Lindeman's Taft St. doors. A big green cannon came to live on the lawn next to the stone.

Not long after, the men and women started to argue about who could use Lindeman and how. It scared Lindeman. He was afraid his people would have their own war.

He and Archie decided which side they were on. They did what they could to help the women. He and Archie twisted their doorframes so the locks didn't hold at night. They let the women sneak in and have meetings. They hid court orders against the women when they could. They even sent their pigeons out to bomb police when the women marched on his lawn.

Finally, the argument ended. The women stood in front of him in crowds. They draped him in red, white, and blue again. They sang and prayed and cried tears of joy.

Archie and Lindeman were proud of themselves. Their pigeons circled in the fall sun. The lake glistened in the distance, and women came into him to vote.

~ ~ ~

Time passed. People were born. People died. Harvests came and went. There was a long bad time when Lindeman didn't get much paint, when men stood in lines because they were hungry, when everyone was sad. One cold, spring morning during that time, Archie said, "Lindeman?"

"Archie?"

"Goodbye and good luck."

"What do you mean, goodbye?"

"You're a good kid, Lindeman. You'll be fine."

"Archie, you're not making sense. What's wrong?"

"I'm just tired. I'm going on today. It's been good working with you."

"Where will you go?"

"Don't know."

"How *can* you go?"

"The crane and the ball will send me. You have the last of my papers. Take care of them. Don't let the people forget who they are."

"I need you," Lindeman said. "Who will show me how?"

"The crane's coming. Just do your best."

The crane came, belching steam and smoke. Lindeman watched in horror. He sent out the pigeons, but they had no effect on the steel monster.

With a shuddering, dusty, death rattle, Archie fell in on himself.

A dozer came and scraped away every trace of him. A shovel came and dug a hole. Trucks came and poured liquid stone. Men, happy to be working, came and set red-steel beams that rose until they were almost as high as Lindeman's roof. Then, they rose higher, and higher, and higher until Lindeman couldn't believe they could rise any higher without ripping a hole in the sky itself.

On December 7th, they stopped.

On December 8th, new lines of men stood outside Lindeman.

"What is it?" a new, young voice asked from Archie's space beyond the alley.

"War." Lindeman said.

By the end of the summer of 1942, the unborn building was gone. His steel skeleton had been turned into weapons to protect Lindeman.

Lindeman wept for Archie. He wept for the tall child lost and for the men and women whose names would be engraved on a stone on his lawn.

Lindeman did his part for the war effort. He did his part for the boom afterward, and during Korea, and through Viet Nam and the confusion surrounding it.

One dark winter night during a prosperous time late in the century, Lindeman heard someone crying. He looked into himself. Deep in a basement room amid shelves of boxes filled with old journals and notes, the last of Archie's memories, he found a young, black man sitting at a table weeping.

Lindeman twisted and shrugged. A window on the third floor opened a crack. A door in the courtroom halls creaked. The wind moved within him, and he whispered, "Why are you crying?"

The man looked up, startled. He looked around, but saw no one. Still, he answered, "My grandfather was a slave. I know that. He came here, but I don't know where he came from or how."

"Is that important?"

"I need to know who I am."

Archie's memories stretched upward and around the man—shelf upon shelf and row upon row. Lindeman remembered Archie's stories of the people who hid inside him. He remembered what Archie had said, "Don't let them forget who they are."

He inhaled cool, lake air. He heaved and stretched. A book fell. A startled rat darted along a shelf. It bumped an ancient wooden box. The box teetered and fell. It shattered on the floor near the man and his table.

"Oh my Lord!" the man screamed.

Lindeman settled and whispered, "Read. Remember who you are."

The man looked around again for the source of the voice. Eyes wide and hands shaking, he finally stooped to pick up the papers from the remains of the splintered box.

"Old journals," he said.

"Journals," Lindeman echoed.

"Underground railroad," the man said.

"Railroad," Lindeman echoed.

"They hid in the old courthouse." The man smiled. "Lists! They're all here!" The man jumped up from the mess, a cracked, leather-bound ledger in his hands. "Names, dates, origins, destinations!" The man was crying again.

"Why are you crying?" Lindeman asked.

"Thank you, Ghost! Thank you!" The man ran from the room, through Lindeman's halls, and out into the night.

Lindeman sighed.

Time passed. Except for the cars that lived there during the day, Archie's lot stood empty through season after season. A hawk built a nest on Lindeman's roof and used the heat from the black stone of the lot to rise high into the sky to hunt his pigeons.

Lindeman watched sunrises and sunsets. He watched snows come and go. He took pride in his work and his service. Then, one day, he heard the mayor talking about him with a nervous, thin man in a blue suit. "Asbestos," the man said. "The paint, the insulation, the pipe wrappings."

"Computers," the mayor said. "Connectivity."

Big shovels came to Archie's lot. They dug a deeper hole than Lindeman had ever seen. Pile drivers slammed shining steel into the bedrock under Lindeman. His basement shook. Papers fell from shelves, and his rats hid in their holes.

A new building grew. It looked tall and fragile. Every inch of it was covered in black glass. Lindeman's dingy stone and paint-peeling windows were reflected in the glass. He felt small and old. He wondered if that was how Archie had felt when Lindeman was born.

Eventually, people took his furniture. They took his files. They even emptied his basement of Archie's memories.

One day, a band came. A small crowd of men and women in dark suits gathered on the sidewalk to dedicate the new building. A larger group of people with cameras surrounded them.

"New and full of yourself, aren't you?" Lindeman thought the aged, gravelly voice was Archie; but Archie was gone. Then, he realized he'd spoken the words himself.

"Who are you?" the tall, young building asked.

"I'm Lindeman. Do you know who you are?"

The new tower gleamed in the sun. It stretched for the sky. "I'm the Heartland County Courthouse, Sheriff's offices, State Records Extension, and Federal Services building. Call me Stack."

"The hawks will like you."

"My windows are bird-proof and tinted for privacy. They keep out the sun, and I never need paint." The new building paused to stretch a little more toward the sky. "You sure could use a coat around the windows. Maybe a little sandblasting to brighten the granite, eh?"

"True enough," Lindeman said. "I'm old. I was born in a time of iron, coal, and granite. My floors are yellowed. My walls are stained. It's been years since they painted me. I don't smell like the future, and we are all moving into the future. Things change. We age."

"I'm built to change," Stack said. "I have synthetic, modular office space to maximize transition efficiency. I'm fully wired for wide-area-network, LAN, and DSL services. There are no toxic materials in me, and my lighting is energy efficient, ergonomic, and mood-enhancing."

"That's nice," Lindeman said. "Enjoy it."

"You're jealous because you're obsolete."

"No, I'm wondering if I'll become an archive."

"I doubt it. You're not wired for databases. Your ducts are probably contaminated. Your paint is full of lead, and your floor tiles are asbestos. You're going to be my parking lot."

"Probably so," Lindeman said. Hadn't Archie become his parking lot? But before that, Archie had helped Lindeman learn who he was and what he could do for his people. Lindeman might be able to do that for Stack.

But there was no time. The crane came.

Lindeman watched as the men set up the ball. He looked away toward the shimmering lake when the crane's motor started. He waited for the impact, but it didn't come.

Lindeman heard women singing. He looked down onto Taft. There was a line of women in front of the crane.

"Who are they?" the new courthouse asked.

"Friends," Lindeman said.

The crane waited, its tall skeleton casting a shadow on Taft.

The women marched and sang. Some were old. Some had marched when Lindeman was young, when Archie still cared for the lists of their children. Some had sons or fathers whose names were on the stones in his yard by the cannon. They covered Lindeman's steps with flowers.

Night and day, the women stayed with him. Others joined them. Whole families of black men and women filled his halls, his steps, and his yard.

"Who are *they*?" Stack asked.

"More friends," Lindeman said.

The crane went away.

"How'd you get so many friends?" the young building asked.

"I'm old," Lindeman said.

Workmen came.

The Friends of Lindeman let the workmen past.

The workmen sealed Lindeman in plastic and wore masks and suits that covered their skin like they were afraid to touch him. They tore at his ceilings and walls. They ripped at his wood.

Lindeman shook in fear. His pigeons fled.

Then, one day, the plastic was gone. The masks were gone. The Friends of Lindeman arrived with paint, new wood, and tile. They fixed, finished, and polished. They brought back his furniture. They brought back his paintings.

Finally, they draped his freshly sand-blasted granite in red, white, and blue banners. A red ribbon once more stretched between the pillars in front of his walnut doors.

Lindeman looked out on the intersection of Ash and Taft where the tree streets meet with the president street that had once been the last. A crowd of people danced and sang to old-time marches played by a brass band.

A woman in a white summer dress addressed the crowd.

A horse and carriage rolled up next to an old motorcar. The polished chrome on both flashed in the sun. An old black man in a black suit put a brass plaque on Lindeman's great walnut doors. The man turned to the crowd. A tear rolled down his cheek.

In spite of his fuller face and gray hair, Lindeman recognized him as the man who had cried in his basement.

The old man said, "My great grandmother hid from slavery in the cellars of the old, old courthouse. I found her journals in the basement of this building. My father was a judge here. I was married here. The lives of my family and all the families of this county have revolved around this building for a hundred years. So, it gives me great personal pleasure to open the Lindeman National Historical Courthouse and Museum. May it stand through the next millennium as a reminder to the people of Ohio and this great Nation. We must never forget who we are."

Together, the man and women cut the red ribbon and opened Lindeman's doors.

"They saved you," the new courthouse said. "Why?"

"I never let them forget who they were," he answered.

"But you're old and—"

"And you're the future," Lindeman interrupted. "So was I, once. So was I."

The long afternoon passed into evening, and the people went home. Lindeman's pigeons were settling their heads under their wings when Stack spoke again. "Can you show me how to help them remember?" He twisted a little to keep a chill wind off Lindeman's granite walls.

"I can show you what I know," Lindeman said. He looked up from his skylights at the first stars in the clear Ohio sky and gave thanks to the powers of imagination, stone, and fire. Finally, he whispered, "Thank you, Archie."

Codependent Spectral Disorder

Originally printed in Shadow Spinners anthology and Short Story America, Vol. V.

My cell hissed. The firemen were coming. That's all I'd gotten from my son. My heart grew colder under layers of sonic snow, each layer made of another second of hissing silence on my cell. Pinching the phone between my shoulder and ear, I plucked another HO model train wheel-and-axle set from the loose pile on my vinyl work mat. The snowstorm hiss assaulted my ear while I examined the wheels and set them into the plastic sorting tray compartment I had hand lettered, *HO. Wheel. RP25. Freight. 33 scale inches. Metal. Flat black. Blunt axle pin.* While my hands moved, my mind worked the puzzle of talking to my son.

"*Use his full name,*" our family therapist, "*Cassandra Victoria Fanterri, Ph.D. Please, Call me Cassie,*" had said.

"*His name can cut through the fog of his sensory overload,*" Cassie had said.

"*Be firm, not angry. That means level tone and relaxed facial muscles.*"

Except, I didn't need to worry about the face thing because I was on the phone.

I picked up another set of wheels and took a deep breath. "Randall Phillip Crawly. Was anyone hurt?"

I hoped my stern use of his full name would shift his focus—jump whatever mental train he had going onto a new track.

I needed him on my track. I didn't have time for his spectrum problems. Not now. Once emergency services arrived, Randy would overload like an antique Rivarossi headlight on DCC rails. He'd get bright for a second, then he'd go dark.

I located the wheels' compartment in the tray—*HO Wheel. RP25. Freight. 33 scale inches. Metal. Flat black. Pointed axle pin.* I had a Bettendorf truck frame it would fit.

If he would just tell me what had happened, I'd know what to do next. If he would give his mother the phone-

I picked up another wheelset.

HO. Wheel. RP25. Freight. 33 scale inches. Silver. Pointed axle pin.

I wanted to scream a dozen questions into my cell. I wanted to know about Alma, Randy's mother, but I held my tongue. Before Cassi had insulted Alma and given up on us, she had taught me that if my son were going to come around to what *I* needed, *I* had to wait. Speaking again would only give him an excuse to retreat, to get back on his track and lose any progress that following the therapist's suggestion had given me.

Somewhere, wires crossed or microwaves tangled. Faint voices held ghostly conversations just beyond my ability to understand. I sorted wheels and waited for my son to answer.

A woman laughed. Even ghosts laugh. In her distant voice, I heard flirt and hope. Guiltily, I wished she were my wife—that I was talking to her. Alma's voice had lost that tone long ago.

Waiting for Randy to speak was a war. The winner would be the one who held his tongue longest.

My neck cramped. I shifted the phone to my other ear and held it with my shoulder.

HO. Wheel. RP25. Freight. 33 scale inches. Brass. Pointed axle pin.

If Alma were hurt, every second mattered, but any words I uttered could add countless minutes to the phone call. I didn't dare heap disaster on disaster. I couldn't, not any more than I could drop my "HO. Wheel. RP25. Freight. 33 scale inches. Black plastic. Pointed axle pin." into the tray for "HO. Wheel. RP25. Freight. 33 scale inches. Metal. Flat black. Pointed axle pin."

If I did made things worse and she died, who would raise Randy?

The waiting and the ghosts had almost beaten me down. I nearly dropped a 36 scale inches wheel in a 33 scale inches compartment. I was drawing breath to try and break Randy's silence again when I smelled oil. While I scanned my workbench for an open, pinky-sized squeeze tube of light, non-conductive axle oil, Randy spoke.

"She was telling me about the ferret she had when she was a kid his name was Loki and he was a rescue from the pet shop in the strip mall down the street nobody wanted him because he was crazy and his name means crazy like a tricky god from the Norse Pole."

New track. Wrong track. I had won the wrong war.

The ghost woman giggled. For just a moment, I understood her words. "I like that," she said.

I couldn't find the open oil. It should be easy. I always put it in the brass pen tray in the upper right quadrant of my workbench. Always! Even if I'd forgotten, the tube was striped like a barber pole in caution orange and fluorescent green. I should have been able to see it instantly.

"RANDALL!" It just burst out of me. I couldn't stop it, and I couldn't get it back. Cold, cell-snow silence filled my ear. I decided I regretted my blurt.

I found the tube of oil, capped it, and dropped it in the pen tray.

I knew my son's atypical brain as well as anyone, except maybe Alma, and while my freezing heart pushed out another slow motion surge of blood, my burning imagination created horrible variations on disaster for Alma.

The Cassie-trained part of me chanted the mantra, *sympathy for poor Randy*. He couldn't help it. For just an instant, my imagined Alma-empty kitchen and silent vacuum cleaner gave way to an image of my son, his high forehead wrinkled in concentration, his eyes watering, his shoulders rolled forward like he was pushing his way into a blizzard to get the mail through to some remote town in the outback of some story world where Alma would reward his heroics with kind words, a warm hearth, and respect.

But it was Randy, and we don't live in a story world. Randy is what he is.

OO. Wheel. Hornby. Freight. Special 40 scale inches. Brass. Pre-war clip mount axle.

The silence was not as long this time.

He began his story again. When derailed, he always had to begin again. He never picked up where he left off like norm—like most people. "She was telling me about the ferret she had…"

I swallowed hard, wondering why my mouth wasn't dry like it was supposed to be, like all the people in the stories mouths were when they were scared. Instead of the emotions Cassie said were normal, anger, fear, and frustration, turning my mouth dry or transforming the spit in my mouth to caustic bile, my mouth felt normal. In fact, once I started thinking about it, it felt better than it usually did—warm, wet, and ready to kiss poor Alma if she had been at home taking care of me like she promised instead of running Randy to the lessons she insisted he have.

The ghost woman spoke in a high, affected, dramatic voice. "I don't *think* so!"

HO. Wheel. RP25. Freight. 33 scale inches. Metal. Flat black. Pointed axle pin.

Ignoring the distant whispering and the cell's electronic hiss, I wondered how my mind could fill the cold silence with thoughts about how my mouth should be? It was a horrible, simple thought, and I wished terrible guilt would chase it away. I wanted to feel different, to feel how I should feel in a moment when lives are changing forever.

HO. Wheel. RP25. Freight. 33 scale inches. Metal. Flat black. Pointed axle pin.

Later, if something really bad had happened, those thoughts about my mouth and the flirting ghost would become recycled regrets intruding on quiet moments every day for the rest of my life. They would intrude unannounced and unwanted the same way Randy's name had leapt from my mouth at the worst possible moment.

Randy started again.

I forced myself to focus—forced myself to listen as if listening more carefully would provide more meaning than his repeated words carried.

"...Norse Pole they took it home and built it a giant cage that you could walk into so you could play with the ferret without it getting-"

HO. Wheel. RP25. Freight. 33 scale inches. Metal. Flat black. Pointed axle pin.

"-out and making things crazy in the house like its name but in a cage instead of everywhere."

Sometimes, I could finish pieces of the story Randy needed to tell. Sometimes, if I saw ahead a little ways and gave his brain a bridge from the now of the tale in his head to a new now, his brain would let him cross that bridge.

Sometimes.

I tried. "And they loved Loki, and Mom was driving while she told you the story. It was raining hard."

"Yeah. Uh-huh."

The ghost woman's background drone solidified. "Terrible weather, but I like that..." It trailed off into the background hiss.

Such a sweet voice, but she was talking to someone else. I should have bit my lip. I should have held my breath. I should have felt tears on my cheeks. I should have felt something instead of worrying about what I didn't feel and how it would bother me later.

HO. Wheel. RP25. Freight. 33 scale inches. Brass. Blunt axle pin.

I shouldn't have been thinking about what the ghost lady said or my breath or my lip. I knew what I shouldn't think, but I didn't know what I should think so I could look back on the moment with less guilt for all my non-Alma thoughts.

I decided to put the phone on speaker and prop it against a locomotive on the workbench, an Athearn AMD F3 in Great Northern livery. Then, I stretched my shoulder before I remembered to bite my lip. The bite hurt, but that's all. It didn't cause me to feel what I should have felt.

Randy said, "...and raining and the windshield wipers were going really fast but it was still raining so hard it was hard to see she asked me about school she said, 'How's school going, Randy?' and I said, 'Okay.' and she said, 'I'm glad. You know you can ask me for help anytime.'"

How could I not love a woman who demanded piano lessons for your spectrum disorder son then drove him to them and back during a tornado-spawning thunder-banger? How could I not feel love for a woman who, even in the storm, was still patient enough to offer Randy kindness that might move him out of his normal, deeply rutted patterns? How could anybody not feel love for a woman like that?

Cassie and her labels. If Alma was hurt, it was Cassie's fault.

HO. Wheel. Flat Flange. Freight. 33 scale inches. Metal. Flat black. Pointed axle pin.

The hissing phone crackled. Ghostly words came to my ear. "Love." Then, all the false coquettishness gone from her voice, the ghost laughed deep and hard. While her laughter faded into the static blizzard, I thought of Alma's hip next to mine the time we were car-trapped on a secondary road near the summit of the Sherman grade on the Union Pacific in a Wyoming blizzard.

Our first time happened that night—my first, ever. I was so grateful. I still don't know what she saw in me. I was almost thirty. No other woman had seen what she saw.

The trooper found us naked in the back seat, our parkas, blue jeans, and sweatshirts folded and stacked on the front seat. Standing in the storm peering in through the gapped window, he laughed at me.

I felt rage. I felt *that*. I started to yell at him.

Alma gripped my arm, nails cutting into my red rage. In my ear, she said, "I know how to take care of you. I will always take care of you."

It didn't make sense, but it grabbed my thoughts and made me look at her. Her dark eyes sparkled in the beam of the trooper's Mag Light. She smiled, looked him in the eye, and said, "We're warmer than you are." He stopped laughing. Still smiling, he said, "I guess you are."

HO. Wheel. RP25. Freight. 33 scale inches. Metal. Flat black. Pointed axle pin.

Randy kept talking. I missed some of his tale. He said, "She said, 'You know your Dad loves you,' and she said she did too."

"I'm almost out of minutes," the ghost said.

Randy went quiet. The phone hissed.

I wondered if he could hear the ghostly woman.

I could hear him breathing faster. He had to say something he didn't want to say. "She said, 'He's hard, you know—your Dad.'"

I know she had said it, tone and syllable-for-sad-syllable, exactly as he had. Randy's mind couldn't let him say it any other way.

HO. Wheel. RP25. Freight. 33 scale inches. Metal. Flat black. Pointed axle pin.

HO. Wheel. RP25. Freight. 33 scale inches. Silver. Blunt axle pin.

"'He's a little like you, Randy. He's hard. You have to know when to listen and when to talk.'"

In sessions, Cassie had said it to me over and over. "Listening is more than being quiet."

Now, I had to listen. I had to listen if I ever wanted a bowl of Alma's chowder on a cold winter day, if I ever wanted her hip next to mine, if I ever-

"'but you can't expect him to hear you, you know Randy? You have to know that.'"

Silence. Not even the ghost lady spoke. New layers of cell phone snow became heavier and heavier until I thought my heart would just stop.

"She said, 'There's a train coming, Randy.' And I said an EMD SD 70 Mac, and she said, 'You can tell from the sound?' and I said yeah."

A distant siren broke through the phone's filters for a second. Emergency vehicles were arriving. Noise. Flashing lights. I knew that soon Randy wouldn't be able to say anything, tell me anything.

HO. Wheel. RP25. Freight. 33 scale inches. Metal. Flat black. Pointed axle pin.

"People." Randy spoke the word like most people would say "spider" or "snake." He knew he was about to be hit by a wave that would drown out all his own thoughts. "People, Dad." It was a plea for help.

"They are going to help." I tried to sound confident.

He said, "It was really rainy really, really rainy she stopped telling me stuff she stopped the car she just stopped no Loki no piano. She said, 'No more enabling, Randy.' She made me get out in the rain she said, 'Your Dad loves his trains.'"

HO. Wheel. RP25. Freight. 33 scale inches. Metal. Flat black. Pointed axle pin.

HO. Wheel. RP25. Freight. 33 scale inches. Metal. Flat black. Pointed axle pin.

HO. Wheel. RP25. Freight. 33 scale inches. Metal. Flat black. Pointed axle pin.

"She drove BANG I'm cold it's wet and rainy."

"Where's Mom, Randy?" I asked.

"People."

"Where is she?"

"Dad?"

"I'm here."

"She was in the car."

"Now. Where is she now?"

"Listen. Listen, Dad. Can't you hear her? Listen."

The phone snow stopped. I held my breath, my hands in my lap, waiting for the ghost to speak.

Whispering Canyon

After four days of hiking the serpentine, dry streambed at the bottom of the Slick Rock Canyon system, certain things began to prick Connie's psyche. It was like the tiny, invisible cactus spines caught in her socks had spread to her whole body.

Towering red stone canyon walls framed the high sun between rims, and she hated the hot flint smell of dust on her tank top and backpack straps. She remembered a very similar dry, hot stench from her father's shop when he sharpened knives on his antique whetstone wheel. At least she could leave her father's workshop. Here, that hot smell would become a cold, damp root cellar and forgotten canned goods smell at night.

Tonight, she'd have to sleep next to Chuck again. At least it wasn't *with* Chuck. It was just near him.

He was a First Nations guy from her American Heritage class. A week ago, he'd been tall, brown, and seriously fit. His shimmery black ponytail had seemed exotic. She wanted to touch it—a lot. His stupid grin told her he wanted just as bad to touch her Irish skin and tight red curls.

It was kinda cool to have an exotic guy like that interested in her. Now? Not so much.

He said his real name was CHA'KWAINA. It meant "One who cries" in the old tongue; he said the old tongue was Anasazi.

Stupid, Connie. She had fallen for it.

And she ended up out here in this damn maze of canyons, dust, coyotes, and rattlesnakes, and he was gone someplace up ahead without her.

She tugged on a water bottle tethered to a D-ring on her back pack harness.

Empty. *Still empty.*

Rising rage froze her. If she had been in her car, she'd have screamed and pounded her steering wheel before she cussed out the other drivers. In the canyon, she didn't have a steering wheel to pound, so she just screamed, "Fuck you Chuck whatsit WYNE goddamn A!" she said.

Then, she remembered another of the things that pricked at her in the canyons—the damn echo.

Stand in the right place and a whispered word can bounce off a cliff wall then take off through the curves of alternating sheer cliffs and sloped amphitheaters until it poured out over the long surface of Lake Powell or came roaring back to pound on your ears.

"Shit," she whispered. "He had to have heard that."

"Everybody from here to Moab heard *that*."

Startled by the unexpected voice, she jumped backward, caught her heel on a small rock, lost her center to her backpack, and fell on her ass.

Chuck had been squatting in a small patch of shade between two dead, brown bushes.

"Asshole!" She was beyond caring what he thought of her. She flipped him off.

"Sorry, Connie," He stood. "Didn't mean to scare you." He reached out to help her up.

His damn *I was just part of the landscape* innocent sincerity poured gasoline on her anger. She ignored his hand and rolled off her ass to one side to center her pack on her back. She pulled her knees up under her and stood to face the dumb shit.

"Really, Connie. I thought you saw me."

"Bullshit," She said. "You blend in, and you know it."

"Hiking here isn't what you thought it would be, is it?"

"How far to the car?"

"Two days by canyon."

She shook her pack to settle it on her sweaty, dirty back, and she marched past him.

"One, if we go over the mesa," he offered.

She knew that. They had spread his maps out on a flat rock, and he had shown her where *her* car was, the car she had agreed to let his cousin move for them. They had come into the canyon system at the headwaters of Owl Creek, and his cousin had taken their car—her Subaru—to the headwaters of Ghost Canyon. The plan was to hike Owl Creek to Slick Rock, Slick Rock to Ghost, then up to the head of the canyon and the BLM road where the car waited. Alternatively, climbing the rough, ten foot strata tiers of a thousand-foot amphitheater to the mesa gave them a flatland, compass line to the car—assuming they could find a path up and through the last tier, the rim rock of the canyon.

She was seriously thinking about climbing, and that was an indication of just exactly how *"not like she had imagined"* this trip had turned out. She had imagined warm, late spring nights under starry skies with a camp fire and s'mores and her exotic First Nations conquest.

Head-down, she ignored him and continued her march along the twisting canyon bottom.

About a hundred yards later, she confronted another thing that really pricked at you when you'd been in the canyon for four days—a man with a gun.

He was tall and broad, and he wore desert camo shorts, military boots, and a floppy camo hat. She knew instantly that if he had wanted to hide, she wouldn't have seen him at all.

The gun was a big, black cop-type gun holstered on his belt. His tanned, whiteman's hand rode on it like it was her Subaru's armrest.

Silent, he stared at her.

She figured he wasn't expecting a skinny, white chick any more than she was expecting some prepper nut case.

Chuck caught up and murmured in his language, which she was pretty sure was not Anasazi. She didn't know what he said, but she knew it wasn't nice.

"Hey," she said to the prepper, and she waved. "Been in the canyon long?"

The way the man stared, she might have just stepped off a UFO wearing a thong.

Part of her watched the gun. Part of her watched his dark, not very kind eyes. In his not-on-the-gun hand, he held a folded map.

She flashed him her best Irish barmaid smile.

He nodded. "A while," he said. "You?"

"On our way out."

He stepped off the trail to make room. Chuck's grinding footfalls were close behind her.

"Local?" The man was looking over Connie's head. He was talking to Chuck.

Again, Chuck muttered in his language. Connie imagined the words meant, "You fucking white asshole."

The man answered in Chuck's language, and Connie froze. Chuck bumped into her from behind. Then, he froze, too.

The man chuckled. "No offense taken, Chief," he said in English, but a finger on his gun hand twitched, and Connie heard the Velcro strap over the handle of his pistol tear loose.

"Mapping ruins?" Chuck asked.

"Research," the man said.

"Which university?" Chuck asked.

"Personal. A book."

The testosterone pouring into the air between the two men was thick enough to ignite if Connie kicked a hot stone through it. She decided that being between these two assholes was not a good idea.

"Come on, Chuck." She half turned and grasped his hard forearm, a forearm she thought would have felt really good around her waist a couple days ago, and she tugged on him. They moved past the man with the cop gun and hide-in-the-bushes fatigues.

He said nothing, and they moved along the trail in silence. It took her half an hour to let go of her fear.

One of the things that pricks at you in the desert after you've been hiking for almost a week is how silence is better than talking until the silence has gone on long enough to remind you that pretty soon you'll have to talk to the guy you're sick of. She knew she was going to have to talk to Chuck about the guy with the gun, but she hoped another half hour of silence might make the man with the gun make sense.

It didn't. Finally, she stopped. She needed water. It pricked at her that Chuck's bottles still had water in them and she'd have to ask him to share, but she still asked. He gave. She drank. Between swallows, she said, "What was that all about?"

"Artifact hunter," Chuck said. "Grave robber."

"There's nothing out here."

"Pots. Bowls. Arrows. Anything he can sell."

She had seen the potsherds. They were everywhere. Three days ago, the first few she had seen made her gasp. They were 700 years old, minimum, and they had been made by the fingers of people who lived in the canyon. After a week of dirt, sunburn, fucking beef jerky, and awkward advances from a guy who smelled like flint and rotted sweatshirts, she was over the whole ancient ancestors shtick.

"Up there." He pointed.

She followed the line of his finger to a point high on a red stone cliff. A strata of almost yellow stone cut across the face then disappeared into a shadow. "What?"

"Anasazi ruins. In the shadow. On a rock shelf."

She couldn't see anything, but that didn't mean they weren't there. She had seen a few during their hike.

Chuck said, "Even a small piece of intact pottery's worth five or six hundred dollars. The right piece could make him thousands. Even arrowheads are worth enough that people come into the canyons to grab them." He spat something in his language, and she turned away.

"Great." she said. "Is that guy dangerous?"

"We should keep walking for a while." Chuck sounded tired. In fact, she thought it was the first time since they started that he had sounded tired. "We'll make Ghost," he said. "We shouldn't see him again."

~ ~ ~

That night, they didn't bother with the tent. A blue tarp on a bed of sand with a little trench around it to catch scorpions and other critters was good enough. They propped up the edges with twigs and stones so anything that got over the trench would go under the tarp instead of joining them on it.

Like clockwork people winding down, they cooked, ate, cleaned up. Chuck went looking for water, and Connie was sand-washing her camp pot when she heard people whispering. She couldn't quite make out their words, but they weren't far away.

She sat very still and listened for a few minutes, trying to get a bearing on them.

The thought she heard three people, two adults and a child. No, four. Two children. No. Maybe just one child—a girl. One of them, the mother, she thought, sounded upset.

A family with kids? Not likely at sunset in Ghost Canyon in the BLM land in Utah. *I don't think so.*

She ignored the urgency in the imagined mother's voice, and she went back to work.

Later, she and Chuck lay side-by-side. Connie stared at the turning stars overhead. The voices came again. For a while, she told herself they were breezes. They, she told herself the desert was affecting her—she was making them up. She ignored the insistent whispers. She even tried listening to Chuck's breathing, which became steady and deep. She was pretty sure he had gone to sleep.

"Hello?" she whispered to the voices. She knew it was irrational, but if she could hear them, maybe they could hear her.

"Talking to the ancestors?" Chuck asked.

She jumped a little. To his credit, he didn't laugh. She said, "I don't believe in ghosts."

"Ghosts." Now, he chuckled. "That's your people. My people don't have that word. Our word doesn't translate."

She tried to head off the *our people* lecture she heard coming. "Then don't try."

"Heart is as close as your language comes." He paused, and the whispering woman lectured her children.

Maybe, Connie thought, the family had met Camo-and-Gun Guy, too.

"No," Chuck said. "Heart's not enough. Maybe you would say, the heart of a person forever and now."

"Soul?" she asked.

"Not like Christians die and go to heaven soul. More like you are here now is the same as you are here forever."

She stared at the moon slowly crossing the star-speckled gap of deeper blackness between shadowed canyon walls. "That makes no sense."

"No. I suppose not," he admitted.

~ ~ ~

In the morning, they'd both had enough. They decided to climb out. Chuck picked one of the outside curves that had collapsed to make an amphitheater. From the bottom of the canyon, it looked like there was a good chance they could make it past the rim rock. The first two hours were too difficult to allow them to talk. They traversed the long curve of a stratum to find a break, then they scrambled up ten to twenty feet of scree before working along the higher contour to find a break in the next stratum. A few hundred feet below the canyon rim, they stopped to rest and drink.

"Another half hour," Chuck said, "and we're out. Less than an hour after that, we'll be in the car."

"Hotel," she said. "Hot water."

"Yeah," he agreed. "Pizza."

While sipping water, a too-straight line in the scrabble of rocks fifty yards away caught her eye. As the curve of the amphitheater continued away from them, it became steeper and steeper until it turned into the cliff walls of an outside curve. Before the cliff, at the steepest part that could still be called a slope, the straight line resolved into a squat, stone building.

"Is that a ruin?" She pointed.

Chuck looked and nodded. "Sentinal camp."

"What?"

"Sort of a guard tower. You can probably see up and down the canyon from there."

"Let's take a look."

"That's another hour before hot water."

"Seriously? It's not that far."

Chuck said, "Sentinel camps are never easy to get to."

She won the argument by dropping her pack and pulling out her camera, a fanny pack containing the first aid kit and protein bars, and a couple water bottles. She headed out, and he had to follow.

It pricked at her that he ended up being right. Just as Chuck had said, it was about a half-hour scramble, one-way. The little hut stood in a stratum niche that was hard to get to, but climbing up a couple layers then down then up again was totally worth the effort.

The little house had been meticulously constructed over 700 years ago. Every stone had been fitted to the one beneath it. No mortar held up the stable little house. It was a simple structure of four walls, three windows, and a door. It was like the people had just got up and walked away a few days ago. Even the grass thatch roof was still mostly intact. Connie crouched down and stuck her head in through the low door. The floor was made of powdery, dry dust.

She said, "If we needed to, we could camp in there."

"No." His voice was harder and more certain than she had ever heard it.

"The roof's almost intact," she said, "and it's not like it will rain this month. The floor's made of soft dust."

He squatted low beside her and reached into the little building. He lifted a stick from the dust of the floor by one wall. As soon as he held it up, she realized it was too straight to just be a stick.

"Sentinal hut," he said. "Arrow shafts." He trailed long fingers through the dust and came up with an assembled arrow. The ragged fletching was loose, and it was so short it was more of a long dart, but it was unmistakably ancient and handmade.

"That what Camo Guy with Gun was looking for?"

Chuck gently placed the arrow back in the dust and covered it over. "Ancestors live here."

"Yeah," Connie wanted to sound sarcastic, but her words came out as more of a whisper. "Hearts without bodies forever and now."

He nodded. "The whispers came from here." He swept a hand out over the canyon below.

She understood. The three little windows let a person see all of the undulations of the canyon for miles. For the first time since they had entered the canyon, she felt the homeness of the place. It wasn't her homeness. It was homeness for *them*—the people who had lived here, here where water occasionally came and where small crops of corn could be grown in the spilled out sands of the amphitheaters in the bottom of the canyon.

"These people were afraid," she said.

"And smart." He moved past the little house toward the steep edge where the amphitheater became a sheer cliff face.

There, a solid stone path continued on, a path cut into the wall of the cliff along a stratum of softer, more yellowish stone. The trail and stratum made for a little half tunnel like an ant farm trail up against glass, but the glass here was open air over a seven-hundred-foot drop to the valley floor.

A ways along the tunnel were two square windows made of mud and stone.

Beyond, the tunnel opened up onto a large ledge. Several stone buildings ran along the inside of the ledge. From above, below, or farther from their vantage point, the buildings would have been completely invisible.

"You couldn't see them from below," she said.

Chuck said, "That's the idea."

He got down on his hands and knees and tested the ledge. "Too narrow," he said. "I don't think I can get through the mantraps."

"Mantraps?"

"The little windows. To get to the dwellings, you have to climb headfirst through those windows. A child sitting on the other side with a stone or a stick could smack you and roll your body off the cliff before you could do anything about it."

Connie suddenly wanted to cross to those buildings, to feel the place that had once been home to children who played on cliffs. She pushed forward. "Let me." They traded places. She crouched and tested the stone path. She was pretty sure she could crawl across to the little homes on the cliff, but the mantraps were small, very small—and very high.

"I can make it," she said, "but not with my stuff." She stashed her fanny pack, camera, and water.

"I don't think you–," Chuck began.

"You found an arrow. You said it was worth a lot. What if there's more stuff over there?"

"Then it stays over there," he said.

"I'm going." She crawled along the narrow ledge on all fours. At the mantrap, she had to push her arms through and twist a little sideways to get her head and shoulders in. For a moment, she had to look down the sheer face of the cliff. She froze and closed her eyes to fight off vertigo. The canyon breeze whispered to her. She took a deep breath and tried to hear the voices in the breeze—tried to understand what they were saying to her. Then, the voices were gone. When she opened her eyes, she was sure she could make it.

At the second man trap, she paused. If she got through, it was only ten feet to the ledge and buildings. She peered through the frame like a window, and a six- or seven-year-old girl peered back.

Surprised, Connie said, "Hello?"

The girl grinned and held up a stick with a stone bound to the end.

Connie imagined herself, arms out in front of her, shoulders twisted, trying to get through the window when that stone came down on her head.

She stayed very still, her eyes on the sparkling brown eyes of the child. Over the little girl's shoulder, she saw several women sitting in a row, rocking, pushing grinding stones back and forth over concave metates. Farther along the shelf, a couple solemn men pressed a flat stone against the wall of the canyon and patted mud around its edges.

Connie blinked hard. She shook tears from her eyes. When her vision cleared, the people were gone. She blinked again. The little girl had been as real as Chuck or her, but that was impossible. She told herself the vision had been caused by adrenaline, dehydration, and lack of sleep. She told herself that she was in no condition to be taking the risk she was taking. She should go back.

Instead, she pressed through the opening and made her way onto the ledge.

A half hour later, Chuck stood beside her, paler than usual and sweating. "The ancestors don't like us messing with their places."

"We're just looking," she said, but she felt people watching her. This was more than just whispers. A lot of people were watching her.

She looked around, expecting to see the little girl and her family, but she found only the ledge, the dust, the breeze, and the empty buildings.

Still, she felt like she was walking down the aisle at her first communion. She was small, really tiny, and she had to walk carefully and make no noise so God wouldn't get pissed off.

Chuck asked, "Where's your camera?"

"It didn't fit through the mantrap."

"The fanny pack," he said, "and water?"

"Nope."

"Yeah," he said, "They didn't let us bring anything from our world."

The wind in the canyon sang. The dust of the shelf danced around their feet. Where Connie had seen the women, they found three grain grinding stations, each with a concave metate stone set into the dirt. The curved grinding stones, manos, sat motionless on top. The three women might have stood up and walked away only a few seconds ago.

The buildings were empty, and a granary set into the cliff at the end of the shelf held only tiny, ancient corn cobs long ago stripped of their grain.

Connie remembered the men and their stone. She looked for the place they had been working, and the stone was there, white against the yellowish background stone. It leaned against the wall, caked mud around the edges holding it in place. She looked closely at the mud. It still held ancient fingerprints. "Look at this."

"Touch them. Right there," Chuck said. "If you touch what they touched, that's where flesh can meet the spirit that is always here."

She pressed her finger into a fingerprint.

The grinning girl was there, her hand under Connie's. She smiled for Connie and winked. Then, the little girl pulled on the stone. As if the stone were alive, it popped away from the canyon wall. Behind it, a dark opening the size of the man traps appeared.

"Wall kiva," Chuck said.

Connie stuck her head in. Just enough light filtered in to show a circular, stone room. A man as old as the canyon sat facing her. He held up a plate, offering her some of the corn paste on it. She reached, and he was gone, but the plate was there next to the stone on which he'd been sitting.

She pulled back, twisted, and fell back to sit in the dust.

"You okay?" Chuck asked.

She shook her head. "I think I'm really dehydrated."

"You don't look real good."

"There's a plate in there," she said. "An intact pottery plate."

He bent and poked his head into the hole. When he pulled back, he was grinning.

"What?" she asked.

"Did he offer you maize paste?" he asked.

She wrapped her arms around herself to fend off a chill that had nothing to do with the breeze. After a few deep breaths, she gave him a slight nod. "How did you know?"

"He offered it to me, too."

"The plate?"

"Pinch pot type. The oldest."

"Worth a lot?"

"Half a house."

"Should we take it to somebody?"

"Sell it?"

"No." It hit her then that even five minutes ago, she might have meant selling it. A day ago, she certainly would have meant selling it, but here, in the singing breeze, with the face of the child still fresh in her mind, she meant take it to a museum or to his people or to… she didn't know who, but she knew it was important.

"They didn't let us bring the camera," he said.

"Yeah," she said. It was an agreement to take nothing.

Together, they carefully replaced the stone. The edges of the broken mud seal fit together perfectly, almost as if they had never been separated. Job done, they sighed together.

Chuck whispered. "Forever spirits. We should go, now."

She nodded, and they stood to leave, to crawl back through the mantraps.

Connie saw him first. She grabbed Chuck's arm and whispered, "Shit."

Camo-and-Gun Guy was through the first mantrap and almost to the second.

The man looked up. His eyes locked with Connie's, and she took a step back. Her heel landed on something hard in the dust, and she stumbled. Chuck caught her in his lean arms, lifted her, and set her back on her feet.

At her feet, turned up from the dust by her stumble, she found the little girl's stick bound to a stone. For just a moment, she saw herself picking it up and hurrying out to the mantrap before Camo got through. Then, sunlight hit the gun at his side.

"No place to run," she whispered. "Gun."

"What do you want?" Chuck called.

"Find something?" The man pushed his arms through the second man trap and started twisting his shoulders.

"Nothing worth a damn," Chuck lied.

Connie stooped and scooped up the child's club. She started toward the ledge.

"Leave your gun there," Chuck called.

The man laughed and pushed harder at the little window. His head popped through.

"You can't bring your stuff here," Chuck said. "Leave it behind!"

"I figured you'd show off for your girlfriend," Camo said. "Followed you. I appreciate your—"

His head jerked up. His eyes went wide—whites surrounding pale blue irises. Then, as violently as it had jerked upward, it slammed down into the stone. A moment later, his whole body twisted away from the cliff and fell.

He didn't scream. He didn't even grunt. He was just gone.

The wind sang. The ancestors whispered. Connie thought she heard a mother sigh and a child laugh.

Gently, silently, and with awe in her heart, Connie returned the child's club to the dust.

By the time she and Chuck managed to get to the body, the sun was down behind the canyon rim. Camo-and-Gun Guy had become part of the whispering canyon forever, though his flesh would soon be gone.

They laid out their tarp and zipped their sleeping bags together. Connie and Chuck held each other through the night. The whispers were kind and quiet and full of love for them.

In the morning, they decided to walk the rest of the canyon. Another day wouldn't make any difference to Camo Guy's corpse, and another day wasn't nearly enough time for them to walk together among the whispers of the canyon.

The Wrong Medium

The sculpting had gone well. Barnes stepped back from the worktable and wiped wet clay on his canvas apron. His creative fever cooled. The world around him returned from the hazy melt of all things outside the intensity of his obsessive fit of concentration.

He didn't know how long he'd been working. He was exhausted. His first awareness of the loud tock of the grandfather clock turned his head. The ornate old clock and its massive brass pendulum guarded the studio door and reminded him of all things regulated, timed, and measured. Its tock brought back to mind all things outside his sublime attempts to bring clay to life.

The dusty door to the studio opened. A brittle, Montana winter breeze swept gray dust across the concrete floor. "Close the door!" he snapped.

Erin flipped the door closed behind her. She smoothed long, straight red hair back over her shoulders, stripped off her long, chic leather coat, and laid it over the padding protruding from the faded blue-floral fabric of the rounded arm of his Goodwill sofa.

In the worn sanctum of his studio, her strapless, black dress, strand of pearls, and heels, looked all wrong. She was like a field hand who had clomped up to the altar of a cathedral wearing dung-covered boots.

Eyes the same pale shade as the sofa flowers peered at him, then they shifted focus to the table then back to him. She pressed her full, painted lips together and let the corners of her mouth droop. "We're late for your showing," she said.

"I did it," he said. "I finished it."

"Only children believe clay can come to life."

"And gods." He knew his excitement had gotten the better of his restraint.

"Is that it?" She gestured toward his creation.

He turned to the workbench. What had been a delicate tracery of dynamically opposed forms, what had been months in the dreaming and perhaps an entire day in execution, had collapsed into a mass of gray sludge. What had moments before been the glory of his highest achievement might now have been the patty cake and rolled worm creation of a child.

"I had it!" he said. "Dammit, Erin, I had it! It was life. It was everything people hope and dream for, it was sadness and joy and power and submission. It was-"

"Be realistic, honey. You're neither child nor god."

"I'm both. I'm an artist," he said. He stared at the mess on the table. It had been so right a moment ago. Now it was nothing. Less than nothing. She couldn't understand the pain of loss he felt. She was only a model. Her gift was to create desire. The desire to buy. The desire to have and hold. Sometimes she created lust, but that was her greatest achievement.

He had given his life to deeper needs, to the dream of living clay. One day, he would get the mix right, move his hands just so, capture the perfect and subtle feelings he held and nurtured.

"Barnes," she said.

He turned. The dry clay on his hands felt tight. He rolled his fingers into fists, and tiny flakes of gray peeled away and drifted to the concrete floor.

She tilted her head. A shining curtain of red hair spilled forward over her bare shoulder. She put on a slight pout. "Please, can't we go? Remónde has spent days preparing the Gallery. New York critics have flown out for it."

Another man might have melted under her pleading gaze. Many men had whimpered and bitten their thumbs when she cocked her hip and tilted her head.

Barnes was immune after living with her for two years. "I can see it. I can feel the life of it. I *can* put that feeling into the clay." He wiped his hands on a shop rag and tossed it past the stained molding table into a 55-gallon drum by the grandfather clock.

She stood up straight and glared at him. "We need the money, Barnes. Our wedding won't be cheap."

"Your wedding." He pulled at the clay.

"We're supposed to be at the gallery now," she said. "There'll be architects. They need status art for their buildings. There'll be gallery owners who want your name to bring customers to their showrooms."

"Not one of them knows what creation is like. Who will be there who has put their hands to stone, or clay, or wood? Which of them has burned themselves pouring brass? Not one of them can see past their bottom line or the hypnotic eye of a computer screen."

"But they can pay for the time you need to bring that clay to life."

He heard the manipulation, the insincerity in her attempt to move him. "I'm close," he said. "I had it for a moment. I'm going to try again. You go. They end up talking to you anyway."

"You have to go."

He looked up from the collapsed mass of clay on the table. Her arms were crossed over her slight breasts. She had replaced her pout with a mother's demanding stance. He laughed.

Erin's face turned red. "Don't you laugh at me. Laugh at your customers. Laugh at your buyers. Laugh at the people on the street, but don't you ever laugh at me!"

He laid his hands on the formless mound of clay. "I can do it, Erin. I can see what it looks like. It's like the bones of time. It's like-"

"You can't laugh at me and expect me to stay in this house. I'll leave you, and then what will you have? Memories of past achievements? Your clay? A few chunks of busted marble? No," she said. She stabbed a long finger in the air. "You'll have a vision of life, but you won't have the courage to walk out that door and live."

He kneaded the clay to loosen it for working. "You're done with me anyway, Erin. You might as well move on. I was fun for a while. You liked being with *Barnes*. You looked good on my arm. People paid attention to the woman with Barnes, but I'll never be more than that to you. Your heart is made of stone."

"Oh, Honey," her voice was soft and her footsteps were quiet as she crossed the workshop toward him. "Oh, Honey," she said again. "I'm sorry. I didn't know you were in a mood. I thought you wanted to go-"

"Just leave, Erin. I need to be alone. I need to put the vision into my hands." He pounded a fist into clay and began to worry a shape outward from the lump.

"You don't mean that," she said. From behind, she pressed against him and slipped a warm hand around his hip.

He spun on her, capturing her probing hands in his. He squeezed until her eyes opened wide in alarm. "I *do* mean it, Erin. Leave. I'm tired of the game with you. It's all a game. You. The galleries. The architects. The interviews. It's a money game. You don't have a clue what I'm trying to create."

She pulled away, her perfect face set like marble. "I know you think you're a god. You think you can breathe life into clay. There's only one way to make life, Barnes, and you'll never get it. You'll never be human, and you'll never be the god you think you are."

"Get out," he said. "When you come back, bring a truck for your stuff." He turned back to the clay.

She pounded on his back. Her tiny blows felt good, like hands kneading clay muscles, loosening knots and lumps long tense from concentrated effort over unresponsive clay. "You bastard," she cried. "You son of a bitch," she whispered.

He barely heard her. The clay was at his fingers. The pounding receded into the distance. The sound of the grandfather clock disappeared. The vision came on him and his fingers brought the vision into the world.

~ ~ ~

The grandfather clock chimed six. Barnes's artistic fit ended, the sublime vision spent. A vague memory of Erin's anger flitted through his head like the ghost of a drawing beneath a watercolor painting. Fatigue crept up from his cramped feet into his thighs and back and every muscle and joint.

Barnes staggered back.

The clay held form.

It was perfect. It was his vision. It felt right. It looked right. It was the thing that drove him, that haunted him. Four feet tall, it was a fluid, twisting mass of tendrils and petals surrounding angles and spars. It reached away from itself, and it never turned back on itself. A line moving outward always drew the eye back to the base. It radiated ancient, impossible, primal rightness.

He nodded and turned away from the work.

Erin lay sprawled on the old sofa. She was beautiful. Her long, red hair lay over her pale arm, and her legs stretched out gracefully from beneath a patchwork quilt.

He was glad she hadn't left. He wanted to show her the... He needed a name. In all the time he had struggled with the image of the thing, he had never considered a name for it.

She stirred. Feathery red lashes rose and pale blue eyes looked up at him.

"Hello, Love," he said. "I did it."

She lifted herself on one arm. Her eyes focused beyond him. "You did," she said. Her voice was empty of pretense. She saw and spoke the fact. "You really did." She sat up. The quilt fell away. She stood and smoothed the wrinkles from her little black dress.

"Maybe I just needed the right level of frustration, or maybe exhaustion," he said. "I'm sorry about the things I said last night. I didn't mean them. I was… Well, you know. I was working."

She nodded, eyes still staring beyond him. "It's unbelievable."

Pride filled him. His work had never evoked such sincere surprise from her before. His work had stripped her of all her practiced poses. She stood before him as a woman instead of a self-conscious image. Exhausted as he was, he wanted her. He wanted to draw her, to sculpt her, to put his hands on her and know the curves of her more completely than he ever had.

He reached clay-encrusted hands for her.

She batted his hands away and stepped toward the sculpture. "What's its name?" she asked.

Confused, he let his hands fall to his sides. He turned as she passed. Her eyes were fixed on the thing. Her breathing was deep and fast.

"Birth from Bones," he said. It came to him. It was just there on his tongue. It was right. It came just like the form itself had come to his fingers during the artistic fugue of the night.

She reached to touch.

"No!" he grabbed for her.

She paused, turned her head, but her eyes never left the clay. Her hand hovered near it. "It pulls at me," she said. "I need to touch it. I need to feel it."

As surely as he knew it was finished, he knew he couldn't let her touch it. He put his hands on her shoulders and pulled her gently back.

"Leave me alone," she said. She shook him away and reached. She caressed.

"I don't think-"

The sculpture moved. One twisting tendril wrapped around her wrist. "Oh," she said. Then she smiled and sighed with pleasure.

"Erin, let it go."

She placed her other hand on the piece. Another tendril wrapped itself around her wrist. "Oh god," she said.

"Jesus," Barnes said. For a moment, he hesitated. It was a hallucination. He was still asleep. Several more twisting lines wrapped around her hands. Petals of clay spread outward and enfolded her forearms. Erin gasped and shook and moved closer to the thing.

Barnes looked around the studio for something, anything. The grandfather clock struck the quarter hour. He ran to it, flipped open the front, and wrenched the heavy, brass pendulum free.

He turned. The thing was alive, growing, climbing slowly up Erin's arms, embracing her, reaching for her heart. Her eyes were closed, her lips slightly parted. Tendrils of clay wrapped themselves around her waist, and she pressed her belly toward the thing.

"No!" Barnes screamed. He brought the pendulum down as hard as he could. The thing collapsed under his blow. He struck again. The worktable shattered. The clay died. It became yet another patty cake and rolled worm mess.

He dropped the pendulum. It clattered on the concrete floor.

Erin swayed and fell. He caught her and tore the remaining tendrils of wet clay from her arms.

She was unconscious. He carried her to the sofa. He sat and held her. He caressed her temples and smoothed her hair. He whispered his love to her. He listened to her breathing and told himself she was fine.

Her eyes opened. She smiled.

"Erin?"

"It was so beautiful," she said. "You did do it. It was perfect."

"No, Erin. It wasn't. It needed you. You're perfect."

"It made me want to touch it, to feel it more deeply than anything I've ever felt." She tried to sit up.

Gently, he held her down. "Be still, Love. Be still."

She relaxed. "Can I touch it again?"

"I killed it."

Tears filled her eyes. "It wanted me to help it be alive."

"I know," he said. "It wanted me to help it be alive, too."

"Can you do it again?"

He brushed her tears from her cheek. "Yes," he said. "But I was working in the wrong medium. I'll need your help to do it right."

She smiled. Her arms snaked up and around his neck. He buried his face in her hair, and they laughed and cried together on the faded sofa.

Mirages

Originally printed online in proofs for Polyphony 7 and by The Writer Magazine.

The desert is never empty. At the worst, it's full of death.

That's a hell of a thought. He wondered at the offering of his failing mind.

Dancing mirages flickered in and out of sight on the horizon. He searched for solid objects like rocks or dunes or even the occasional dead bush—something on which to hang his hope.

If he could make it to that stone, he might live.

If he could touch that dune crest, he might see another soul.

Maybe that scraggly, dead bush meant water.

The rhythm of his trudging matched the slowing of his heart.

What kind of thought was that, that would keep a man's mind dark and occupied under the sun, under the relentless onslaught of dehydration and the slow, sweating loss of life through his pores.

Pausing in his trudging only added to the desert's fullness.

Pausing only plopped one more drop of life into the bucket of sand.

The mirages, though—they appeared and disappeared. They flickered into and out of and into existence again. Sometimes they revealed the object of his hope. Sometimes they swallowed it; and when he had dragged his feet through enough sand, they dispersed and left only sand behind as if they were real water and had somehow, in the course of a few minutes or hours, eroded away whatever hope he had chosen to pin his life on.

In those moments of despair, he still understood that to pause was to die. Even still living, he could be counted as fill in the vast bucket of death, so he chose a new hope and moved on.

Minutes, hours, life, death—time and sun made him start to wonder if he would know the difference between one and the other.

When a man dies, does he know it? Can he know it?

What kind of thoughts were those?

He thought he had heard that a man's feet became cold when he died—first the feet, then the fingers, then the calves and forearms.

His feet were cold. Cold feet, but he knew they couldn't be cold. The sand had to be near a hundred degrees, perhaps more. He'd seen a lizard two days back, when he was still fresh, still certain of his direction. It had balanced on two legs: front left and rear right. It had quickly shifted to front right and rear left. Like a man juggling a hot egg, it juggled itself over the sand.

Another mirage covered the sand ahead. Beyond, a single tree, dead as any bush or stone, pushed up through the wavering, silvery ripples.

He blinked. The tree resolved into two objects: a dead tree and the dark form of a tall man standing next to the tree.

A man. Another human being. A companion. A savior. At the very least, someone to talk to.

He would have laughed if his lips hadn't been so dried and blistered and cracked that they were fused closed in a grimace of determination he hoped would not become permanent—not be his death mask.

Cold feet, a dead tree, and a living man. People saw dead relatives when they died. He was dying. Perhaps he was dead.

He looked down.

The silvery, liquid flow of the mirage crossed the sand and wrapped itself around his ankles.

His feet moved of their own will. He felt no attachment to them at all.

With each push, each lift and slide over the sand, the mirage splashed. Ripples and droplets rose and danced and fell back into the silvery shimmer.

Now, he chuckled. His lips cracked. His own blood wet the tip of his tongue.

The desert played with him.

It cooked his brain in his skull.

Like a child, he pushed on through the illusion, through the puddle, across the shallow lake toward the dead tree and impossible man. He even allowed himself the foolish luxury of kicking at the water, of playing along and taking pleasure in the ripples and splashes, even though he knew, or at least part of him believed, the game would only hasten the filling of the desert with another grain of death.

The cold illusion rose up his calves, and he believed he was dying. He wondered if he were lying down, if he were lying down and staring at the sun through lidless eyes now blind. If he were, his brain, his cooked and beleaguered mind, played this game to give him some relief in the moments of passing. For that, he was grateful, though he resented the fact that illusion filled his last minutes.

The cold had risen to his waist when he found himself staring at the feet of a man. The man seemed to fly, to hover a few feet above the sand.

The mirage still held him, cold up to the waist, but it ended abruptly against a shore of sand mere inches away. He reached out and grasped hot sand beneath the booted, flying feet. It sifted and poured through his fingers and into the watery illusion where it created clouds of chocolate that drifted around his waist.

He looked up.

The man stood on air above the sand. Boots, black and scuffed and scalded, twisted slowly in a breeze so gentle that he couldn't feel it.

He stepped forward, but his feet met resistance, a wall, the end of movement.

So, he thought, flying men and feet that think they are underwater. This is my end.

The sun, merciless as ever, unblinking, poured heat and burning rays down into the bucket of death.

He reached up and touched the boots.

His hands believed the boots were real.

He touched the mirage, and his hands believed the water was real.

If he were dying, he decided, he might as well enjoy what little comfort the illusions of death brought him. He cupped his hands and splashed mirage on his face.

Cold. Cold and hot at the same time. His cracked and blistered lips burned as if the water were real, as if they were touched by cold, clear spring water.

He licked his lips, and the illusion was complete. His swollen tongue felt the water, believed in the water.

Perhaps, he thought, that's all anything is. Perhaps if he believed in the water the way he believed in stones and bushes and dunes…

Perhaps.

He closed his eyes. He let his feet feel wet. He let his legs feel cool. He let his hands dangle in the pool he imagined himself in. He knelt and immersed his head, and for the first time in three days, he was cool. The sun was no longer an enemy. The desert was less full.

He dared to open his eyes, and the cold continued, caressed, and healed.

He laughed at himself, and his mouth filled with water. He coughed, sputtered, stood back into hot air and scalding sun. Spitting and retching, he emptied bile into the mirage, and the bile floated on the surface, orange and green on silver and blue.

Water. Belief. He believed in the water, and it was real. Not a mirage.

A desert spring.

Or perhaps it was death, and in death water came to a man in the desert.

He immersed himself again. This time, he sipped. Slowly. Only a little.

And again.

And again.

And finally, he moved along the wall of sand. Along and away from the flying man until he stood once more on smooth, dry sand.

His pants, what was left of them, dripped water onto the sand. Where the water touched, the sand swallowed and the sun created short-lived puffs of steam.

He dripped, and he marveled at how quickly the sand dried, at how quickly the little droplets died.

Finally, he looked back to the tree, to the flying man, to the spring that might be a mirage or death.

He walked the edge of sand and silvery water until he stood beneath the dangling man, a man hung by the neck, a man much like himself.

The man was dead, not flying—hung from a dead tree by his own belt.

So much work to hang yourself in the hot sun, he thought. The water was so near.

The boots turned slowly.

He sat in the shade made by the hanged man and sipped from the spring in which he now believed.

Forgotten Lore

Second Place Prize, Short Story America Festival Award, 2013. Printed in Short Story America, Vol IV.

The windows of his drafty room rattle. The gales have come, and the winter storms break full against the cold sands and basalt walls of the Oregon coast.

The long night comes to every man, and Ash believed his life no different than the life of any other man. Storms had raged through his life, as storms rage through every life. His were not hurricanes spawning a thousand tiny tornados, though they seemed so to him at the time.

Of course, every man's storms must be weathered, and all storms seem to the man battling them to be the worst ever spawned by the gods; but even so, when the weather is calm, most men know deep down that worse storms hide in the clouds of the lives of other men.

Ash, like most writers, knew this. He had spent a lifetime of days and nights imagining lives filled with terrible storms to place on the page.

In his bed he persists, even in the tempest of the darkness of his last nights, in spinning yarns about himself, about his own importance in a world that long ago gave up the written word in favor of flickering lights and promises of bigger, better, happier, and newer.

He imagines that somewhere a child hides beneath wool blankets, safe from storms blowing and howling beyond stretching, rattling window panes. He imagines the child inhales the scent of yellowed, brittle pages and explores worlds penned in manuscript before the child was born.

He imagines this, and his own feeble hands grasp the satin edge of his blanket and pull it upward to his bristled chin. Then, with determined effort, he pulls it again until it comes upward to cover his face.

The remembered security of darkness is still there beneath the blanket.

For a moment, he thinks he will let the silent darkness take him now. After all, he is seventy years away from his childhood, and his flashlight rests on bookshelves beside dusty volumes—friends and teachers long ignored or forgotten by the children of the new world: Winston Smith, Guy Montag, and Bernard Marx.

Youthful vision has given way to eyes that no longer resolve the black letters on yellowed pages. His fingers, locked in permanent hooks by swollen, bulbous knuckles, no longer obey his mind. He can neither tap at keys to type nor curl thumb and fingers around a pen to scratch away at yellow pads.

Submitting to the darkness will protect him, leave his dream to live forever in the imagined silence, light, and safety of the child who reads.

Imagined.

Tapping filters through the wool battlements he has drawn around himself.

Tapping.

Poetry breaks into his fantasy of oblivion.

Take thy beak from out my heart and take thy form from off my door.

Tapping.

…as if someone gently rapping…

He pulls his blanket down to his nose and inhales his own ancient smell. He pulls the blanket down farther and breathes in cooler, cleaner pre-dawn air. For a moment, he wonders how long it has been since he slept through a sunrise, since dreams came to him and gave him reason to sleep beyond the coming of light.

Then, the tapping again.

He turns his head and finds a friend—not a raven bringing more darkness. This friend is an old gull, a bird who has come to him for food every day for…

He has forgotten when he first befriended the bird, first tossed bread into the air and saw it swoop down to neatly snag the morsel in beak at the moment when gravity and momentum fought one another to a standoff.

Long ago—before his hands could no longer tear at a loaf, before the bird's claw was injured, before the other birds had learned they could run it off from crab carcasses and dead fish.

His friend perches at the sill, one gnarled foot tucked up under its white belly and the other gripping the sill against the push and pull of outside winds.

Ash smiles and pulls his blankets down. He moves his spindly legs out into cold air.

"You have come for a story?" he asks.

He knows his hope is false. No one comes for a story. They come to steal from him now. He supposes they always have. Since his hands curled and froze, they have discovered that they can run him off from his work, that he has no lawyer, no money. There have been films. The titles and names have been changed, but he has seen his pen in the settings and dialog. There have been collections and reprints. Thieves have gotten fat, but somehow there have been no profits to share—no morsels for him.

The bird cocks its head as if to question his thoughts.

Ash laughs at himself. The bird knows the truth. That thought, too, was fantasy. They don't come at all. He flatters himself that he has anything left worth stealing.

The bird comes for bread, and Ash won't let it down. He has never missed a deadline in his life, and he won't miss this one.

He reaches for the sash, hooks its cold, steel handles with his deformed fingers and lifts. The bird, white and gray and battered by gales for so many years, hops into his room, flaps once, and lights atop the wrinkled pile of wool. It shakes itself free of the rain it brought in.

Ash ignores the musty feather spray, secures the window, and shuffles off toward his kitchen to find breakfast for himself and his friend.

Only old loaves.

He doesn't mind eating the loaves from the Goodwill food bank himself, but he regrets not having better fare for his friend. Still, he will share what he has, and he comes back to his room with half a baguette, stiff and hard in the crust but still soft enough in the center.

The bird waits. It has settled on its belly, making a sort of nest for itself in the blanket.

"That blanket," Old Ash tells his friend, "was my father's. I had it in my bed as a child. I worried the satin while sucking my thumb. I wore it out. After my first book, I had new sewn on."

The bird nods, but the old man knows it is only following the up and down of the bobbing loaf while he shuffles toward the bed.

The wind rises and wails outside. The glass rattles in the sash. The bird, wary with age and weakness, turns beak and eye toward the sound.

"I won't send you back into the tempest," the old man says. "Neither you nor I are fit for this night's plutonian shore."

The bird turns back.

He sits beside it.

The bird nods.

He breaks the loaf in half. It's the best he can do. He holds half out for the bird, who pecks at the white core, pulling soft tufts away and snapping them down, beak clicking. Wings spread a little, as if pumping the bird's throat, as if the movement is needed to get the bread down.

"I understand," the old man says. "I do. I have to take much smaller bites now. And I have to turn my head to swallow. It's all so much work. Once," he continues, and he offers the bird another bite, "I wrote a story about a man who never had to eat and never had to sleep."

The bird eats and nods and pumps.

"Someone out there is reading that story right now," Ash says. "I can feel it."

The wind howls.

The bird pecks.

"Maybe not." He looks out the window. The gale is in full force now. The window glass itself bends. His face and the bird's are reflected there, bowing in and out as if the room is breathing.

"Bad weather."

The bird makes a noise. It sounds like an ancient, steam foghorn—a broken, miniature foghorn.

"Sorry," he says, and he offers the bird another bite. "Do you remember the skating pond when we were young?" he asks the bird. "When the winds of Lake Erie swept down from Canada into Ohio? Where we all spent our winter days?"

The bird eats and nods.

"What was the name of the pretty girl? The one I wanted before I knew what the wanting meant?"

It seems to Ash that his good friend settles into the blanket to listen. The wind bends the glass. Rain coming in from the ocean spatters and clatters against the pane. He should have closed his shutters, he thinks, but then he would not be sitting safe with his friend enjoying fine French bread. "It is a good thing to breakfast with a good listener," he says.

The bird nods and snaps its beak.

"Andrea," he says.

"I remember now. Her brother was little and very cold. The ice was thick. Her parents were late, and the night was coming. I built a fire on the ice for her and her brother. She was so surprised that I could build a fire from the sticks and ashes of the fire made by older boys earlier in the day."

The bird shakes. It nods. It eats.

"Or did I write that?" He tears off a bit of bread for himself. "It has become so hard to know what is memory and what is story."

Tapping.

He looks to the window. Another gull perches outside. Wind and rain lift its feathers from behind. It is a white and gray feather ball with a yellow-beaked face painted in the middle.

"Oh, Lord," he says.

His friend, settled deeply in the blankets, snaps its beak and makes its foghorn noise.

"You invited a friend?"

The foghorn sounds again.

"I see." Ash places his loaf where his friend can get it, and he moves once more to the sash. He lifts. Wind and rain tear at his thighs.

The new arrival leaps inward.

He closes the sash.

The new friend moves quickly to the bread. It touches beaks with the older friend then settles itself in the blanket as if it has come to this bistro every day for all its life.

"Family?" the old man asks.

Two foghorns sound.

"I hear the resemblance," he says, and like any good host he offers what he has to the second bird as well.

For a time, they sit together in comfortable silence, eating and thinking thoughts that mingle in the air between them. He wonders if he is thinking bird thoughts, and he wonders if they wonder if they are thinking man thoughts, and wind outside howls and whistles and rattles the windows.

"There was a bookcase in the basement of our house," the old man offers.

The birds are attentive.

"I remember the first book I took from that case. I remember it was the first novel I ever read that had no pictures."

His two friends snap up the last of the soft bread, leaving the crust like an empty, brown crab shell.

"I have it here." He gestures toward the dusty tomes and resting flashlight. "Shall I read to you? I would be glad to."

The birds flap and hop to the sill. The elder taps at the bowing, rattling glass.

"The storm," he says. "It's terrible out there. Stay a while and hear a tale."

The older of the two taps at the glass. The old man knows what it means. It means he will be alone again. It means the night is closer. It means that he has nothing left for them to take.

He stands and shuffles to the window. "You can stay if you like." He knows his hope is false.

Tapping.

He hooks his fingers into the sash handles. The wind howls. The window bows. He lifts.

In spite of the blast of rain and wind, the birds are gone into the pre-dawn darkness.

The old man closes the window.

Deep into the darkness peering, long I stood there, wondering, fearing.

The window breathes. His reflection is now fleshy, corpulent, and youthfully smooth; now it is narrow, skeletal, and wrinkled parchment dry.

He turns away.

Cold, he shivers.

He shuffles across the room to his bookcase, lifts a worn and yellowed paperback from the shelf, and gathers up his flashlight.

He climbs back into his bed and blanket refuge and manages to convince his hooked and crooked fingers to turn on the flashlight. He pulls the blankets once more over his head. By flashlight, he opens the book. He imagines he is a boy again and that he has a boy's vision. He pretends to read.

Even after all the years, the words remain burned perfectly into his memory, the words of that first book—words that helped him weather his first storms, that fueled the dreams, and that even through the last nights of life keep the darkness from his heart.

"It was a pleasure to burn..."

To Build a Boat, Listen to Trees

Originally printed as a stand-alone eBook by IFD Publishing.

Chapter 1: To Save Your Home, Teach Your Enemy

Port Corwald's Master Shipwright, Venerré, opened his shop window and lifted his spyglass to one ancient eye.

Every morning, he scanned the bay, beginning in the south at his abandoned assembly barns where once hull, mast, sail, and rigging were joined together by a small army of his trained craftsmen. Built during the war, they squatted like giant sea turtles in the shadowy, winter-wind lee of Shashka Peak. Black piers, dry docks, a forest of scaffolds, and spider-web lines still covered the southern curve of the bay—all empty save for ravens and wind—a monument to drowned men.

No man dared disturb the spirits of that place.

He scanned northward along the long breakwater of fitted stones separating sea from bay, across the channel gap, and onward to the opposite side of the bay where merchant shipyards built new cargo and fishing vessels. Following the curve of the bay inland along the northwest shore, his glass passed over busy trade docks, warehouses, and salting houses.

Every day, he took up quill to record the winds, the clouds, the temperature, the position of the sun, the state of the tide, surface conditions, and sail movements. He wrote notes about the people of Port Corwald who did business along the seawall causeway that linked merchant docks and trade houses to Venerré's shop and the darker shipyards beyond.

This morning, he returned his glass to the wave-lapped breakwater between ocean swells and the smooth bay. A mute named Sill fished there. Taller than most men in Corwald, his parents had blessed him with skin as golden as fallen oak leaves and with eyes as gray as misty horizons. His strength brought him work on the docks, but his silence kept him from deck and sea.

Sill's willow pole, the thick butt tucked into the rocks, pointed seaward. Sill stood, back to his pole, watching single-masted skitters race across the morning-glass surface of the bay.

The pole tip dipped nearly to the sea. Eyes on the rainbow sails, Sill casually lifted one bare foot and grasped the butt of the pole between toes. He pressed his heel into the pole to steady the thick end against a rock.

The pole jumped and swayed.

Sill's attention followed the sails in the bay.

A landward, northeast breeze filled triangular sails of all colors, bent the pole masts, and honed the strength and sea-cunning of boys and young men.

Fishing and cargo were the life of Port Corwald, and every boy older than five had his own boat—if they weren't mute and doomed to solitude by sailors who believed a man who couldn't call out couldn't be useful.

Clearly, Sill loved sea and sail. Another year, and he would be eighteen, old enough to enter the annual regatta. Though Venerré no longer built ships, men came to him every year hoping to learn. Venerré wondered if Sill would come to him.

Venerré laughed at himself. He had promised himself to leave off watching human hearts the way he watched water, wind, and sky.

He put his spyglass away and finished his notes. Then, he settled himself at his stool and bench to work on Mrs. Andrell's rocker, a simple chair for a simple woman who would soon want nothing from the world except to sit with breast to children's lips until they slept.

He picked up a wave-worn stone to rub smooth an armrest.

Four tiny, golden ship bells tinkled over his door.

A man spoke, his voice full of swagger and authority. "Venerré, Master Shipwright of Port Corwald."

Venerré looked up. A tall, lean shadow blocked the light from his doorway. He went back to sanding.

"I will build a boat," the man said.

In eighty years, Venerré had heard people plead for help while bragging. He had heard fear in courageous bluster. He had heard yes in the word no. In all his years, he had never heard so much fear hidden by contempt and certainty.

Venerré changed to a smoother stone. A mother's elbow might touch just there on the armrest.

"In two years time, I will win the regatta and the hand of the King's daughter, Marletta. I will become King of your city and country."

"Skill to you," Venerré answered. "Coming or going will free the light. Standing at the threshold only wastes your life."

The man crossed to the center of the floor.

Venerré looked up again.

Light from the door and windows played over the man's red silk vest and burgundy cape. He stood in profile to Venerré and stared at the stone forge in the center of the shop. Nearer the windows, heavy bellows suspended from the ceiling entered the brick, bee-hive cover. A quarter turn around the forge, on the side facing the stranger, open iron doors gave access to the cold coal bed.

The stranger straightened, turned to Venerré, and pointed his arrogant chin. "Did you hear me, Old Man?"

Venerré looked back to his work. "You will build a boat."

"Yes."

Venerré blew on the armrest. Dark wood dust danced across his oak workbench. Sunlight caught the swirl, and Venerré paused to watch the tiny spectacle.

"As fast as the wind," the man said.

"What will fill the sails?"

"I mean…" The man paused—coughed. "Very funny." He forced a laugh.

"So, you lied."

"A figure of speech."

"Go away." Venerré rubbed at the armrest.

"You are Venerré, Master Shipwright."

"So you say. Do you doubt yourself?"

"No."

"A pity."

"I am Agon of Kusk."

"Hm."

Agon crossed in front of a window. A new shadow covered the rocker.

"You are determined to ruin my light," Venerré said.

"You will help me."

"I build chairs."

"My father says you conjured boats that sliced the water like a skinning knife cuts milk, that your sails took wind like a falcon's wing, and that your ships turned like a dog cutting colts from the herd. He said your tiny fleet sank the combined might of Bormell, Kusk, and Suthar."

"Open the shutters wider." Venerré tested the armrest with his thumb.

"I am to learn the wizardry of wood, water, and wind."

Venerré sighed. He looked up. Agon had a long, hard face—the kind of face short-sighted men followed. His dark, nearly black eyes held certainty—the kind that sent men to die.

Venerré set the rocker's arm aside. He pressed against his knees to straighten his back and stand from his stool. His knees popped and his back cracked. He crossed to his open front window. "I poured seawater on the forge coals of my shipyards thirty years ago. Look." Venerré pointed out his window. "Do you see men? Smoke? Ships?"

Agon nodded. "I do not need a war ship. I only need to learn your wizardry."

"I'm not a wizard. Never met one. Don't take apprentices. Don't build boats."

"I am a genius."

"More's the pity."

Agon pulled a long roll of paper from beneath his cape. "My proof. Templates for the Corrigan Keel. I have added my own modifications."

Venerré's many years had stolen the strength to toss a young horseman from his shop, but they had gifted him with patience enough to humor the man until he left. He took the offered roll, opened it, and examined the drawings within. "I see."

"You appreciate my genius."

"I see you have no experience."

Agon grabbed his plans. "That keel will move ten percent faster than Corrigan's original design. As the boat's speed at quarter-to-wind increases, the boat will heel but the cord will not increase."

"When you tested the design, at what speed were the gunnels pulled under?"

"My design will not capsize. Your jokes are wasted. It will beat any boat built by you."

"If you believe I joke, then you do not need me. Go away. My light will thank you." He returned to his stool, picked up the rocker arm and a curved blade to deepen an ornamental groove in the hand rest.

"The armrests are too fat, splayed, and uneven. They won't be symmetrical." Agon pointed out the difference in length and height on the two arms. "You see? I have a young man's eye for the wood."

"True. They will not be symmetrical, and you have a young man's eye. Now, go away. I'm working."

"I'll be back tomorrow. I'll not remind you I helped with the chair."

Venerré said nothing. He had long ago outlived his days of ships and politics. A rich man from Kusk could join the regatta. Any man could. Certainly, this fool posed no threat to Marletta. Venerré lost himself in the feel of sharp blade in tight grain.

~ ~ ~

Each day, Agon returned to repeat his brags and boasts.

Each day, Venerré ignored him.

The sixth day, Agon brought two soldiers. He produced a scroll sealed by the King.

Venerré broke the King's seal. He read the document. Then, he read the faces.

Agon glared.

The Corwaldian soldiers would not meet Venerré's gaze.

"I see," Venerré said.

"I doubt a mere shipwright understands affairs of state," Agon said.

"You may waste my time and the King's, but I will not become young or build boats. You yourself have said you can do better."

"You *will* teach your magic. I *will* marry Marletta."

"You must love her very much."

Agon's hard face softened and flushed red. He seemed for a moment to peer into a possible tomorrow where he could be a different man, then his eyes cleared, his face hardened, and he said, "Love has no place in a king's heart."

"Sad, Kuskan philosophy." Venerré wrapped himself in a gray robe against the chill breezes of spring and left the shop to obey the summons of his king.

~ ~ ~

In the marble-pillared throne room of the King of Port Corwald, Venerré encountered the unexpected—a rare thing in his waning years. Atop the King's red-carpeted dais, against the purple velvet curtains separating the throne room from the King's antechamber, three thrones sat where only one had been in years gone by. The one on his right, Venerré had long ago made for the King. It was lovingly hewn from tight-grained blackwood cut in the foothills to the east of the city. Venerré remembered the smooth give of the blackwood under his blades and stones. The King's throne gently curved and sloped back to allow him to sit at court for long hours without pain from his war wounds. Venerré had made the back short enough that the King could turn his head and see behind him or rest his neck in the curve of the back without appearing to be at rest.

To the left of the King's throne sat a smaller blackwood throne. Venerré touched callused fingers to his throat, as if his aging hands could stop the sigh rising unbidden from sad memories secreted in his heart. He remembered crafting that throne for Marletta, daughter of the King and Venerré's God Daughter. Farther right still, towered a golden throne with a tall, straight back. Venerré's hands had never touched its sharp edges, straight lines, and carvings of sword-wielding horse soldiers butchering footmen.

Agon strode past Venerré and up the marble stairs of the dais. There, he sat in the golden throne. His stiff, pained posture suited his seat. "Now, Old Fool," Agon said, "We will see what you will and won't do."

One of the escorts marched up to the dais. He stomped his leather boots. Mail and sword jingled. He did a precise about face. "The King of Port Corwald," he announced. "Ruler of all lands between Venture Pass in the east and the Westward Sea—between the White Wall range on the north and Salten Dunes in the south."

The purple curtain behind the thrones parted, and the King took his place on his blackwood throne.

He was as old as Venerré. They had played together as children, long before the King won the last regatta of succession and was taken into service to be trained to rule. Later, they fought together against Bormell, Kusk, and Sothor. From that time, both wore scars that could be seen. Venerré knew well that both also wore scars that could not be seen.

The King, his aging bones barely filling out his leathery face enough to make him look alive, nodded to Venerré. A crack of a smile lifted the corner of his mouth.

Venerré nodded to his old friend.

"The Princess Marletta," the guard announced.

Marletta, seventeen now, glided through the draperies. Her beauty brought a smile to Venerré's aged lips. Her eyes shone green like the sunset flash on the ocean horizon. Her hair was a shimmering sheet waterfall of copper silk bound loose with a leather strip and pouring over her opalescent décolletage. On her twelfth birthday, the throne had seemed too large for her, and now it seemed too small. She had grown so. Her smile warmed him and wounded him with memories.

Venerré, childless, had outlived only one wife. The King had outlived three, and the third had given up her flesh to bring this beautiful child into the world.

Deep behind her smiling eyes, a shadow moved.

Venerré peered into her oceanic eyes the way he might peer into a storm cloud on the horizon to seek its depth and speed and force. He found a shadow of dark water—perhaps the shadow of betrayal. She had lost some of the innocence he remembered. Not all, but some.

She sat. She rested her pale hand atop Agon's darker hand. Her smile slipped away, disappearing behind the still, thin mask of a politician. The way her eyes took in everything except Agon showed from whence the betrayal had come and that it had taught her contempt.

The King sat. The skin of his brow folded between his eyes more deeply than could be accounted for by his age.

"This is the Master Ship Builder, Venerré," Agon said.

"I can see that," the King said. "Ven, old friend, I'm sorry to have sent for you this way."

Venerré enjoyed Agon's confusion. "You are not from here, Agon," Venerré said. "Our kingdom is small."

"Your majesty," Venerré said. He bowed as best his bones would let him. "I would have come at a word. Guards were not needed."

"I sent no guards." The King glanced at Agon.

Agon met the glance with thin lips and narrowed eyes.

"I see," the King said. "My apologies."

"No matter," Venerré said. "I am here."

"Venerré," the ancient King said. "I desired your presence so I might ask you to save our kingdom once more."

Agon stiffened. "You ask? Is he so great a wizard as that?"

The King smiled. Marletta, to her credit, was not so dulled by courtly life that she did not need to bite her lip to stifle her laugh.

The King stood. "His golden throne is not so comfortable as the one you made for me, Old Friend."

"My memory is not gone," Venerré said. "I'm not so old as you by two years."

"Insolence!" Agon said. "How can I apprentice with this arrogant old man?"

The King leveled his gaze at Agon. After a moment, the younger man bowed his head—but the bow was in his neck and not his eyes.

"Walk with me then, my younger old friend," the King said. "Please."

Venerré nodded.

~ ~ ~

The King and Venerré walked silently in the palace's walled garden amid the heady scents of blooming heather and rhododendrons. At the center of the garden, a tall oak shaded gravel walks and overflowing fern beds.

"We brought this tree," said the King, "from our eastern forests. It was only twice the height of a man."

Venerré touched the bark. The rough skin of the tree warmed under his hand. "Your wedding," he said. "We were children."

"I was twenty-three when you taught me to build my boat."

"*Admiral's Flag.*"

"I'm honored. You remember my boat's foolish name."

"I remember many things," Venerré said. "Some, I wish to forget."

"So now you refuse to teach or build?"

Venerré held up his hands. Sun, filtered through spring oak leaves, lit yellowed calluses on his palms and fingers. His joints and fingers looked like oak galls and twisted twigs. The small finger on his left hand wanted for knuckle and fingertip.

The King took Venerré's hands in his. "Calluses well kept."

Venerré pulled his hands back. "I build furniture for families."

"Stripped of catapults, your ships yet sail in our merchant fleet. They are fewer every year."

Venerré pressed palm to oak again. "They should be scuttled. Men are prideful fools."

"Pirates and privateers will lose ten ships to capture one of yours. Your ships are lost because even after thirty years men will fight to the death to man them."

"In my heart, I hear the gasps of each drowning sailor."

"Your skill saved us from slavery. You saved my life—many lives."

"What need for ships if we are saved?" Hand on warm wood, Venerré listened through fingertips to the flow of sap within.

"Old enemies return." The King placed his ringed hand next to Venerré's. "This tree will become a ship."

"Then a fool builds your ships."

"Why say that?"

"Listen."

The King closed his eyes.

"Hear the tree's heart? Hear the stretch of limbs in the wind?"

They stood in silence before the King opened his eyes. "No, Old Friend. I have never had your ear for such things."

"Untested by our seasons, cared for by gardeners and children, its rings are thick and broad. Boats built from this tree will sink in their first gale."

"We planted it at our kingdom's heart," said the King. "Like us, it has grown weak."

"You are stronger today than you have ever been." But how many days, Venerré wondered, before he or his old friend would leave this world?

"Marletta inherits," said The King. "She is wise and well taught, but her rings are not so strong and tight as I would wish."

"The regatta," Venerré said.

"Yes, Old Friend. Your mind is still as clever as your hands."

"She loves this Kuskan?"

"She tries."

"Why? A hundred strong men might win the race just as you did. Why give advantage to this fool?"

"He is the second son of the King of Kusk."

Venerré rested his forehead against the oak. He whispered, "You want me to teach *him*?"

"Yes."

Venerré faced his King. "What has happened to you?"

The King looked upward.

Venerré followed his gaze. In the tree's crooked maze of branches, squirrels chased one another. The chatter of their courtship mixed with the whisper of spring breezes.

"The law," said the King. "Rule passes to the youngest daughter and her husband. She must wed the winner of the regatta in her nineteenth year."

"But him?" Venerré said. "Son of Basslik, King and Warlord of Kusk?"

"Most especially him. To save lives."

"So," Venerré said, "even after thirty years the war has not ended."

"Agon brings alliance with all the lands on our northern and eastern borders. Marletta brings a warm water port to Kusk."

Two male squirrels chased one female. They bit and clawed at one another even while they chased her fluffy tail in spirals around the trunk of the oak.

"Our mountains still protect us on the east," Venerré said. "We still hold Venture Pass. Yes?"

"Yes. Basslik moves goods overland to Suthar. It takes nearly a year. To move goods onto ships through our tiny kingdom is only a matter of weeks."

"Sell passage."

"He calls it tribute. Instead, he trades for a fleet of warships in Suthar."

"To make this evil pact, you will give up Marletta's hand?"

"What choice?" The King rubbed his hands over his wrinkled face. "This marriage saves thousands of lives."

"The oldest ills live longest."

"As do the deepest friendships."

"I would," Venerré said, "ask Marletta her heart in this."

"I will send her." The King bowed and retreated.

~ ~ ~

Venerré sat and rested his aching bones on a marble bench near a long bed of roses. Sunlight baked dark loam. Steam rose from the earth between cropped, thorny stalks. Squirrels chattered. Scrub jays, resplendent in spring blues, squawked and scuffled over bits of twig and grass, the makings of homes hidden in tree or shrub.

Venerré's gray cloak warmed him, but he rubbed his sore hands as if washing them in sunlight.

"Master Venerré." Marletta's voice seemed to braid itself into the spring sunlight. She wore a loose, blue gown the way spring wears blue sky. Jays saluted her with silence. Squirrels danced to the ends of the smallest twigs to watch her. She curtsied, though her station demanded Venerré stand and bow.

He patted the bench.

She sat. The breeze danced stray, copper hairs into her eyes. She swept a hand up under her hair and pulled it over her shoulder. Sunlight made her hair a shining wave rolling over her pale neck like sunset surf along white sand beaches.

"You have your mother's beauty," Venerré said.

"Thank you, Master Venerré."

"Venerré," he said.

Ocean-green eyes narrowed. "I remember you." Warm light seemed to glow behind her eyes the way sun shines through the back of a wave.

"You were twelve," he said.

"Yes. My own throne."

He nodded and looked at his empty, life-worn hands.

"Even before that," she said.

"Long ago," he said. "You were perhaps three."

"A toy," she said.

He nodded. His throat closed around his breath.

"A boat," she said. "No bigger than my hand. So detailed. Long and thin with a tin roof over the decks and many oars and a clever clockwork spring to make them row."

Venerré took a deep breath. "A small version of a ship I once thought to build."

"It made many daring fountain crossings. I still have that strange little boat," she said. "It reminds me of a happier time."

"Are you not happy?"

"My father was happy then."

"Did you learn evasion at court?"

"Excuse me, Sir?"

"My question was not about your father."

She smiled. Sun flashed on pearl teeth.

Heat rose in Venerré's chest—love and hope for the child of a friend. "What do you think of Prince Agon?"

Venerré read the truth in her tight smile before she spoke.

"A good man." She stared at her clasped hands. "Strong. He has clear eyes, and he is very sure of himself. I will wed him."

He touched her chin and lifted until her eyes met his. There, he saw her future with Agon. Her green eyes would lose the beauty of ocean and sun and harden into cold, sharp emeralds.

He released her. "Thank you, Milady. Tell your father I will answer him now."

She sat back. Her face showed her puzzlement. Still, she stood and curtsied. "Thank you," she said. "Your gifts have always been cherished in my family."

Venerré admired her eyes, once more fluid and alive.

~ ~ ~

"I pray," the King said, "you will do more than teach him boat craft. I need you to make him into a King worthy of my daughter and our people. Marletta is my blood. My flesh. My life. Can you bring sun and wind into him? Can you give my daughter a worthy husband?"

"Two years is a very short time to change a man's soul. For most men, it requires a lifetime."

"Please, my friend. Can you do it? Anything you ask of me will be yours."

Venerré watched the squirrels dancing in the tree. "When two months time has passed, send your daughter to my shop to check on his progress."

"You will help us," the King said. "Thank you, old friend. Thank you."

Venerré nodded. "As I always have, I will do what I can to save our people."

The King sighed. "We will once more rule the sea," he said.

"The sea rules the sea," Venerré said. "The heart rules men."

"Yes." The King's weathered eyes sparkled with hope beneath the oak they had planted together so long ago. He smiled and clasped Venerré's gnarled hand. "It will be done as you say, my friend. You lift a great weight from my heart."

The old King's skin was brittle paper in Venerré's hands, but his grip was firm and his gratitude strong.

Chapter 2: To See a Heart, Dance with the Wind

On the new apprentice's first workday, an occasional light North-by-Northeast breeze pushed the smell of Corwald to sea rather than the smell of sea into Corwald—a rare day.

A silk kite, off-square and striped in three bands—red, blue, and green, the colors of sunset, sky, and forest—danced above low surf. From his window, Venerré marveled. The kite lifted like a nighthawk rising in swooping steps against the breeze, then it fell like a turning leaf through still air, then it once more swooped upward against a puff of breeze.

He had never seen the like, so he studied shape and movement. The front of the keel curved like a ship's bow. Tugged string pulled that keel into the breeze, and the kite jumped upward. Slacked line let the kite fall like a leaf, the nose sawing back and forth, ever seeking a new direction. Thus, the kite rose more than it fell. The kite flew even though the breeze barely blew or at times blew not at all.

Venerré decided he would go out to meet the man who built that kite and knew faint breezes so well he could take their lead in a dance of string and silk.

The door's bells chimed.

Agon once more blocked the light from the doorway, a shadow casting a shadow on worn floorboards. "I am here, old man."

"You may begin work."

"You may look at my drawings again." Agon thrust rolled papers at Venerré like a sword.

Venerré took them and crossed to the forge he used to make tools, cleats, fasteners, buckles, pulleys, and rings. He hooked the iron firebox door with his callused hand and swung it open. Heat rolled outward into the shop. Agon stepped back. Venerré tossed the roll onto glowing coals. It burst into flames.

Agon lunged past Venerré. He yanked tongs from a hook by the forge and grasped at ash and fiery coals.

Agon turned on Venerré. He waved the tongs like a club. "The King ordered you to help me!"

"Do you plan to kill your teacher on your first day?"

Shamed, Agon froze. He lowered the tongs. He returned them to a hook by the forge.

Venerré sat on the rocker he'd been building. He settled his hands on the odd curves of uneven rests. "You said the King ordered me? What were the words you heard?"

"The words do not matter. He is the King."

"The words do matter, *Apprentice*." Venerré stared at the flushed face and hard jaw of the Prince of Kusk.

"He said you *agreed*."

"Yes."

"Those designs were perfect. I will send to Kusk for new ones."

"You told me those designs were yours. Why do you need to send to Kusk for something that lives in your mind?"

"I will win the race whether you help or not, Old Man."

"To win Marletta's hand, the design must be your own, the trees chosen, cut, milled, cured, and fashioned into a boat by your hand. Friends may sew sails and carry loads, but no craftsman may touch your boat before the race."

"I know the rules. Order or request, you are honor-bound to your King to help me."

"Humor an old man, Prince of Kusk. Tell me what I am honor-bound to do."

Agon put a hand on the tongs. "I could just kill you."

"Yes," Venerré said. "It would certainly let you continue to believe in your designs and skills. Would the King approve?"

Agon's angry flush grew deeper and redder. Tight muscles sharpened his chin. He settled the tongs on their hook.

"Would Marletta?"

Agon's hand fell to his side. His eyes sought a path in the grain of the floorboards.

"Better," Venerré said. "Now, *Apprentice*, speak my King's words."

Agon mumbled quiet words. "Venerré agreed to take an apprentice."

"And your own father's words in sending you here?"

Agon spoke clearly. "Win the regatta."

"Your boasting tells me you fear something."

Agon's eyes came up. A storm flashed in them once more. "I fear nothing!"

"Yet an old man's quiet words bring the blood to your face. Come, now, Prince of Kusk. Tell your new master your father's true words."

Agon turned away and paced back into the shadows between the forge and the rear of the shop. "You know nothing of me or my family."

"I know your father. I fought against him in the war. In my mind, I hear him say, 'Win their race or die before setting foot in my yurt again.'"

Agon spun back to face Venerré.

"Ah," Venerré said, "Just so, then."

Agon stepped back into the light. His face pale, he whispered, "Trickery."

"I know your family, Agon of Kusk. My ships sank your father's navy thirty years ago."

The angry color returned to Agon's face. "Old ships made by old ways, old tools, and old men."

"So, *you* came to teach *me* new designs?"

"My designs are better."

"You've built ships from your designs?"

"Of course."

"Tested them against my ships?"

Agon glared.

From his workbench, Venerré picked up a piece of wood. "Here." He tossed the wood to Agon. "What is that?"

Agon caught it and turned it over in his hands. "Scrap blackwood."

Venerré laughed.

Agon hurled the wood back.

Venerré lifted his gnarled hand and snagged the wood from the air. "This is a pair of spoons for babies' soft mouths. See the length, the curve of grain, the way two spoons nestle within this *scrap*. I have not yet brought them out of the wood, but they are spoons none-the-less."

"Trick questions."

"A test for my apprentice."

"Teach me before you test me, Old Man."

"Walk with me. You may not learn, but I will teach."

~ ~ ~

Venerré steadied himself against the causeway seawall along the curve of Port Corwald's beach. The colorful little kite danced over the sea—now a leaf floating downward on still air—now an arrowhead shooting skyward. He was not surprised to see that the man holding the string was Sill, the mute who loved the sea but could not sail with other men.

"Are we going to waste the day staring at a mute and his toy?" Agon said.

"*You* might." Venerré said. "I waste nothing."

"I have only two years to learn your tricks."

"Then watch Sill's kite."

Sill tugged line, and the kite shot upward, pulling line through sun-browned fingers. He tugged again. The kite shot higher. The wind died. The kite fell like a leaf, rocking on the air, falling and twisting. Slacked line looped and piled in the sand at Sill's feet. The breeze puffed. Sill pulled. The kite shot upward. The line followed.

"Could you fly that kite, Apprentice?"

"A child can fly a kite. What has that to do with regattas and my future wife?"

Venerré hobbled down stone stairs and across the sands. Agon followed, carrying his contempt like a black cloak wrapped against a gale.

Sill nodded acknowledgement. Venerré smiled his response. "May I fly your kite, Sill?"

Silent as ever, Sill handed Venerré the string. "Ah," Venerré said. "Wax on the string. I wondered how you kept the loops on the sand from tangling."

Sill nodded. He held a hand up against the breeze, his long fingers bent and loose. Suddenly, he snapped his fingers open as if they were a sail blown taught in a fresh breeze.

The breeze tugged lightly on Venerré's line.

Sill mimicked a pull.

Venerré looked at the colorful little diamond in the sky. He tugged. The keel caught air, and the kite shot upward. It rose higher, and string flowed over Venerré's calluses. Venerré laughed.

"I will not tolerate this treatment," Agon said.

"Go home, then," Venerré said.

"Teach me, and I will."

"The lesson is to fly Sill's kite."

"I've flown much larger kites than this! In Kusk, the plains winds are so strong that our kites need ropes and horses to hold them. I have seen them drag men and horses."

"No doubt." Venerré handed the string to Agon.

Agon took the string. The breeze died, and the kite began to fall like a leaf, rocking and twisting. Agon pulled in slack. The string piled at his feet.

The breeze returned, but the kite fell.

Agon ran backward, trying to keep the kite up. He tripped on driftwood and sprawled in the sand.

The kite settled to the surf.

"The wind died," Agon said.

Venerré stooped. His knees popped and cracked. He scooped up loose, dry sand. He struggled to stand again. Sill's trong hands helped him up. "Thank you, my quiet friend," Venerré said.

Sill nodded then extended a hand to Agon, who refused his help.

Venerré let sand slip through his fingers. The light breeze feathered it and scattered it along the beach. "Same breeze as when we arrived."

"Then the kite would have flown," Agon said. "You're too prideful to admit you're wrong." He stood and brushed sand from his clothes.

"Would it be a fair test to see if Sill can fly the kite again?"

"It would be if the wind had not dropped the kite in the sea."

Venerré took the string from Agon and handed it back to Sill. "Please?"

Sill nodded.

Agon laughed and batted sand from his waistcoat.

Sill gathered slack until the kite pulled against seawater. Venerré could not see the kite, but he trusted Sill's hand on the line.

Sill tugged gently, pulling—letting the string go slack—pulling again, slowly, gently, clearly timing tugs with movements of waves.

"He thinks he's flying the kite in the ocean," Agon said.

"He is," Venerré said.

"That doesn't count."

The kite appeared on the back of a wave. Sill stepped backward and yanked hard, timing the kite's rise against the curl of the wave. The kite leapt upward to the height of five men. Then it fell like a leaf.

Sill gathered slack, he pulled hard. The kite shot upward again. He let line slip through his fingers.

Again, it fell.

Sill danced with string and breeze and kite. He tugged. The kite soared. He slipped line. The kite tumbled. Thus he worked his kite higher and higher while sunlight made ribbons of steam trail the dance of silk high in blue skies.

"My knees are too old to test the breeze again. Do it for me, Apprentice."

Agon stared at the kite.

"Hm," Venerré said. "This apprentice has been struck deaf. Perhaps a mute will be better. Would you apprentice to me, Sill?"

"You can't take another apprentice," Agon said.

"While Corwald is free, I do as I please, and the apprentice I have isn't very good. Will you join me, Sill?"

Eye ever on the kite, hands tugging on waxed string in time with the rhythms of the breeze, Sill smiled and nodded.

Chapter 3: To Build a Boat, Listen to Trees

Weeks passed, and Venerré taught hammer and forge.

Sill's strength made hammer and bellows easy.

Agon hired out his shifts at bellows to Alexander, a short, powerful Corwaldian so deeply into his drink no seaman trusted him with line and sail.

Venerré hoped the good work might redeem Alexander, so he allowed it.

Venerré taught use of the bow to spin a forge-heated spindle auger to drill hot peg holes for joining.

Agon refused bow and spindle. He favored Kuskan, sword-steel drills. "Perfect holes and always the same," he said. "Wood pegs are weak." He used iron screws and nails to make his joints. "Modern techniques," he said.

Venerré nodded. "You are right. They are rigid and strong as steel."

Sill practiced bow and spindle. He rocked with his patient push and pull.

Alexander made the bellows sound like a storm wind through mountain passes, and Venerré took pleasure in the activity in his shop. After a few weeks working bellows, when Alexander's sweat no longer smelled like ale, Venerré gave him a true wage worthy of a hard worker.

Mid-day, near the end of the second month, Venerré took pity on Agon, who seemed to have replaced common sense with vanity. Wearing only the leather apron and breeches of the shop work, the horseman's chest and arms had poured sweat every day because the heat of the forge filled the shop. That day, however, the outlander had traded leather kilt and apron for red silk tights and a purple leather vest.

Venerré shook his head as he fastened back the shop shutters to release the heat of the forge and invite in cool ocean breezes. The shoreward breeze smelled of clean, high tide, and the noon sun steamed a morning shower from the cobbled streets.

Agon stopped work and watched the door.

Four soldiers arrived, all wearing mail, helm, and saber. The bells tinkled. Two came in. Two stayed outside. The two who entered broke into sweat. They stood on either side of the door like statues dripping rain from chins and hands.

Princess Marletta swept into the shop like a spring breeze into an oak grove. She wore a loose, blue gown of imported silk. With her hair netted, she looked more like her mother than she had in the garden. Venerré smiled and bowed.

Agon's odd clothing for the day suddenly made sense. The Kuskan Prince had known Marletta would grace the shop to check his progress. Spycraft, no doubt.

"Welcome, Milady." Agon bowed.

She extended a hand for Agon's kiss. While he pressed lips to pale flesh, her eyes found Venerré's. Desperate questions lived in the ocean swells of her irises.

He had no answers. A heavy, cold darkness grew in his heart.

Sill glanced up from his hot-spindle work. He smiled and nodded toward the lady. His short breeches and leather apron were normal for forge and spindle work. His golden skin and sensibly shaved head glistened. The muscles of his arms rippled in time with the push and pull of his spindle bow. Smoke rose from the drill hole.

"Don't mind *his* manners," Agon said. "A simpleton—a mute peasant."

"Welcome, Marletta," Venerré said. "I'm glad you have come."

"Old Man," Agon said, "she came to see skilled work."

"Indeed?" Venerré said. "One of my apprentices is truly gifted."

The princess nodded slightly to Agon.

Sill lifted his red-hot spindle and blew away charred shavings. He lifted a peg from a keg of water, examined it, and tested it against the smoking hole. He set the peg, lifted a mallet, and slammed the peg home.

Marletta jumped.

"He makes his holes too tight," Agon said.

Steam rose from the hole and peg. Sill ran his thumb over the smooth joint. He nodded then stood from his stool. He crossed to a short table, lifted a pewter pitcher and poured a small cup of water. From a bowl of fruit, he selected an apple.

Agon said, "And he stops to eat more often than a chicken stops to scratch,"

Sill crossed to Marletta and handed her the cool water and apple. Then he went back to work.

Agon glared.

Marletta sipped.

Venerré watched her oceanic gaze follow Sill back to his stool. Ripples in Marletta's eyes lit like the phosphorescence of a gentle bow wave in moonless, southern seas.

Marletta sat in the blackwood rocker.

"You see, Milady." Agon held up his drill. "My holes are exactly the same every time. Steel bolts and nails are stronger than wood. The wise men of Kusk—"

Marletta bit her apple. The crunch rendered Agon silent.

Venerré bowed. "If it pleases the Lady Marletta, care creates the difference in each hole. Steam expands pegs and plank to create joints that let a boat bend with the movement of the sea. Peg and beam bend as one. Iron and steel work against the beams, loosen, rust, and eventually fail."

"Ah," she said. She handed Agon her apple core.

Venerré turned to face the forge so his smile would not fuel Agon's anger. The man had enough difficulty hearing wisdom without his teacher taking pleasure in his humiliation. As it was, it would be days before the man would try Venerré's techniques without an argument. Passion was, he mused, the strength of the young. Patience and experience were the disrespected strengths left to old shipwrights. The day might yet come when Agon would be able to see and hear, but it would not come this week.

~ ~ ~

Venerré chose a fair, fall day on which to take his apprentices into the eastern forest to select the trees they would harvest, mill, dry, and eventually craft into skitters for the regatta.

"You have said we would cut trees on Solstice Day. Why go to the forest now?" Agon asked.

Sill lifted Venerré's pack from the old man's shoulder and slung it over his arm so it rode alongside his own.

Venerré answered, "To listen to the trees talking to one another and preparing for the winter. To learn which among them wishes to sail the sea."

It pleased Venerré that in a quarter year Agon had learned enough to ask questions and keep his contempt to himself—at least until events had begun to unfold.

In the King's oak forest, Venerré led them to a great oak too thick through the trunk for six men to surround with stretched arms and joined hands. The canopy of the ancient giant stretched above them, a maze of angles, tangles, and squirrel nests. Below, lay a carpet of golden brown leaves the color of Sill's skin. Spotted galls and scaled acorn caps lay scattered amid the leaves.

"Such a tree!" Agon said. "No wonder your ships beat my father's. One tree like this could build ten ships."

Venerré settled himself on a flat, worn root at the ancient tree's base. "Vanessa," he said to the tree, "meet Sill."

Sill spread his arms as if embracing the grove. He turned and stared into the canopy where smaller trees joined their branches to the old tree and where squirrels leapt and capered. He pointed upward then laced the fingers of his hands together. He broke the lacing and put one hand low as if patting the head of an invisible child. He looked at Venerré, tilted his head, and raised one eyebrow.

"Yes," Venerré said. "Her children."

Solemnly, Sill bowed to the ancient tree.

Agon laughed. "Her children! Insane old man, they are trees."

Venerré sighed. At least Agon had held his tongue on the walk. "Yes, Vanessa," Venerré said. "The loud one is from another land."

"You *believe* the tree talks?"

"To a man who listens, many things will talk."

"Even if the trees could talk, why would a man listen to anything they said?"

"Perhaps because he wanted to learn the secrets of wood to build ships."

Sill sat at Venerré's feet. He crossed his legs and rested his large hands in his lap.

"I know your secret now," Agon said. "Trees like this!"

"No," Venerré said. "Vanessa is a mother tree. Like other mothers of Port Corwald, she sacrifices some of her children to protect our land and to protect her other children. A man who harms her will be put to death by the King's own blade."

"I will change that law," Agon said.

A small branch fell and hit Agon's head. He jumped back and looked up.

Sill slapped his knee.

Venerré chuckled.

"You want me to think the tree threw a stick. It's like the kite. You wizard the wind, then you insult me."

"As with Sill's kite, I am showing you how to win the regatta. If you learn, you will also learn to build ships that can out sail any other, that can win any battle, that can live with the rule of the sea and ride swells as if borne by magic."

Agon became silent for a moment, then he said, "This listening to trees better be useful."

Venerré closed his eyes. Nearby, Sill breathed smoothly. The sound soothed Venerré's frustration. His own breath came and went, not quite so smoothly as in years past. He listened to the hiss and rattle of leaves, the creak of limbs and trunks— to the susurration of Vanessa's conversation with her children and the wind—and to Agon pacing, cracking twigs, and scooping up leaves to make a soft seat.

~ ~ ~

Solstice Day came. Venerré presented his apprentices with two wooden boxes, each as long as a tall man's leg: one ornately carved, the other rough-hewn and worn.

"Of what wood are these boxes made?" Venerré asked.

"Oak," Agon said.

Sill nodded and pointed at the worn and weathered box. He flashed fingers in the air. All ten—twelve times. He pointed at the ornate box. He flashed fingers again. All ten—five times. Then, on his right hand he held up two fingers.

Venerré laughed. "Yes, my friend. Exactly!"

"Exactly what?" Agon said.

"This box was made from 120 year-old oak. This one from fifty-two year-old oak."

"More jokes at my expense," Agon said. "There are no rings to count."

Venerré smiled. "You are a very certain man, Agon."

"I know what I know."

"But not what you don't know."

"No one can know something until he knows it."

"Ah. Just so." Venerré turned back the lids. "Your certainty wins you first pick."

In the ornate box, nestled in velvet, lay an axe. Its polished, double-bladed head reflected light, as did its straight, lacquered handle.

In the older box lay an older axe—a single-bladed head, broad and heavy at rear—the cutting edge showed marks from many whettings. The worn, curved handle cradled a steel file, a whetstone, and a vial of oil.

"This axe," Venerré tapped the shiny axe, "was a gift from a Tintran merchant. The other, I made during my apprenticeship."

"Tintran is known for great blades," Agon said. "The file marks on the old axe tell me it cannot hold an edge." He hefted the pretty, Tintran axe like a weapon. "Balanced well, of course." He stepped back from Sill and Venerré and swung it in the fashion of a horseman in battle, once overhead then sweeping to strike down his right side then back to ready.

Sill took his axe by the neck. He offered it to Agon.

"What's this?" Agon grinned. "You want to trade?"

"He offers a chance to reconsider," Venerré said.

"A weak trick." Axe in hand, Agon turned and left the shop.

Sill tucked whetstone, oil, and file into his pack.

Venerré rested a hand on Sill's shoulder. "It was a kind offer."

Sill shrugged. He pulled on his deerskin gloves and headed out.

Three days later, Sill had brought back two trees, milled them to the lumber he would need, and stacked planks and beams on spacers to dry for the next year.

Agon and his shiny axe had failed to cut the single tree he chose, so he hired a team and men to fell a great tree—not Vanessa, so he would not be punished, but perhaps a sister acorn.

Venerré cried for the death of an ancient mother who had been given no choice in her passing.

Sill pulled a small, leather pouch from under his shirt. He gave it to Venerré.

Venerré opened the pouch. Inside, he found three acorns—one to replace each tree Sill had cut, and one for Agon's.

He smiled, and Sill made him tea.

Chapter 4: To Make Good Bread, Build a Crooked Chair

One cold, spring afternoon, Venerré smoothed the final polish on a baby's spoon. Agon poured over scrolls, seeking advantage in keel and sail. Sill worked wood and brass, testing each with silent eye and sensitive thumb. Daylight streamed in through the shop's windows.

The door chimes rang. A petite, young woman with dark hair braided down one shoulder and a babe swaddled and cradled in her arms entered the shop. Mrs. Andrell wore the long, cotton walking gown popular among the ladies who attended Marletta. Red ribbon bound her waist and crossed her shoulders to support milk-swollen breasts.

Her husband, a baker by trade, followed. A long-armed, thin man, his quick eyes could catch a lad stealing cookies, and his broad smile could free the child of guilt. Mr. Andrell carried a second babe.

Dark rings under Mrs. Andrell's eyes, her shuffling step, and the way her husband touched her arm to steady her, told of her exhaustion.

"Welcome," Venerré said.

Sill moved the kettle nearer the forge coals. Alexander added muscle to the bellows to heat the tea more quickly.

"My light," Agon called. "Out of the doorway!"

"Agon!" Venerré scolded. "Up from my stool so Mr. Andrell can sit."

Agon looked up and scowled. "I'll not give my seat to a peasant."

Venerré shot his hard, gnarled hand into the forge, lifted a hot coal, and threw it at Agon. The coal caught the prince on the side of his cheek, careened off his face, and fell into his lap.

Agon leapt from his stool, slapping at the coal. He staggered back. "You son of a goat!" He started toward Venerré.

Sill stepped between them. Agon swung hard and hit Sill on the jaw. The blow might have felled a horse, but Sill's head only turned slightly. A silent storm gathered in Sill's gray eyes.

Dark eyes wide, Agon backed away.

"We should come back," Mrs. Andrell said.

"I won't have it," Venerré said. "A disrespectful apprentice will not stop me from giving you my gift."

"Gift?" She glanced at her husband.

He shrugged. His thin lips stretched into a crooked smile. "Master Venerré came to me a year ago. He told me we would have twins."

"How could he know?" she said. "I wasn't even–"

"Indeed?" Agon glared. "How? Here are proofs you are a wizard. You predict twins before they are conceived. You grasp red-hot coals and take no burn."

"My hands are quick and not as soft as yours," Venerré said. "This morning is about this young woman and her children. You'll not ruin it. Be quiet, or I will tell the King you are an unfit apprentice and husband who should be sent home."

Agon paled and stepped back into the shadows near the wall.

To Mr. and Mrs. Andrell, Venerré said, "Please, stay." Then, to Sill he said, "Would you please get Mrs. Andrell's gift?"

Sill moved quickly into the assembly area in the rear of the building. He returned with the crooked rocking chair.

"This will be rich," Agon said.

Venerré gestured to a space next to the stool Agon had vacated. "I fear our baker will not sit before his wife."

Sill placed the chair.

Husband and wife stared—his mouth open, her eyes wide. "Crooked," she whispered. The babe in her arms squirmed and squeaked.

Agon chuckled from the shadows.

The bells chimed. Marletta, out of breath, swept into the shop.

"Milady!" Mrs. Andrell said. "I didn't expect you."

"You have always attended me. I owe at least this." She smoothed her dress. "Have you seen your chair?"

Agon crossed from the shadows into the light beside Marletta. "Milady–"

She started at his sudden appearance. "Agon!" She backed away.

His face flared crimson. He stepped back and turned his gaze to the floor.

Venerré said, "Sill has just shown them. She has not yet tried it."

Sill motioned for Mrs. Andrell to sit.

"I don't know," she said.

"Please," Venerré said. "I have made this chair especially for you."

"Go ahead," Mr. Andrell said. "Try it."

"She can see it's shoddy work," Agon said.

"Hush." Marletta held out her arms for a child.

Agon stiffened. His deep, black eyes narrowed.

Venerré noted the dark fire smoldering within.

"Please," Venerré said to Mrs. Andrell. "Humor an old man."

Mrs. Andrell handed Marletta her child. Her thigh touched the edge of the seat, and the chair rocked forward to receive her. Surprised, she looked over her shoulder. The chair waited. The worry lines in her face smoothed. She smiled at her husband then settled into the seat. The chair rocked back, supporting her. When her feet rested flat on the floor, it stopped.

A smile marked her surprise. "Soft," she said. "Wooden but soft."

"Blackwood," Venerré said. "Rare and wonderful to work. Take the children."

Mrs. Andrell reached. "Please."

Mr. Andrell handed her one babe. The movement woke the child. Tiny, pink hands grasped at the air. A healthy wail filled the shop.

Sill smiled.

Agon grunted.

Marletta glanced from one to the other. Her troubled gaze found Venerré.

He winked.

Sill touched Mrs. Andrell's elbow. He moved it gently to the side to rest on one tilted arm of the chair. He moved her other arm to hold the babe near her breast. Marletta approached and handed her the second child. By use of her lap, her arms, and the crooked armrests, she held both children to suckle. "Ah," she said. She smiled and nodded. "So clever! The armrests are perfect."

She bared her breasts, glanced at her husband, then settled the children to feed. Each took hold and sucked. She pressed down with one toe, and the chair rocked. Heel to toe, her feet rose and fell. Her weight settled. The crooked back welcomed her shoulders; the uneven arms cradled her elbows, arms, and babes. Her head rested against the curved back.

She let her eyes close a little, and she sighed.

"I cannot pay for this, Master Venerré," Mr. Andrell said.

Mrs. Andrell's eyes opened wide.

"A gift," Venerré said. "You wake and work before anyone in Port Corwald. You feed a fleet every day. Of us all, we can least afford for you to lose sleep."

Mrs. Andrell's eyes closed. The chair rocked. The babes sucked. Mr. Andrell stood tall and proud behind his wife.

Sill knelt before the mother and child.

Marletta crossed to Sill and put her elegant hand on his shoulder.

In the shadows by the wall, Agon smoldered.

Venerré took it all in and nodded his satisfaction with his work.

Later, in a shop empty except for Sill and Alexander quietly at work, Venerré pulled a copper chest from under his workbench. He opened it. The bellows held its rhythm and Sill's hammer marked time on a brass sail ring, but Venerré felt them watching. He removed a small scroll. "Alexander," he said.

The bellows stopped. The hammer stopped. Alexander came to Venerré.

"I have grown to trust you," Venerré said. "I hope you have grown to trust me."

"I owe you much, Sir."

"You owe me nothing, but I now ask much. This is a list of men. Find them and tell them I need them."

Alexander unrolled the scroll. "Some of these men are dead."

"Find their sons or grandsons, though they have scattered on the wind like fluff seeds. Gather them. By the end of the first spring bloom, bring as many as you find. I have summer crops to plant."

Alexander bowed low. When he stood straight again, Venerré saw his clear eyes, and in them, his determined heart. "I will do this." He left the shop.

Venerré faced Sill. The young man cocked his head to one side. His eyebrow rose in question.

"We will need a new man for the bellows," Venerré said. "Alexander will be gone for some time."

Sill nodded, and they returned to work.

~ ~ ~

After the Andrells took their rocking chair, Agon appeared less and less in the shop, though he still pretended to be an apprentice. He bought a warehouse at the south end of the causeway. Whisperers in taverns oft said Agon hired men in secret to mill and shape lumber for his skitter. If the rumors were true, the Kuskan was clever. No man but he was ever seen to put hand to wood, sail, or line for the skitter. Sill worked alone on his skitter.

Venerré watched both men, and from time-to-time he spoke equally to both about their plans, suggesting improvements as he saw the need.

A day came when Venerré visited Agon. He examined Agon's tables, plans, and elegant tools. All around, men in the leather and wool of Kusk busied themselves at bench, forge, and fabric.

Venerré shook his head. "This is not what I taught."

"You favor that mute," Agon said, "but I will still win."

"Who can say?"

"This is the workshop of a true shipwright. These are the tools of my homeland. These are the plans of my own mind. I will put your mute's skitter to shame."

"Apprentice, I still offer my services," Venerré said. "I cannot touch your boat, but the regatta is a mere three months away, and I can teach."

"You lied." Agon turned his back on Venerré.

"What was my lie?"

"You have not taught me to wizard ships."

"I cannot teach what does not exist."

Agon turned on Venerré. He held an awl like a knife. "The rocker was on your workbench the first day I met you."

"Yes. You wanted me to improve it, to make the armrests even."

"That peasant wasn't yet with child."

"What has that to do with your boat?"

"You could not have known she would bear twins."

"I have known her family for three generations. I have known his as long."

"You have shown me none of your wizardry."

"I have shown you. Have you seen?"

Agon turned back to his bench. "As King, I will bring the justice of Kusk to Port Corwald. Do you understand me, *Wizard*?"

"To name a man wizard to hide fear and ignorance is not justice."

"We burn wizards. You'll wish you'd never met me."

"I am glad I met you," Venerré said. "If I had not, I could not have learned many things I have learned in the last two years."

Agon faced Venerré again. "I *have* shown you many advancements, many new techniques. I didn't think you were paying attention."

"It is my curse to pay attention," Venerré said. "I have learned you may never understand the people of Port Corwald."

"I understand them," Agon said. "They've grown fat and lazy on trade. They think themselves better than others because this country is surrounded by high mountains, has an open port, and had a crazy wizard's ships to protect it."

"Your words or your father's?"

"Truth no matter whose words. Your ships are nearly gone. You refuse to build more. You've learned nothing."

"I have learned blossoming love can see the deeper soul."

"Marletta does not love me."

"Nor you her."

Agon put the awl down. He looked at his hands. "I've tried," he whispered. "She is a rare creature. She will not look at me. She does not see how hard I have worked to rule here."

"What is her favorite spring blossom?"

Agon looked up.

"What makes her laugh during the short, dark days of our rainy winters?"

Agon's face hardened. "Get out. I'll not have you spying here. Not now."

Venerré nodded. "In my long life, I've learned that a man who serves can rule, and men who wish to rule never serve."

"Out!"

Venerré pointed at a rack of long willow poles in the eves. "The willow for your sail battens is too soft."

"You cannot know that."

"Nor can I know a girl will have twins."

Agon scowled. "How stiff will they need to be?"

"The winds on the day of the race will be from the southwest—as fast as a trotting horse. On days like that, the wind can stiffen before a sailor is ready."

"You want me to make a mistake. You taunt me."

"Make another set of battens from ash. Choose the stiffness according to the winds on the day of the race. A wise man would make a second sail as well. A taller, deeper sail for low wind and a shorter, tighter sail for stronger."

"There is no time in a race for changing cloth."

"Stack your mast rings to allow a cutaway of your first sail. The second sail will lift the empty rings." He left Agon alone with his designs and his wise men.

Chapter 5: To Win a Heart, Serve Those in Need

Regatta Day in late summer found people from several kingdoms gathered on the causeway above the beach. Vendors sold candies and banners with colors and symbols that marked the sails of favored racers. Skitters, long and sleek, covered the beach. Men busied themselves preparing mast, sail, and rigging. Fully fifty boats would race, but not all would race for the hand of the princess. Older boats, passed down from father to son, raced for pride and family and fun. Still, more than half were newly built by hopefuls vying for Marletta's hand. Young men manned some. Older men, seamen of many years, manned others. Young or old, seaman or spectator, many eyes searched for signs of Marletta.

Venerré watched from his front window—so much ambition in so many hearts. Behind him, Sill and Marletta pressed to finish a new sail. A pair of mailed soldiers stood near his forge to see that Venerré did not help. One soldier, a Kuskan, watched Venerré. The other, Corwaldian, watched the Kuskan. Both rested hands on hilts.

"The boats are on the beach," Venerré said.

"Fifty gold says Agon will be the next King of Port Crumble," the Kuskan soldier said.

The Corwald soldier nodded. "Done. No one has ever beaten a boat built in this shop."

The Kuskan laughed. "And in the spring, Agon will plough the virgin fields of Corpsehold."

Marletta spit at the man's feet.

He lifted his sword.

The Corwald soldier responded with his.

Sill stood.

"Enough!" Venerré commanded blood to cool.

Swords returned cautiously to sheaths.

Sill returned to sewing.

"Agon is a thief," Marletta said. "If he were a man, we would not have to stitch new sails."

"He was with me all night." The Kuskan soldier chuckled.

Marletta's attention stayed on her needle. "He hasn't the spine to steal a sail himself."

Sill put a hand on Marletta's arm. She looked up. Their eyes met. She took a breath and tied off her stitch. "Done," she said.

"Quickly, then," Venerré said. "We must get it to the beach." They hurried to the back of the shop where skitter and mast rested.

"Touch the boat, Wizard," the Kuskan said. "Please. Disqualify your mute so I can dance at your pyre when Agon is king."

"Sill can't carry the boat himself," Venerré said.

"I will help," Marletta said.

"*I* can touch it," the Corwald soldier said.

"Thank you," Marletta said.

"My honor, Milady." The soldier dropped his sword and removed his helmet and mail. He and Sill lifted boat and mast to carry into the streets. Behind them, Marletta carried their sail.

On the beach, fifty skitters ready for sail bobbed in the surf at the water's edge, each with its mast set, its sharp nose in the sand, and its rudder in the low surf.

In very few minutes, at tide's turn, a horn would sound. The men, arrayed along the breakwater causeway, would sprint through sand to their boats and push off. They would sail a great triangle: against the wind from beach to buoy near the northwest corner of the breakwater where maritime mason's stone joined the mainland, then south and west out of the bay to the channel buoy in rougher, open seas, then round the buoy to sail before the wind into the bay and finally to the beach. The first eligible man to run up the beach to the wall below the King's pavilion would snatch Marletta's silk from a pole.

That man would wed her and become King.

On the sand, Sill laid out the patchwork sail of blue, green, and red silk diamonds. He began slipping his battens into the sheet.

Agon, accompanied by several craftsmen, strode up to the sail where Sill worked. "He made a sail of kites!" Agon kicked sand onto the sail. His soldier laughed. "I imagine you are tired from sewing, Fishmute. Best leave this race to men."

Sill looked up.

"Prince Agon." Venerré distracted Agon. "You are ready, then?"

"No thanks to you."

Sill returned to work.

Venerré said, "Winds from the southwest as fast as a trotting horse."

"Wizard work."

Marletta and Sill ringed the sail then lifted the mast to socket, seat, and pin. They set the rigging.

"Milady." Agon pointed down the beach. "Here is the boat that will win your hand."

Six men carried his boat to surf and lowered it to the water. Bleached white oak glistened. The smoothly lacquered wood grain made the hull look like rippling water. A golden horse-and-rider on red silk, a pennant flag of Kusk, flapped in the breeze from the top of the mast. The sail, gathered and loosely bound to the mast, shone whiter and brighter than any other sail in the regatta. It was clearly made of silks imported from kingdoms beyond the borders of Kusk. The craft's long, low line and deeper draft set it apart from all the Corwaldian skitters.

"It takes more than a new boat to win my hand," Marletta said.

"There," Agon pointed to sea, "is my protection against wizard winds or curses."

From behind Mt. Shashka, a square-sailed warship pushed against the swells outside the breakwater. The ship had four catapults mounted on its wide deck. Within its broad belly, no doubt, 200 Kusk swordsmen readied armor and blades. To Venerré's dismay, two more ships appeared, following the first.

"Kuskan treachery," Marletta said.

"You must be very sure of losing," Venerré said.

"My boat is perfect."

"Your boat," Venerré said, "is certainly *pretty*."

"It looks fast," the Corwald soldier said. "Did you teach him to build that?"

"No," Marletta said. "Venerré did not teach him to build *that*."

"I taught," Venerré admitted. "Who can say what he learned?"

"You see your fate now, Old Man," Agon said. "Fame and magic are nothing. Only the wind and the sea matter, and I rule the sea."

Venerré smiled. "To fight the sea is to drown; to join the sea is to touch the shores of the world."

Agon grunted.

Sill and the soldier slid the boat into the water. Shorter and wider than Agon's, its shallow draft exaggerated the unusual upward flair of the stern.

"Old kites!" Agon said. "A bent stern! A fool's boat!" His sycophants guffawed.

Sill stood tall and strong, like a headland against Agon's wind.

"Goodbye, Fishmute." Agon strode away. He called over his shoulder, "I will see you soon, Wife."

Sill stepped after him.

Marletta caught Sill's arm. "Blowfish are a waste of hook and line."

"Marletta," Venerré said. "Your father and many hopeful men await your appearance at the pavilion."

Marletta stood on toes and kissed Sill's cheek. Sill's face turned the red-gold of a good-sailing sunset.

Marletta grinned. "And you?" she asked Venerré.

"A moment with Sill, then these good soldiers will escort me."

Marletta left them.

Venerré touched Sill's arm. "Give me your boots," Venerré said.

Sill's head tilted.

Venerré pointed to the southwest sky.

Overcast moved northeastward like a pale curtain closing out the blue sky.

Sill looked, nodded, and gave his boots to Venerré.

"Now, more than ever before, Sill, listen to wind, wood, sea, and heart."

Sill gripped Venerré's shoulders. Loyal, strong hands spoke Sill's readiness.

~ ~ ~

The King, Marletta, and Venerré sat beneath the blue awning of the King's pavilion. A row of six King's soldiers stood behind their chairs. The Kuskan soldier stood amid the King's men.

Below, Marletta's silk flapped from a pole in the sand. Flanking the pole, backs against the causeway's stone, men waited in a long line.

"Tide's turn," the chamberlain said.

The trumpeter sounded one clear note. Fifty men sprinted across the beach.

Sill ran at one edge of the crowd. Agon ran at the other.

Agon and several other men reached their boats at the same time.

A great roar and applause went up from the spectators on the causeway.

Sailors pushed off.

Agon and others used paddles to turn bows to the sea.

"Agon will win?" asked the King.

"I will not wed him," Marletta said.

"Venerré, you trained him as I asked?" asked the King.

"I've worked hard to save our people." Venerré squinted to see better. "It is now a matter of wind, wood, sea, and heart."

Sill leaped into his boat without pushing off.

"Ha," the Kuskan soldier said. "Pay me now."

Sill's full weight landed on the water-borne stern. The stern dipped, and the bow lifted from the beach sand. His weight and momentum launched the boat. Powerful arms hauled lines. The patchwork of kites rose. Wind caught the silk diamonds. Sill held his centerboard ready with one hand. With the other, he hauled hard on his boom line to rotate his sail fast enough to catch air and pull the boat to sea, finishing what his leap had begun. Then, sail against the wind, the skitter pivoted under the mast. When the bow pointed N-by-NW, Sill dropped his centerboard. His skitter leapt forward, cutting over the surf and across the sterns of boats still lifting sail.

Agon's boat cleared the sand. It caught wind and cut in behind Sill.

"He *can* sail," said the King, watching Agon.

"Of course," Marletta said, watching Sill.

"Good, Venerré," said the King. "Is his boat worthy of your craft?"

"We shall see." Venerré checked the closing curtain of clouds.

Sill sat on his gunnels and leaned back to hold his skitter deep in his N-by-NW cut across the wind.

"The mute runs too long to the north," said the King.

Agon, as if he had heard, tossed his tiller, ducked his boom, and set his sail again. He shot back across the open bay.

Sill held his tack.

"My prince has the idiot now," the Kuskan said. "Agon has found smooth water. So much for the legendary sailors of Port Corwald."

"Silence," Marletta commanded. One of her soldiers pressed the man from Kusk.

"The mute is not sailing well," said the King. "Was he not also your apprentice?"

Venerré nodded. "Remember thirty years ago when the enemy fleet entered our bay under full sail?"

The King frowned. "Many died."

Sill, nearly to the merchant shipyards, finally turned.

Many other boats followed Sill's lead, running long on tack, almost to the north shore, and turning late. Sill led them all, and his skitter and patchwork sail opened the distance between them. He crossed the bay behind but farther out than Agon.

Agon hit smooth water. His bow dipped. His sail slacked. He slowed.

Sill closed the apparent distance and gained the advantage of passage farther from shore.

"Yes," Marletta said.

"The dead water," said the King. "It *was* a day such as this."

"Dead water?" the Kuskan asked.

"Wind from the southwest," said the King. "Shashka Peak makes a hole in the wind. The water is smooth near Agon because there is no wind there. See how the wind chops the surface near the mute."

"His name is Sill, Father."

Venerré caught the King's glance at Marletta. The King turned from her to him.

"Exciting," Venerré said.

"I see," said the King. "You know the stakes in this race, Old Friend?"

Venerré nodded.

Agon broke from the dead water, but Sill had already rounded the buoy at the breakwater where Venerré had once watched him fish.

In the next tack, Agon held long to give chase.

"He's winning," Marletta said.

"No, he's not," said the King.

Their eyes met. The King's eyes hardened. Marletta's eyes hardened in exactly the same way. "My glass," said the King. "And for my daughter and friend as well."

A soldier handed long spyglasses to the King, Venerré, and Marletta.

"It is one thing," said the King, glass to eye, "to sail a small boat in the bay. It is another to put to sea."

The white sail of Kusk followed patchwork kites into open sea.

"This mute's sail is made of rags," said the King.

"Marletta sews well," Venerré said.

"Agon's keel cuts well," said the King.

The white sail gained on Sill. It passed him.

"Someone stole his sails in the night," Marletta said. "We did our best."

The soldier chuckled.

"Ah," said the King.

Venerré glanced at the sky.

Beyond the breakwater, beyond the warships of Kusk, a line of darkness rolled along the surface of the green sea.

Venerré tapped Marletta's shoulder. He pointed.

"No," she said.

"A new wind," said the King.

Other boats cleared the breakwater. None challenged Sill or Agon—Agon leading, but Sill only a length behind. The two men worked sail, line, and rudder for advantage.

They turned as one. Sill cut inside but angled wide—tacking loose on the wind. His speed dropped.

"That cost him a kingdom," said the King.

The freshening line hit the two boats. Sill's skitter heeled hard. He leaned outboard. His centerboard held. His boat leapt forward. His slower heading suddenly became the fastest.

Agon's boat, already heeled deep, took the wind against full sail. He stretched and leaned over his gunnels, but the running board broke water. The boat rolled. Mast and sail hit water.

Fully a third of the racers capsized in the new wind. Still upright skitters had no time to slow. Many came on hard, keels to upturned hulls. The race became a chaos of mortal dangers.

The King stood.

Men and women screamed in the crowd.

Sails dropped. Men in upright boats worked to pull brothers and outlanders from cold, growing swells.

Agon, raised a horseman, thrashed in the cold water. Only Sill could save the Prince of Kusk. He threw his tiller and turned his skitter back.

"No," Marletta said.

"A brave man, this Sill," said the King.

"Agon would not turn," she said.

"No," said the King. "I think not."

Venerré heard his King's sadness.

Sill came alongside Agon. He tied his boat to Agon's. He helped the man from the sea. Together, they loosed the sail. Together, they top-lined the mast. Together, they stood on the gunnels, leaned, and heaved against the line on the top of the mast. They lifted the mast from the water and righted the boat.

Agon kicked Sill into the water. He cast off Sill's boat. The wind pushed Sill's boat away.

Through the glass, Venerré saw Agon bite his thumb, mast a second sail, a smaller, stiffer sail, and move away.

"Father!" Marletta cried. "He cheats!"

"No, my dear. He breaks no rule. He merely dishonors himself."

In only a few minutes, the race had changed completely. Some boats were righted to race on. Others carried two or three men and ran low in the water. Still others towed swamped boats to shore, abandoning the race, which was now Agon's.

Sill's boat drifted on. Behind it, white foam followed.

Marletta cried out. "He holds his line!"

Sill gripped the long line that had bound the boats. His skitter dragged him, but he pulled himself toward it hand-over-hand.

"Come on, boy!" said the King.

Marletta dropped her spyglass and hugged her father.

The King glanced at the Kuskan soldier. Then, he returned his daughter's embrace. "Marletta."

"Father?"

"You are my heart."

"I know," she said. "As you are mine—and Port Corwald is our charge."

The King gently stroked his daughter's cheek. Each nodded silently to the other, then they joined hands and returned their attention to the race.

Sill climbed his skitter's stern. Quickly, he set sail and turned to a new heading.

Cutting deep into the wind, he wrapped a hand in his haul line to adjust the angle of the sail. Barefoot, he stood on the gunnels with one foot and leaned outboard. With his other foot, he held the tiller. He balanced speed, wind, swell, line, and body all as one, as if his heart beat to the rhythms of sea and wind, as if he danced to their lead.

Where he had merely matched Agon before, he now appeared to fly across the tops of waves.

"I've never seen the like," said the King.

"Nor I," Venerré laughed.

"Wizardry," the Kuskan said. He pulled his sword.

Six sword tips rose to the man's throat.

He let his sword fall back into its scabbard and held his hands away from hilt.

Sill's shallow draft lifted to the crests of the chop and skipped across the surface. He closed on Agon.

They rounded the buoy—Sill's bow almost touching Agon's stern.

"Sailor's skills show in tacking," said the King. "Builder's skills show in the run with the wind. I hope our man has learned well, Venerré."

"He has, my Lord."

Sill and Agon settled to their tillers. Agon's beautiful boat attacked waves. Spray rose over the rising and falling bow. Agon kept his head low, his sail at a right angle to wind. He aimed true for beach and Marletta's silk.

Sill aimed true as well, but his skitter seemed to rise up the swells, bend upon them, and race down them. The swells drove his boat forward faster than the wind.

"The curved stern," said the King.

"He built for this day on this bay," Venerré said.

"He shifts his weight and loosens his sail," said the King. "He lifts the bow and rides the power of the surf. He tightens the sail for the run up the back of a swell. Masterful."

"Yes," Venerré said.

Sill's boat pulled ahead slowly, steadily, surely.

He rode wind and wave across the bay. He let surf and wind drive his boat hard onto the sandy beach. He dropped his sail and trotted to the sea wall. Beneath the King's Pavilion, he looked upward to King, Shipwright, and Marletta.

"He awaits your permission," Venerré said.

The King nodded.

Sill waited.

Marletta looked seaward. Venerré followed her gaze. "Milady," Venerré said. "Who will best serve you and your people?"

Agon's boat hit the beach. He leapt out. "No!" he cried.

"Marletta?" said the King.

"She's mine!" Agon said.

She looked at the warships of Kusk. She glanced at Venerré. The fear in her face cut at his heart. He forced a smile. He winked.

To Sill, she said, "Please, Sir."

He snatched Marletta's silk and ended the race.

"NO!" Agon leapt toward Sill.

Sill side-stepped.

Agon went down in the sand.

The King gestured. Two soldiers leapt the wall and landed on the sand below. One put a blade to Agon's throat.

"I was to win!" Agon stood.

"The best man was to win," said the King. "You failed to become the best man."

"They wizarded the wind!"

"Bind him," said the King. "Round up his men."

"I may spend an hour in your dungeon but not a day," Agon said.

"True," said the King. "Take them to the pass and send him home to his father with empty hands."

"I will present you and your wizard in chains." Agon pointed seaward.

The three warships entered the harbor under sail. Alarm bells in the city rang. Soldiers scrambled along the shore to defend.

The King turned tired eyes and gaunt face toward Venerré. "I wish you *were* a wizard. Now would be the time to show your true power."

"In two years," Venerré said. "Sill and I have learned much from Agon of how his people think."

Rhythmic booming echoed across the bay. From the dark barns in the shadow of Shashka Peak, three long, sleek ships emerged. Each surged forward under the power of forty oars. Each had a peaked roof of oak armored with thin, shining brass to protect oarsman from arrows and catapults. At each stern, a captain stood tall next to his tillerman. From each bow, a long spike rode above the water, dipping and cutting through swells with each surge of the oars.

Agon said, "Tiny. They have no catapults. They are nothing against the might of Kusk." His voice shook, and his pale face betrayed his fear.

"Certainty is a habit for you," Venerré said.

"I've never seen such ships," said the King. "What are they?"

"Toys." Marletta's tone expressed her admiration.

"Harbor rams," Venerré said. He lifted glass to eye. In the stern of the first ram, Alexander stood, eyes fixed on Kusk's flagship and one bellows-strengthened hand on his tillerman's shoulder.

Strong and steady, the battle drum sounded across the water. Corwaldian oars lifted and fell in unison, and the defending harbor rams sliced across the bay like narwhales moving to feed on a school of salmon.

The bloated Kuskan warships turned inward and across the bay as one to bring catapults to bear on the shoreline. Their bows hit slick-water wind-shadow. Square sails flapped. Bows dipped. Catapults set to attack shoreward could not defend against the oncoming rams.

"This battle is over," Venerré said, "We must prepare to save the Kuskans."

The assembled people of Corwald watched rams shatter the hulls of the sluggish warships. Skitters and rowboats moved to save drowning men. Alexander and his rams saved those who would take help. Others drowned because of pride.

When the silence of the drums marked the end of the battle, Agon stood tall and said, "Sinking these ships will not save you. Your only hope against my father is to marry Marletta to me."

"Go home, Agon," Venerré said. "Tell your father if they send a fleet to Port Corwald, they will lose their ships to the wizard shipwrights here."

"Wizard!" Agon cried. "The old man admits he is a wizard! He witched the waters and the winds. He capsized my boat. Is this the honor of the King of Port Corwald?"

"I noticed," Marletta said, "that the best sailors remained upright."

"I could have drowned!"

"Then you are lucky," she said, "that Venerré trained his apprentice to be compassionate enough to return for a floundering horseman."

Agon said, "I call on your honor, King of Corwald. You apprenticed me to this wizard. He refused to teach me his dark arts."

"What do you say, Venerré?" The King grinned. "You are accused of wizardry and withholding craft from your apprentice."

"Look at his boat!" Agon said. "It is bent in back. It has a patchwork of kites for a sail. It bends in the waves. I had the best builders of Suthar, the best minds of Kusk. Wizardry, I say!"

Venerré stood and looked across the water. A dark line of smooth water moved toward them, calm spreading across the bay.

"Sill," Venerré said, "I tire of yelling so this fool can hear. Will you stop the wind?"

Sill cocked his head. He faced the sea, glanced skyward, and turned back. He raised his hands.

The dark line of calm hit the beach, and the wind died.

"Much better," Venerré said.

The King and Marletta laughed.

Agon stared, open-mouthed and wide-eyed.

"You say you cheated?" Venerré asked. "While your soldiers watched me, artisans from two countries helped you?"

The King shook his head. "A grave matter."

"You taught him to rule the wind," Agon said. "The kites are bewitched. I've seen it!"

"I taught him to listen to trees. I chose him because he already knew waves and wind. The kites proved it."

"A mute cannot rule!" Agon spit in the sand.

The soldiers holding him shook him.

"Perhaps," Marletta said, "he has learned to listen because he can't interrupt."

"You, Marletta! You chose *him*? He waited for your choice. You chose the lesser man. I learned everything he did. Everything! And I did it better!"

"No, Agon." She stood. Her noble beauty held the eyes of all around her. "He learned a man must be the boat, the sea, the wind, the city, and the kingdom. He served Venerré while you plotted. He listened to wind and sea and struck a truce where you sought to conquer. He served you when you would have died. He served me where you would have ruled. Because of his heart, by the rule of the regatta, he will be my husband and sit beside me as King of Port Corwald."

Sill clapped his hands. All eyes turned to him.

Marletta smiled and nodded to him.

He held up her silk and shook his head.

Marletta's smile faded. "No? No, what? You'll not marry me?"

Sill climbed the seawall. He knelt before Marletta. On one knee, he held up her silk.

"Sill," Venerré said, "it is law."

He kissed the scarf and handed it to the Lady Marletta. She reached for it. He held her hand, and they gazed into one another's eyes for a long moment. Sill nodded and released her.

He stood. From the pouch around his neck, he produced an acorn. It rocked in the palm of his strong hand. He cupped his other hand over the acorn. He lifted his covering hand, rolled it palm up, opened the fingers wide and made a graceful sign of growth unfolding.

"I understand," Marletta said. "And I already love you."

"Understand what?" Agon said.

"Time and growth," Venerré said. "If in the spring when this acorn sprouts she will have him of her own heart and not by law, he will wed her."

"I don't understand," Agon said.

"No," Marletta said. "You don't."

The King laughed. "Truly, Venerré, you *are* a wizard."

"Merely life's apprentice," Venerré said.

Sill opened his arms. Marletta slipped into them and lifted her lips to his.

"Go, Agon," said the King. "You have safe passage through Venture Pass. Go home to your father's love."

"I think," Venerré said, "Your father will respond more kindly to tales of wizardry than to the news his son, who had the help and resources of two countries, has failed in love, war, and sailing."

The soldiers turned Agon to begin his march to disgrace.

A long-reaching wave dropped a bit of shattered wood in the sand. Agon knelt and lifted the wood. He laughed.

"You laugh at your kinsmen's broken ships?" said the King.

"Ironwood," Agon said. "Fastened with bolts. A good plank for war carts but too broad in grain for the sea."

Sill tapped Venerré's arm. He pointed at Agon, then to himself, then to Venerré. He cupped an ear and made the sign of the growing tree.

"Wait," Venerré said. "Sill offers a trade."

The soldiers, Agon between them, looked to the King.

"Agon has sealed his own fate," said the King.

"Then war is our future," Venerré said.

"Please, father," Marletta said. "Sill has earned the right."

The King nodded.

Sill signed. Venerré spoke, "Sill says we have much to learn from one another, Prince of Kusk. You know ironwood and the ways of horses and the wind of the plains. He offers you a place here—if you will learn to listen to trees."

"How?" Agon asked.

"Sill will take you as an apprentice."

"Do not insult me with pity."

Sill pointed out over the water. The rams were making their way back to the shipyards. The mainmast of one warship still showed above water. The flag of Kusk blew in the freshening wind. He made a motion of letting out string, of pulling it in, of flying his kites and dancing with the wind. Finally, he set out his hands, one on the side of the sunken ships and one on the side of the city, Marletta, and the wind dance he had made.

Agon looked from Sill to his country's flag. He nodded. "Many will die," he said.

"The future King gives you a choice, Prince of Kusk," said the King. "It is not the alliance you came for, but your choice here—your hard work and honorable actions—may yet save many."

Agon nodded, swallowed hard, bowed to Sill, and covered his heart with one hand. "I swear my service on my debt of life to Sill and on the lives of my people."

Venerré read the eyes of each of his friends.

The horseman's new eyes saw wind, wood, heart, and sea.

Sill held Marletta. Their eyes spoke love for one another.

The King frowned and shook his head, but his eyes shone like morning sun on calm seas.

Venerré winked at a childhood friend who had once become King, then he turned to begin the long walk to the forest. He would sit with Vanessa for some time before they chose the tree from which he would make his Queen's new rocking throne.

Vincent's First Bass

Originally printed as a Father's Day story by Daily Science Fiction.

"Go ahead," his father said. "Stand up."

Vince was a Vanderpender ninth-grader, and he'd seen flat-bottomed punts in his art history courses. Not that he liked art history. He was a math boy, but he'd seen pictures of men fishing from boats like his dad's.

They'd started rowing before sunrise. Now, they floated on glassy water in a back bay of Oleanta Lake in the rolling hill country near the Ohio river. Wisps of steam rose off the water, and a bird somewhere made a really spooky cry. At least his father told him it was a bird. "A loon," he'd said. Vince wasn't sure if the name was a joke or not. The cry sounded crazy, and he supposed someone might have named a bird that made that sound *the loon*.

"It's safe to stand," his father said.

He nodded. The boat moved if Vince moved. He could feel it. It was action-reaction—simple Newtonian physics. He should be able to compensate. The variables were known: his weight, height, angle of lean, center of mass, the friction coefficient of the surface area of the bottom of the boat against the lake water.

"Fish are waiting," his father said. "Daylight's-a-wastin', and they won't wait forever for us to pluck 'em out'a the lake."

His father? Vince barely remembered the man. He was weather-tanned and tall, broad like a weight-lifter but dressed in his olive green game warden's uniform. He was a myth, a wild country legend that Vince's mother despised.

Feet braced wide for a better center of gravity, he slipped his blue-jeanned butt forward off the front bench of the punt. Knees bent to create springs to absorb movement, he managed to stand.

"Good." His father sat, hands on oars, making casual, micro-movements to steady the boat. "It's really just physics," he said. "I hear from the school you're really good at that stuff." His father handed him a fishing rod.

Vince managed to nod without falling out of the boat.

"The reel goes on the bottom," his father said. "Open faced-reels hang down below the rod for balance."

Vince let the reel drop low. The stem that held the reel to the rod slipped in between his fingers.

"Don't worry, Son," his father said. He let go of an oar and adjusted his cap. "I'll teach you what you need to know."

Vince was sure he looked like a rank beginner. He hated looking like a beginner in front of this man, which was pretty silly since they'd only just met. But his father was a Fish and Wildlife Warden, and for the first time he could remember, he was spending time with his father like other kids. Of course, he'd seen the look in his father's eyes in the eyes of kids at school and in the eyes of other kids' fathers. The look said it all. Vince was a geek.

"The rod is a spring," his father said.

"Cool." Vince heard the shake in his voice. *A linear spring*, he thought. *Knowable variables. Calculus. No worries.* He measured the length and taper with his mind's eye. He bounced the tip to test material tensioning against the weight of the bulbous gold and fluorescent gold lure at the rod tip.

"Let a little line out," his father said.

He bounced the tip again. The bright lure bounced. The silver, oval plate spinning on its side tinkled and flashed in the morning sun. No line came out. He tried to pull the line out.

"No," his father said. "Throw the bale, Son."

"The what?"

"The wire around the edge of the spool."

Vince nodded. "Oh." There was a rigid chrome wire around the edge of the reel. The line left the spool and slipped under a little guide on that wire. "Do I throw the whole rod?"

His father laughed at him.

Not good. Hot embarrassment burned his face. He should have said no when the lawyer came to Vanderpender for him. It was a moment of decision. He had created

274

the wrong universe with his decision. He should have picked the universe in which he went to the chess tournament in New Mexico, but some other Vince was in that universe now.

"Sorry," his father said. "You'll learn. Try to relax. Hold the rod in your right hand and lift the bale away from the face of the reel until it clicks."

He listened. He did exactly what he'd been told. The bale clicked open, and the lure dropped like the lead weight it mostly was. It hit the bottom of the punt and made a metallic clank. Vince wanted to melt away and hide from the steady eyes of his father. "Sorry," he said.

"No need," his father said. "That's supposed to happen."

"Really?"

"Yup."

He searched the tanned lines of his father's face for signs of suppressed ridicule or judgment. All he saw was joy and confidence.

His game warden dad said, "Now, crank the handle with your left hand."

He did. The bale snapped back over the reel face and picked up the line. The spool turned, and the lure lifted from the bottom of the boat.

"Stop." his father said.

Vince did. The lure hung a foot or so off the rod tip. Vince started to feel a little confidence. He thought he was getting it. A counterweighted lever: reel underslung, fulcrum at his wrist, tapered fiberglass spring, eighteen inches of eight-pound test monofilament with plus or minus 3 percent elasticity and a two-ounce weight dangling like a pendulum.

Manageable variables.

The boat rocked.

Vince almost lost his balance. It was a lot to keep track of: rod, reel, line, boat, balance… The equations danced in his head, but he managed to keep the numbers clean and ordered.

"It's okay," his father said. "My fault. We were drifting near a submerged stump."

"We could crash?" Vince asked. "And sink?"

His father laughed again. The laugh echoed off the Ohio hills. The weird bird trilled its eerie response. "Bump and maybe rock," his father said. "Even if we had a hole the size of a basketball in the bottom, the boat would float. The seats are full of buoyant foam."

"Do I cast now?" Vince had once seen a guy cast while clicking through YouTube videos. The title of the video had been, "Surface Tension," and Vince had thought the video was about molecular cohesion. Instead, it was about a man who went fishing after a fight with his wife.

"Yeah," his father said. "There's big bass in these stumps. With a little luck, you'll pick one up."

He swung the rod tip back and let the pendulum weight ride its arc. He felt the rod-spring load. He calculated the rate of load and the point of maximum arc. He pushed the rod forward against the maximum loading to increase the loading. He snapped his arm forward and let the rod tip unload.

The weighted lure came forward, swung fast around the rod tip, and spun in a quick eighteen-inch circle around the whipping tip. The lure went nowhere.

This sucked. He was sure he had done the calculations right. The weight should have pulled line out and gone approximately thirty yards in a rising twenty-degree arc over the plane of the water's surface.

"Try again," his father said. "This time get ready for your cast by hooking and holding the line with your index finger then throwing the bale."

Vince nodded. He considered tossing the whole rod into the lake. He could probably get away with it. His father wouldn't know it wasn't just a stupid kid's accident. Instead, he opened the chrome wire covering the face of his spin-caster. It rotated out and clicked into place. The gold and fluorescent lure dropped to the punt bottom again.

His father chuckled.

Vince's face warmed. He avoided his father's gaze; instead, he looked away and off across the misty pond. Cold, wet air filled his nostrils with the smell of algae, muck banks, and the surrounding forest. This wasn't his world. It was all wrong. He sniffed and blinked back tears. He'd made the same mistake with the bale twice.

"I'm sorry, son. I should have said to pull your finger in tight. Like this." His father reached up and wrapped a large, calloused hand around Vince's small, pale hand. He positioned Vince's hand and finger. "Like you're squeezing a trigger so the line doesn't fall away."

Vince reeled in his line. He pulled his finger tight against the line. He threw the bale again.

"We need to get out together more," his father said. "Too much time in those math books makes you forget how to explore possibilities. If everything is by the numbers—all formulas and figures, physics and calculations—you start thinking you have to have a right answer *every* time. It's just not true, Son. Some things don't have right answers. Some things, you just have to feel to really understand."

Vince set the tip of the rod back. He flipped it forward. He pointed his finger at his target. The line released, and the lure arced out over the lake. He said, "Twenty degrees. Three meters of rise. Sixty meters of travel." The lure splashed down.

"Perfect!" his father said. "That was perfect. You've been practicing."

"Conservation of angular momentum augmented by the spring loading of the fiberglass tip resulting from momentum. The lure weighs 2.5 ounces, according to the package. The tensile strength of the line is 8 lbs. The thickness is negligible. Elasticity is maybe 3% over three meters. The coil friction in unwinding is a primary variable in achievable distance and must be weighed in a function against the acceleration imparted by unloading the fiberglass spring."

His father stared at him, his olive green cap high on his forehead. "What?"

"Formulas and figures, Dad. A right answer."

"Uh-huh." His father recovered a bit. "Maybe there's math for that cast, but there's no math for the brain of a fish."

"The Rule of Very Large Numbers. Chaos Theory and I suspect a certain amount of quantum synchronicity could be applied." Vince grinned. Fishing was starting to make sense.

"You're saying you can tell how to catch a fish using math?"

"I'm saying that if a person really needed to, he could probably figure out where the fish are and when they would bite by knowing a lot about where the fish aren't and when they don't bite."

"I have to get you away from your mother and her damn boarding schools before you're ruined," his father said.

Vince was confused. He thought he'd done it right. He cranked his reel, and the bale locked shut. The rod tip dipped, and Vince jerked his arm up.

"Easy, boy. Take it easy. That's just the lure hitting bottom. Water's not deep here. Only about ten feet. Just reel the lure in."

He nodded. He reeled. The line cut a V-shaped wake in the water.

"Feel the tip bumping? That's the lure action, son. You want that. Reel too slow, the rod tip gets quiet. Reel too fast, and the lure spins differently. You need to get the lure to look like a fish moving along with a gimp fin."

"Point five revolutions of the crank per second. Spindle rotation is 3.5 RPS. Tip bob at 2 BPS."

"BPS?"

Vince grinned. "Bobs per second. I made it up."

His father actually laughed at his joke.

The rod tip pulled hard. It went down almost to the water.

"Lift the tip." his father said.

Vince lifted the tip of the rod over his head. He felt the deep drag of something heavy on the line.

"Okay, now reel enough to keep the line taught but not enough to drag the fish in."

"How big is the fish?"

"I don't know."

"Then how do I know how hard to reel?"

"Feel it in your hands."

"How?" Vince was frantic. He had no math for this. His numbers left him, and the line was darting to one side, the tip following. He tried to reel, but the rod bucked in his hand. He lost his grip on the crank.

The V slipped sideways one way, then the other. The bent rod tip followed like it was alive.

"Feel that?" his father asked. "You have to feel the fish now. Keep the tip high. Lead him."

"How!? Where!?"

"It's a big fish, boy. A damn big one."

Vince recovered the crank. He reeled. He felt the pull of the fish, but it didn't mean anything. It was just pull. His reel clicked. Line dragged out against the gears of the reel.

"I'm reeling, but the line goes out."

"Good. That's good. Just keep tension on the line."

"The line's still going out."

"The drag is set to let a big fish pull without breaking the line."

"How strong is the drag?"

"I don't know."

Vince didn't like it. He didn't like it at all. There were too many variables, too many possibilities. If he lost a big fish, his father would laugh at him again. He couldn't lose the fish. *Couldn't!*

The fish darted left hard.

"Keep him out of the logs!" his father called. He pulled on the oars. Vince almost fell. He lifted the tip to the right as high as he could. His mind raced. He wanted to see the fish, to know what he had hooked.

The answer came to him in a blinding flash, a white hot thought born of the need to see his father smile. It wasn't Newtonian at all. It was a probability alignment problem. Quantum geometry. He had to force the correct configuration of line, rod tension, and fish movement. He might be able to create a synchronous probability point and access universal potentials.

He led the fish with the rod tip. He didn't have time to crunch the numbers. A perfectly correct answer would take years and computers he didn't have. He had to approximate, to find the configuration. Odds were stacked badly against him. The dark energy rip expansion death of the universe had better numbers than him landing this fish.

He had to try.

"Feel it," his father yelled.

Of course, he thought. His father understood fishing—could feel it. So could he.

The rod tip dipped. The fish turned. The boat twisted. The line made a sound like a piano wire breaking.

A universe Vince did not want to live in was about to be spawned by his failure. Vince's mind raced, searching for the feel of the thing, the way of it, the moment of solution.

He found it in a white-hot flash of understanding, and the sound of the loon bird stopped. The tiny lapping of waves against the side of the boat went silent. He and his father stood on the still deck of the punt. The line went out from the tip of the rod to the surface of the water. Tendrils of motionless mist hovered in the silent air. Breeze-driven ripples stood in long wave lines, motionless, even where interference effects cancelled or amplified the intersecting wave forms. Fifty feet from the boat, a large-mouth bass hung in the air, frozen, surrounded by motionless water spray and refraction rainbows.

"What the hell?" his father said.

"Hold this," Vince said. He handed his father the rod. "Keep the line tight. Don't let the rod tip dip."

His father's mouth gaped. Still, he nodded and took the rod.

Vince stepped out of the boat and walked across the surface of the lake to the fish. He carefully unhooked the bass then walked back to the boat. He put the bass in the five-gallon paint bucket they had brought for their catch.

"Okay," he said, "Give me the rod."

Silent, eyes wide, his father gave the rod back.

Vince gave the reel a sharp crank. The rod tip snapped upward. The line streaked up out of the water, slicing a line of spray across the surface of the lake. The lure shot back toward the boat, a steaming red-hot streak. It hooked his father's cap and dragged it right across the boat and into the lake. Hat, lure, and lake boiled and steamed.

"What in Sam Hill?!" His father put a hand to his bare head.

"Sorry, Dad." Vince reeled in the cap.

"Holy Mary and Joseph!" his father said.

Vince unhooked the warm, wet hat and handed it to his father.

The mist twisted. The ripples rolled. The weird bird called out across the empty lake.

He'd done it. Vince inhaled a lung full of the fresh, lake air. He'd caught his first fish, and his father seemed impressed. Finally, he looked in the bucket at his fish. It was a big one. Maybe six pounds. The fish thrashed its tail and splashed water up out of the bucket.

"You got it," his father said. "It's real."

"Did I do it right?" Vince asked.

"You walked out there and got the fish." His father pointed out over the water.

"I did okay?"

"How?"

"I didn't do it right?"

"What did you do?"

"Are you mad at me?"

Vince's father let the oars float free in their oar locks. He twisted his cap to get the water out. He put the wet hat back on his head. "No, Vince. I'm not mad. I just don't understand what you did. It all happened so fast. The sun must have gotten to me. I could have sworn you walked out on the water and picked up the fish. Hell, it looked like the fish just waited in mid-jump for you to come and get it."

"I was afraid it would get away," Vince said.

"So you walked out and got it?"

Vince nodded. Embarrassed that he hadn't done what his father had wanted. "How was I supposed to do it?"

His father looked at the fish in the bucket. Then he looked at his son. "Boy," he said, "You did it exactly the way you were supposed to. I just didn't know you had it in you. I've never been more impressed by anyone or anything in my whole life."

Shocked, Vince looked at his father. "I mean, I just did what you told me. I was afraid I'd lose him. You told me to just feel it."

"You did great," his dad said.

Vince beamed. He reached in the bucket to touch his fish.

"Can we let it go, Dad?"

His father grinned at him and nodded.

"Son, you've got a feel for it you didn't learn from your old man, and if you're willing, I'd sure love to learn it."

"Sure, Dad." Vince lifted the bucket and let the bass slip back into the lake.

About the Author

If you enjoyed this book, please let the author know by rating the book or leaving a review at the purchase site and on Goodreads.com (or the review site of your choice).

Eric Witchey lives in Oregon where the fly fishing is good and deer like to sleep in his yard. He has made a living as a freelance writer, communication consultant, teacher, and speaker for over a quarter century. In addition to many contracted and ghost non-fiction titles, he has sold more than 100 stories. His stories have appeared in multiple genres and on six continents. He's still working on Antarctica. He has received awards or recognition from New Century Writers, Writers of the Future, Writer's Digest, The Eric Hoffer Prose Award Program, Short Story America, the Irish Aeon Awards, and a number of other organizations. His how-to articles have appeared in The Writer Magazine, Writer's Digest Magazine, and other print and online magazines.

Other stories written by this author and published by IFD Publishing are listed in the next section, and you can find even more by searching on "Eric Witchey" in your favorite search engine.

You can contact the author through the publisher at www.IFDPublishing.com or through any of the following:

Email: eric@ericwitchey.com

Web Site: www.ericwitchey.com

Shared Blog: http://shadowspinners.wordpress.com/

Twitter: @EWitchey

Other Books from IFD Publishing

You can find the following titles at most distribution points for ereading platforms.

Ebook Novels:

Bull's Labyrinth, by Eric Witchey

Beyond the Serpent's Heart, by Eric Witchey

How I Met My Alien Bitch Lover: Book 1 from the Sunny World Inquisition Daily Letter Archives, by Eric Witchey

Lizzie Borden, by Elizabeth Engstrom

Lizard Wine, by Elizabeth Engstrom

Northwoods Chronicles: A Novel in Short Stories, by Elizabeth Engstrom

Siren Promised, by Alan M. Clark and Jeremy Robert Johnson

To Kill a Common Loon, by Mitch Luckett

The Blood of Father Time: Book 1, The New Cut, by Alan M. Clark, Stephen C. Merritt & Lorelei Shannon

The Blood of Father Time: Book 2, The Mystic Clan's Grand Plot, by Alan M. Clark, Stephen C. Merritt & Lorelei Shannon

Candyland, by Elizabeth Engstrom

Baggage Check, by Elizabeth Engstrom

Death is a Star, by Christina Lay

D. D. Murphry, Secret Policeman, by Alan M. Clark and Elizabeth Massie

Black Leather, by Elizabeth Engstrom

York's Moon, by Elizabeth Engstrom

Jack the Ripper Victims Series: The Double Event, by Alan M. Clark

A Parliament of Crows, by Alan M. Clark

Ebook Collections:

Suspicions, by Elizabeth Engstrom

Professor Witchey's Miracle Mood Cure, by Eric Witchey

Ebook Novelettes:

The Tao of Flynn, by Eric Witchey
To Build a Boat, Listen to Trees, by Eric Witchey
Beware the Boojum, by Eric Witchey

Ebook Children's Illustrated:

The Christmas Thingy, by F. Paul Wilson. Illustrated by Alan M. Clark

Ebook Short Fiction:

"Brittle Bones and Old Rope," by Alan M. Clark
"Crosley," by Elizabeth Engstrom
"The Apple Sniper," by Eric Witchey
"Seducing Storms," (erotica) by E. M. Arthur
"Diver's Moon," (erotica) by E. M. Arthur

Ebook Non-fiction:

How to Write a Sizzling Sex Scene, by Elizabeth Engstrom

Trade Paper:

Professor Witchey's Miracle Mood Cure, by Eric Witchey
Bull's Labyrinth, by Eric Witchey
Baggage Check, by Elizabeth Engstrom
How to Write a Sizzling Sex Scene, by Elizabeth Engstrom
The Surgeon's Mate: A Dismemoir, by Alan M. Clark
Death is a Star, by Christina Lay

Over-sized Paperback:

Pain and Other Petty Plots to Keep You in Stitches, by Alan M. Clark and Friends

Over-sized Paperback and Hardcover Full-color Art Book:

The Paint in My Blood: Illustration and Fine Art, by Alan M. Clark

Hardcover Limited Editions Anthology:

Imagination Fully Dilated, Volume II: Edited by Elizabeth Engstrom

Hardcover Limited Editions Collection:

Escaping Purgatory, Fables in Words and Pictures, by Alan M. Clark and Gary A. Braunbeck

Audio Books:

The Surgeon's Mate: A Dismemoir, by Alan M. Clark

The Door That Faced West, by Alan M. Clark

A Parliament of Crows, by Alan M. Clark

Jack the Ripper Victims Series: A Brutal Chill in August, by Alan M. Clark

Jack the Ripper Victims Series: The Double Event, by Alan M. Clark

Jack the Ripper Victims Series: Of Thimble and Threat, by Alan M. Clark

Jack the Ripper Victims Series: Say Anything but Your Prayers, by Alan M. Clark